CRITICS PRAISE *PINK VODKA BLUES*

"With a little sex and a lot of wit ... Barrett finds his best inspiration in bars and dry-out farms, places he can size up the clientele and crack bitter jokes, the kind that leave bloody tracks behind."

—*The New York Times Book Review*

"Hits the ground running and never lets up ... sharp, irreverent humor and nonstop action make this a surefire winner!"

—*Publishers Weekly*

"Breathlessly paced, hard-boiled caper, peopled with tart, charming, sad drunks ... Barrett gives us his best shot—of wry."

—*Kirkus Reviews*

"... Really a romp ... reminiscent of several Hitchcock movies ... Barrett has a wonderful way with words and has created a very funny crime story."

—*Mystery News*

"A fast-paced, breathless novel. Barrett will keep you on edge."

—*The Houston Post*

Also by Neal Barrett, Jr.

THE HEREAFTER GANG

THROUGH DARKEST AMERICA

DAWN'S UNCERTAIN LIGHT

SKINNY ANNIE BLUES

BAD EYE BLUES

DEAD DOG BLUES

PINK VODKA BLUES

Neal Barrett, Jr.

Kensington Books
Kensington Publishing Corp.

http://www.kensingtonbooks.com

For Ruth, from the Prince of Toad Island.

KENSINGTON BOOKS are published by

Kensington Publishing Corp.
850 Third Avenue
New York, NY 10022

First Kensington Paperback Printing: December, 1997
10 9 8 7 6 5 4 3 2 1

Printed in the United States of America

Chapter 1

A designated drinker is going to wake up and wonder where he is. This is bound to happen sometimes. A bottle doesn't always point north. Sometimes it goes the other way. I knew I wasn't home. The spot on the ceiling where the water leaks through looked like a horse. A roach I didn't know crawled down its back. My spot looks like a duck. I like to wake up and see a duck. It's the little things that make a house a home.

The lamp by the bed said cheap hotel. The lamp was bright orange, which is not a good color if you drink. You wake up and your head's a can of nails, you don't want to see a lot of orange. You want to see a color like black.

Past the lamp I saw a table and a chair and bad pictures on the wall. A window with a dirty lace curtain and a dull square of daylight after that. I decided it was still September and Chicago outside, a solid foundation for the day. If you don't know where you've been, you can work around that. Knowing where you are is the thing. If you know where you are, if you know your last name, you'll do fine. So the hotel bit was nothing new. I have wound up in hotels before. Even serious drinkers have to sleep. The girl, though, the girl was something else. The girl was a big surprise.

I turned to put the window at my back and there she was. She had kicked the covers off and they were tangled in her legs. She was curled in a pleasant little nest, arms wrapped around each other, knees tucked in below her waist. Her ebony-colored hair was tousled in sleep about a young and nearly perfect angel face. I saw the tip of a perfect nose. I searched for a blemish or a mole. In this sort of thing, thoroughness is the key. This girl was Heffner clean. She was perfect and young, a very small and fine-boned girl with a tan that didn't come from September-in-Chicago afternoons. Her nails and her toes were coral-pink. Wrapped about a very nice foot was a tiny pair of white bikini pants. I admired this foot a lot. A very fine and perfect foot. A very young foot. Just how young was a matter for concern. There are laws we must obey.

I tried to recall the night before. I might have dropped by the Oasis and jawed with the regulars awhile. Surely I didn't find her there. The ladies in Artie's place tend to show a little wear. Some, if you ask, will display a small tattoo. I had not found this girl in any bar. This little honey was the girl next door, untouched by boozy nights. The places I went she wouldn't go.

Maybe I had kidnapped a cheerleader squad and the others got away. Maybe she only looked thirteen. Some girls look a lot younger than they are. I wondered if I'd practiced safe sex. I wondered if I'd practiced sex at all.

Drawing the covers around her neck, I slid quietly out of bed. I nearly made it to the chair. I eased onto the floor for a break. Travelers need to rest. My jeans were nearby, tangled in a very small bra. I got both feet in the jeans and decided I could make it to the john. Two minutes flat is lousy time for the morning-after four-foot dash. Certainly not a personal best.

The bathroom door wouldn't close all the way. If anyone cared to watch, there was a bull's-eye view from the toilet to the bed. Maybe the girl wouldn't look. Maybe she'd stay asleep. I could pee around the rim, and then flush when she was up.

I didn't want to think about that. She had to wake up some-time, and I wondered what she'd do when she did. Several likely scenes came to mind. "I want to call Daddy" led the list. I could dress very quietly, and simply sneak out and leave her there. It didn't seem the right thing to do. It seemed like the smart thing to do, but I knew I probably couldn't handle that.

The window right above the pot was slightly open, just high enough to let cold air slice into the room. Buildings appeared through a dreary mist of rain. Drops of moisture beaded on a rusty fire escape. I could smell smoke and garbage, the fumes of passing cars. I was still in Chicago somewhere. I was not in Cozumel.

The mirror showed me nothing I cared to see. Single malt eyes, a stubble maybe three days overdue. I turned on the tap and an iron-brown trickle found the sink. I brought cold water to my face. The water felt fine and I tried another splash. Closing the eyes was not a good idea. Something went wrong inside my head. Balance stepped out for lunch. Nausea rushed in to fill the gap. My hands began to shake. My legs gave way and I held on to the sink. My mouth was as dry as a page of Henry James and I knew what I needed was a drink, a shot to jump-start me on the day.

This had happened several times before, but this time it nearly took me down. I started to sweat and the shakes raced up my arms and down my chest until everything was churning like a tremor rolling quickly through a fault. There was nothing I could do but simply stand there and watch and hold on, and hope to God the thing would go away. It had gone away before. Maybe it would go away again.

When the moment finally passed I sank down to the floor and hugged the pot and threw up. I hoped the girl didn't hear. This is not the way it happens on the soaps. It is not a pretty thing to wake up and say hello to a jerk you don't recall, and find he's got his head in the commode.

I was weak but the scary part was gone. More cold water seemed to help. I didn't try the mirror again. I sat down on the edge of the tub. The sweat-and-shake business had happened

to me before. And lately it was happening a lot. There were
too many places I didn't know I'd been. Too many days on
my calendar were clean. I had skipped a lot of squares. The
way it happens is, you drift along fine in the social-drinker
class and then something tears loose one night and there you
go. You wake up where you're not supposed to be, barfing in
a fleabag bowl. I did not want to do this again.

What I needed was a break. The idea had crossed my mind
before. Everybody says they're going to get out of town, but
there is always something else to do. Now seemed a very good
time to *really* do what I knew I ought to do. I would go
somewhere and catch a fish. Catch a lot of fish and read a lot
of books. If I wanted a drink I'd have a beer. I could make
certain rules. Each fish I caught would entitle me to a beer. If
I caught over ten, I would divide the fish by two. In the evening,
I would have a glass of wine at a local woodsy inn. No hard
stuff at all. Pacing is the key. Artie always talked about a lake
north of Chisholm, Minnesota, where the fish were apparently
the size of golfing carts. I could fly up there, rent a car and
find the lake. Can you fish in September? Maybe not, I'd have
to ask. Maybe I ought to go south.

The fishing idea felt good. And Tony Palmer wouldn't care.
If I was off somewhere a week or two, *The Chicago Literary
Times* wouldn't crumble into ruin. We are not *The Chicago
Tribune*. Our last big scoop was a lost line from Edgar Allan
Poe, circa 1842. I could wrap up a few loose ends and be out
of town in three days. "Russell Murray Sobers Up, Lands
Record Lake Trout. 'What I did was ease off,' Murray stated.
'I still have a brew now and then, but that's it. Fishing is a
way of life with me.' Murray currently lives on Maui, where
he is finishing a book."

The interview was going real fine and the very attractive
lady from *Field & Stream* said she hoped I'd be in town for a
while. I said I surely would. That's when I heard a slight sound
somewhere and decided the girl was up. I stood to take a look
through the door that wouldn't close. Someone tried the knob

on the door across the room. Someone tried again. I decided they'd gone away, then the chain lock ripped free from the wall. Wood splintered, and the door to the hallway exploded into the room. The girl screamed. Two men moved quickly inside. They looked just alike. Both wore dark denim jackets and dirty jeans, oversized lumberjack shoes. They had bad haircuts and linebacker necks, little piggy eyes, and brows that went all the way across. The girl kept screaming and wouldn't stop. I caught a flash of bare legs. One of the men paused at the foot of the bed. He brought his hand up from his side and calmly shot the girl twice. The gun made tiny little sounds, like someone had opened a pair of 7-Ups.

The man with the gun looked at his friend. The friend said something, and they both looked at the bathroom door. I have read about frozen in fear. Someone is too scared to move, he is rooted to the spot. To hell with all that. I was across the bathroom to the window in one second flat. I gripped the wood and heaved. No one had opened this mother since Truman sold socks, and it wouldn't budge now. No more fun nights with Artie at the bar. Kiss the record trout good-bye. I squeezed the frame again. I wasn't even there anymore, it wasn't me. Captain Marvel and adrenaline took command. The window gave way and slammed hard against the top, showering me with flecks of dried paint. I pushed off the pot with one foot and threw myself over the sill. I heard the bathroom door fly open and hit the wall. Somebody yelled and grabbed my foot. I kicked out and found a piggy face and didn't stop. My shoulder hit the fire escape hard, turned me around on wet iron and sent me sprawling down a flight of metal steps. Something sliced into my foot. I couldn't take the time to look. I pulled myself up and bounded down another flight of stairs, gripping the railing and taking four steps at a time. A quick glance down said three flights to go. One of the piggies let loose with a gun. This time the weapon made noise. Mortar sprayed off a brick wall and stung my cheek. When I hit the last turn I could feel the vibrations from above and I knew the two men were on the stairs. I rode the ladder down to the alley. My bare feet hit a broken pint. I yelled in pain and hopped around on one foot. The gunmen seemed to like that. They started firing at me again. A cop I used to know said shooting either uphill or down was a tricky thing to do. I kept this in mind, bolted up the alley to the street and turned quickly to my left.

I figured I had about a ten-second lead and it wouldn't be enough. My foot was hurting bad. I couldn't outrun the two hoods. Hell, I couldn't outrun a fireplug. I felt the pocket of my jeans and found the comforting bulk of keys. A quick pat on the butt said my wallet was intact. Okay, I had a car. But where the hell was it? Maybe I'd left it home. Maybe Lolita and I took a cab. I risked a look back. This was not a good idea. Two hefty tanks in Li'l Abner shoes turned out of the alley, spotted me and took up pursuit.

I decided last week was the ideal time to leave town. That I really liked fishing a lot. That I could surely learn to like the local beer. As ever, good planning is the key.

Chapter 2

My ten-second lead was shrinking fast. I was down to maybe five. There were people about, and the two guys behind me had put their guns away. Very thoughtful and discreet. They walked at a fairly brisk pace. They knew they didn't have to run. I took this as a personal affront.

The long block came to an end. I looked to the left and saw my car. It was halfway down an alley, skewed at an angle that did not speak well for driving skills. The Toyota was a derelict, rusted and bent. It seemed to have an aura like the Grail. I hopped around the corner and broke into a run. I couldn't walk but I could run. Fear makes milers of us all.

Another stroke of luck. I had been too drunk to lock up and there was no need to fumble with the keys. I threw myself inside, and found the ignition first try. The manual says it is wise to let the engine warm up on cold days. This will greatly increase the life span of your car, and lead to miles of highway fun. I slammed my bad foot down hard, popped the clutch and backed up fast, jerked the car straight and squealed down the alley, scattering garbage in my wake. One of the piggies shouted from behind. A shot pinged the top of the car. Another shattered glass and I was gone.

I knew the hoods would have a car. They were probably in it now. Theirs was likely better than mine. Your criminal types tend to go for classy cars.

Familiar streets appeared. I knew where I was. Two quick turns and I was headed west on Fullerton toward the Kennedy Expressway. I didn't know where I was going and didn't care. If I didn't know, the guys on my tail didn't know. Ignorance is the key.

I bullied the Toyota into semi-heavy traffic heading north. Everyone was going too fast. I looked for a cop. Chicago police have very little time for minor crimes. Murder and mayhem keep them fairly occupied. If I wanted to get attention, I would have to run over someone or have a major accident.

On sober second thought, I wondered if attention right now was such a good idea. Supposing I found a cop, what did I want to say? Officer, this girl in my bed got shot. No, I don't know who she was. You might check the local Girl Scouts, see who missed the cookie sale. The piggie brothers wouldn't be around to back me up. Maybe the cops wouldn't feel they had to look. Maybe they'd be satisfied with me. A bird in the hand helps the caseload disappear.

Hard time was on my mind and I didn't see the Old Milwaukee truck. I whipped the Toyota over hard, into the passing lane. The guy in the Chrysler on my left squealed his brakes and shook his fist. I sat up straight and watched the road. Good safety habits can prevent a major tragedy in your life. If you drive, don't think; if you drink, don't jive.

The beer truck brought a pressing need to mind. I was starting to sweat again. My throat was getting dry. My hands shook when I raised them off the wheel. This was not a good day to taper off. I needed to find a drink, get my head clear and stop the shakes and try to figure something out.

A great many questions needed answers and I didn't have anyone to ask. Mainly, what did the goons want? Or, more specifically, who? Were they after me or the girl? Next question, why? One of us had pissed somebody off. If it was me, I didn't have the foggiest idea what I'd done. Which didn't prove a thing, of course. "Foggy" was the order of the day. If you don't know where you've been, there's no way to tell who you've offended along the way.

Another probing question came to mind. How did they know where we were? We had obviously been in bed at least part of the night. If the two hoods had known we were there, they wouldn't have waited till morning to do us in. Which meant they'd been looking—and the only thing to look for was my car. Find the car and find us. They knew who I was and they spent the night looking for the car. It wasn't where I lived, or anywhere I drank, so they started to look around. Or somebody found it and called the muscle in.

A trickle of sweat found the center of my back. That had to be the way it went down. Nothing else made a lot of sense. It was me they were after, and I didn't know why. All I knew was that someone had gone to a hell of a lot of trouble to track me down.

The Lake Forest Oasis is built on the overpass right above the Tollway. The name seemed a lucky omen, same as my regular bar. I parked the car behind a large RV and found the john. While I stood before the urinal, a man came out of a stall. He wore a double-breasted blue blazer with gold buttons, white pants and a natty sailing cap. He took one look and decided he didn't need to wash his hands. No one at his club went around with no shirt and bleeding feet. I was not his kind of guy.

I wiped off the blood as best I could with paper towels. My left foot wasn't bad. The right one hurt like hell. I opened my wallet and checked the cash. Four twenties and a five, a Visa card. I wandered outside around the front. There used to be a Howard Johnson's here but it was gone. The restaurant was now cafeteria-style. The gift shop was open. A pretty black teenager stood behind the counter and pretended I wasn't there. There were T-shirts on a rack. I picked out a blue one that said: Chicago—Convention City. There was booze in a big glass case. Half-pints, fifths and quarts. I told the girl I'd have a quart of J&B.

The girl shook her head. "Not till twelve o'clock, man."

"Why not?"

"Sunday morning, what you think? No booze till noon."

I stared at the girl. "It's Sunday? Are you sure?"

The kid looked at my feet. "You could use a pair of thongs. Looks to me 'bout a medium'd do."

"Good. Medium is fine."

"What color you think?"

"Surprise me."

She picked out blue. Very chic. Color coordinates, shirt and shoes to match. I paid her and left. I was starting to shake so bad I could scarcely find the ground. I knew where I was going. Your serious drinker remembers the things he needs to know. I remembered Wisconsin has early opening on Sundays. I remembered it was fifteen minutes away. I could wait. I could do fifteen minutes standing on my head. Sure I could. If the Christmas-tree lights behind my eyes would go away. If my grape-jelly legs didn't melt and leak out through the clutch and disappear.

The sign at the Wisconsin border reads: "Warning! Wisconsin Arrests Drunken Drivers!" To help bring this about, an impressive number of taverns line the roads. Other states have Mom and Pop groceries, shabby little stores that sell bad lunch meat and stale bread. Wisconsin has Mom and Pop taverns—more taverns per capita, locals boast, than any other state.

I pulled in at the first one I saw, Sid and Ann's, just off the exit ramp. Nothing very special. A sagging converted house with a barnlike room, a scarred bar. Good. I wasn't looking for decor. I laid a twenty on the bar and asked for a fifth of J&B. The bartender was perched on a high-legged stool, reading a gun-and-ammo magazine. Without looking up, he reached for a bottle on the shelf and set it on the bar. It was a Scotch I'd never heard of before. The Black Watch soldier on the label looked vaguely oriental about the eyes.

"Fine," I said, "I'll take it."

The bartender nodded, hauled out a bottle that matched the first and poured me a shot to the brim.

"You get a free sample when you buy a bottle here," he explained.

"A very fine tradition," I said.

I downed it before he could change his mind. Half the shot was lost to shaking, but enough got through for a start. The second promised relief. Warmth began to work its way out of my stomach and into the blood.

Nothing kicks in like the second shot. It left me reasonably calm and relaxed. Life might continue on earth. The species might survive. From experience, I knew this rush was a lie that wouldn't last, but I was glad to go along. You go with what you've got.

There were three other customers in the bar, two old men and a woman, all chasing morning shots with beer. Sporting a brand-new T-shirt and thongs, I saw I was overdressed. The possibility of living in Wisconsin all my life had some appeal. I might go into cheese. I could blend in with the dairy crowd and change my name to Sven.

The pay phone and the cigarette machine were in the back. Armed with a handful of change, I got a pack of Marlboros and tried to remember Tony Palmer's number at home. I couldn't think of anyone else to call. Barry Hague was a cop I might trust, but this didn't seem the time to find out. Nobody answered at Tony's home. He wouldn't be at the office on Sunday, but it wouldn't hurt to try.

Tony answered halfway through the first ring.

"Tony, listen," I said, "this is Russ. Tony, I'm in a little trouble and I—"

"Where the fuck are you, Russell? Where you calling from?"

"What?" I frowned into the phone. "Are you mad or something, Tony? You sound upset to me."

There was a fairly long silence. I could hear Tony breathing in the phone.

"Tony, are you there?"

"I'm right here, Russell."

"Well, I thought you were gone."

"I'm not gone, I'm right here."

"I still think you're mad about something."

"I'm not mad, okay?"

"Well you sound mad to me."

"Russell. I'm not mad. I'm a little disturbed. I am not mad."

"You sound a little disturbed."

"I am a little disturbed. I believe that's what I said. Where the fuck are you, Russell?"

"You keep saying that. I said I'm in trouble and you keep asking where I am. What you sound like to me, you sound like you're mad about something, you're trying to sound like you're not. That's how it sounds to me."

"For Christ's sake, Russell—"

"Tony, I don't know what you're disturbed about. I honestly don't. I'm the one ought to be disturbed. See, I woke up this morning, I'm in a hotel. These guys come in and shoot a girl. I'm in the john and they try to shoot me. I cut my feet real bad. This is why I'm calling you. So far, Tony, I can't say you've been a lot of help."

Tony was silent again. This time the silence was different, and I knew he'd put his hand across the phone.

"Tony, you're covering up the phone. You want to tell me why you're covering up the phone?"

"Russell, I heard about that. I mean about the girl."

"My God, is it on the TV? What did they say?"

"Russell, here's the thing. I'm in a little trouble and I kind of need your help."

"No. That's what *I* said, Tony. See, I called you."

"I know you did, Russell. And I'm very glad you did. What I need, Russell, here's what I need, I need the briefcase. That's all. You just tell me where you are, I'll come and pick it up."

"You need the what?"

"I need the fucking *briefcase* Russell."

"I don't have any briefcase, Tony."

"Russell. Tell me where you are. Tell me where you are right now."

"I don't think so," I said, and hung up.

My hands shook as I put up the phone. It didn't have a thing to do with booze. I wanted out of there fast. Chicago suddenly seemed too close to Sid and Ann's.

I made my way back up front. The bartender gave me a look. "You okay? You don't look real good to me."

"I'm fine. I guess I got to go."

"You buy a bottle at Sid and Ann's, you always get a free shot."

"I'll keep that in mind, Sid."

"Huh-uh." The bartender shook his head. "Sid's dead. Caught one going in at Iwo Jima."

"I'm sorry to hear that."

"Now we got to buy their fucking cars."

"It doesn't seem right," I said. I picked up my bottle and left. I didn't ask about Ann.

Chapter 3

North seemed a good way to go. South was Chicago and I knew I didn't want to be there. If I drove straight ahead, the Expressway would take me right into Milwaukee, but I planned to pull off before that. I would find a small motel somewhere, get something to eat and go to bed. Not a very long-range plan, but it would do. What I needed was time to think, so this is what I did. I drove and watched the road and took a comforting nip now and then and wished I'd fixed the radio.

Mostly I thought about Tony Palmer. I thought I knew Tony pretty well, and this worried me a lot. The Tony I had talked to on the phone was definitely not the Tony I knew. Tony Palmer is an easygoing guy, more like a friend than a boss. As sole owner, publisher and managing editor of *The Chicago Literary Times*, he takes long lunches, goes to New York now and then, and generally charms the highbrow set. I sit in my hole with my Apple PC. I am chief writer, editor, and all around person in charge of whatever Tony Palmer doesn't like to do himself. I have done this for over two years and it works out fine. We both do what we like to do best. We run a very proper paper, a 24-page bimonthly, devoted, as it says below the banner, to "literary reviews and the arts." I have never figured out who buys our respectable rag, but apparently someone does. My paychecks are always on time.

Tony is perfect for his end of the job. He doesn't look it but he is. What he looks like is a jockey, if jockeys wore three-piece suits, hand-tooled Italian shoes and Sulka ties. The first time your literary type sees Tony, this is exactly what he thinks. Here's a jockey in a three-piece suit; he doesn't know John Milton from Elton John. Tony sets them straight with no effort at all. A minute later they're Tony Palmer fans. I don't know how he does it but he does. And if a literary person is of the female gender, that's that. Especially if the person is very tall. Tony has the power to cloud tall women's minds. I've met Tony's wife. She's very striking and very short, and Tony goes out of town a lot.

I think I know Tony. I've made up stories when he goes to New York to meet someone who does not resemble John Updike at all. And he has returned the favor more than once when I was not exactly sober on the job. Correction: When I was not exactly on the job, period.

So what was wrong with Tony on the phone? First, Tony wasn't mad, he was scared. He was fighting for control, but he was scared. Second, and the part I didn't want to think about, he wasn't in the office alone. Someone else was there. Someone was there and they wanted their briefcase back. I didn't know a thing about that. I had tried to put the pieces together since I left Sid and Ann's, but everything was blank. I could take it back as far as Wednesday morning. I was a few days late, but I wrote Maid Marian an alimony check. Wednesday night I stayed home. I remembered TV. I think I went to work the next day, maybe around noon. And that's it. If there was a briefcase in my life, it appeared after that.

I wanted to think the briefcase wasn't real. The fear in Tony's voice wouldn't let me out of that. The famous fucking briefcase was there, all right, it just wasn't real to me.

And something else . . . When it hit me, it raised the short hairs on my neck. I wanted to toss it out, but it wouldn't go away: When I told him about the girl, Tony knew. He didn't see it on the tube, he just *knew*. Tony was in the office on a Sunday because of me. They knew I was still alive, and they were fairly pissed off about that.

I knew I was hitting the bottle hard, so I started easing up for a while. What you want to do when you drink is learn to pace yourself right. This is doubly important when you drive. Driving is a skill, and safe drinking is too, and you've got to learn how to match them up. You need to come out even, this is what you've got to do. Caution is important, but your inexperienced drinker tends to overcompensate. Don't be too careful, you don't want to stand out. Normalcy is the key. What you've got to remember is the harder you try, the farther from normal you're going to be. A good cop can spot a careful driver a mile away.

I tried to watch the road and not do everything right. The trouble was, I kept thinking about the girl. I didn't want her in my head but she was there. It was easy enough just to set her aside before. I had enough to think about without that. Now I kept seeing that sleepy angel face and the guys coming in and what happened after that. I didn't even know her, I didn't know her name. And she was dead because of me. I didn't kill her or anything, but she was there where she wasn't supposed to be.

The road looked blurry, sort of fuzzy and out of sync. I knew I was starting to cry. That's the worst thing you can do. If you drink, don't cry, it gets everything out of whack. But I started and couldn't stop. I thought about that perfect little girl. She probably had a new red bike. She maybe had a dog. I thought about the dog. It sure was a cute little dog. She'd come home and play with that dog every day, she'd pet it real good and brush its hair. Now the dog was all alone, it didn't have anyone at all. They'd probably take it off and gas it at the pound.

I tried to dry my eyes with my new T-shirt. I took another drink. I cried for that dog. I didn't even know its name. I cried for the poor little children overseas. I wondered if the girl had a cat. She might've had a cute little cat. Oh Jesus, that kitty was all alone. It had a little bowl where the girl gave it cream, and the girl wasn't ever coming home . . .

Chapter 4

I woke up and saw the guy sitting on the foot of the bed. Standing, he'd stretch to five-two. He had a baby-pink face and tiny ears, Easter-Bunny eyes with the drive and intensity of 2 percent milk. A road-map nose dwarfed every other feature on his face. It was a nose any San Diego wino would be proud to call his own. A fringe of red hair circled the frontiers of his head. It wasn't a lot of hair, but a good-looking guy like that, he doesn't want to spoil the image, he doesn't want to think he's going bald. So he lets about six red hairs grow two, maybe three feet long, then he folds them real neat in a circle on top of his head. Hey, now he looks fine! He's dressed in red slacks, the kind you order through the mail. Slacks, and a polo shirt with some kind of little animal on the front.

The guy saw I was awake. He smiled, and I got to see his overbite.

"Hi, Russell. How you feel?"

"Who the fuck are you?" I said.

"I'm Les. I'm your roommate."

"No, you're not. Exactly where am I, Les?"

Les thought this was a riot. "You're in detox, pal. Wilson

Rehab. Bet you don't remember a thing. *To*tally zonked.
Blacked out the whole time. Oh, man. You were something
else, you know? Took two cops to bring you in.''

"Two cops."

Les nodded. He was blinking and laughing and sucking air.
He was having a great time. "They said you were—Jesus—
doing eight miles per hour on the Expressway. Might be a new
state record.''

"Have you got a cigarette, Les?"

"God, no. I've got enough problems, Russ. I've fouled my
body temple with abuse.''

"I don't want you to call me Russ. Is that okay with you?
My friends call me Russ.''

"Right. Whatever's fine with me." Les got up. "I'm headed
down for breakfast. Don't guess you're ready for that. Which
is fine if you're not. Nobody cares. They'll bring something
up if you want to eat.''

I told him I'd think about that. Les headed out the door and
I sat up on the edge of the bed. I liked the natty robe. Now
that I was traveling a lot, I seemed to be picking up some really
fine clothes. When I stepped on the floor, the pain hit my foot
hard. I looked and saw heavy wrappings on the right, a few
smaller bandages on the left. Better than paper towels. I wondered where they'd put my new thongs.

The john was at the far end of the room. I hopped in to the
sink and drank six paper cups of water, then threw up on the
floor. Another new day.

When I turned back to the room, a nurse was waiting by the
bed. She had dark hair and lipstick the color of Mickey Mouse
pants. Her uniform was starched and white and a size too big.

"Someone's got to clean that up," she said. "Someone
throws up, someone else has got to clean it up.''

"I come from a broken home," I said.

"Get back in bed," she said.

"I feel like I ought to sit up."

"Fine. Sit up. Take these."

She showed me a small paper cup full of pills.

"What are they for?"

"The green-and-black one is Librium. The orange one is a vitamin pill. The gray is Dilantin. It's an anticonvulsant. If you'd taken it before you got up, you wouldn't have vomited on the floor."

"Do you care which one I take first? I'm in the decorator trade. Color means a lot to me."

"If you'd like, you can stick them up your nose."

"I think you and I could be close."

She left the pills on a tray and walked back out into the hall. I looked out the window. It was bright outside, the kind of bright that said cold. On the lawn was a single skinny tree with half a dozen yellow leaves. Two of these fell as I watched. A new nurse came in with a tray. She was hefty and blond. She took my temperature and blood pressure and looked at my card.

"Which comes first, Murray or Russell?"

"Russell Murray."

"They've got it backward here."

"Everybody gets it wrong."

"I'm Nina. Eat some breakfast, Russell."

"I don't think so right now."

Nina smiled. "You don't want to fuck with me, Russell. I am not an easy touch."

"Nina, Jesus hears everything you say."

"Clean your plate, Russell. You are going to get with the program, babe. Nina's going to help."

Nina left me with coffee, fried eggs and bacon, and a wedge of dry toast. I kept the coffee and nibbled on the toast. I wondered where they'd put my clothes. Even if Nina beat me up, I did not intend to hang around for lunch. I did not intend to get with the program. What I intended to get was out.

I already knew about the program. Anyone who hangs around Artie's Oasis knows someone who's been there and back. We used to watch these ads on the color TV Artie keeps above the bar. Some over-the-hill movie star comes on the tube looking sober and sincere. He tells us how he had a problem once too and how you owe it to yourself to get help, and then they'd flash the number to call. All the places had names like cemeteries. Everyone would get real depressed, and Artie would pour drinks on the house.

Hey, I think a program's fine. Someone needs help with a problem, that's fine. I don't happen to like the idea of hanging out in a place like this, everyone telling you what to do. Sometimes I drink too much. Big surprise. I knew that before I *had* a shabby robe. And I've been cold sober without Nina the Nazi nurse.

An elderly couple was walking along the grounds. They were bundled up tight against the cold. The man was slow and lagged behind. Every time he caught up, he grabbed the old woman on the ass and she leaped half a foot. Then the man hung back, and they ran the scene again.

I didn't think I'd care for the happy institutional life. Even if I had a little talk with the chef and we learned other ways to do eggs, it wouldn't last. Les could devote a lot of time to the problems of abuse. I had other things to do. Every cop in Illinois knew finding Russell Murray was the road to promotion and success. Two very ugly thugs wanted to rehabilitate me in a box. I didn't know where to go, but I saw no problems with this. I had no destination when I ended up here, so all I'd lost was a little time. Leaving is the key. When you feel you need to go, the first thing to do is find the door.

The afternoon was chock-full of fun. Les took me to the lounge and introduced me to his friends. The social center here was a coffee urn the size of New York. Everyone seemed a little nervous. Maybe OPEC had control of caffeine. Maybe they were about to shut us down.

"Just wander around," Les said. "You're free to do anything you like. They're real soft on you the first couple of days."

"And then what?"

Les grinned. "Oh, well, *then*, I mean, when you're up to it, the good part starts. Whammo! They sock it to you, pal. Group stuff, lectures, seminars, the whole works. What they do, Russell, is pick you apart and put you back together again. You learn to respect your body temple is what you do. You've been crawling on the ground, friend. I know, I did it too. Now you're going to learn to fly. My God, it's the greatest experience you'll ever know."

"Do I get to take Nina to the prom?"

"You don't *need* booze, Russell. You think you do, but you don't."

"I think I'll find a cigarette machine."

"Search your inner self for control."

"I'm doing that right now, Les."

Les left me alone and found his way through the crowd. Les was in his element here. He had the restless urge to interact. A very short John the Baptist. Charlie Manson on a Nutra-Sweet high.

I didn't have my wallet, but they had kindly allowed me a little money to carry about. Ten dollars, to be exact. They knew I was a responsible adult, and could probably handle that. I fed two bills into a changer and got a pack of Marlboros in return. When I got my allowance, they said I had another twelve bucks in my wallet. This didn't seem like enough. Maybe I had bought some more clothes. Maybe Nurse Nina was dreaming of a new Chevrolet.

The wallet business pissed me off, but no one seemed to care. Rules are rules, Mr. Murray, we all have to understand that. These people knew their guests well. Some uncanny sense told them people needed wallets and keys and credit cards if they wanted to go anywhere besides the lounge. Like down to the 7-Eleven for lemon snaps. Or out to the nearest liquor store for a case of Gordon's Gin.

The first order of business, then, was learning how to get my stuff back. Get my belongings and find the door. Try not to yearn for Les. Mingling seemed the right thing to do. In

every semi-organized group there are dissidents about, people
who know the score and think the group is fucked up and
do everything they can to sow the seeds of revolt. There are
Kiwanians who really hate business, and Shriners who don't
care for kids. This is the kind of guy I had to see.

Easy for me to say. Two gallons of coffee later, I wasn't
certain my man was here. Twenty or thirty people wandered
in, drank coffee and wandered out. They all seemed cheery
and clear of eye. Everyone wore real clothes except me. When
they gave me my allowance, they said my clothes were "badly
soiled" and I would get them back soon. So I shuffled about
in my robe, and everyone knew I was the new kid on the block,
unclean and ravaged by drink. In case anyone didn't know,
Les pointed out that I still had the shakes and couldn't eat, and
I would likely throw up for a while. This helped me flow
smoothly into the group.

Most of the people I met were named John.

"Hi, I'm John, and I'm an alcoholic. Now I can say that out
loud. I'm breaking through denial real good."

"You got to be proud," I said.

"And this guy here," Les said, "this is John. John was very
big in industrial pipe. You maybe saw his picture in *Time*."

John said he thought his wife was taking him to a very nice
resort. He said he was really fucked up.

"Boy, I was really fucked up. I'm telling the man at the
desk to take my luggage upstairs. I'm passing out twenty-dollar
tips to all the nurses and the aides. I'm looking around, I'm
saying, hey, where's the bar?"

This got a big laugh from the group. They had heard this
story before.

I decided I was having a lot of fun. I met some more Johns
and had two or three hundred more coffees and smoked a lot
of cigarettes. I was spilling a great deal of coffee down the
robe, but no one seemed to mind. I thought it was a good idea
to cut down, but there was nothing else to drink. I thought

about that. I asked Les where I could get a drink. Les got a big laugh out of that.

"What I used to do," John said, "I used to do it all the time, I'd run out to the store for some bread and I'd wake up outside of Detroit. I'd wake up, I'd think to myself, what the shit am I doing here? And I'd still have that goddamn sack of bread. I'd gone to the store about April and this'd be July."

"Bread won't keep a long time," I said.

"Jesus, you got that right. You ought to've seen some of that bread."

My bladder was about to explode. I cut loose from the group and found the cigarette machine. I forgot that I once found it before. I searched my robe for change and found a dime. How much did cigarettes cost? I wasn't sure about that. The cigarettes could wait. First I had to pee. I couldn't see the urinal at all. I couldn't find the zipper on my pants. Tony Palmer said, "Crissakes, Russ, quit hopping around. I want to talk."

"Good," I said. "I can talk just fine."

"Listen, what I'd like you to do," Tony said, "I'm supposed to go to Dallas, you know? We've got a writer down there, he's kind of what? He's a kook, he's a Texas Salman Rushdie's what he is. He doesn't want anyone to see his galleys, he doesn't trust the mails. Hell, he doesn't trust *me*. The thing is, something's come up. I need to take these galleys to the guy, I don't see how I can go."

"Something's come up."

"That's the thing."

"So what's her name?"

Tony grinned and said he couldn't fool me. The girl's name was Gloria, and this was a lady I wouldn't believe.

"So you make the trip. I've got the tickets, and I throw in spending money on the side."

It sounded okay. A free trip, a couple of days off, and it's easier than lying to Tony's wife. By late afternoon I was up in the air, downing double Scotches and telling the flight attendant she was a ringer for Cheryl Ladd.

Things get a little hazy after that. I stayed somewhere Thursday night. Friday is a blank. I got back to Dallas—Fort Worth on Saturday and did what Tony said to do. At one forty-five, I took the briefcase to the American ticket counter and told them Mr. Mason would come by. Then I went back to the bar and had a drink. The idea was, the writer shows up, takes his galleys out and puts some more work in for Tony and goes away. I pick up the briefcase at two and get on the plane. Nobody sees the kook writer and everything works out fine. The whole thing seemed crazy to me, like something Len Deighton might do. But Tony's right. All writers are nuts, and some are a little screwier than the rest.

And that's when Karla came along. She was in the seat next to mine. Younger than springtime and a smile that wouldn't quit. I knew I was the luckiest guy on the plane. I was half-looped, but Karla managed to catch up fast. She was young, but she'd seen a few empties in her life.

By the time we hit O'Hare, we both knew exactly what was going to happen next. All I had to do was find my car in the lot and drive straight a few miles, and Karla would bring joy to my life. First I had to pee and the urinal didn't look the way it should, but that didn't bother me a lot. Then Les said, *"Uh-oh,"* somewhere down a very long hall, and that was apparently the end of that.

When I opened my eyes it was dark outside. The girl was sitting on a chair beside my bed. Her mouth was too wide, and her eyes behind wire-rimmed glasses were a color I couldn't see. A cotton-candy machine had gone berserk around her head.

"I'm Sherry Lou Winn," she said. "You're Russ. Nina says you pissed on the cigarette machine."

"You look a lot like Cheryl Ladd," I said.

"You look like a man who could use a drink."

Hallelujah. This is how Poland got free. I knew I'd found my rebel with a cause.

Chapter 5

"I thought I'd drop by and say hello," Sherry said. "I missed you when the cops brought you in."

"Probably something you won't regret," I said.

Sherry grinned. "The way I hear, you did not go gentle into that good night."

"Heaven be praised. Literary allusions at the detox farm."

"I do a couple of card tricks too."

"Well, sure, but can you dance?"

"We don't want to wake Les."

"Jesus. No one wants to wake Les."

It was stone-cold dark outside, but a dim bulb burned in the hall. As my eyes got used to the light I could see Sherry Lou was a very striking girl. She was one of those women whose features are less than outstanding on their own. Her nose was too sharp and her eyes were set a little too high on her cheeks. A prominent jaw framed a mouth that was much too big for her face. Mix all this under a startling explosion of apricot hair and she was a stunner and a half. This is the way real beauties are put together, and they leave all the Barbies in the shade.

"You're off to a kinda shaky start," Sherry said. "What

you want to do is at least sort of act like you're getting with the program. Just for a couple of days, anyway. Do that and they'll leave you alone.''

"Makes sense," I said. I wanted to tell her I didn't plan to stay long enough to do anything of the sort, but I didn't know her well enough for that. I wasn't even sure she could dance.

"Watch out for Nina. You're number one on her shit list now. Which is okay with me in a way. Means I drop down to number two.''

"Listen, if you're some kind of troublemaker, you can hie yourself out right now. I have Les to think about.''

"Hie?''

"Absolutely. I will not brook shabby behavior, Sherry Lou.''

"Brook and hie. Wow.''

"I'm of a literary bent myself.''

"You're sweeping me off my feet.''

"Don't get any ideas. Nina is carrying my child.''

Sherry grinned. "She isn't carrying it real well.'' She leaned down and planted a very nice kiss on my cheek. "I gotta hie myself to bed. I expect we'll talk.''

Sherry got up and quickly slipped through the door. The sweet scent of her hair lingered on. And so did something else. Vodka's not supposed to give itself away but it does. Sherry Lou had wit and charm, and she also had a secret stash.

It was there on the edge when I woke and found Sherry in the dark, vague bits and pieces, the leftover shreds that a bad dream leaves behind. Drinkers tend to lose a lot of things and sometimes they get them back. My lounge act had shaken something loose somewhere, found the missing days where I'd tucked them all safely out of sight.

While Sherry was there, it was fine. Everything managed to stay away. When she left and I lay there by myself, there were Tony and the missing briefcase and a lot of things I didn't want to see. I knew a little more than I had before, but it still didn't make a bit of sense. I knew where I'd been, but I didn't know why. I didn't have the slightest idea what I'd done with Tony's briefcase, or why he was desperate to get it back. Maybe I'd find some answers or maybe not. Maybe the two hoods would walk in and I wouldn't have to face Nurse Nina another day.

I could think about Tony, and hanging out at airport bars, and wonder if I'd enjoyed Big D. I couldn't think about the girl. I couldn't handle that. Seeing Karla clearly again, remembering her alive, was something I simply couldn't do. Maybe some day. But not now.

Les saw through us from the start. I decided on breakfast with the gang, mainly because I figured Sherry would be around too. She was. She sat down beside me, and instantly earned an icy glance from Les.

"We have a saying here, Russell," Les said. "Stick with the program and the program will stick with you. Go slack and you fall right back."

"That's two sayings," I said.

"What?"

"You said, 'We've got a saying here.' But then you did two sayings. Things like that throw me off, Les. You start tossing out multiple saws, I'll lose control of my urinary tract."

"I kinda like saws," Sherry said.

"Adage is good too," I said. "It's not as good as saws."

Les turned a shade of red that did not go with his hair. "You can fool around all you like," he said. "It's your life, Russell. If you don't really want to get well, then you won't. You want to make sport of someone who's trying to help, well go ahead."

With that, Les picked up his tray and stalked out.

"Why does the Easter Bunny hide his eggs?" I asked Sherry.

"I don't know, why?"

"So no one'll know he's fucking chickens."

"You get into racial jokes, you're going to lose my respect real quick."

"Rabbits aren't as good as us. That's a proven fact."

Sherry took a bite of dry toast. "Les doesn't care for me a lot. He figures I'll bring you down."

"You just might," I said. "I have no will of my own. I am easily led astray."

"I sure do admire that in a man," Sherry said.

We talked for a while and the room began to clear. We decided we would split Les's orange. We decided that breakfast was clearly the very best meal of the day, especially if the food was fit to eat. When we finished, we walked together down the hall. I hung back when I could, subtle and ever sly, admiring the way Sherry Lou fit into her stone-washed, label-on-the-butt designer jeans. She fit quite well. In the jeans, in the blue denim shirt and everywhere. A fine-looking lady in all respects.

"That's one thing I think about here," Sherry said. "Good food. I look at that tray and I think about all the good restaurants I been. I say to myself, I say, 'Sherry Lou Winn, you could be in New York City sitting down at Four Seasons right now. You could be eating a fat Maine lobster at Maurice. And here you are suckin' shit on a shingle at the detox farm.' "

"I sure do admire a rich drunk," I said.

Sherry grinned. "Les says I ought to be ashamed of myself, all the advantages I've had. He gets real mad, he calls me a remittance person."

"Les said remittance? Wow. I'm sorry I put him down. So are you?"

"Am I rich, you mean? Am I the black-sheep daughter of the clan? You bet. The checks come every month, long as Sherry Lou doesn't darken the door of the old ancestral home."

"You ought to be ashamed."

"I guess I sorta am. But I cash those checks all the same."

We walked the long hallway and started back again. It was too cool to go outside, and too depressing in the lounge. Breakfast was scarcely a memory, but the coffee machine that ate the world was already going strong. Guys named John were lining up to confess their sins. I could see Les square in the middle of all this, and Sherry saw him too.

"It isn't just the money," Sherry said. "Les doesn't like me a lot 'cause I'm the only one here remembers how he used to be before he got to be a saint. I was in my first time when they poured him through the door. Lord God, that was an awesome thing to see. He thought he was being eaten whole by wild hogs. All you had to do was say *oink* and off he'd go."

"So you've been in here before."

"Three times." Sherry Lou made a face. "That's just in *here*, I mean. I've been about everywhere, Russ. I have flat made the rounds."

Sherry gave me a very thoughtful look. The look said maybe I want to tell you all this, and maybe I really don't.

"Russ, I am not exactly your all-American girl," she said finally. "I've been in all the finer farms from coast to coast. I am basically suicidal, chemically dependent on booze and several of your major recreational drugs. The shrinks say I'm sexually addicted but I'm not, so don't let your hopes go astray. I'm awful cute, that's a fact, but I'm not as good a lay as I likely look."

"How am I supposed to answer that?"

"I'd let it go if I were you."

"Right. I think that's what I'll do."

Sherry shook her head and smiled. "You're a first-timer, I can tell. You got that rookie stare. Desperation and surprise. You don't know what you're doing here. Last time you looked, you had a job somewhere and you frequently knew your name. You're wired so tight right now, you'd run down a paraplegic nun to get a drink."

"Now that's not fair," I said. "A nun on a crutch, okay. A nun she's maybe got a broken foot, something like that. Listen, Sherry, you don't mind me asking, what the hell are *you* doing here? You've got plenty of money and you've got a lot of class. You could go about anywhere you want. You're really into this detox stuff, so go dry out at Saint-Tropez. Go down to Cancún. I think I could get a lot of help at Cancún.''

"Oh, good thinking, Russ." Sherry crossed her arms and leaned against the wall. "That's what you want to do. Find a nice big resort with a lot of sun and sand. Everyone's dressed up nice and having fun, scarfing down drinks with umbrellas on the top. And you're saying, 'Golly, no thank you, Mr. Yacht, see I'm dryin' out, I don't guess I'll have a thing.' ''

"Okay, I get the point."

Sherry looked a little sad. "They say I've got an institutional personality, Russ. That's something else they say I've got."

"Well, maybe you don't. Just because somebody said it doesn't mean it's so."

"Doesn't mean it isn't, either," Sherry said.

Chapter 6

Nurse Nina said I could slip into my freshly laundered clothes if I'd agree to take my pills. I told her that was fine with me. I'd had a little round of cold sweats before lunch and I knew the shakes were creeping up fast. All the signs of a major scene were there, and I didn't care to go through that again. So the pills couldn't hurt. Reason said pills or a good stiff drink would do the trick. As near as I could tell, there was not a bar in sight. In order to escape from the Alcoholic Arms I would have to go out standing up. Barfing through the halls like a snake likely wouldn't do at all. They would see through this at once.

Sherry wasn't around for the noonday meal. I wanted to see her, and thought about looking up her room. Then I remembered the vodka on her breath the night before, and decided this was not a good idea. Maybe Sherry didn't care for veal cutlets and lima beans. Or maybe she was having a liquid lunch. In either case, it was better if I let her find me.

Sherry worried me a lot. She was a very attractive lady with a very large monkey on her back. Possibly a whole tribe of monkeys, and Sherry Lou knew them all by name.

It didn't seem right. Sherry Lou looked great. She didn't

look anything at all like a drunk. All the other goofs in the lounge fit the bill, but not Sherry Lou Winn. So maybe that's the way it goes. Maybe that's what everybody thinks. Everyone else is a drunk except you. You see a guy pissing on the cigarette machine, you say this jerk's a drunk, not me. The thought left me with a chill. Me and Les and a roomful of boozers named John. Jesus, I didn't want to think about that.

Tony Palmer and a ghost named Karla were never far away. They followed me through the halls, demanding answers I couldn't give. Every time I tried to stop and work the thing out, I met a blank stone wall. I had to get out of the detox farm, I knew that. My plans were very clear up to there, and then everything came to a halt. Where the hell was I going to go? Nine bucks won't take you very far. If I had a little money I could run for a while but in the end it wouldn't help. Two crazy hoods and every cop in Chicago wanted Russell Murray's hide.

I went through a mental list of everyone I knew. Artie, who ran the Oasis, and didn't know me all that well. A couple of drinking-buddy cops I couldn't trust with a problem like this. A few other people who didn't count and couldn't help. Which left me with a handful of quarters in the late afternoon, trying to recall Jane Kowalski's private number at the *Trib*.

I felt a lot better the minute I thought about Jane. Jane Kowalski is a fine reporter. One of the best. She knows the crime scene in Chicago, and has a fair idea where all the bodies are buried at city hall. At one time, we were briefly entangled in romance. I had some very nice memories of winter weekends by a fire, of porcelain-blue eyes and dark hair. And possibly the longest legs in the world outside of the NBA.

Jane picked up the phone and said, "Jane Kowalski here."

"Jane, listen," I said, "this is Russ."

"Oh my God!" Jane said.

"Jane, I'm in a little trouble. No, I'm in a *lot* of trouble, Jane. I guess you already heard about that."

"I work on a newspaper, Russ. All I ever do is read the funnies and check my horoscope, but sometimes I'll catch the front page."

"Okay, I'm sorry. So you know."

"Russ, I think it's safe to say everybody knows."

"You maybe want to not say *Russ* so much? I mean, someone could walk by the desk, they could pick up a phone . . ."

"Russ?"

"What?"

"Just shut up, Russ, okay?"

"I didn't kill that girl. You ought to know that."

"I didn't think you did."

"Jane, I wake up, I go into the john. These two guys break in and shoot the girl. I go out the window fast. Christ, they were trying to kill *me*. I'm out the window, I'm running down the street—"

"Wait a minute. You saw these guys?"

"Of course I saw 'em, what do you think?"

"What did they look like, you remember that?"

"Big guys. Very big and ugly guys. Blue jeans, big shoes. Little piggy eyes. They looked just alike."

"They did what?"

"I said they looked just alike. You know, like twins. Jane, are you still there?"

"Irv and Mort Wacker," Jane said. Her voice was an octave lower now. I liked it better when it was high. "They *are* twins, Russ, and they are very heavy dudes. They work for Ritchie "Bones" Pinelli. And Ritchie Pinelli works for Frank Cannatella, who is, as we say in newspaper land, reputed boss of the Chicago mob. What the fuck are you into, Russ?"

"I am not into anything, Jane." The name Cannatella made my throat go dry. "I don't *know* people like that. I never knew people like that."

"People like that know you."

"Well, I can't help that. Whatever this is, it's a mistake. I think that's what we've got here, a mistake."

"Russ. Frank Cannatella doesn't make a lot of mistakes. He's made two, maybe three mistakes, and all of them are dead."

"Don't tell me that. Don't tell me things like that."

"Deposit another two dollars and thirty-five cents, please," the operator said. I dinged more quarters in the slot.

"Russ," Jane said, "what were you doing in that hotel with the girl? Okay, I'll rephrase that. What were you doing right *before* that?"

"I'm not sure," I said. "This whole thing has been a shock. I've suffered a little memory loss."

"Right. You were drunk."

"I didn't say drunk. You said drunk. I maybe had a couple of drinks."

"Russ. This is not the tooth fairy, this is Jane."

"Okay."

"Okay what?"

"Okay, I don't remember right before that. I remember Thursday fine. Things get a little hazy after that. I went on a plane trip for Tony. Thursday afternoon or Thursday night. Tony Palmer at the *Literary Times.*"

"I know who he is, Russ. Little short guy, comes up to my crotch."

"Tony likes tall girls a lot."

"Russ, if a toy poodle winked at Tony Palmer, he'd fly it to Bermuda overnight. So you went on a plane. You remember where you went?"

"Of course I remember where I went. Why wouldn't I remember where I went?"

I took her very quickly through the trip. How I flew out of O'Hare to Dallas, hung around somewhere Thursday and Friday night, then flew back Saturday afternoon. I told her about the briefcase and the paranoid writer, how I left the briefcase at the airline desk and went back and picked it up. I told her how

I met the girl named Karla on the plane, and that I didn't recall a lot after that. I told her that I'd talked to Tony on Sunday and he seemed very nervous on the phone. He wanted very much to get his briefcase back, and I didn't know a thing about that.

Jane was very quiet for a while. I could hear people talking at the *Trib.* I could hear the clack of hundreds of fingers typing accidents and rapes, break-ins and the latest big news on the Russell Murray case.

"Russ," Jane said finally, "that is the dumbest fucking story I ever heard. I mean, if they ever give a Nobel for dumb, what you want to do is pack a bag. You ought to get your ticket now, book yourself a Stockholm flight."

"Jane, thank God I called. This is what I need right now."

"Will you wake up, Russ? Jesus. You take this briefcase to Dallas. Some guy you don't know, you don't see, he takes something out of this case, then he puts something in. You fly back to Chicago, and two of Frank Cannatella's prize hoods make a very earnest effort to do you in. And your boss wants this briefcase back. He wants it back a lot. Does this tell us anything, Russ?"

"It tells me someone made a big mistake. That's what I said before. This is all a big mistake."

"Did you look inside the briefcase, Russ?"

"I maybe took a peek."

"And what was inside?"

"Galley proofs. Just like Tony said."

"And that's all."

"Of course that's all. What else you think was inside?"

"Well, gee, I don't know, Russ. I can't think of more than four or five hundred things someone'd hide inside a briefcase, and then maybe con some jerk into taking whatever that was on a plane to Big D. This sure is a puzzler, all right."

"Now wait a minute," I said. "I'm not about to buy that. Tony Palmer wouldn't have anything to do with the mob."

"You know that, do you?"

"No, I don't know. I mean I *know*, okay? Look. I lose a briefcase somewhere and Tony wants it back. Two guys try to knock me off. That doesn't mean the two things are connected in any way. Just because they both kind of happened at once, that doesn't mean a thing."

"I think I've got it," Jane said. "Frank Cannatella sees you in a bar. He puts out the word, he says hit this guy, I don't like the guy's tie."

"Fine. That makes sense to me."

I heard Jane sigh into the phone. "Where are you, Russ? Where are you right now?"

"I'm in Wisconsin. I'm in a sort of—it's an institutional setting is what it is."

"I'm not going to ask," Jane said. "Look, Russ, I'm going to ask around, see what I can find. Call me back tonight."

"Jane," I said, "tell me about the girl. I want to know."

Jane didn't answer for a moment. "Her name was Karla Stark. She was twenty-two, a pediatric nurse. Her family lives out near Rochelle."

I thought about that. "She didn't seem that old," I said. "She looked real young."

"We ran her picture, Russ. She was a very pretty girl. Listen, I think you ought to know we ran your picture, too. I don't know if any copies of the *Trib* will show up over there . . ."

"Oh, shit." I hadn't thought of that. "I'll call you," I said. My hands were really shaking. I managed to get the phone back in the cradle the second try.

I got back to my room and flopped down on the bed. Les wasn't there and I was grateful for that. I didn't need Les. What I needed was time to think. The clock on the wall said twenty after four. It would get dark soon. I could leave after dark. I didn't know where to go but I couldn't stay here. I thought about my picture in the *Trib*. A nurse or an aide or someone could be looking at my picture right now. Hey, that's Russell

Murray, the guy who pissed on the cigarette machine. Jesus Christ, he killed a girl in Chicago, it says right here.

I fought back the urge to get up and run right then. Never mind the fucking dark, just go.

Okay, Murray, take it easy, I told myself. Take a deep breath and try to think. I couldn't leave without my wallet. I had to have that. My call to Jane had taken a very large chunk of my last bit of cash, but I still had the credit card. I wouldn't get anywhere without the credit card.

I thought about Tony, and what Jane had said. She couldn't be right about that. Tony was real uptight when I called, and he wanted his briefcase back. But that didn't mean he was connected to the mob. I could see Tony hijacking a Vegas chorus line. I could see him maybe cheating on his taxes. I couldn't see him in the mob. Mob guys are ugly and they always need a shave. Tony looks good and he always dresses nice. Besides, if Tony Palmer's in the Mafia, what's he doing at *The Literary Times?* Emily Dickinson is not a big favorite with your average family hood. Your name ends in a vowel, you're going to read the racing form.

None of what was happening seemed to make a lot of sense. And if it didn't, I thought, so what? Someone wanted me dead. In the end, it really didn't matter why.

Chapter 7

"What you've got to think about," Les said, "see, it isn't just you. I mean, you're saying to yourself—don't tell me you're not, I know you are—you're saying, 'Hey, I'm all alone. I'm stuck in my head place here and there isn't anyone can understand what it is I'm going through.' That's what you're thinking. That's what's in your head. What I'm saying, Russell, is it just isn't true. I have been where you are, friend. I know, because I've been right there, I have stood in your shoes."

"Les," I said, "you better not be in my fucking shoes. I don't want you in my shoes."

Les showed me his overbite grin. He nodded like a chicken picking gravel off the ground, quick little dips that brought his whole body into play. I was standing at the sink, running a wet comb through my hair. It wasn't even my comb. I had found it in a drawer. I could see Les in the mirror, standing at the bathroom door. He didn't look better in reverse. There was some kind of static in the air and the red mess of hair on his head was coiled to strike.

"See, what that is, Russell, that's a very common figure of speech. I am not actually *in* your shoes. What I'm saying is, I have been caught in foul abuse the same as you. I know exactly where you are.''

''I'm in the bathroom, Les.''

''You're in trouble is where you are. You are swept up in addiction and despair. You have lost control of Self.''

''It might be in my other pants. If I had some other pants.''

''Your Self is still *in* there, Russell. Believe me. You know where it is? It's hiding down there below the booze.''

I put the comb down and turned around. ''So if I locate the Self I find the booze? Now we're getting somewhere.''

Les didn't seem to be amused. ''I don't have to be here. I don't have to put up with this.''

''No you don't, Les.''

''Every time I try to help I get reviled.''

''Reviled is real good. 'Maltreat' is good, too. Not a lot of people use maltreat anymore.''

''Sherry Lou Winn is not the kind of person we need in this place.''

''How did we get on Sherry Winn?''

'' 'Rum' rhymes with 'dumb.' Did you ever think of that?''

''It has never crossed my mind.''

Les turned and left. I decided to keep the comb. It had suffered foul abuse and loss of Self, and several vital teeth were gone. Still, it was the only comb in town.

Before Les came I was stretched out on the bed, wondering if you could still get on a tramp steamer and sail to foreign climes. Bogart or someone used to do it all the time. A guy gets in a jam, he takes a tramp steamer and leaves the world behind. You might have to fuck with Peter Lorre on the way, but you could learn to live with that. You know Myrna Loy shows up looking great in Borneo. She's wearing this stuck-up little smile that says 'I don't think I will but I might, I guess we ought to have a drink.' Which is just about the point where Les shows up, flying low on a caffeine high. Myrna says I'm real sorry, Russ, but I guess I better go.

How did a guy fat as Sidney Greenstreet wear a white suit and tie all day and never sweat? He's sitting in a Malay bar, it's a hundred and forty-two in the shade. A guy like that, you figure he's got to go through twenty, maybe thirty suits a day. Peter Lorre weighs, tops, eighty-two, he's sweating buckets all the time. But the big guy sits there, he doesn't sweat at all.

Nurse Nina stopped me in the hall and I downed my evening pills. She wanted to know what I'd done to Les. I told her I hadn't done anything at all.

"Les has been through it," she said. "He could help you a lot."

"The man's already changed my life."

"Bullshit. I spotted you right off. I've seen your kind before." Nina glanced at her watch and frowned at me. "You better get to supper. It's macaroni night, you don't want to miss that."

"If I clean my plate, do I get an extra pie?"

"You're an asshole, Russell. I don't much like that in a man."

"There's a moon out tonight. You and me in a canoe."

"What I want you to do is leave Les the fuck alone."

"I can handle that," I said.

I waited until Nina was out of sight, then I walked to the nurse's station two halls down and looked up Sherry's room. Sherry Lou Winn was in 184, which the handy map said was at the end of Wing 2. Wing 2 was to my right, so I wouldn't have to go by the dining room or the lounge. I took this as an omen of better days to come.

Sherry's wing looked considerably better than mine. The carpeting in the hall was fairly new. I spotted a few cigarette burns, but very few people had thrown up since the decorators came. There were the usual tables and lamps, and fake oil paintings of the Seine. We're not at a drunk farm, folks, we're staying in a shabby hotel.

I knocked very lightly on Sherry's door. Faint music came from inside, then Sherry opened up without taking off the chain.

"Hey, Russ." She tried to look past me to the hall. "You by yourself or what?"

"No," I said, "I brought Les and all the gang. We've got a lot of onion dip and funny hats."

"Wow, sounds good to me." Sherry slid the chain free and stood aside to let me by. "Watch your step," she said. "It's kinda like a mine field in here."

"No problem," I said. A polite little lie. Sherry's room looked as if a major tornado had recently wandered by. There were great mounds of old newspapers and stacks of books. A pile of fashion magazines had toppled from a chair to form a slippery avalanche across the floor. Cardboard boxes bearing labels from famous stores were everywhere. Some of these were open, the contents still inside, or carelessly scattered nearby. Most of them had never been touched. The closet was full of clothes. Bras and panty hose exploded from every open drawer.

"You maybe noticed," Sherry said. "Housekeeping's not a big thing with me. I can't handle order of any sort."

"Listen," I said, "don't apologize. This is just right for me. I'm into disarray. I was raised by ferrets till I was ten."

Sherry gave me a look that said that was about enough. She swept a tangle of clothes to the floor and offered me a chair, then flopped down on the bed.

"I got a little worried," I said. "You've been here awhile, so you've got to know it's macaroni night. I hear they stole the Four Seasons recipe."

"They did if the chef's name is Boyardee." Sherry made a face. "I flat can't take that trash all the time. The guy that owns this place has got a starch mine on the side."

"Yeah, but you've got to eat."

"My, aren't you sweet to care." Sherry grinned, then leaned

down and pulled a long flat box from under the bed. "I like to keep some goodies on hand. Case anyone drops by."

"My God, Sherry." I stared at the box. "Where the hell did you get all this?"

"I like to order stuff. I figured you noticed that."

"Never crossed my mind."

The box was packed with cans of smoked trout, caviar, truffle pâté, candies from Belgium, and thin little crackers from France.

"Boy, everything from your major food groups. Chocolate and salt."

"What are you, Mr. Health?" Sherry waved vaguely across the room. "I've got a little fridge in the closet. There's a microwave somewhere, too. I think it's in a Neiman-Marcus box."

"They let you keep this stuff in your room?"

"Not your common folk, they don't. The pay's real low in this place. People got to live, and money talks."

"I heard about that."

"It's true as it can be. The idle rich are just the same as you, Russ. 'Cept we can keep shit in our rooms."

"Seems fair enough. The social order breaks down, where are we going to be? People like me'll start wanting foreign shoes and new cars."

"I wouldn't care for that," Sherry said. "You want some Cranapple juice? I got a bottle in the fridge."

"I hate Cranapple juice."

"Me too."

Sherry stood and went to the closet. She hummed to herself as she parted racks of clothes to find the fridge. She poured herself a glass and brought the bottle back with her and sat cross-legged on the bed. I thought Sherry Lou looked great. Her very tight jeans were still tight. Her blouse was unbuttoned far enough for a peek. Her feet were bare and her toes were painted red.

Sherry caught me watching and gave me a little wink. "You

ought to have some juice, Russ. You're looking sorta uptight. Sorta wan and uptight, seems to me.''

"Wan's good," I said. "Wan's better than waxen or pale."

"You want to watch out. You're going to get sallow before long. Russ, you've got something on your mind, I know that. And it isn't all me."

I leaned forward in my chair. I didn't look at Sherry, I looked at a stack of books across the room. "Sherry, I am up to my ass in trouble, okay? I got mixed up in something awful right before I landed in here. I called up a friend a while ago. Now I think I'm in a lot more trouble than I thought. Which doesn't seem possible but it is. I need help."

"Well, shoot." Sherry pretended to pout. "And I thought you were worried 'bout me."

"I was. I mean, I thought you ought to eat. I didn't know you had a gourmet store."

Sherry shifted on the bed. She put her elbows on her knees and cupped her hands beneath her chin. "What kind of trouble are we talking here, Russ?"

"You don't want to ask."

"I thought I just did."

"The kind where I end up dead."

"Oh." Sherry raised a brow. "*That* kind of trouble."

"That kind of trouble," I said. "Or maybe worse. Maybe I don't end up dead, I just wish the hell I was."

I got out a smoke from the crumpled Marlboros in my pants. I didn't see an ashtray around, but I found an old anchovy can on the floor. My stomach was feeling queasy. Even macaroni sounded good. Sherry didn't offer any caviar or trout. The rich can be cruel, even when they're cute.

"So what can *I* do?" Sherry said. "You need a little dough?"

"Sherry, I didn't come in here for that."

"I didn't say you did."

"Okay. Since you asked, you might set me up in South America for a while. And you can tell me how to get the hell out of this place."

Sherry looked surprised. "What are you talking about?"

"I mean I can't stick around, I've got to go. I need to know how close they watch the doors. Maybe you can—what? Get out through the kitchen after dark. Shit, I don't know. I've just got to get *out.*"

"For Christ's sake, Russ." Sherry shook her head and poured herself another drink. "You want to leave, you want to go? So go. Walk out the door."

I looked at Sherry. "They let you do that?"

"What do you think, you're in prison or something? Tell 'em you're taking off. Tell them you're going AMA."

"What's that?"

"Against medical advice. They'll bitch and moan how you're making a big mistake, you didn't give the program a chance. Tell them fuck you very much. Wave when you drive away."

Her words tripped an alarm somewhere. God, I'd forgotten about my car. It simply never crossed my mind. I probably didn't even *have* a car. The cops had picked me up and brought me here. That meant the car was impounded someplace. They had my car and they had my name. They had my Illinois plates.

Something cold crawled up my back. The Chicago police would have an APB on the car. So the cops in Wisconsin would have it too. All they had to do was drop my name in a computer and I'd pop right on the screen. They'd know exactly where I was.

"Russ," Sherry said, "you look kind of sick to me."

"They send you to the chair in Illinois, or what?" I told her I thought the cops had my car. I told her I thought I ought to go, that I didn't have a lot of time to talk.

Sherry grinned. "You've got a car, Russ. It's in the parking lot."

"How do you know that?"

"I know a lot of things, friend."

"Sherry, don't pull the gypsy bit on me, okay?"

"Right. A guy at the desk knows the cop who brought you in. The guy told me. What you did, you lucked out. You're a first-time offender. They didn't file charges. One of the cops who picked you up, the friend of the guy I know, this cop is AA. He gave you a break.''

"So they don't have my name anywhere?"

"I don't know what cops do. I'd guess they maybe don't.''

I felt a ray of hope. I could check out and go. I wouldn't have to run through the Great Midwest, I could flee in my very own car.

"I need my wallet and my keys," I told Sherry. "How do I go about that?"

"Ask for them at the desk.''

"And that's that?''

"That's it, pal." Sherry gave me a funny little grin. "I guess I'll miss you, Russ. You're a little bit goofy, but you might've been fun.''

"Thanks. I've been fun before. I sincerely hope to be fun again."

"Stress'll bring you down. Do it every time.''

"That's a fact.''

"I can fix you up a stash. Crackers and a couple cans of stuff for the road.''

"I guess not.''

"I've got an extra bottle of juice.''

"Sherry," I said, "I appreciate the thought. I think I'd better go.''

Sherry blew a strand of apricot hair from her face, and there was that silly smile again, that lopsided grin, that sly and lazy look behind the eyes that said "I've got a secret and don't you wish you did." I hadn't caught the look before. Maybe I was thinking how I had to break out of the detox farm before the SWAT team met me at the door. Or maybe other parts of Sherry Lou were on my mind and I didn't see the smile. I missed it once but I didn't miss it twice. I have seen that smile a thousand times, looking back at me from a mirror behind the bar. It's a laid-back hazy kind of look that says, 'Fuck you, pal, I've got the fires banked up, I've got the glow, I'm feeling fine.' And there was the look on Sherry Lou. The girl who woke me up with vodka on her breath had been sitting right in front of me slugging it down. And I was so out of it, I never even knew.

"Sherry Lou," I said, "why do I get the idea you're not getting with the program here? I feel you're letting down Les and the team."

"I feel kinda bad about that. Les has sure been good to me." Sherry's crooked grin told me that she knew I'd caught her act, that she thought I was kind of slow.

"Let me guess," I said. "You send out for the juice, then you pour about half down the john and put the booze on top of that."

"God, no." Sherry made a face. "I pour it *all* out. Can't stand the stuff. What I do is I add a little maraschino juice to get the shade. Think pink, Russ. Shoot, you can drink this mother in the lounge. Sure you won't have a little sip?"

"What I'd like, Sherry Lou, is not a sip. What I'd like is about a quart. That'd do me for a start. What I'm going to do, what I've got to try and do, is drive my car somewhere. I will drive, and hope to God my eyes don't fall out. That, and try not to throw up on a major interstate."

"Right," Sherry said, "you don't want to throw up. I'll drink to that."

Sherry drained her glass. She looked at me a very long time, or somewhere past me to the wall. Then she slid off the bed and put her feet on the floor and made her way toward me through the clutter and debris. When she stopped, the crotch of her jeans was maybe half an inch away. She stood there and didn't say a thing and didn't move, just waited to see if I could possibly imagine what I ought to do next, if I was smart enough to figure out a play.

What I did instead of that was give her fairly solid proof I was as goofy as I looked. I stood and said, "Sherry, I'd honest to God like to stay. I hope you know that."

Sherry gave me a lazy grin. "I *know* you've got to go. But you don't have to go right now."

"I really think I do. I mean, that's what I ought to do."

Sherry laced her arms around my neck and brought her face up to mine. Her kiss was soft and easy. Her lips teased the corners of my mouth, daring me to catch her before she got away. She pressed herself against me, letting me know clearly she was there. Every part of Sherry Lou moved at once. Nothing ever stood still. Her pelvis made a tight little circle, looking for the perfect place to light. One long leg found its way between mine. I decided Nurse Nina and Les were likely right. I had not given the program a chance. The institutional life might be the thing for me. I reached up and found Sherry's arms and gently pushed her away.

Sherry blinked in surprise. "What the hell's the matter with you, Russ?"

"I don't know," I said. "I think I'm going nuts."

"Fine. You want to go nuts, do it on your own time."

"Sherry, all I want to do right now is pick you up and toss you in bed. That's what I want to do. But I've got to get out of here now. I am flat out scared is what I am. I don't think I want to be dead."

"Jesus, Russ." Sherry stood back and put her hands on her hips. "Nobody's going to find you here, you're not going to be dead."

"You don't know that."

"Yes, I do know that. Who's going to look for you at the boozer hotel?"

"I've got to go, Sherry." I moved past her to the door.

"Well this is just fine," Sherry said. "You get a girl all worked up, you leave her standing at the door."

"Now, you worked *me* up, Sherry Lou. I hardly did a thing."

"That's the damn truth."

"Besides," I said, "you told me you really didn't care about sex."

"I *told* you I wasn't a sex addict's what I said." Sherry gave me a withering stare. "I didn't say I never got the urge."

I opened the door. "I've got to go, Sherry. I want you to know I feel bad about this, I really do."

"Fuck you, Russell," Sherry said.

I walked into the hall. Sherry slammed the door at my back. The fake pictures shook on the wall. I could still feel Sherry's mouth. Every inch of her body had left warm indentations on mine. Vital parts below the waist were still screaming red alert, unaware that there was nothing to attack.

Russ, you are in the wrong institution, I thought. No man in his right mind would leave a lovely and willing girl behind to go drive across Wisconsin in the dark. Even if the radio worked. Even if you had a fifth of Scotch by your side, and the station played all-night jazz.

Chapter 8

Nina wasn't around. Even angels of mercy have to sleep. A middle-aged guy dressed in whites manned the nurses'-station desk. He had a sad horse face and bleary eyes. He was drinking coffee black as road tar and checking charts. I waited and he didn't look up. A man who loves his work doesn't need to watch the world go by.

"Listen," I said, "I'm leaving. I want to check out."

"What for?" He didn't take his eyes off the chart.

"What do you mean, what for?"

"I got to ask. They like me to ask what for."

"Okay," I said, "you asked."

The name tag on his shirt said "Clyde Bob." Next to the tag was a twenty-year pin. I was glad I was dealing with a pro.

"Clyde Bob, I'm in a little hurry," I said, "I need some help."

"It's just Clyde," he said.

"What?"

"I said it's just Clyde. Bob's my last name. You don't have to say Clyde Bob. A guy's name is Fred Jones, you wouldn't say 'I'm in a little hurry, Fred Jones,' you'd say Fred."

"Fine. I'm in a little hurry, Fred."

Clyde finally looked up. He studied me a moment, then showed me a crooked grin. "You're Murray Russell, right?"

"Russell Murray. Everybody gets it wrong."

"Guy that pissed on the cigarette machine."

"I'll bet you know Les."

Clyde frowned. "Jesus, you just got here, pal."

"I just got here, Clyde. I'd sure like to stay, but I've got to go. Is that okay with you?"

"Hostile attitude. I see it all the time." Clyde shook his head. "You've got a lot of anger inside. You're wound up like a two-dollar clock. Your body's crying out for strong drink. You can't get the booze, so you figure what the hell, I'll pass out a little strong abuse. I'll strike out and hurt my fellow man. I bet you'd like to hit me in the face. I got to warn you I'm into martial arts. Here, sign this."

Clyde found a form somewhere and slid it on the countertop. There was a pen chained to the desk. I didn't stop to read, I just signed.

"What the fuck do I care," Clyde said. "Go get yourself beat up a little more. You'll come barfing back soon, they all do."

"You've been very kind," I said. I folded the paper twice and stuck it in my pants. "Now, I'd like to have my stuff. I've got a wallet and some keys."

"Can't do that," Clyde said.

"You can't do what?"

"Can't get your stuff. Come back in the morning about eight, you get your stuff."

I looked at Clyde and gripped the countertop. "I don't want it in the morning. I want my stuff now."

"Your stuff's in the safe," Clyde said.

"So get it out."

"Can't. Day shift's got the key."

I tried to look sincere. It's hard to look sincere when your stomach's doing flips and the shakes are coming back.

''Clyde, listen,'' I said. ''I got a call a while ago. My mother's in the Peace Corps. She's had a bad accident. I need to be by her side.''

''No kidding?'' Clyde grinned and showed me bad teeth. ''Shit, I got to write that one down. Go to bed, Murray. That's what you ought to do.''

''I don't want to go to bed.''

''I bet you do,'' Clyde said. He looked below the counter at something I couldn't see. ''If you don't, I bet you will. Nina gave you a big ol' Seconal. About half an hour ago.''

''I took a sleeping pill? I don't want a sleeping pill, I got to drive.''

''If I was you, I'd pick me a soft place to land. You don't want that sucker to hit you standing up.''

''Oh, Jesus.'' I turned and left Clyde Bob and started back down the hall. I couldn't go to sleep. Not now. I had to get out.

Somewhere in the back of my mind I knew Sherry was right. There wasn't any reason to think the cops were on my tail or had the slightest idea where to look. But reason didn't cut it any more because fear was in there fucking with my head. Fear said get your ass out of here, Russ. If you go to sleep now, you're going to wake up dead.

When I turned the first corner I stopped and stuck a finger down my throat. I gagged and hugged the wall. The heaves started coming and tore everything apart. I wanted to quit but the throw-up gear was in drive and my stomach didn't know how to stop. It kept on doing what I'd told it to do and not a damn thing came up.

When it finally let go I was too weak to stand and I was sweating like a hog. All I wanted to do was sit and rest, and if I did I knew I'd never get up. The pill was still in there and all I'd done was wear myself out. Which just about figures, I thought. When you need it, nothing's there. You want to hold it down, everything from last Christmas spills out on somebody's rug.

* * *

There were still a few people in the halls, but everything was closed except the lounge. The happy old couple I'd spotted on the lawn were dozing by the TV set. The clock said nearly seven. I tried the dining room door but it was locked. There was a door marked "Emergency Exit Only" down the hall, and it was locked too. I stood there shaking, wondering what the hell to do next. I could fake a heart attack. They'd have to take me somewhere and I could knock out the driver on the way. I could set the place on fire. When the engines came I'd run outside and steal a truck.

The thought suddenly hit me and I felt like a dope. I didn't have to do anything at all. I could do like Sherry said: You want to go, go. Walk out the front door. Fine. Arson would be a lot of fun, but I didn't really have the time for that.

The guy at the front desk looked a lot like Clyde. When I handed him my paper, he frowned at it and gave me a surly look and went back to *Plastic Man*. I'd made him lose his train of thought. Now he'd have to start from scratch.

It was cool outside, and I didn't have a coat. The night was pitch-black. There were two dim fixtures filled with bugs above the door. A long gravel drive circled the entryway. The drive was lined with bare-limbed trees. A broad lawn disappeared in the dark. I spotted the parking lot, off to the right of the drive. I couldn't see a thing beyond the trees, not a light from a house or a glow up in the sky. Okay, so Wilson Rehab was in the country somewhere. If I followed the drive, I would probably end up on an interstate, or at least a road into some town.

Since I hadn't arrived in a conscious state, I didn't have the slightest idea where I was. Why hadn't I asked someone? Sherry knew where we were. Why didn't I think of that? Why didn't I think of a lot of things I never thought about?

When I reached the parking lot, I was tempted to find my car. I decided there was no need for that. What could we do, sit and talk? I wished I liked to watch TV. You catch a bunch of cop shows, you learn how to hot-wire a car. Every cop show, someone wires two or three cars.

I was nearly past the lot when the lights swept through the trees and cut a bright path across the road. I left the drive fast and ducked behind a van. It was probably a nurse coming on for the late shift. Or someone bringing in Uncle Ed, who couldn't stay off the kerosene. The car was a big white Lincoln Continental. It came on slow, squeezing gravel beneath the tires. The lights arced past the van and turned into the parking lot. All I had to do was wait. They would park and then they'd go inside. I'd wait till they were gone, then I'd start back up the drive.

The car didn't stop. It slowed to a crawl, passed the first row and started on the next. What were they waiting for? I wondered. The lot wasn't full and there were plenty of places to park. The driver left the second row and started on the third. Halfway down the row he pulled up. A guy on the passenger side got out. He looked around awhile, then walked in front of the headlights and shined his flash on a car. The flash found the hood and then the plates. The plates looked familiar and so did the car because they both belonged to me. I could see the man clearly in the Continental's lights. He was thick as a side of beef and wore Li'l Abner shoes and there are only two guys in the world look like that.

For some reason, I wasn't scared at all. I wasn't shaking anymore and my heart didn't stop. There was something wrong with that, but I was grateful for whatever it was that kept me intact.

The Wacker with the flash said something to the one in the car. The driver got out. He wanted to see the plates too. Okay, I thought, all you've got to do, Russ, is sit tight. Sit there and wait. The hoods would go inside. I would disappear into the night. I wouldn't stick to the drive, I'd take off to the left or the right. By the time they came out, I'd be gone. It was dark and they wouldn't know where to look. It was a very sensible plan. Hide and run. Go from town to town. It used to work for "The Fugitive" all the time.

And that was the moment when my stomach said, okay, we're ready now, Russ, and I threw up on my souvenir shirt. You could have heard me in Chicago. Jesus, you could've heard me in Cozumel.

Chapter 9

I got up and ran. One of the hoods yelled, but I didn't look back. When I hit the gravel road, both my thongs disappeared. My bad foot hit a sharp rock and I nearly fell. I limped to the lawn and started running in a lopsided gait. The building was to my left. Motion caught my eye and I saw one of the Wacker boys sprinting for the entry, trying to cut me off. I could hear the other one cursing and puffing at my back.

I had a fair head start, but my form wasn't great. No Olympics for Murray this year. A patch of grass exploded ten feet off to my left. I didn't hear a sound, so the Wackers were being discreet. Good, I thought, we don't want to wake the drunks.

I made the corner of the building and jumped a flower bed. Two nurses were standing in the dark by an open door. They looked up, startled, and backed off. All they wanted was a ten-minute break and a smoke. They didn't need a guy with vomit on his shirt.

The hall inside was too bright. Ten yards down it split off to the left and the right. Arrows pointed to Wing 1 and Wing 2. Wing 2 was Sherry Lou and I hopped off to the right. The carpet felt good to my foot, the hall seemed a hundred yards long. I knocked on 184, looked over my shoulder and waited for a Wacker to appear. Sherry opened up. She saw me and her eyes turned flat.

"Russ," she said, "you got a lot of fucking nerve—"

The chain wasn't locked and I pushed my way inside. Sherry went sprawling on a stack of French fashion magazines. I shut the door fast and threw the lock, turned and helped Sherry up and grabbed her arms.

"Don't talk," I said, "just listen. I went outside. Two guys who want to kill me were in the lot. Now they're inside. I mean they're in the goddamn building right now. I hurt my foot again. I don't have any shoes."

I could tell she wasn't sure. "You making this up?"

"No, I'm not making this up."

"You ought to get out of that shirt. It's not goin' to set a trend."

"Right." I peeled off the shirt and tossed it across the room. Someone yelled out in the hall. A nurse screamed, and someone threw a lamp against the wall.

"For God's sake, Russ." Sherry looked at me in alarm, then went to the door and pressed her eye against the little hole. In a moment she turned around, glanced about the room, didn't find anything she liked, and started digging in the closet debris. Expensive underwear and alligator shoes began to fly, then Sherry reappeared. She dragged out a backpack and tossed it on the bed and turned to me.

"Russ," she said, "you stay right here. Turn off the lights and lock the door. The windows aren't supposed to open but they do."

"Sherry—"

"Just shut up, Russ. I'll get the car. You come out the window when you see me flash the lights. Don't forget the pack."

I shook my head. "You can't get the car. I haven't got the keys. They wouldn't let me have my wallet or my keys."

Sherry rolled her eyes. "Jesus, Russ, you think you're the

only one here's got a car? I've got a car. We don't need your fucking car.''

Sherry started for the door. I cut her off past the bed. "What do you think you're doing? You can't go out there."

"Why not? Everybody else is out there."

She switched off the lights and left me in the dark. I turned the lock as quietly as I could and put my ear against the door. The chase had moved off down the hall. I thought about the Wackers, and what they'd try to do. They couldn't kick in every door. They knew someone would call the cops. They didn't have time to mess around. Maybe they'd find my room and shoot Les. Maybe Clyde Bob would subdue them with martial arts.

I found my way to the window in the dark, then kneeled down and opened it half a foot. The detox farm had come to life. There were people in shabby bathrobes wandering everywhere about, up the drive and out across the lawn. The nurses and aides were going nuts, trying to herd everybody back.

From Sherry's window, I could see a small corner of the lot. I couldn't see the Wackers' car. It occurred to me I should have said something to Sherry, like the hoods were driving a white Continental and to stay away from that. I should've said, "Sherry, I don't want you getting mixed up in this," like the good guys do on TV. That's two things I should've said.

I wondered what the Wackers were doing now. They were probably talking to Les. Les was saying, "Listen, if I were you guys, I'd check out Sherry Lou Winn."

A dark shape appeared on the drive, a car without lights. The driver hesitated for an instant, then hit the accelerator hard. The rear wheels whined on gravel, the car gave a jerk and went hurtling off the drive across the lawn. People scattered in its path. An old guy stopped and threw his slippers at the hood. The driver cut the wheels sharply left; the car skidded on grass and nearly ran down a nurse. I blinked and took a second look. Unless the rich craved battered red Toyotas, the car Sherry was driving wasn't hers, it was mine. Clyde Bob had the keys, so how the hell had she managed that?

Sherry wrenched the wheels and came straight at me across the lawn. She hit the lights and smashed a row of shrubs, then braked to a stop maybe twenty yards away. I threw the pack to the ground and pulled myself over the sill. I seemed to be going out windows a lot without a shirt, something I'd have to stop.

Sherry blinked the lights and honked the horn. I picked up the backpack and limped across the lawn. Sherry popped open the passenger door. I tossed the pack in back and threw myself into the seat. Sherry ground the gears and took off.

"Listen," I said, "you're not giving this car proper care."

"Shut up," Sherry said. "I don't want to talk to you, Russ, I gotta think."

"What's the hurry? Who could've noticed that sly approach?"

We hit the curb hard and bounced back on the drive.

"What kind of car are those guys driving, you know?"

"A white Continental. It's over on the lot."

"Good."

"That's good?"

Sherry didn't answer. She spun up the drive, past the entry way. We caught Les and Clyde Bob in the lights. Sherry sat on the horn and didn't stop. Clyde and Les dived for the safety of the steps. I looked up then and saw the front doors swing open wide, and there were two fireplugs dressed just alike.

"Oh, shit," I yelled, "it's them!"

Sherry gave the Wackers a glance, then raced up the drive and made a hard turn into the lot.

I stared at her and nearly threw up. "Sherry, what the *fuck* are you doing? Let's get the hell out of here!"

"Right," Sherry said. "Got to handle this first."

I tried to grab the wheel. Sherry made another sharp right and slammed me hard against the door. I looked and saw the Wackers in our lights. The driver was in his seat and the other hood was reaching for the door. Sherry stepped on the gas and went straight for the Wackers' car. I braced my hands against the dash. Sherry hit the brakes and we smashed into the Lincoln head-on. Glass shattered and something like a fender hit the ground. The Wacker on the passenger side went sprawling out of sight.

"Sherry," I said, "for God's sake—"

Sherry backed off, squealed the tires and raced down the row, made a left and then a sharp left again. She stopped, backed up, and turned the Toyota around, heading back the way we'd come, scraping the ends of three cars along the way. She stopped again and killed the lights.

I let out a breath. Sherry turned to me and glared. "Russ, I just peed in my pants, okay? You say one word and you are *out*. I will dump you in rural Wisconsin on foot."

"You get a chance," I said, "you need to learn to parallel-park."

Sherry waved me off. The Continental screamed around the corner the way we'd come. Sherry hit the gas. The Lincoln appeared and she hit it broadside. The front of the Toyota caved in. The radiator hissed and blew steam into the air. Sherry backed off and rammed the car again. I could see the face of the driver over our hood. He looked startled and betrayed. He couldn't believe some maniac with apricot hair was attacking him with a Japanese car. It wasn't even December and we were doing Pearl Harbor again. Sherry struggled with the gears and finally shoved us in reverse. The car shook and made agonizing sounds but wouldn't move. Sherry jammed her foot to the floor. Rubber shrieked against asphalt and filled the car with the smell of burning tires. Through the radiator steam I caught the Wacker on the far side of the Lincoln stumble out and slam his door. He grinned at us and leaned across the hood, bringing his arms out straight before his face.

"Sherry, look out!" I yelled, but Sherry had seen him too. She threw herself down in the seat. I tried to jam my body through the floor. Three large holes suddenly starred the safety glass. Sherry was twisted like a circus acrobat, but she never took her foot off the gas. She shouted something at me and her elbows hit me in the face. Metal gave a torturous groan somewhere and the Toyota jerked free. The car hurtled wildly across the lot in reverse. Sherry struggled to untangle herself and find the wheel. I stared through the frosted windshield. Something large and white was stuck to our grille. It looked very much like a Continental door.

We weaved across the lot, hitting every other car. I figured we were going maybe sixty, sixty-five.

"Sherry, you want to sorta straighten out now," I said. "You want to find another gear?"

"We haven't *got* another gear," Sherry said. "What we also don't got's a fucking brake. Russ, I think I better stop."

"How do you plan to do that without a—*Jesus,* Sherry!"

Sherry rammed us into the front of a Chevy van. My knees hit the dash. I looked at Sherry Lou. "Parking's not a big thing with you, is it? I want you to think about that."

Sherry looked straight ahead. She still had her hands on the wheel. "I smell gas," she said calmly. "You want to sit here and talk to yourself, that's fine. I feel I have to go."

I sniffed the air. I smelled it too and the hair started climbing up my neck. I jerked the pack out of the back. For some inane reason I took the car keys.

Sherry was already out the door. She ran past the van to the next row of cars and I limped along behind. I didn't want to think about the Wackers, so I didn't look back.

Sherry stopped at a bottle-green car, yanked open the door and got in. I jumped in beside her and tossed the pack in back. Sherry burned rubber and roared out of the lot. She headed up the drive, then made a sharp right, bounced across the curb and out across an empty field. We weaved through second-growth trees for a while and then stopped. I heard sirens somewhere, looked through the trees and saw red and blue flashers to our left. Suddenly the sky grew bright and a hot blast of air hit the car. I twisted around and saw an orange ball of fire far behind us in the lot. So much for the red Toyota. My insurance company wasn't about to buy this.

In a minute we saw the white Continental racing up the exit drive without lights. The right front wheel was out of whack. Vital parts dragged along behind, making sparks. The cop car squealed past the entryway and wailed around the circle in hot pursuit.

Sherry leaned past me, flipped open the glove compartment and found a half-empty pint.

"There's a back road somewhere off past the trees," she said. "It'll put us right on the interstate. Where you think you'd like to go next?"

Chapter 10

"Good question," I said. "How about Brazil? I've never been to Brazil."

"I have," Sherry said. "It's a whole lot of fun. But we're sort of in Wisconsin right now. We ought to stop off and fill up and maybe buy some tropic wear."

"You sure know how to stomp on romance."

"Well you'd know all about that." Sherry unscrewed the bottle and started to take a drink. I took it from her and put the cap back on and tossed it on the floor by my feet.

Sherry gave me a puzzled look. "What the hell is this?"

"I just thought we ought to hold off until we figure out what to do next. Sort of keep our heads straight, so to speak."

Sherry gripped the wheel. "You sure picked a great fucking time to take the cure."

"Sherry, I am not taking the cure. I'm taking a precaution, that's all."

"I should've brought Les. Les is a hell of a lot of fun compared to you." Sherry gave me her best hard look. "Russ, tell me you don't want a drink. Tell me that."

"I didn't say I didn't want a drink."

"Aha."

"That's not the point. I want a drink as bad as you. The point is, my record's not looking too good. I've been on two drunks in the last few days. The last time I blacked out, I ended up in Wilson Rehab, which is not too bad, considering I could have killed somebody instead of running off the road. The time before that, I woke up in a hotel room with a girl I didn't know. The two goons you saw back there broke into the room, Sherry Lou. They walked in and shot the girl dead. She was there because of me. They wanted me, not her, but that won't do her a lot of good now."

Sherry turned away from the road and stared. "My God, Russ. You never told me about that."

"I didn't see any reason why I should."

"My God," she said again.

Sherry didn't look mad anymore. She looked a little scared, a little ragged around the eyes. Sherry Lou put on a very tough act, but there were soft spots underneath she didn't want the world to see. I wondered if she'd ever even known anyone who hadn't died in a bed.

I told her the story, as much as there was to tell. Maybe I thought if I laid it out again, it would make some sense to me. I took her through my Thursday meet with Tony, and the plane trip to Dallas after that. Then the briefcase bit on Saturday afternoon, and meeting Karla on the plane. How I'd gone out the window ahead of the Wacker boys. I even told her about the T-shirt and the thongs. I told her how I'd managed to phone Tony before I got back on the road and blacked out. How I'd phoned Jane Kowalski from the Wilson Rehab, and that I ought to stop and call her up again.

Sherry didn't say a thing for a while. She let me take the wheel while she pulled back a headful of frizzy auburn hair and tied it with a string. She tapped her fingers on the wheel and worked her tongue around her lips. Two little frown lines creased between her eyes, and then she nodded as if she'd worked it all out.

"Okay," she said finally, "we need to stop somewhere and get you in some decent clothes. And yeah, you ought to make that call. We better find the *Trib* somewhere, see if they've got anything new. I'm not sure about the car, what do you think? The cops'll figure out you're with me. If they don't, Les'll fill 'em in. I guess we ought to eat. I'll find us a—"

"Sherry Lou . . ."

"I'll find us a—what?"

"Sherry, you keep saying *we* and we're talking about me. I am up to my ass in this shit, and I don't want you in it too."

Sherry laughed. "Didn't you notice? I'm already in it, Russ."

"I know you are. And I don't want you in it any more. You can let me off at a bus station whenever we hit a town. You don't have to worry about the hoods. If the cops don't get 'em, they won't be coming after you. You can tell the police I forced you to drive the car. They can't prove I didn't. They'll have to take your word."

"Russell . . ." Sherry gave me a grin. "That's all very noble. If I didn't have to drive I'd throw up. I feel I'd better stick around. I keep thinking you've got real potential for fun and I want to see how it comes out."

"Sherry, I know exactly how it comes it out."

"No you don't. What you are is overwrought. I'd say you've got a lot of stress."

"Les thinks I do too."

"Les ought to know. A man pursued by hogs is going to have a good handle on stress."

I lay back and watched Sherry drive. The car was a brand-new BMW. The showroom smell was still intact. The radio sounded great and the heater worked fine. Everything probably worked fine. I could keep my feet warm, but I was a little cool on top without a shirt. Sherry told me to get a sweater from her pack. I dug it out and put it on. It was ten or twelve sizes too small, but it helped.

Sherry found a highway, which was 15 South. It would take us into Beloit, Wisconsin, and then across the line to Illinois.

We drove for a while and then Sherry decided there was too much traffic on the road and we might run into cops. We turned west on 20, and a sign said we'd passed East Troy.

I thought about Wilson Rehab. Everyone in bathrobes running from Sherry Lou. I thought about the Wackers, and wondered where they were. I thought about my car going up in a fireball just like they do on TV.

"Sherry Lou," I said, "you want to tell me about the keys? I'm a little bit fuzzy on the keys."

"Oh, right." Sherry dug into the pocket of her jeans. "I forgot. Got your wallet, too." She tossed the wallet in my lap.

I looked at Sherry Lou. "Clyde Bob said my stuff was locked up."

"Everybody's stuff is locked up."

"But Clyde Bob can fix that."

"Clyde Bob and me are kinda close."

"You and Clyde Bob."

"I told you, Russ. Those folks have got to supplement their income some. Who do you think smuggles in my booze?"

I shook my head at that. "I've lost a lot of respect for Clyde Bob. You expect a little more from a twenty-year man."

"Clyde Bob expects a little more too," Sherry said. "A new guy'll shoot the head nurse for maybe thirty, forty bucks. An old hand like Clyde is going to run you twice as much. The thing is, you deal with Clyde, he isn't ever going to tell."

I stuck my wallet in my pants. "You know where you're going, Sherry Lou?"

"Haven't got the foggiest idea."

"That's good to know."

I leaned back and closed my eyes. My head felt as big as a cantaloupe. I itched all over like bugs were crawling in and out of my pores. I thought about the bottle on the floor. Mr. Big Mouth. I'd cut myself off at the pass.

Something like Aunt Jemima syrup filled my head. The lights on the road wore white halos, as if we were driving through a

fog. The dash looked like a Christmas tree. Sherry Lou said
something about Bermuda or Brazil I couldn't hear.

"That's fime," I said.

"What's that, Russ?"

"That's gool. Hassa lassa bahm."

"Russ?" Sherry Lou was somewhere far away. "What the
fuck are you *talking* about, Russ?"

I woke up feeling like a fifty-pound guppy in a five-gallon tank.
My head was wedged under the dash and I couldn't find my feet.
I managed to sit up and get the right end on the floor. The sky
was a dirty gray outside and a squirrel stared at me from the
hood. It looked a lot like Les, except the squirrel had better teeth.

The car was sitting in overgrown brush under two dead hack-
berry trees. I stepped out on the cold ground and saw the backside
of a house. The house was officially white, but the paint had
peeled off to basic gray. Sherry Lou sat in a lawn chair on a
former patio. A rusty iron table was covered with Big Mac debris.

Sherry Lou waved a french fry at me and grinned. "Hey,
old sleepyhead's arisen from the dead. Coffee's in the carton,
burgers in the sack."

I got out and joined her, sat, and reached for coffee and one
of Sherry's cigarettes. "Where the hell are we, Sherry Lou?
Jesus, I'm freezing to death."

"We'll get you some gear when the stores open up. We're
in somebody's backyard, couple of miles out of Whitewater,
Wisconsin. The house has got a 'For Sale' sign, which I figure's
been up since 1942. What happened to you, pal? You conked
out on me like a rock."

"I guess my Seconal kicked in. I thought I threw it up."

"Shoot, you get within a mile of one of Nina's sleepy pills
you're lucky you're not flat-out dead."

The aroma of mustard and grease made me want to throw
up, but hunger said you better take a chance. I wolfed a burger

down, dissolved the mess with coffee, and started on another cigarette.

"You feeling okay?" I said. "You get some sleep?"

"I'm 'bout as good as I can be."

"Where'd you sack out, the back seat?"

"No, Russ. I piled in on top of you. I didn't think we ought to be apart."

"I appreciate that."

I tried to fold my feet up under me on the chair. The chair was colder than the ground. Sherry saw my problem and motioned at the car.

"You want to get back inside? It's six forty-five. We got a couple of hours before they open up the stores."

"I'm tired of the car," I said. "I think I'd rather freeze. You know what? I forgot to say good-bye to Les."

"You think a postcard'll do?"

"It's better than him thinking I didn't care." A thought suddenly hit me and I looked at Sherry Lou. "I need to find a phone booth somewhere. I'd like to catch Jane before she gets off to work."

"She real hot for early-morning calls?"

I shook my head. "Anytime she hears from me is a bad time. I should've called her last night. My schedule got kind of screwed up."

"Where you think you went wrong?"

I tried another sip of coffee. It was cold, but the caffeine was still intact. Sherry Lou was inspecting her nails. She played with the little blue strip from the cigarette pack, winding it around her Bic lighter and letting it flip back. She looked up and saw me watching and looked away. She played with the lighter awhile, but she wouldn't glance at me.

"Russ," she said finally, "I guess this is something you've got to see. I kinda—you know, wanted you to get waked up a little first. Get a little coffee inside."

She reached behind her and picked up a paper from the ground and handed it to me. "It's a day old," she said. "They had a copy left out in front of the Dairy Queen. I guess they'll have today's real soon but I didn't want to wait around.''

I wasn't listening anymore. The second I saw the *Trib* my heart clutched up in my throat. I didn't want to look, I knew exactly what I'd see.

The story was at the bottom of page one. The headline said, "Killer Still Sought in Brutal Slaying of Rochelle Nurse." They ran a very bad picture of me. I'd had it taken the year before when Tony made me speak to a bunch of librarians somewhere. Karla's picture showed her the day she graduated from nursing school. She had longer hair then, and she looked close to thirteen.

The story didn't tell me much I hadn't heard already from Jane. The cops were looking into "several possible angles" but the major suspect was still me. Nobody mentioned the Wacker boys. Nobody saw the guys chasing me down the street. No one seemed to wonder why I'd knocked down the hotel door when I was already there in the room. Why muddy things up, when you've got Russell Murray on a string?

I can't handle journalistic schmaltz. An ugly kid never gets run down by a bus. It's always the "handsome sixth grader" or the "attractive cheerleader who had the best grade average in school." Women who get murdered are "striking redheads" and "lovely blue-eyed blondes." All the dogs are still running around alive.

This time it was different. This time it was someone I knew. Karla was the "raven-haired beauty who didn't have an enemy in the world" and it was true. She looked like an angel, and the Wackers didn't hate her at all, she had simply been in the way. In the way and in a hotel room with me.

"Russ, listen," Sherry said, "we can go find a phone if you like. Or we can just drive around somewhere. You want to sit tight, I can get the heater on."

I wasn't listening real good. I wasn't too much there, I was back in that hotel room with Karla Stark.

"All right," I said, "maybe that's what we ought to do . . ."

Chapter 11

Jane Kowalski answered on the very first ring. I said, "Listen, Jane, it's me."

"Jesus, who else would it be? You son of a bitch, I told you to call me last night. This is fucking morning, it's not last night."

"I got tied up last night."

"Oh, right. Doing what? They have a class picnic at the detox farm?"

"It's a real long story," I said. "I'm not there anymore, I'm on the road. I wish you weren't mad. I really hate it when you're mad."

"I am not mad, Russ. Several other emotions come to mind. There's not a lot of room for mad. Russ, I haven't got real good news. You're in a lot of trouble, pal."

"Boy, you newspeople are right on top of things."

Jane breathed into the phone. I looked out of the booth at Sherry Lou. She was perched on the hood of the car. She'd changed into lavender jeans and an off-white blouse and combed her hair.

"See, here's the thing," Jane said. "Yesterday I thought

you maybe had a little problem, like running from the cops on a bum murder rap, something simple like that. That's the good news, Russ. The bad news is, you remember your buddy Tony Palmer who couldn't possibly be connected to the mob?''

''You're going to tell me something, aren't you?'' I said. ''You're going to tell me something I don't want to hear.''

''Tony Palmer's real name is Antonio DePalma. Tony hails from New York. He came to Chicago nine years ago. He's related to the Frabotta bunch in Jersey and Manhattan, cousins with cute names like Sal and Fats. He's never been mixed up in family business, at least as far as anyone knows, but with connections like that—''

''Antonio DePalma?'' I stared into the phone.

''You got it.''

''But he's not mixed up in anything, you said that.''

Jane groaned. ''Wake up, will you, Russ? Have a cup of coffee. Have another drink.''

''Jane, I have not had a drink.''

''Too bad. Maybe you ought to have one now. Russell, Tony Palmer dash Antonio DePalma is married to a woman named Felicia. Felicia's maiden name is Cannatella. Her uncle is Frank Cannatella. Possibly the name rings a bell.''

''Oh, shit.''

''There you go. Tony's wife's uncle is the boss of the Chicago mob. Irv and Mort Wacker work for Ritchie Pinelli, who works for Frank. Tony Palmer sends you off to Dallas with a funny briefcase. And you can't figure what's wrong and why everyone's picking on Russ.''

''You want to hold the phone?'' I said. ''I think I'm going to throw up.''

''Hold it in awhile,'' Jane said. ''It gets worse. Russ, I don't know if this has anything to do with you, but I'll go ahead and pass it on along. There's been a lot of talk about Cannatella's connection with Senator Jack Byron of Texas. Nothing in print anywhere, just courthouse and newspaper talk. Byron is a possible presidential hopeful next time around. Everything looks like they're gearing him up for the number-one job. The thing is, Byron and Frank Cannatella went to the same boys' school here in Chicago. All this was a long time ago, but you get in the public eye, people start nosing around, they start looking for things to dig up. Jack Byron is rich as God. Made a lot of money in oil and real estate, but he had a nice nut before that. It seems he got his start right here in the import-export trade.''

I could see this one coming down the road. "And you think this Byron is mixed up with Cannatella?"

"*I* don't think anything, Russ. I'm telling you what a lot of people say. Where there's smoke, there's maybe fire, okay? What I am thinking is this. Jack Byron lives in Dallas. Russell Murray takes the now mysterious briefcase to DFW Airport and forgets to bring it back. Maybe it all figures in, maybe not. The Cannatella family's fairly pissed, we know that."

I patted my pants for a smoke, and remembered Sherry Lou had all the cigarettes. "Jane, what the hell am I supposed to do next? I can't just drive around forever, I don't know where to go."

"You ask me, which you didn't, I think I'd have stayed put at the boozer farm. At least for a while. The cops aren't very likely to look for you there."

"I don't guess I mentioned that."

"Mention what?"

"That the Wackers tried to shoot me again. See, Clyde Bob wouldn't let me have my keys, so this friend sort of helped me get away. I hurt my foot again. The car blew up and we—"

"Russ, goddammit, *hold* it, okay?" Jane took a deep breath about eighty miles away. "The Wackers showed up? In *Wisconsin* somewhere?"

"In a big white Continental."

"I don't care about the car. Who gives a fuck about the car? Russ, what are you doing now? Right now."

"I'm talking to you, Jane. I'm in a booth at the Dairy Queen. We're right outside of—"

"Don't tell me where. I don't want to know where. I don't

mean right now, I mean after right now. Like where are you
going next? Russ, listen. How did you get to the detox farm?
You never told me that."

"The cops brought me in. I was driving a little slow."

"They just dumped you at the farm."

"That's right. They didn't charge me or anything. One of
the cops was AA. They didn't take the car. Jane, that's not real
important now, is it? I don't live there anymore."

I listened to the silence for a while. Finally, Jane said, "You don't
get it, do you? You don't see this at all. The cops didn't find you,
but the Wacker boys did. How did they manage that, Russ?"

"We didn't talk a lot, Jane, I didn't ask."

"They found you through the cops, that's how. The cop who
picked you up didn't charge you, okay, but your name went
on the record in a computer somewhere. So any other cop in
the country who can type can find your name and where you
are. Only that didn't happen. Someone in the Cannatella family
called someone on the force they're paying off and said, 'Say,
any word on Russell Murray? We'd sure appreciate it.' "

I thought about that. "The cops maybe had my name and
they didn't pick me up."

Jane's voice took on a little kinder edge. "That's what I'm
thinking, Russ. Maybe your name showed up and then someone
took it off. After they told the family where you were. Chicago's
got a lot of good cops, but there's not a city anywhere that's
squeaky clean. Russell, it gets worse. Take it a step further and
say the fix is in higher up, and no one is working real hard to
pick you up for a murder rap. Someone else is willing to pay
to get you first."

I could hear other voices on the phone. Someone named Phil
said he didn't like the deal, he'd have to check with L.A., they
could get siding cheaper out there.

"So what you're saying is I'm dead, right? I walk out in the
traffic and save everyone a little time."

"That's close," said Jane. "Go somewhere, Russ. Go anywhere and stop. Get a shabby motel and stay off the major roads.

You don't want to drive, you want to keep off the roads. I'll try and talk to some people, find out what I can. I don't know how much I can do if there are really big fingers in the pie.''

"I appreciate this," I said, "a whole lot."

"You are a pain in the ass, Murray. They ought to lock you up for rude behavior and treating all your friends like shit, but I feel this other rap's a bit much."

"That's a nice thing to say."

"That's what you think, isn't it? You really think that."

"Think what?"

"That I gave you a fucking compliment. That I think you're a really swell guy."

"You've got a lot of hostility," I said. "You're under a lot of stress."

"I wonder where I got that?"

"Jane, I think it's good you're kinda letting this out. Maybe the way you feel about me, I mean, what you're saying to me now, this is why we never got married or anything."

Jane laughed. It was a very nasty laugh. "We *did* do the anything, Russ. We did a lot of that. Whenever you showed up. When you *remembered* to show up. You even proposed to me once. I doubt you recall this big event."

"Of course I do," I said. I didn't remember that at all. "I just don't remember what you said."

"I said no. Jesus came to me in a dream and said, 'Jane, you can have a brain tumor or marry Russ.' And I said, 'Hey, give me some time to think.' "

"You made that up."

"Call me," Jane said. "Not in the fucking morning or the middle of the night."

She hung up the phone. I limped back to the car, where Sherry Lou was tapping her foot and looking cross.

"So what did your friend say? You sure talked long enough."

"She said stay off major roads. Hole up in a shabby motel."

"In a pig's eye."

"Right. Let's go try and get some shoes."

Chapter 12

Sherry was a little put out Harrod's hadn't thought to open up a branch in Whitewater, Wisconsin, so we settled on a J.C. Penney store. I made her park in a spot where no one would likely see our plates, but I still felt edgy about the trip. Being a fugitive killer's like anything else—it takes a little while to get used to something new. I was sure nearly everyone north of Mexico had seen my bad picture by now, and was hot to turn me in.

Sherry had her own ideas about how I ought to look. She picked out underwear and socks, a pair of five-pocket jeans, a plaid flannel shirt and some steel-toed boots, a fleece-lined denim jacket and a semi-Western hat. I told her I never wore a hat. She said you've got to have the hat. I put my foot down on the steel-toed boots. I didn't think I'd be fixing any telephone lines, and the steel toes hurt my feet. We settled on some high-top desert boots that gave me that rakish Aussie sheepherder look.

My new image seemed to please Sherry Lou. She said the jacket made my shoulders look broad, a hint that they hadn't been overly broad before. She said the outfit gave me a healthy outdoorsy kind of look that would be a good disguise. We topped off my new fashion statement with a pair of green aviator shades. I didn't much look like me, which I guess was the whole idea.

The lady who waited on us was a double for my third-grade teacher Mrs. Kranz. She let me know right off she didn't care for men who came in the store with bloody feet. She didn't like the sweater I'd found in Sherry's pack, and I couldn't much blame her for that. It came up to my chest, and made me look like a poodle in his new winter suit. Hey, somebody, take me for a walk.

Her suspicions were confirmed when she took my credit card, punched it in the phone and gave it back. The card was no good. I wondered how the hell I'd managed that. You blow over fifteen hundred bucks somewhere, you like to recall a little fun.

Sherry gave me a look that said, what a big surprise, and presented her American Express. It was one of those colored solid gold, and Mrs. Kranz liked it fine. She gave Sherry Lou an A-plus.

I felt a lot better in my brand-new clothes. A bath and a shave would help, but I could do without that. Us outdoor types live on the edge. We've got better things to do than sissy stuff like keeping clean and sprucing up. I leaned back in the seat and closed my eyes. Riding in the BMW felt fine. It was a snooty little car with an engine as slick as an Elmore Leonard plot. A new car, a pretty girl and a gold credit card. If I cast all reason aside, I could dream I had a life.

"Where to?" Sherry said, and I told her anywhere but Illinois, that I needed time to think. She took 59 from Whitewater, heading roughly southwest. A sign said "Milton" up ahead, to be sure and see the Milton House Museum. I thought about Les. Les would probably like to do that.

Before we started on our gala shopping spree, I had filled

Sherry in on my phone call to Jane. Sherry didn't say much at the time, but as we toured Wisconsin, I knew she was mulling things over in her head. You could tell when Sherry mulled. She got a very mulling look, complete with deep frown lines and serious action about the mouth. I knew better than to try and interrupt. When Sherry Lou is mulling, that's that.

I tried to mull myself, but I wasn't sure where the hell to start. Jane had hit me with some terminally odorous stuff. Somewhat more than your daily sack of coffee grinds and peels. Jane had pulled her garbage truck right up to the phone, and dumped the whole load in my ear.

I couldn't spend a lot of time on Frank Cannatella, or a senator from Texas who was Uncle Frank's boyhood chum. I didn't know these people. They were names in the papers and the news magazines. I couldn't believe they had anything at all to do with me. Tony Palmer, okay. I could think about Tony just fine. And in spite of what Jane had just said, I couldn't pin the bad-guy label on my friend. In my head, Tony's image was still intact. Antonio DePalma I didn't like. DePalma had sent me off to Dallas and dropped me in some very deep shit. And, if Tony's voice on the phone meant anything, I wasn't there all by myself.

So why me? I wondered. I'd already asked myself the question a hundred times. If the briefcase was so damn important to everyone, why didn't Tony make the trip himself? He'd said he had something lined up, but I couldn't buy that. There was always a hot new lady in Tony's life, but I couldn't believe he'd bring a second-string player off the bench just to get some honey in the sack. What the hell kind of thinking was that? I wasn't even on the team.

Sherry Lou looked right at me, as if she'd been peeking in my head.

"You and this guy you worked for, you and he were pretty close? I mean, not just someone like a boss or anything."

"We didn't do a lot together," I said, "if that's what you mean. We had a drink now and then. I went to dinner at his house maybe twice. We got along fine. Tony never acted like a boss.''

Sherry lit a smoke. ''It's kind of strange, you know? It seems to me like you could tell.''

''Tell what?''

''Someone you know like that, he's mixed up in the mob it's going to show. I bet I'd know. I knew a guy like that, I bet I'd know.''

''He never brought his brass knucks to the office, Sherry Lou. That's what threw me off.''

She caught my irritation and reached over and squeezed my arm. ''Hey. Don't get mad at me.''

''I am not mad at you.''

''You're sorta vexed.''

''I might be irked or peeved. I'm not vexed.''

''What *I* think,'' Sherry said, ''is this friend of yours is right. This old school buddy of Frank what's-his-name wants to run for President. So this Frank Cannelloni—''

''—Cannatella.''

''—Whatever, this mob guy says, 'Hey, I'll blackmail my senator friend. Fuck him. We aren't that close anymore. I'll threaten to expose his lurid past.' ''

''What lurid past is that?''

''You know. Like your friend said. Way back he made his dough in the mob.''

I shook my head. ''He made his money in the import-export business, Sherry Lou.''

''Right.'' Sherry Lou raised a finger to make her point. ''And where did he import stuff *from?*''

''I don't know where from.''

''Sicily,'' Sherry said.

''Sicily.''

''Sure. That's what's in the briefcase. Incriminating evidence. He hid the dope in olive-oil cans. You wouldn't want something like that to get out if you're going to run for President. This is scary shit, Russ. I'd find that briefcase if I were you.''

"Damn. Why didn't I think of that?"

"Well, you should. Really. This newspaper friend. You two have some kind of hot interlude?"

"Did we what?" I was looking out the window at some black-and-white cows and sort of caught the tail end. "That's none of your business, Sherry Lou. They make a lot of cheese around here or what?"

"Sweat and lust on Sunday afternoon. She dumped you but you've still got embers in your heart."

"Oh, for Christ's sake."

"You been married once or twice?"

"Once. Her name's Marian. Dark hair, brown eyes, five-four. We divorced six years ago. Anything else?"

"She caught you doing what?"

"Having a sort of hot interlude with her very best friend."

"Nice move."

"It seemed like the right thing to do at the time."

"So then what?"

"So then she moved in with her very best friend."

"Uh-oh."

"I believe that's exactly what I said at the time."

Sherry grinned. "Mine was named *Anton*. God, what a name. Race-car driver. Real good on the track, couldn't think of anything but cars. He'd try and fine-tune me now and then and I wouldn't stand for that. 'Listen,' I said, 'you want something runs just right all the time, go stick it in a Porsche. I got other needs as well. I'm your wife, I'm not your pit-stop pal.' "

"Sounds like a winner," I said.

"In everything but love."

"I'll bet you've got embers in your heart."

"I'll be goddamned if I do."

Sherry shook her head and paid attention to the road. She was thinking on something, and whatever it was, it brought a smile. Anton, maybe, or somebody else. It's occurred to me once or twice before that the person you moan about the most is often the very same one you can't forget. The times I spent with Marian were the best and the worst years of my life. We did everything wrong and we did everything right. We cut each other up and made up and went to bed. Jesus, Maid Marian and Robin Hood. Baby, we've got to try and treat each other right.

For a while, midnight romps heal the wounds you inflict in the day. But that's too easy, so the daytime bouts begin to crowd into the fun time after dark. You fight because there's nothing else to do after Leno says good night. It's not important anymore to stop and work things out. Now you've got to win. You can't just let her get away with saying women are more reasonable than men, what kind of shit is that? And since you've both learned drinking tends to loosen up your head and lets you slice a little deeper than you should, things get said that there isn't any way to take back. So you down another anesthetic shot to dull the pain of knowing that. And when the last big title match is over and you're both out flat, you ask yourself, "Now what the hell was that all about? Who said which about what?"

You always hurt the one you love, and why's that? Easy. There's no one else around to fight. And then she's gone and you don't have anything to do after dark. Well "fuck her," you say, and the lady down the bar says, "Hey, I'll drink to that."

Sherry stopped for gas somewhere. Maybe the famous Milton, I didn't ask. A high school boy who manned the pumps fell in love with her at once. While she pranced around the station buying peanuts and Cokes and showing off her tight denim jeans, I hunched down in the seat behind my shades. That's how us killers get caught. Some guy pumping gas watched "America's Most Wanted" the night before and that's that.

I picked up trash off the floor for a while, then tried to fold

our map. A simple IQ test I failed right off the bat. I tore off
a tag I found hanging from my brand-new hat, a little Minnie
Pearl effect. I'm sure Sherry saw it, and wondered how long
it would take me to discover it for myself.

I went through my wallet to see if Clyde Bob had left everything intact. Two one-dollar bills. A parking ticket for a car I
didn't have. My driver's license with a picture that was better
than the one they used in yesterday's *Trib*. And two things I
didn't know I had. A receipt from the Fairmont Hotel in Big
D. And, squirreled away behind a leather flap, an unfamiliar
key. I stared at the key. I held it up and turned it in the light.
One of those tingles you hear about started racing up my spine.
I didn't know where the key was from, but I knew what it
was for. It was a standard locker key. "M-2765" was deeply
stamped on one side. So a locker. Maybe an airport locker.
Most likely, an airport locker at O'Hare. I had come in roaring
drunk with Karla and put the briefcase in a locker at O'Hare.
Now why had I done that? And who cares? I could get myself
out of this briefcase mess and get Frank Cannatella off my
back. Maybe Uncle Frank would be grateful and pass the word
along to the cops.

I don't know why I cared at the time, but it struck me that
I'd have to start looking for a job. I couldn't share an office
with Antonio DePalma anymore, and I felt a little sad about
that.

Sherry was excited about the key. With her usual zeal, she
wanted to get started right away. She fumbled with the map
and said, "Hey, it's only maybe four or five miles down to 90
and on past Beloit, and the Tollway to O'Hare after that."

I was anxious too, but I didn't like driving on a major thor-
oughfare. Maybe no one was looking for the BMW plates. But
if they were, the Northwest Tollway would make it real easy
to check on passing cars.

"So what do you want to do?" Sherry said. "Tour lovely Wisconsin till it's dark?"

"Hell, I don't know," I said. "Probably dark won't help. We stop at a tollbooth, they can easily check us out. Illinois's still got electric lights."

"There's that."

If the traffic's not heavy, I thought, it won't take more than an hour and a half on the Tollway to O'Hare. Say two hours, go ahead and make it three. It wasn't even noon, which meant at the outside we'd hit O'Hare at three.

"I don't like it," I said. "The road's bad enough, but the airport's something else. There'll be cops everywhere, Sherry Lou."

"That's right, Russ." Sherry gave me a look. "And if we wait till dark, all the cops'll go to bed. They'll leave the place open to muggers and thieves."

"So it doesn't make sense. Does it have to make sense? I'll feel more secure at night."

"You don't have to go in," Sherry said, "did you ever think of that? *I* can go in, you can stay out in the car."

I shook my head. "I couldn't let you do that."

"Why couldn't you let me do that?"

"I don't know. It doesn't seem like you ought to do that."

"Oh, for Christ's sake, Russ!" Sherry gave me a look of sheer disgust. "Good. That's fine. We'll drive around the state. Maybe we'll find some cheese. Maybe you'll see another fucking cow."

Sherry revved the engine to a Grand Prix scream, then roared out of the station flinging gravel in our wake. She gripped the wheel hard. Her jaw stuck out like a rock.

"Okay," I said, "why are you mad at me?"

"I'm not mad."

"I can tell mad. I'm sitting next to someone in the car, I can tell that person's mad."

"Good for you, Russ. You get out of this mess, you can save up your boxtops and get a shrink degree."

"I'm sorry, Sherry Lou."

"Okay, you're sorry."

"No, I mean, I *know* what's wrong, okay? Besides all the shit we went through last night."

"And what do you think's wrong with me, Russ?"

"I didn't say *you*. I didn't say wrong with you, I say that? For God's sake, I guess I ought to understand. You want a drink is what, I guess I ought to know that. I know you got the bottle off the floor last night, Sherry Lou. I cleaned up the floor, it wasn't there. Okay. That took off the edge, but not enough. You're strung out bad right now, you're—Jesus *Christ*, Sherry Lou!"

Sherry jerked the wheel hard. Air horns blasted in my ear and a semi nearly sliced us in half. Sherry jammed her foot to the floor and tore off 59 down a dirt road on our right. We were passing the tip end of a lake. There was a small grocery store beside a fishing-tackle place and an empty laundromat. Sherry braked and got out and slammed the door, and marched across the lot. In a minute she was back, clutching a paper sack. When she got back in, she turned in the seat and ripped the sack apart and brought out a quart of vodka and a quart of good Scotch.

"Okay, you son of a bitch," Sherry said. "Here's yours and here's mine."

"Hey, Sherry—"

"Shut up, Russ. Just shut *up!*" Her eyes were full of anger and tears. Her fists were clenched tight and she was maybe half a second from hitting me in the face.

"I know you, Russ," Sherry said, "I know exactly who you are. You've tried to pick me up with your real nice smile in about a hundred bars. Hey, buy the little lady a drink, this broad's so fucking tanked I'm goin' to spin her like a top. You're the drinker and I'm the drunk, right? I'm the cute little trick at the detox farm, and you're a guy just sorta dropped in. You go on a toot now and then, but me, I got a problem, I'm sick. I'm the freaky boozer and you're a lot of laughs."

"Sherry, I don't like you doing this, I don't—"

Sherry slapped me hard. "Tough shit, pal. Look in the mirror, Russ. Who's got the shakes, you want to tell me that? You're *strung out,* Russ. You got nerves hanging loose on the end of every hair." She gave me an awful smile and tapped a bottle with her nail. "Well fuck you, okay? Let's see who goes bananas first."

Sherry spun out of the lot and steered a dizzy course back to 59.

It looked like a very long drive to O'Hare.

Chapter 13

There's nothing much worse than getting pissed at someone in a car. It's a lot like you and Godzilla in a phone booth together, waiting for the start of round one. When he starts punching, where are you going to run?

Maid Marian and I used to do this all the time. We'd get boozed up and start a fight, then take it on the road. We'd scream at each other for three or four miles, then we'd both shut up at once. That's rule number one when you're fighting in a car. You can't stomp out and slam the door, so you run out of nasty stuff to say. Then the silent part begins and you get to look at road signs and cows.

This can go on for some time. Nobody wants to talk first. Talking first is a sign of giving in. Open your mouth and you might as well admit that you're wrong. That's rule number two. Cave in first and you're dead.

I didn't want to fight with Sherry Lou, but I wasn't about to tell her that. I didn't want to talk, and I didn't want to think about her brown paper sack. What I did was take the coward's way out. Sherry's slick little car hummed along smooth and easy as single-malt Scotch, and I leaned back in the seat and conked out.

Sleep was a bad idea. I dreamed of Karla Stark. We were running buck naked down Michigan Avenue, Irv and Mort Wacker in pursuit. The Wackers rode French racing bikes. After a block or two, Karla turned into Jane Kowalski. Jane turned into Sherry Lou. Sherry said we ought to stop off and have a drink. I said I wasn't real sure we had the time. The Wackers switched to skates. They both wore bright-red Roller Derby hats.

Things got confused after that. Brando starred as Frank Cannatella, with Les as the Beaver, and Diane Keaton as Nina Nurse. We ran through *The Godfather IV,* and I got all the shitty parts.

I woke to the glare of the afternoon sun. My mouth tasted worse than Iraqi underwear. I recognized the Tollway, which meant we were back in Illinois. The fugitive returns to the scene. Cut to evening news. Cut to Joliet, Russell and his cellmate Red. Red says, "You're a sweetie, Russ, you and me are going to get along fine."

"Must've been a doozie," Sherry said. "You moaned and flipped about. I'd say you've got some acrobatic skills."

"Don't get your hopes up," I said, "I'm not that good when I'm awake. Where do you think we are?"

"That was Elgin, so O'Hare's about twenty miles ahead."

"Are we still mad at each other, Sherry Lou? I don't much want to do that anymore."

"I wasn't mad at you, Russ," Sherry said. "I was furious and hurt. I was piqued. I might've been incensed. I never was mad."

"Piqued is good," I said.

"I was also rankled. I was rankled quite a lot."

"You might've taken umbrage, too."

"I'm pretty sure I did."

Sherry's grin was somewhat reserved. It told me she was possibly amused. That I wasn't to assume I was totally off the hook.

"Russ, I think you're a pretty nice guy," Sherry said.

"You're real fucked up, but I don't take points off for that. You can't help being what you are."

"Thanks a lot," I said.

"You just listen, okay? I'm not even half through. You want to know what set me off back there? It's your goddamn rookie attitude is what. You sober up two or three days, you read a slogan on the wall. You think, hey, this is fine. I guess I'll maybe straighten up. I'll bring all the rummies back to Jesus and I'll start with Sherry Lou."

"Sherry, I never thought any such thing."

"Sure you did, Russ. You got the first-timer glory in your eyes."

"I've got the what?"

"I don't blame you, friend. Guy comes in the first time, it's a shocker and half. He's never seen so many drunks without a drink."

"I can't argue that."

"Makes you think, right? Maybe you could do it, too. You want to sober up, Russ? You want to live the good life? Look at me and tell me it hasn't crossed your mind."

I didn't look at Sherry Lou. I looked out at the Tollway where it crosses high over Golf Road and Busse Woods. The reservoir was up and the water looked cold.

"Everybody drinks too much thinks they'd like to give it up, Sherry Lou. So what's wrong with that?"

"Not a thing," Sherry said. "Get you a Salvation Army suit, Russ. Wear a funny hat. Only don't shake your tambourine at me. I'll take that stuff from the detox farm, but I sure won't take it from you. And don't you ever, *ever* go poking under the seats for my empties anymore. I am not going to tolerate that."

I didn't say a word. This seemed the wise thing to do. We were sort of on speaking terms again, but one false move would mess our truce up real quick.

Sherry Lou sat straight, looking at the road, her hands just right on the wheel. An example of good driving posture for us all. Possibly she'd learned this from Anton the race-car king. We all bring habits from the past. You hang around with someone awhile, you're going to pick up a habit or a trait. That person goes out of your life, but the trait is still there. I used to comb my hair straight across instead of back. Marian taught me that. In turn, I introduced her to Travis McGee. I also taught her to enjoy oral bliss. John D. MacDonald is dead, so he isn't writing books anymore, but I'd guess Marian's parts are still intact. It doesn't seem right that the business with the hair is all I got. Hell, I could've thought of that myself.

It was twenty after five when Sherry turned off the Tollway and into the traffic for O'Hare. Short-term parking was nearly full, but she aced out a guy in a Caddie and pulled into a spot on Level 2.

Sherry opened her door and got out. I tried to move but nothing seemed to work. Oh, Christ, I thought, now what? "Killer Found Paralyzed in Getaway Car. Crime Spree Comes to Bitter End."

Sherry poked her head back in. "Russ, I figured you maybe noticed that we're here. You want to get out of the car?"

"I think my foot's asleep," I said.

"Huh-uh. I don't think it is."

"Let's talk about this. We could have a smoke and talk."

"What do you want to talk about, Russ?"

I looked at Sherry. "For God's sake, what do you think? Every cop in Chicago wants my ass. Not to mention assorted hoods. My picture's in the papers. They've probably got the place staked out. They do that in cop shows all the time."

Sherry looked pained. "Russell, what we've got here is real life. It'd take about five hundred cops to watch every single person in O'Hare."

"It only takes one. One of those guys is on the ball, that's it."

"You want me to do this? You want to wait in the car?"

It sounded like a good idea. "Of course I don't," I said, "what do you think I am?"

Sherry didn't move. I looked at our paper sack. A drink would get me back on my feet. One or two slugs and old Russell would be just fine. I took a deep breath, opened the door and got out.

We walked forever down the long rows of cars. The entire population of Chicago was out of town. At the terminal, I fished out my key.

"I guess I took American," I said. "At Dallas—Fort Worth, I left the briefcase at the American ticket counter. That was Saturday afternoon. It stands to reason I took American out of Chicago Thursday night."

"That'd be the sensible thing to do," Sherry said. "It doesn't mean that's what you did. American, Delta, and Continental fly out of Chicago to DFW. We'll try those first."

"How do you know that?"

"How do I know what?"

"Where all the airlines go."

"Rich folks fly a lot, Russ. That's the kind of thing we do."

"Right. Why didn't I think of that?"

Sherry led me off down the concourse. I thought about putting on my shades, then remembered that's exactly what criminals always do. The cops would be looking for guys in shades. I was hoping my fleece-lined jacket and my hat would throw them off. I didn't look like I worked for the *Literary Times*. I looked like a man who thought a lot about cows.

We checked all the airlines I could possibly have taken to DFW from O'Hare. None of them had any banks marked "M," or lockers numbered 2765.

"Now what?" I said.

"How much were you drinking when you got here, do you know?"

"I don't know, why?"

"You might've used a locker at Lufthansa or Iberia."

"Why would I do a thing like that?"

"Why did you piss on the cigarette machine?"

"I'm going to call Les right now. I'm going to tell him what you said."

Sherry sighed. "I'm serious, Russ. If you *knew* where you'd left the fucking briefcase, I wouldn't have to ask dumb questions, now would I?"

"No, I guess not."

"Okay. So let's—" Sherry stopped, looked past my shoulder and grinned. "Oh, officer, can I talk to you a minute?"

My heart dropped down into my brand-new boots. I turned and saw the security guard walking our way. He was a middle-aged guy with chubby cheeks and beagle eyes. He had put on weight since he bought the uniform. His zipper popped out and he was strangling in the shirt.

Sherry Lou turned on her smile and laid a hand on his arm.

"Ah am so glad Ah *found* yew?" she said. "I mean, yew sure could help me if you would?"

The guard beamed, stricken at once by Sherry Lou's impression of Alabama Boll-Weevil Queen.

"I'll sure help any way I can," the guard said, and I was certain that he would.

"Where can I find the lockah this little ol' key goes to?" Sherry said. "I left some real *personal* items here this mornin' and I don't recall what section it's in."

The guard took my key and turned it over several times. "Tell you the truth, miss, I don't think it fits any of the lockers 'round here. See them squared-off edges? The keys at O'Hare are all round. You sure you left your stuff here?"

"My goodness, I just don't *know*," Sherry said.

"Wish I could help," the guard said. He glanced once at me, grinned at Sherry Lou and left.

Sherry gave me a nasty look. "So much for the great locker caper, Russ. Now what?"

"That was a dumb thing to do, Sherry Lou. That man's

probably got my picture in his pocket. I'll bet he's going for the cops right now."

"He didn't even look at you, Russell. He was looking at me."

"That's what he wants you to think. They're trained to do that."

"Okay, pal." Sherry folded her arms and tapped her foot, the way mothers do when a kid acts up in the mall. "Where would you like to go now? How about the bus station? How about the YMCA?"

"I want to make a couple of calls," I said.

"Fine. The phone booths are right over there."

"You didn't sound a thing like Scarlett O'Hara to me. If I were you, I wouldn't do regions you don't know anything about."

"Fuck you, Russ. Go make your calls."

I tried Tony's office and his home. I called Jane Kowalski at the *Trib*. No one answered anywhere. A little kid came up to the booth and pressed his tongue against the glass. An old lady gave me the evil eye.

Sherry had picked up the latest Chicago papers. I was still in the news, but the stories were just a rehash of previous events. There was nothing about my daring escape from Wilson Rehab. Nothing about the shoot-out with the Wackers, and no mention of Sherry Lou.

"I don't like it," I said. "The cops know what happened out there. They know who you are and they know we took off in your car. So why don't they say anything about it?"

Sherry shrugged. "I don't know, why?"

"Because Jane was dead right, that's why. The mob's got a lot of clout, and so has this Senator What's-his-name. They've got the cops and the papers on a string. They want Russell Murray to disappear, and they don't want to raise a lot of fuss.

Christ, Sherry Lou. What I ought to do is save a lot of time and throw myself in front of a truck.''

Sherry didn't answer. We walked outside and started back to short-term parking. The sun was down and the wind had picked up. My fleece-lined jacket felt good. I thought about Wyoming. I'd been there once and it looked kind of nice. Sheep couldn't be a lot of fun, but my new outfit would work fine.

Sherry stopped at her BMW, opened the door, and crawled in the back seat. She pawed around awhile, found a coat hanger, and started off up the line of cars.

''Sherry,'' I said, ''you want to tell me where you're going?''

''Just sit tight, Russ,'' Sherry said.

She walked down the row, peered into windows and tried several doors. I followed close behind. Finally, she stopped at a faded blue Chevy four-door. It looked like about a '72 or '73. I could see this car had not had proper maintenance. There was duct tape on the windows and the tires were nearly bald. Several collisions had occurred.

The window on the driver's side was half an inch down. Sherry wormed her hanger inside and very quickly flipped the lock. Then she lay down on the seat and poked her head beneath the wheel. Moments later, the engine came to life. Sherry sat up, backed the Chevy out, and squealed to a stop behind her car.

''Toss our stuff in the back,'' Sherry said. ''Let's get a move on, Russ.''

''Sherry Lou,'' I said, ''I hate to see you leave your car here. It's almost brand new.''

''Russ, it's just a car. Okay?''

I started hauling out our gear. It seemed I kept forgetting that the rich don't view life as other people do. A car is not a payment every month. A car is just a car. Your background will betray you every time.

Chapter 14

Sherry got us through the airport maze and onto the Kennedy Expressway toward town. The lights of Chicago turned the low-hanging clouds a dull red. Chicago's a city you either like or you don't. I like the place because it's still kind of rough around the edges and doesn't care. New York and L.A. pretend to be a lot of things they're not. Chicago says like it or leave it, pal, what you see is what you get.

I wondered where Frank Cannatella called home, and figured maybe Lake Shore Drive. Frank probably had a boat. All your big mobsters have a boat. You can take a bunch of girls on a boat and have fun. Or you can dump some guy in the lake in a cement overcoat. Some jerk forgets where his briefcase is, he gets a nice ride in a boat.

I put this happy thought aside and studied Sherry Lou. She hadn't said a lot since we'd left O'Hare. Maybe she was having second thoughts about taking up the outlaw life. I couldn't much blame her if she did. We made a pretty dreary-looking team. Abbott and Costello could've done a better Bonnie and Clyde.

"You're a girl with hidden talents," I said. "Where'd you learn to break into cars?"

"I watch a lot of cop shows," Sherry said.

"No way. I'm guessing you served some hard time."

"I had a big brother. When Dad wouldn't let him take the car, he'd hot-wire it anyway and drive till he ran out of gas. Sometimes he'd take me along."

"Any other brothers and sisters, or just you and him?"

"Just us."

"So where's your brother now?"

"He's dead. He flew a chopper in 'Nam."

"I'm sorry, Sherry Lou."

"So am I. No one else in the family would put up with me but Ed."

So much for lively conversation. I sat back and watched Sherry drive. The Chevy shook at thirty-five and had a most peculiar smell. I missed the BMW and its smooth and silent ride. It doesn't take long to grow accustomed to a rich and better life.

I opened the glove compartment to pass the time. Inside were two cheap condoms, a box of .22 shorts, and half a Lucky Strike. Next I inspected the back seat, and found empty beer cans, gun and ammo magazines, and several publications that fostered romance between busty girls and dogs.

"Don't hit anyone," I advised Sherry Lou. "I doubt if this guy's got real good coverage on his car."

"Don't worry," Sherry said, "this mother won't run long enough to have a wreck. Where am I supposed to be taking us, Russ? You got a destination in mind?"

"Five-hundred block, Michigan Avenue," I said. "I want to stop by the Oasis for a minute. See if Artie's there."

Sherry gave me a dubious look. "Sounds good to me, friend. We're on the run, we drop by your favorite bar. Who'd ever look for you there?"

"No one's going to see me," I said. "I've got a plan."

"Oh, well, then . . ."

"Sherry Lou, don't get uptight on me now, okay? I've got a lot to think about."

"I am *not* uptight. Don't you tell me what I am."

"You are too. You're doing your mouth real funny. You do your mouth funny when you get uptight."

Sherry turned on me and glared. "I do *not* do my mouth funny, Russ. Don't you tell me what I do with my mouth. I will not put up with that."

"Okay. Your mouth looks fine."

"Well, I'm sure relieved to hear that."

"Sherry Lou, I know you don't believe it, but I can think fairly clear now and then. I want to see Artie because I don't know what I did Saturday night. I got off the plane with Karla Stark. I'm a blank after that. Maybe I took her by the Oasis. That's something I'd probably do. Maybe I talked to Artie. Hell, maybe I left the briefcase there. It's a logical place to look."

Sherry Lou looked straight ahead. What she did was do her mouth up funny, but I didn't mention that.

"All right, it makes sense," she said. "But you could just as easy call this guy. You don't have to go in."

"You don't talk to Artie on the phone."

"Why not?"

"Because that's the way he is. He's got a thing about phones."

"I don't like this, Russ."

"Don't worry," I said, "I've got a plan."

I showed Sherry Lou where to park about two blocks down, and walked to Artie's place. I half-expected some hassle, like she didn't want to stay in the car, but she didn't say a thing. She didn't say "See you later, Russ," or "Lots of luck." She sat with her hands on the wheel and her mouth uptight.

I had seen her getting itchy before we left O'Hare, all the signs you get when you're running on dry. The nerve ends start to unravel and the skin gets tight around your eyes. You want to scream and smash somebody in the face, but you know it won't do you any good. The only thing that helps is a drink; you know it's the only cure you've got. I hated to leave her like that. I knew how she felt, because that's the way I was feeling too.

Artie's Oasis isn't "Cheers." It's an old-fashioned bar left over from prehistoric times. Al Capone and Mayor Daley would feel right at home in Artie's bar. There aren't any games that light up and sound like World War III. The folks who come in Artie's don't much want to be fighter pilots, what they want to do is drink. There's a jukebox from the forties, but Artie doesn't like to plug it in. The TV is set for sports. You can see about any sport you want except golf. Artie won't put up with golf. The *Trib*'s a block down across the street, but no one from the paper comes in. I took Jane Kowalski in once but she wouldn't go back. She said newspaper people didn't have a lot of class, but they maybe had a little more than that.

Artie's isn't built like a lot of bars you'll see. The pay phone and the johns are in the hall out front instead of somewhere in the back. I dropped in a quarter and punched in Artie's number at the bar. He can't stand phones, but he can't stand to listen to them ring. I said, "Artie, it's me, I'm up front." Artie said, "you better not be," and hung up.

A minute later he appeared, looking fat and unhappy, nailing me with buckshot eyes. He didn't speak until he'd led me to his cubbyhole office past the john.

"What are you doing here?" he said. "You got to be out of your fucking mind."

"Thanks a lot," I said. "I've got a lot of problems and I could use a little friendship and support."

"Oh yeah, what problem's that? You out of work, your mama's sick, what? I didn't know. How'm I gonna know?"

I sat down in a straight-back chair. "This isn't funny, pal. The situation's fraught."

"You know what's fraught?" Artie rolled his eyes and ran pudgy fingers through his hair. "*I'm* fraught, is what. I got cops in here on the hour. I got guys in sunglasses need a shave. Hey, you seen Russell Murray? Everybody wants to know. You know where he is? He shows up here you better call. You see this fucker, you better call. This is real good for business, you know? People come in for a drink, that's what they want to see, cops and hoods. What I got is a fuckin' theme bar. You look lousy, Russ. You look like you could maybe use a drink."

Artie brought a bottle of Scotch and two glasses from a drawer in his desk. I thought about Sherry in the car. An image of Les came to mind.

"Maybe one," I said, "to kind of take off the edge."

I'd like to say I hesitated, that Jesus stepped up and said, "I'm walking with you, Russ." What I did was leap on Artie's drink in maybe half a second flat. The shot was the first I'd had since Sid and Ann's. It went down fine, spreading good cheer and oiling all the rusty inner parts. Guilt flowed along with the syrupy warmth, but I drowned that mother in Artie's second shot.

"I'd look into Alaska, I was you," Artie said. "I been reading how there's big opportunities in fish."

"I don't see Alaska," I said, "I maybe see Mexico. The thing is, you can run but you're going to get caught. Maybe you're fine for a while but that's what you're going to do. Those guys on my back, they don't forget. Artie, I didn't kill anyone, you know that."

"Sure I know that. So what?"

I didn't wait for Artie, I poured my own drink. "I think I was in here Saturday night. Was I in here or not? I think I brought the girl."

Artie raised a brow. "You don't remember, right? Figures. You was hanging one on pretty good."

"But I was here."

"I'm thinking, what I'm thinking is, Russ ought to get that sweetie home. I bet she's got homework to do."

I let that one go. "So I was here. Did I leave anything for you to keep? I maybe had something with me, I asked you to keep it for a while."

"Like a briefcase," Artie said. "Something like that."

My heart did a flip. "Jesus, you mean you've got it?"

"No, I haven't got it." Artie's tiny eyes squeezed nearly shut. "But the wiseguys in shades, they figure *you* got it, Russ. Fucker breathes garlic in my face, says maybe Murray give you something, pal. He says, how'd you like to try and run a bar with your arm in a cast? He says, this Murray shows up you give me a call. You give me a call, you're all right."

"I'm sorry, Artie. I really am."

"Some jerk's going to break my arm, that's it? 'I'm sorry,' that's goin' to make it okay?" Artie reached over and took his bottle back.

"You think about Alaska. Go catch a fucking salmon or a trout. I won't get my feelings hurt you don't write."

I could hear the car radio half a block away, the sound of heavy metal, or badgers in cardiac arrest. The passenger door was unlocked. I slipped in and punched the radio to "off."

"Sherry Lou," I said, "I've got about enough offenses now. I don't need a sound violation on top of what I've got."

"Hi, babe," Sherry said, "how'd it go?"

Hi, babe?

I took a good look at Sherry Lou. The radio was off but she didn't seem to mind. Her head bopped along with the beat. She had a squirrelly little smile and her eyes were out of sync. Clearly, this was not the same woman I'd left a few moments before. In my absence, she had overcome anxiety and stress. I had broken the pact of the sack, but I had surely not acted alone.

"So, Russ," Sherry said, "how many did you have?" Sherry knew I had sinned. She didn't have to look.

"Two, maybe three or four."

"Hey, we got a tie here, folks."

"Yeah, that's great."

Sherry gave me a crooked grin. "Jesus, Russ, don't be such a drag. You're going to feel just fine."

I already did. The old Murray engine was coming back to life, ready to shift into drive, ready to burn up the night. You walk in this really nifty spot, the girl at the piano starts to play. Every tune she does is your very favorite song.

Okay, I thought, hold it right there. A drink or two's fine, but you got to get it right, you got to stop while you're ahead.

That's the way it works. You tell yourself you'll stop while you know where you are, while you still recall your name. All you've got to do is quit when you get right where you want to be.

Sounds good, right? Hey, I'll drink to that.

Chapter 15

Once or twice a year, your social drinker wakes up and wonders what he did the night before. His wife says, "Nice going, Fred, I doubt if Bill and Edna will ask us back again." Fred says, "Sure they will, kid," and remembers that he had a lot of fun. He thinks he got his hand up Angie Baker's dress. He thinks he did his Garbo bit, either that or maybe Cher. Coffee and seltzer do the trick, and by noon he's feeling fine. The guys at the country club say, "Hey, you were something else, pal," and Fred's a legend for a week.

Your serious drinker wakes up by himself, or with someone he's never seen before. He thinks it's May or June and his name is Bob or Phil. His exes call up and say hello. They say, "Listen, motherfucker, you working yet or what?" Men in plaid jackets bring legal-type papers to the door. He knows he's not a legend anywhere. He knows if he wants to stop the shakes he'd better throw up quick and get a drink.

So Sherry Lou was right. My stay at Wilson Rehab had shaken me up a lot. The bathrobe-and-coffee crowd did not seem a happy way of life. A rose is a rose, and a serious drinker is a drunk. You want to straighten out, the best time to start is right now.

I reflected on the new, improved Russell Murray while Sherry toured Chicago in our stolen vintage car. Now and then, I allowed myself a medicinal slug of Scotch, just enough to keep the glow. The trials of real life began to blur, and it seemed a true wonder that drinking itself had shown me the way to sober up. With stress on the run and the cold light of reason in control, the answer was perfectly clear. Booze had gotten me into this mess; I would use booze itself to set me free. Pacing is the key. You drink, but you don't get drunk. What you do is keep the edge, keep the shakes away and keep the nerves from freaking out. You don't fly out of sight, and you never sink down where it's dark. Jesus, I wondered if anyone had thought of this before?

"I am flat going to do it," I announced to Sherry Lou. "I'm going to get myself right. I'll shave every day and brush my teeth. Get a job with a good dental plan. I might get a three-piece suit."

"Black's your best bet," Sherry said. "I'd start with your black and kinda work your way from there."

I wasn't sure I'd heard her right. "What are we talking here, suits? We're going to talk about suits?"

"Black's good for your work situations and it's fine for church too. I expect you'll want to go to church a lot."

I looked at Sherry Lou. "What I'm doing, I'm detecting some lack of conviction in your voice. Listen, I am going through with this. I intend to change my life."

"Starting when, Russ?"

"Okay. Okay, I see your point. I got this bottle in my hand, you're thinking, boy, what's this all about? It's the bottle threw you off. See, that's the key to this thing. The detox farm set me straight, Sherry Lou. I learned that I don't *have* to drink. I did without a couple days, I did fine."

"I bet I know what," Sherry said, without turning her head. "I bet you're going to taper off."

"Now there's that tone coming out. You get that tone, I can

tell what's in your head. What you're going to tell me is you can't. Your serious drinker takes a drink, that's it.''

"Jesus Christ, Russ."

"Hey, go ahead," I said, "I deserve this rebuke. Gave you a whole lot of flak, now I'm drinking too. Only now what I— now what I got is a different altitude.''

"Attitude."

"What?"

"You've got a different attitude."

"Right. I most certainly do."

"Fucking rookie," Sherry said, and shook her head. "I could be in Paris, France, I'm driving a fucking rookie in a car.''

"You're a good driver, too. You got good posture at the wheel. Did I tell you that you got good posture at the wheel?''

"Don't talk to me, Russ," Sherry said. "And quit lookin' at my posture all the time. I don't want you doing that.''

I settled back and took another therapeutic slug. No use arguing anymore with Sherry Lou. It was clear we lacked rapport. The lights from other cars seemed hazy at best, pleasantly obscure like Christmas in a fog. We were crossing the river at Dearborn going north. I felt we had done this several times before. North on Dearborn, then south on Clark and back again.

"Listen," I said, "I might be wrong, but I think we're driving aimlessly about.''

"You noticed," Sherry said.

"What you want to do is turn around and head south. Get on Michigan, block past City Hall. Hit Madison, take a left.''

"What for?"

"Want to stop by the office. Take a look around."

"You want to do what?" Sherry looked directly at me for the first time since we'd left Artie's place.

"If Jane's right, Sherry, if Tony's mixed up with mobster types, he's maybe got something at the office could help get me out of this mess.''

"You mean like a clue."

"I'll bet that's a joke. I'll bet that's what it is."

Sherry didn't answer. She pulled off into a side street and stopped.

"Russ, I sure don't mean to offend, you being reborn and all, but this sounds like whiskey talk to me." She spoke with her face turned off at an angle somewhere, as if she were speaking to the dash. "What I mean is, turning up at old haunts doesn't seem like a smart idea. That's how they track your major crime figures down. They show up places they shouldn't oughta be."

"Huh-uh, no way," I said. "If there wasn't anyone at Artie's bar, they won't be watching where I work. See I might show up at the Oasis. I wouldn't go back to where I work, they wouldn't think I'd do that. That's not, like you said, it's not a haunt. A haunt's not where you work. I might go back to my apartment, try and sneak in and get a shirt. Guy on the run he wants what? He wants to get some socks and a shirt. He wants some clean underwear. I might show up at Jane's, they might think about that. No, wait, maybe not. We haven't been close for a while. If I was a cop or a hood, I'd check out Eddie Grant. Eddie's a guy makes book sometimes lives down the hall. You know who I'd check out? I'd put someone on Bambi Dear, you can bet they'll do that. They'll check out Marian, they always see your ex. Like hey, that's what I'm going to do *first* thing, right, I'm dropping in to see the ex. I'm saying, 'How you doing, babe,' she's saying, 'Hi there, Russ, wait here, I'll get the car. I'll get the car I'll drive you to the pen. The least I can do, I can drive you to the—' "

"Stop it," Sherry said. "Just *stop* it right now."

"What? What'd I do now?"

Sherry closed her eyes and pressed her fingers against her head. "I'll take you there, okay? You don't talk, I'll take you anywhere you want to go."

"Listen," I said, "I appreciate this. I'm encouraged by your support. Your understanding means a lot."

"Russell, just shut the fuck up."

"Fine. I can handle that."

Sherry ground the Chevy into life and turned east or maybe south. I tried to read the signs. The streets were all Chestnut or Oak or some other kind of tree. I think we passed Washington Square.

I took another sip, leaned back and watched the world go by. The Russell Murray plan was going fine. I felt alert, yet perfectly at ease. I might want to dance. I might want to get a little sleep. Balance is the secret, moderation is the key.

Everything was the way it ought to be. Still, something nibbled at the edge of my thoughts, threatened to disturb my peace of mind. I remembered what it was. What it was was Sherry Lou. Sherry and her dumb idea to break into the *Literary Times*. This, I thought, is not a good idea. That woman isn't thinking straight at all.

There's a place behind the building, a loading zone where Tony always parks. Tony gives the local cop passes to the Bears and he never gets a ticket on his car. I showed Sherry Lou where to stop. We went up the concrete steps, past the day's garbage and through the back door. It's supposed to stay locked, but all you have to do is hit it hard up near the top.

Sherry seemed unsteady on her feet. She drove just fine, but walking was a chore. I'm just the other way. I can drink and walk, but I'm not real good behind the wheel.

The elevator shuts down at night, so we walked up to three. A two-watt bulb lit every floor. Halfway up, Sherry wobbled and nearly fell. I reached out to help and she jerked her arm away.

"You going to be okay?" I said.

"Yes I'm going to be okay."

"Fine. I just asked."

"Well don't."

"Okay then I won't."

Sherry took off her shoes and held the rail with both hands, and I pretended not to look.

The third floor smelled like disinfectant soap. The only light was a glow from the dirty frosted window at the far end of the hall. I had been up here before in the dark, working late to get a story done, or making up for coming in at noon. Tony worked late a lot too, but not at the *Literary Times.* I'd wrap up a critique of Henry James, while Tony went off to meet a friend. I did all the dead writers. Tony did all the horizontal interviews.

Sherry got a penlight from her purse and held it on the lock while I opened up 303. The lock's pretty old, and you have to keep jiggling the key until it works. Tony wouldn't ever get it fixed. This time it seemed to take forever and I had time to think how I shouldn't be up here at all. How I ought to be somewhere far from Chicago, on my way to anywhere else. The worst part was, by the time we'd crossed the river again heading south, the whiskey fog had lifted and I suddenly remembered this was my idea. Nice going, Russ. If you drink don't think. Words to live by for us all.

The lock finally clicked. I opened the door and took Sherry's penlight and waved it across the room.

"Oh, Jesus!" Sherry's hands closed around my arm like a vise. I could feel her breath in shaky little bursts against my neck.

I didn't move. I stood there with the light. I could see past the small waiting room to my own cubbyhole. The place had been thoroughly trashed. The floor was ankle-deep in manuscripts, memos, canceled checks and broken coffee cups. I waded through debris to my desk, Sherry clinging to me like ivy on a wall. My desk drawers were empty, their contents dumped on the floor. The walls were lined with shelves. Every book had been removed and ripped apart.

"Russellll, let's *gooo,"* Sherry said. "Let's get the fuck *out* of here!" She spoke through her teeth without moving her lips. Her voice had the high-pitched sing-song quality that makes all the ventriloquists in the world sound alike.

"Just a minute," I said, "I want to look around."

"Look around at what? You think you're going to *find* anything in all this?"

"I've got to look, Sherry Lou. You want, you can wait right here."

"To hell with that, pal."

I could feel the complete Sherry Lou, every curve and hollow pressed against me in desperate embrace, a pleasing sensation at nearly any other time or place.

A narrow hall leads from my place to Tony's, a slightly larger office with windows on the street. The hallway used to have autographed pictures of people Tony knew or wished he did. Now there were frames and broken glass and torn glossies on the floor. I spotted half an Updike and part of Saul Bellow, then I swept the flash up through Tony's open door and saw him sitting in his chair behind his desk, sitting there looking right through me in perpetual surprise, hurt and bewildered to find himself alone, working late forever in the dark, no cozy suppers or six-foot sweeties in the wings, nothing but the faint, cold light of the city at his back, and the tiny blue hole in his head.

I quickly turned the flash from Tony's face, but not before Sherry got a look. I waited for a scream. That's the way it happens on the cop shows, the guy finds the body and the girl starts to scream.

Sherry didn't scream. Sherry said, "Oh, goddamn shit," and turned and fled through broken glass. She made it to my office before she threw up. The retching mechanism took control. I waited, but once she got started she couldn't stop. The crazy thought hit me that Tony wouldn't like this scene at all. Tony liked girls the way they look in magazines. Their eyes always sparkle and their hair is always clean. They drink but they never get drunk. They hardly ever have to throw up. We live in troubled times, and romance isn't what it used to be.

Chapter 16

The last thing I wanted to do was look at Tony Palmer again. It was something I knew I had to do but I wasn't sure I could. Someone you know, he's sitting there looking like he's had a bad night, he maybe needs a little sleep, it's not the same as if you find some guy you never knew.

I moved across the room to the desk, making sure I kept the light off Tony's face. I didn't want to see his face, I didn't want to see the back of his head. The hole between his eyes wasn't bad, it was smaller than a dime, but legend has it that a bullet does a lot more damage coming out than going in.

The smell hit me ten feet from Tony's desk. My throat went tight and I nearly let everything go. I swallowed hard and started breathing through my mouth. My light swept the top of Tony's desk and settled on his chest. He wore a nice blue blazer, a light blue Oxford shirt, a gray paisley tie. Good old Tony, I thought, right to the end a natty guy.

Something shiny caught my eye and I looked at Tony's hands. His wrists were bound with silver duct tape to the arms of his chair. The veins stood out on the backs of his hands, and his fingers still gripped the arms tight. I squatted down and looked at his legs. They were bent at a wide, awkward angle, taped to the base of the swivel chair. Someone had taken off his black Italian loafers. Or maybe Tony had kicked them off himself. They'd taped him up and he'd tried to get free. He'd kicked off his shoes and dug his fingers in the padded leather arms of his chair.

That was the part I didn't like to think about. You don't have to tie a guy up you're going to shoot him in the head. They taped him in the chair, then they did something else, something that scared Tony bad enough to make him fill his pants.

I stood back and thought about that. Whatever it was it didn't show. No marks or bruises anywhere, nothing but the hole in Tony's head. I thought about Sherry, barfing down the hall. There was nothing much more I could do for Tony Palmer. I could get the hell back to the car and away from the *Literary Times.* We could drive due west through Cedar Rapids and Des Moines, and make Nebraska by tomorrow afternoon. Who's going to look for a felon at the ass-end of the Platte?

Great idea. Only that was the moment when my light strayed past Tony's chest and hit his lap. Something like a tire tool hit me in the stomach and brought me to my knees. My eyes began to sting and I bawled like a kid. I wanted to tell him how we'd get him fixed up and we'd go have dinner somewhere and everything would be fine and how goddamn sorry I was about this whole fucking mess and how I wasn't even mad anymore. We'd put out a special on the minor English poets, like we always said we'd do. I'd do all the hard parts myself and I'd let him change anything he liked, and Jesus Christ, why'd they have to go and do that?

I made myself look. I pulled back Tony's chair and shined the light between his legs. They'd pulled Tony's pride out of his pants and used some kind of tool that left ugly purple ridges on the flesh. Ordinary pliers came to mind. Everybody's got a handy pair of pliers in the trunk or in the bottom of a drawer.

They hurt him maybe half a dozen times, mostly in the very

same spot. They asked him what Murray had done with the briefcase and Tony didn't know, and they knew he didn't know, but they had to make sure, they had to ask. And when they were through they said, Tony, you know we had to ask, and they shot him in the head. Tony must have known—he had to know right from the start—that even if he had the right answers it would end up just the same. He didn't know a thing, he told the guys he didn't know a thing, but he had to go through it anyway. And maybe that's when it hit him really hard, and everything began to come loose and fall apart.

I turned off the flash and walked out and closed Tony Palmer's door. I took a deep breath but the smell was still there, and I wondered how long it would take me to get to the bottle in the car.

Sherry was slumped in my chair staring listlessly at the floor. In the half-light from the corridor outside, her features seemed flat and drained of all emotion. A lock of apricot hair hung down across her brow.

"I threw up in your filing cabinet," she said, without looking up. "I hope you don't mind."

"I don't mind," I said. "I don't think I work here anymore."

"That was your friend in there, right?"

"Yeah, it was Tony."

"I'm sorry. That's about all I can say. Can we go now, Russ?"

I told her I thought this was what we ought to do. I helped her up, and this time she didn't back away. She rested against me for a moment, then leaned down and picked up her shoes, and said she was okay now, she'd be fine.

I locked the door to the office and we walked down the stairs to the outside door. A light rain had fallen, and the broad alleyway behind the building reflected a flashing stoplight from the street.

"Russ, I am not very good in traumatic situations," Sherry

said as we reached the car. "Some people are, I'm not. What I am is fucking scared. You want to keep looking for clues, take a cab. I'm going to find someplace that's got a bed."

"Fine," I said, "we can do that."

"So where you want to stop? Somewhere close would be okay with me."

"I'm thinking, Sherry Lou, I don't know."

"Well I don't want to meet any more of your friends. If it's a friend you got in mind, I don't want to do that."

"I wasn't even thinking about friends. Did I say we were going to a friend?"

"I'm just saying, I'm saying that I won't put up with that."

"We're not going to stay with a friend. I don't think I have any friends."

"Good. I'm real pleased to hear it."

Sleep sounded great, but I wondered where the hell we could go. With my picture in the paper everywhere, hotels and motels were out. At least close to home. We could drive over into Indiana, stay off the toll, or go up the Michigan coast. Getting out of state seemed a good idea. Of course the cops would likely think of that too. They probably had a roadblock out. Those sawhorse things they put up with flashing lights.

Sherry started to get in the driver's side. I stopped her with my hand on the door.

"I'll drive this time," I said, "you can get some rest."

She turned on me and frowned. "You think I can't drive? I can drive just fine."

"I know you can drive. I didn't say you couldn't drive. I just said I'd do it for a while."

"You want to drive, fine. Go ahead and—"

Sherry didn't finish. A car whipped into the alleyway, taking the corner fast. It came right at us, blinding us with its lights. Sherry said something I couldn't hear. I grabbed her by the shoulders, ducked her head and shoved her inside the car. The other car squealed to a stop, turning halfway around on the wet cement. Two men spilled out of the front, another from the back. The man in the back was tall and thin and I knew I'd never seen him before. He wore a dark gray suit and a porkpie hat. His skin was as dead as Tony Palmer's, and his nose was as sharp as a deli knife. Black circles rimmed his eyes like he hadn't slept a day in his life.

I knew the other two at once, I didn't have to look twice. You're watching the Bears with maybe thirty thousand people all around, right off you'll spot the Wackers in the crowd. Sherry yelled, "Russell, get in the fucking *car*," and I tried but my feet wouldn't move, I couldn't get the message through. I stood there staring at two sides of beef in overcoats and my goddamn feet wouldn't budge. The Wackers came at me, taking their time, like what's this jerk going to do, where's he going to go? The thin guy stood and watched, leaning on the hood of his car. Sherry kept shouting and beating on my back. The Wackers kept coming and something exploded with a burst of white light and a sound that ripped the night. The Wacker to my right looked surprised. Sparks stitched the ground and ran up his overcoat and tore his face away. The other Wacker stared, stumbled back and jerked a .45 from his pocket and emptied it at the dark. Lead whined past him and thunked into the hood of his car. The thin guy yelled and hit the back seat fast. The Wacker who was still on his feet turned and ran, lead dancing at his heels. He threw himself behind the wheel. He didn't bother to close the door.

Bullets shattered the car's front window, marched down the hood and took out the left headlight. The car burned rubber and squealed through the alley for the street. The open door hit a telephone pole, ripped off and slid along the ground.

I don't remember getting in the car. I remember backing off, bouncing off a Wacker, slamming the car into drive, and hitting a beefy speed bump again.

"Oh, *God*," Sherry moaned, and clapped a hand across her mouth.

I finally got the car going straight, and headed out of the alley for the street. My right front tire hit the curb and an old lady stepped into my lights. I jerked the wheel to miss her, hit a rack of garbage cans, and bounced onto Madison going west.

I checked the old lady in the mirror, and saw she was still on her feet. She wore a big shoulder bag looped over one arm, a pillbox hat with a feather on the top. She shook her fist at me and yelled for me to stop. I didn't think I cared to do that. In her other hand she gripped an Uzi submachine gun.

You don't see a lot of old ladies carrying automatic weapons on the street. I told myself it could have been a short umbrella, that I hadn't really seen her that well, but I knew I wasn't wrong. I also knew that I'd seen this old lady once before. She had walked by my phone booth at O'Hare, given me a cold-eyed look and wandered on.

So what the hell is going on here? I thought. Whoever the old lady was, it was clear she had saved us from the mob. I was grateful, but the idea that someone was on our side didn't make a lot of sense. There were cops, hoods, Russell and Sherry Lou. Old ladies with machine guns didn't seem to fit.

"Well, I don't want to hear any more 'bout *my* driving skills," Sherry said. "It's a wonder you're licensed to drive a car."

"There's nothing on the test says what you ought to do under fire, Sherry Lou. It doesn't say a thing about that."

We passed South Wells and I turned on Franklin going north. Two cop cars passed us headed the other way, sirens wailing as they rushed to the scene of the crime. Sherry turned in her seat to look. She stayed in this position several blocks, peering out the back.

"Turn off somewhere," she said finally. "Next time you can, take a right."

"What for?"

" 'Cause someone's following us, Russ, that's why."

"How do you know that?"

"I just do, okay?"

"Jesus," I said, "I bet it's that crazy old lady with the gun."

"What old lady's that?"

"You saying you didn't see her or what? The old lady in the alley, Sherry Lou, the one with the—"

"Russ, will you turn the fucking *car?*"

We had just crossed the river, past the Apparel Center. I made a hard right on Grand, drove a few blocks and hooked a left on LaSalle.

"He's turning right with us," Sherry said, "he's still there."

"Is he wearing a pillbox hat, with a feather on the top?"

"Is he what?" Sherry gave me a curious look. "Are you all right, Russ?"

"I'm just fine," I said, and let it go at that. It was clear we were out of sync again. Sherry hadn't seen the old lady. She wasn't into pillbox hats. Okay, we could go into that another time. For the moment, I concentrated on losing our tail. I turned on Huron, took a right on Orleans, and another quick right on Chicago Avenue. I knew the North Side, and I knew all the alleys and the lights. In three or four minutes, our tail was out of sight. When I was certain we were free, I pulled off the street and parked behind an all-night convenience store.

"I guess you think you're pretty smart," Sherry said. She leaned against the far door. Her eyes reflected green from the dash.

"I shook 'em off," I said, "I know that."

"So this is it, this is where we're going to sleep?"

"No, it's not where we're going to sleep, Sherry Lou. I'll find us a good place to sleep, okay? First I got to make a call."

"Oh, Jesus," Sherry said. She sat up straight and pressed her hands against the sides of her head. "Russ is going to *call* someone. Russ is going to call another friend."

"Take it easy," I said, "it isn't what you think."

"You know what, you know what I think?" Sherry thrust out her chin in defiance. "Look at me, Russ, okay? You make another fucking *call*, I won't *be* here when you get back."

"Fine," I said, "get a cab. That's just fine with me."

I took the keys and got out and walked toward the store to find a phone.

"You come back with those keys," Sherry yelled at my back. "*I* stole this car, you didn't steal this car!"

Nice going, I thought. I guess everyone in the store heard that. "Hey, look, Murray the killer's coming in to rob the store." I wished to hell I'd remembered to take a drink.

Chapter 17

Jane Kowalski answered halfway through the first ring. She said do you know what time it is, you son of a bitch, and I said I had no idea. Jane said it's half past one, is what it is, and where the hell are you right now. I told her and she said don't tell me, I don't want to know, don't tell me where you are.

When she cooled down a little, I learned the shooting on Madison was already on the news. I learned the cops didn't know which brother was dead, since the Wackers didn't carry IDs. I also learned some astute Chicago cop had noticed that the shooting took place behind the office of *The Literary Times*. Now the police knew Tony was dead as well. And guess who they figured had killed both Tony and the hood?

"Great," I said, "what else is new, Jane?"

"They're using 'crazed' and 'savage' a lot," Jane said. "They weren't doing that before."

Sherry was still in the car, slumped down with her feet on the dash. She pretended not to notice I was there. She looked straight ahead, and took a nip from her bottle now and then. Take a nip, *beat,* one-two ... She drank as if she might be competing in some event.

I joined her and we drank in silence for a while. A skinny dog crossed in front of the car, sniffed at the dumpster, and decided to try across the street.

"I didn't mean to say what I did," I told Sherry. "You got a lot of stress in your head, it makes you say things you don't mean. A person says something he isn't thinking straight, it's bound to come out a lot different than he means."

"A person *thinks* before he talks," Sherry said, "he doesn't have to worry 'bout what's coming out. You might want to ponder on that."

"I said I was sorry, Sherry Lou."

"I heard what you said."

"Listen, I got us a good place to sleep. Don't say anything, it's not like what you think. Jane's got a friend who takes pictures for the *Trib.* He's off somewhere in the Middle East. I don't even know the guy, no one's going to look for us there."

Sherry Lou considered this news and took a drink. "This guy, he better not be dead," Sherry said. "I won't put up with that."

"You didn't listen," I said. "The guy's out of town, he's not dead."

"Uh-huh."

"And you're right about the car. I apologize for that. You stole the car. By rights it's your car."

Sherry lowered her bottle and gave me a puzzled look. "I don't *want* the car, Russ. Why would I want this stupid car?"

"Well, if you do, you got the right."

"You better go in and get some smokes, we're about out. And get a couple of packs of beer."

"The TV says I'm savage and crazed. I don't much appreciate that."

"Crazed is kinda strong," Sherry said. "I'd go along with

crackers and loony either one. Unhinged and out of whack comes to mind.''

Jane's friend lived six or eight blocks from where we were, not far from the campus of Northwestern. The apartment was on the second floor in the back, and the key was where Jane said it ought to be, under the second flower pot. I wondered how Jane knew that, and felt a brief moment of envy and regret.

The place was your basic bachelor pad, small living room, smaller kitchenette. Two bedrooms and a bath, one of the bedrooms full of darkroom equipment, boxes of picture files, and the shiny gadgets photographers keep around. The whole apartment had the empty, dusty look of a place where a person doesn't spend a lot of time.

When I finished my tour, I saw Sherry Lou had found the bar. She grinned like a kid who's found the prize Easter egg.

"I like your friend a lot," she said. "A man who drinks Polish vodka is a man who might win Sherry's heart."

"He's not my friend," I said, "he's Jane's. And we shouldn't drink all the guy's booze."

"Yeah, I think we should."

Sherry poured herself a hefty glass and set a bottle of Chivas out for me. The message was clear. I didn't have to sin, I could sit around and watch. I found a Mickey Mouse glass in the cabinet and filled it nearly up to Mickey's neck. Mickey seemed pleased, and why not? He didn't have the cops and the mob on his back, all he had to do was grin.

I turned to speak to Sherry, but Sherry wasn't there. Taking my drink across the room, I inspected the bookshelves and found our host's taste ran to professional catalogs and books. He also liked Robert Ludlum, and lesser-known writers who specialized in intrigue and lust. A lot of the paperbacks dealt with former Nazis determined to retrieve hidden gold. I wondered what the writers would do when all the old Nazis died off and left them without any plots. Most of these gold-crazy

Huns were seventy or eighty by now. This is kind of late for escapades and larks. You want to have a lark, twenty-five or thirty is about the right time. You get to be eighty, adventure is pissing twice a week.

Still no Sherry Lou, so I freshened up my drink and wandered down the hall. I thought she might have found the john and gotten sick. I found her in the bedroom, sitting cross-legged on the bed, holding her drink and watching TV without sound. Her clothes were on the floor, where she'd dropped them in various states of undress. Now she wore a man's white shirt, the sleeves rolled up and the front tucked down between her legs.

Sherry was intent on the screen, and I wondered if I maybe ought to knock or simply stand there and look. There is something quite heady and appealing about a small and shapely woman in an oversized shirt. The thought comes to mind that since a man's shirt belongs to a man, you might have some basic right to take it off. You don't, but the thought is still there.

"Hi," I said, for lack of anything to say. "You disappeared, and I thought I ought to come back and look. You okay?"

"I'm okay," she said. "I could use a refill, you don't mind."

She handed me the glass without looking up from the screen. I glanced at the picture, and saw it was an ancient Lash LaRue. Lash was rushing across the plains in black and white, several hundred outlaws in pursuit.

"You got a real oldie there," I said. "I can't remember when I've seen a Lash LaRue."

"What's a Lash LaRue?" Sherry asked.

"It's not a what, it's a who. Lash LaRue. That's who's on the screen."

"Oh, right. You going to get that drink, or what?"

I took her glass and got a drink and brought it back. Sherry had shifted on the bed, and the shirt now revealed a patch of thigh. I wondered if I went out again and came back if something more might appear.

"I guess you're kinda beat," I said.

"I guess I am," said Sherry Lou.

"It's been a real rough day."

"I noticed that, Russ."

"We're both pretty tired. We'll get a night's sleep."

Sherry didn't answer. She watched Lash LaRue, who had now shot thirty or forty bandits without reloading his .45.

"Well then, Sherry . . ." *One,* two, three, four—"I'll be on the couch. Out in the other room. I'll be right out there. You want anything . . ."

"You're hovering, Russ," Sherry said. She looked up and squinted and blew a strand of hair from her eyes. "I'm getting real dizzy, watching you circle the field. I'm hopin' you'll settle down and light. You think you might consider that?" She patted a spot on the bed.

I wasted little time getting off my new boots. The bed sagged when I joined her, forcing her knee against mine. Sherry turned and gave me a very thoughtful look. She focused on my eyes and then my chin. She frowned and worked her mouth and scratched her nose and then broke into a grin.

"Russ, you got a lot of dirty thoughts in your head. I sometimes admire that in a man."

"Now you've gone a little too far," I told her. "I'm about as pure as I can be."

Sherry grinned again. She picked up the remote and the picture fell in upon itself and left a dot.

"Lash LaRue, huh?"

"The man's a pillar of moral strength. I hear he kept his mind and body clean."

Sherry shook her head and scooted around to face me. "Russell Murray, mostly you're a pain in the ass. Sometimes you're as cute as you can be. You don't have to sleep on the couch. And you don't have to sit there wondering what I'll do if you make some sneaky little pass."

"If I do, you'll do what?"

"I think I'll give my body up to lust. I guess I'll fall prey to base desire. It can't do any harm and it might help a lot. We're both into tension and stress.''

"Listen," I said, "therapy's as good as romance."

Sherry put her hands on my shoulders and came in for a kiss. We held on to that for some while, then I took our drinks and set them on the floor. Sherry leaned back and clicked off the lamp by the bed. I got up and peeled off my sheepherder wear. When I joined her again, she was starting on the buttons of her shirt, and I told her it would give me some pleasure to finish that myself.

Sherry looked delightful in the light from the window and the hall, shadow patterns shifting as she moved, following the contours of her flesh, changing as the darkness touched her breasts and her stomach and her thighs. I brushed back her hair and kissed her mouth, and the hollows of her throat. Her eyes focused intently on mine, as if my eyes might tell her some secret she didn't know; about me, about herself, about what our encounter might reveal.

We didn't speak at all. We were good to each other, giving what we had to give, wanting to meet each other's needs. But when we were done and we lay there and smoked obligatory cigarettes, I felt this event owed more to good manners than longing and desire. We were fairly nice people and we'd had a lot to drink. Making love was the natural conclusion to the time we'd spent together, the courteous and social thing to do.

It happens this way all the time, and there's a sadness here you'd like to put away and deny. You are not indifferent or unconcerned; you both do your best and there's a spark, but there's very little fire. You know you'll get together sometime and try again. Maybe you'll get to know each other, and bring something better back to bed.

Or maybe, I thought, you shouldn't bitch and moan a lot, Russ. You're Murray, you're not Sir Lancelot. You won't curl up and die with a broken heart. You've got a friend who'll let you hold her in the dark, and there's nothing wrong with that.

Chapter 18

The doorbell brought me up out of sleep, fully awake, my heart pounding rapidly against my chest. Jesus, I thought, the cops or the mob? Had to be the cops. The mob wouldn't bother to ring. The clock on the table said a little after six. Sherry muttered to herself, and burrowed out of sight. I pulled on my pants and made my way down the hall. The doorbell rang again. I stopped and leaned against the wall. Maybe it wasn't the cops. They want me to think it's the cops, they ring the bell. Sudden vision of a Wacker, a black mourning band around his gun . . .

I looked around for a means of self-defense. A hockey stick, possibly a bat. Nothing in sight. Photographers don't go in for sports. I picked up a lamp, tossed the shade aside, and jerked the plug out of the wall. The door had one of those holes you can look through and see who's standing outside. Holding the lamp behind my back, I risked a look. A fun-house image of Jane looked back. Jane Kowalski, who else? Jane was the only one who knew I was here. Why hadn't I thought of that before?

I opened the door. She stood there a moment, giving me the Jane Kowalski look number nine. It's the one that wilts waiters when she finds a dirty fork.

"My, you're just as lovely as ever," Jane said. "No shirt, no shoes, no shave. If I were you, I'd avoid Chicago's finer restaurants."

"My tux is at the cleaner's," I said. "You coming in or what?"

"I'm thinking about it," she said.

Jane stepped in and took a cautious look around, to see if everything was intact. Maybe I'd burned all the furniture to cook a side of beef, or scrawled dirty slogans on the wall. You let a barbarian in the house, you can't tell what he might do.

"I don't suppose you've got the coffee on," she said. "I can't stand to talk to you, Russ, without six or eight cups."

"This isn't my apartment," I said. "I'll have to look around."

"That lamp doesn't go with your pants. Coffee's in the left-hand cabinet, the one above the booze."

A double-play for Jane. She let me know she'd seen the bottles strewn about. She made sure I knew she'd been up here before.

I set the lamp aside. I found the filters and the coffee and the pot. While I searched for coffee cups, I sneaked a look at Jane. She sat on the sofa, arms crossed in disapproval below her breasts. The window was behind her and the morning tossed highlights in her hair. She wore a rust-colored jacket and skirt, very no-nonsense and correct, but cut to fit her lean and lanky frame. Jane is six-two in high heels, and most of that is legs. She has the uncanny knack of looking totally professional and slightly depraved, a combination that leaves men confused and uncertain what to do. Do you ask her about the state budget, or see if she'd like to go to bed? Guess right the first time or you're dead.

The sight of her stirred me as it always had, and likely always would. Our affair had been a short one, but you couldn't say it hadn't been intense. We disagreed on everything from politics to sex. We clashed in every way we could. We were made for each other, like Andrew Dice Clay and Barbara Bush. Still, we

kept on coming back for more, hanging on to what we had,
Jane forgiving me for showing up drunk or not showing up at
all, until we used it all up and there was nothing much left to
forgive.

When the coffee was ready, I filled up the cups and set them
on a Budweiser tray. A very classy touch. I set the tray on the
table by the couch, and pulled up a straight-back chair.

"There's sugar if you want it," I said. "There isn't any
cream."

"I never use cream," Jane said.

"You used to use cream."

"I used to do a lot of things, Russ. A lot of things I don't
do now."

"This is what we're going to do, we're going to get into
that?"

"Let's not. What I'd like is to stick to the business at hand."
Jane tested her cup and set it down. "Whatever you're into,
Russ, and I don't have any idea what it is, we're talking very
deep shit. The Karla Stark thing made the papers, but they left
nearly everything out. Like why, if you killed the girl, you
broke down the door to your room, when any rookie cop could
see that's where you spent the night. Or why the Wackers
chased you down the street. People saw that, Russ, but the
Wackers don't appear in this scenario at all. And there is absolutely *no* record anywhere of your run-in with the Wackers in
Wisconsin. I've got to believe this happened like you said. You
are not what we call a reliable source, but even you wouldn't
dream up a thing like that."

"Oh, well, I appreciate that," I said.

"Shut up and listen, okay? I don't think you have any idea
what that means, a cover-up like that. You cover up something
like that, this is not an easy thing to do. The fix is in big, which
means some big people are involved. This escapade last night,
they couldn't very well fix that. A guy gets shot, they find a
stiff in the building next door, they can't smother something

like that. But they're doing what they can, that's the thing, they're calling in a carload of favors on this.''

Jane paused and gave me a painful look. "You understand this, Russell, you getting this at all?"

"You can stop that anytime you like," I told her. "You want to talk, you can do it right now."

"Stop what?"

"I am not fucking four-years-old."

"Oh, right. Well see, sometimes I forget. I keep—" Jane stopped. She let out a breath and closed her eyes, as if she was counting up to ten. "I'm sorry. I am not being nice. We bring out the worst in each other, Russ. We always had a talent for that."

"We brought out the best sometimes, as I recall."

Jane looked away and nodded. For a moment, I thought she might say something else, and I think she thought she might too.

"Okay," she said finally, "you want to tell me what you were doing at the *Literary Times?* I can't wait to hear that." There was still a very slight caustic touch to her voice, but she was Jane and she couldn't help that, and she covered it nicely with a smile.

"The briefcase wasn't at O'Hare," I explained, "so I went to Artie's place . . .''

"Hold it." Jane held up a hand. "What were you doing at O'Hare? You didn't tell me this."

"You just got here, how could I tell you that?"

"Right, you're right." She folded her hands to show me she was exercising patience and restraint.

I told her about the key I'd found, and how it didn't fit the lockers at O'Hare, and that Artie didn't have the briefcase either, so I went up to the office and found Tony dead. I told her how the car pulled up with the Wackers and the skinny-looking guy, and how the old lady with the Uzi showed up and shot one of the Wackers dead.

"Wait, wait a minute now." Jane stopped her cup in mid-air. "An old lady, she's shooting someone with a what?"

"With an Uzi," I said.

"An old lady. Not a guy? You maybe think this guy's an old lady, you see him in the dark."

"An old lady," I said. "With a pillbox hat."

"Jesus Christ, Russ." She gave this revelation some thought. I knew what kind of thought it was, like is Russell hallucinating or what?—and I couldn't much blame her for that. And since we'd decided not to give each other physical or verbal abuse, she let the old-lady question rest.

"This skinny-looking dude with the Wackers," Jane said, "he looked—what? What did he look like, Russ?"

"Skinny. Gray suit and a porkpie hat. What he's got, he's got black rings around his eyes. He looks like Ronnie Raccoon."

"Ritchie Pinelli," Jane said at once. "Ritchie Bones. He's Frank Cannatella's main man."

Jane shifted on the couch, unwinding silky legs, a process that takes some time.

"They want this briefcase back. I don't know what's in it, but they want it back bad. The old lady, I don't think I care to tackle that. Except there's someone else in the game and I don't know where they fit. Russ, since the shit hit the fan, the briefcase bit and Karla Stark, a lot of very strange stuff has been going on in this town. Everyone I know is clamming up. All of a sudden, I don't have sources anymore. No one's got a source. Cops and street guys, guys who'd what, they'd sell their mothers for fifty bucks, it's got anything to do with this, they got nothing at all to say."

Jane paused, and ran a red fingernail around her cup. "People at the *Trib,* they know I know you, I get a lot of funny looks. And people come in, they come in to the office, I don't see 'em all myself but I hear. They don't stop where us peasants hang out, they go right to the top. I'm talking local politicians and cops with lots of braid, and guys I've never seen before. A couple of dudes they come in, they've got suits, they're wearing cowboy boots and hats. One of these characters I know, he's a local party guy, the same party that's pushing this Texas Senator Byron, the one we talked about has some kind of ties with Frank Cannatella. The word is, the brass upstairs tells these guys in a very nice way to fuck off, but that doesn't help a whole lot. The fix is in at the *source* of the news, so nothing gets out the papers and the TV people can use, or anyway not much.''

"Artie said I ought to think about Alaska," I said. "I told him maybe not, I was thinking Mexico."

Jane shook her head. "This is not entirely hopeless, Russ. There's a couple of things we know."

"Like what? I may have already won a case of cement?"

"We've got your former boss, who's got vague connections with the Frabotta Family in Jersey and New York, his wife's uncle is Frank Cannatella." Jane frowned and bit her lip. "How well do you know Tony's wife, uh, widow, what's her name?"

"Her name's Felicia. I don't know her at all. I've met her once or twice, why?"

"I don't know. I'm looking for someplace to start, and there aren't a lot of people who'd give the time of day to Russell Murray right now."

I stared at Jane. "And you're thinking Felicia, I ought to talk to her? For God's sake, Jane, she probably watches TV. She's maybe heard Russell Murray shot her husband in the head."

"If Tony was mixed up with Felicia's uncle, she's got to know better than that."

"And she's going to discuss this with me."

"Maybe. I don't know. I am grasping at straws, Russ."

"Well, I am not about to mess around with Felicia Palmer's straw," I told Jane. "Besides, it wouldn't do any good. The mob, they don't talk business in front of their women. A wife asks a guy something, he tells her, 'Hey, don't ask me nothing about my business.' That's the way they do."

"Russ . . ." Jane rolled her eyes. "This isn't *The Godfather,* this is fucking real life!"

"Uh-huh. And where you think they get this stuff? You think a writer, some writer he makes that up?"

"Okay, Russ."

"What am I *doing* mixed up in this shit? I don't *know* these people, I've got nothing to do with all this."

"You've got their briefcase, Russ."

"I don't have their briefcase."

"You don't have it now, but you did. You had it, and they don't know you don't have it now. They don't, they don't, they don't . . ."

I followed Jane's eyes, and watched her mouth lock on the very last word, unable to let it go.

Sherry had hovered at the edge of my mind from the moment I opened the door, and every time she popped up again I said *no,* I will not take part in this sitcom plot where the old girlfriend drops in, and the guy has a new girlfriend in his bed, and everyone knows what happens next. So here comes Sherry down the hall, medium close-up, girl dressed solely in black bikini panties, standard pose for strumpet of the year, looks at me (startled) with one sleepy eye behind a veil of red hair.

Sherry Lou: "Oh, I am so sorry, didn't know y'all had company, hon."

Russ: "That's Sherry Lou. She's been a lot of help."

Jane: "I'll just bet she has." (Jane rises, pours coffee in Russ's lap. Exits stage left.)

Life reflects art, or maybe it's the other way around. All the world's a stage, and let me off when we get to Cheyenne.

Chapter 19

"Thanks a lot," I said, "that was some performance, Sherry Lou. You ought to take that act on the road, that's what you ought to do."

"I'll bet a nickel that lady was your lost love, Jane," Sherry said. "The one that's still burning like an ember in your heart."

"You know damn well who it was. And I haven't got an ember in my heart."

"Yes you do."

"I said I don't."

Sherry laughed. "My God, Russ, you're turning red as bad credit. You ought to see your face."

"It's real hot in here," I said.

"That's those embers warming up. That's likely what it is."

I left Sherry Lou and went out to check the fridge. There was nothing there to eat. Nothing was there when I'd looked a few minutes before. I do this at home all the time. I'll look in and see something green from outer space, shut the door and leave and then come back again. Like the food fairies maybe dropped in and left a cold jar of pickles and half a roast beef. It's never happened yet but that doesn't mean it won't. Faith is the key.

"There's nothing here to eat," I told Sherry. "I guess I'll run out and get some food."

"Get quail if they got it," Sherry said. "And some good pâté."

"Pâté."

"And don't get me any Saltines. I like those crackers from England, 'bout as thin as a diaphragm."

"I'm not going to Paris, France, Sherry Lou. I'm going to the neighborhood store. I was thinking ham and eggs."

"Well of course you were, Russ. You can't help being what you are."

When I walked out the door, Sherry was propped up on the couch with the pillows at her back. She wore the white shirt she'd put on the night before and her hair was wrapped up in a towel. The granny glasses were perched on the end of her nose and she squinted intently at *People* magazine. I had to admit she looked fetching, very close to cute. There were no fine lines about her eyes, and nothing seemed to sag. She didn't look like a lady who'd killed a fifth of vodka the day before, started on another, and was into her morning booster shots— coffee laced with our absent host's Puerto Rican rum. People get the wrong idea about drunks. They aren't all sleeping in doorways on the street. Some of them are sleeping in high-rise condos and driving Bentley cars. One man's Old Tennis Shoe is another man's single-malt Scotch. Still, there's a kinship between all drunks. It cuts through every social stratum with the same understanding of priorities and needs: You don't let the tank get empty, not if you want to keep your edge. Sherry knew how to handle that. I'd only seen her sweat and shake once, after our escape from the detox farm. Now she was on a roll again, boozing just enough to keep the glow.

Sherry said I was a rookie, and she was right to some extent. When I go on a toot, I drink up everything in sight. Then I black out and wake up somewhere, and I'm too sick to drink for a week. Then the shakes show up and I start on a bender again. So, compared to Sherry Lou, I am definitely an amateur lush.

I knew I didn't want to turn pro, and I doubt if anyone ever does. You don't come out and say, "Listen, I think I got the talent, I think I can make it as a full-time drunk." You don't say it, you just go ahead and do.

Outside the apartment, with happy coeds all about on the way to morning class, with the sun shining bright and the streets clean from yesterday's rain, the decision to make a run for sainthood and walk the straight line seemed the proper thing to do. But daytime promises are easy to keep. Hell, even vampires keep out of trouble till it's dark.

The first thing I did was get rid of our stolen car. If the owner flew in from out of town he'd report his missing car to the police, and the cops would put his plates on a list. I didn't want it found in the neighborhood, so I drove a couple of miles and left it in a supermarket lot. Then I did my shopping and took a cab back. This is how your criminal mind works. We're thinking all the time.

"One of these things I been reading," Sherry said, "they say Pee Wee Herman's got his eyes on Lady Di. You reckon that's true?"

"Sounds like a matchup to me," I said.

"I've partied with the stars now and then. You can't tell what those people are going to do."

I had cooked up some bacon, scrambled eggs with cheddar cheese, and half a loaf of toast. I mixed up a pitcher of orange juice, the kind that comes frozen in a can. It wasn't quail or pâté, but Sherry managed to adjust. She scarfed down her share and started on mine.

"I picked up a paper," I said. "There's nothing in it we

didn't know before. It says I'm still at large. I already knew that. It says I'm wanted for the brutal torture-murder of Tony Palmer. It says I also killed Mort Wacker, a resident of Chicago's North Side. You like that, a resident? It doesn't say he's a hood. People read that, they think the guy's maybe a lawyer or a dentist. Maybe he went to church a lot. Some guy offs a busload of orphans, you know who did that? Russell Murray did. That's what the paper's going to say. That's the—''

"Brutal torture what?" Sherry blinked and poked a piece of toast in my face. "What's this torture-murder shit, what's that?"

"They roughed Tony up. They hurt him real bad."

"You didn't tell me that."

"I didn't think you'd want to know."

Sherry bit her lip. "They hurt him bad *how,* Russ? What'd they do? Jesus, don't tell me, I don't want to hear about that."

Sherry stood abruptly, left her plate and poured herself a drink. She walked to the window and looked out at the street. I couldn't see her face, but I knew she'd be working her mouth real funny and staring out of state. I hadn't told her what they'd done to Tony Palmer. She didn't need to know. Now she was thinking of all the things the Wackers might have done, playing back all the horror shows she'd ever seen. She was thinking how she'd been there and seen Tony dead, and what they'd done was there too, so close it could have touched her, left a shadow of its awful pain behind.

I had seen the real Sherry once or twice, and I knew that behind that cocky mask, behind the polish and the wit was another Sherry Lou who was scared someone would discover she was made of Silly Putty and spit, and had all the self assurance of a mouse caught in a trap. Rabbits wear tiger suits, and chipmunks pretend to be bears. We all play tricks on ourselves, and we seldom fool anyone else.

*   *   *

I left Sherry Lou and went into the bedroom and looked up Felicia Palmer's number at home. Felicia said hello, and I said, "Felicia, it's Russ. Please don't hang up."

Silence. I could hear the ghosts of other conversations on the line. I could hear people talking at Felicia's, and I pictured a houseful of relatives and friends. Editors and writers, poets and artists, and guys named Vinnie and Sal.

"Felicia," I told her, "I don't know what to say to you. If I'd thought, if I'd figured something out, I wouldn't have gotten up the nerve to call. I didn't do anything to Tony, Felicia, I hope you know that. I don't know if you know that or not."

"I don't know what to think, Russell," Felicia said. "I don't know anything anymore."

Her voice was calm and distant, with no tone at all. The way people sound when they're still in shock or the doctor's got them taking heavy drugs.

"Listen," I said, "I want you to know what happened. I mean, you believe me or not, I'd understand if you didn't, I'd understand that. Tony sent me to Dallas with a briefcase, Felicia. I was supposed to give it to a writer at the airport, only something happened to it and I don't know where it is. I honest to God don't, only people think I do."

"I don't . . . I don't know anything about . . . briefcases," she said. "I know Tony's dead, I know that."

"I didn't think you did. Know anything about it, I mean. I'm just saying, what I'm saying is this briefcase thing is what happened, that's what this is all about."

"I kept thinking, it kept going through my head, I thought when they said on TV that you killed that girl, I thought, Russell Murray wouldn't do that. When I heard about it that's what I thought, that you wouldn't do that . . ."

"I appreciate you thinking that," I said, "I really do. And I didn't have anything to do with Tony's death either, Felicia. I found him, that's all. I went to the office and I found him and I left."

A long silence on Felicia's end of the line. "You were there? Last night?"

"I was up there, that's all."

"They said you shot another man, too."

"I know they said that."

I heard Felicia let out a long sigh. "Russell, I'm—I am terribly confused right now. I don't know what to do and I don't know what to think."

"Tony was my friend, Felicia. I cared about Tony a lot."

"Tony . . . cared about you."

"I know he did, I know that."

"Russell?"

"Yes?"

"Russell, I think we . . . I think we need to talk." I could hear her voice breaking, catching in her throat. "I want to see you, I think, I think there's . . . I think we need to talk. There's some things we— We can meet somewhere and talk."

I took a deep breath and thought about that. "You mean, getting together somewhere."

"Is that all right with you?"

"That's good," I said, "that's fine, we can do that. You tell me where and when."

Felicia said three, Lake Shore Park and East Chicago Avenue, which isn't far from where I was, but I didn't tell her that. I said fine and hung up and sat there and looked at the phone.

Cautions and concerns came to mind. The cops show up and Felicia isn't there. The cops *don't* show up. Uncle Frank sends Ritchie Bones and Irv Wacker instead. I didn't know Felicia at all. I had seen her maybe twice. Twice is not enough. You need to know what someone will do, you got to know them better than that.

Felicia said she didn't know a thing about the briefcase bit. If she did, though, that's what she'd likely say. She wouldn't talk about the briefcase on the phone. Not with a house full of people, maybe someone standing nearby. I told myself that it wasn't a trap, that she wasn't mixed up with Uncle Frank, that the fear in her voice was very real.

I had never bought the story that Tony was a hood. Tony wasn't smart enough to hide a thing like that. He bragged about everything—who he slept with, who he knew, how much he paid for a suit. He couldn't stand to keep anything to himself.

The Cannatella family used him, I was certain of that. I couldn't guess the reason, but they did. Tony was flattered. He thought the idea of taking the briefcase to Dallas was a lark. Hey, rubbing shoulders with the mob. Only Tony found a brand-new sweetie, and gave the job to me. Uncle Frank didn't know what I knew: that Tony *never* passed up a chance to add another tall lady to his list.

I was hoping my watch would say twenty to three. It was only a quarter after twelve. I didn't want a lot of hours in between the time I had to meet Felicia in the park. You go to the dentist, he's got to pull a tooth, you want to wait outside forever, but you also want to get it done. Time is a bitch. When you want her she's never there. When you don't, she's right behind you breathing down your neck.

Chapter 20

I took a peek at Sherry on the couch, and saw she was still asleep. A nap seemed like a good idea. A nap would pass the time. I could wake up and go and see Felicia, and eliminate the thinking in between.

I closed the shades in the bedroom and stretched out on the bed. The clock said twelve thirty-two. The sounds of traffic in the street lulled me quickly into sleep. I dreamed of Jane Kowalski. The dream was a replay of an actual event. On an October weekend we'd driven up the Michigan coast and holed up in a cabin north of Little Sable Point. Jane had brought her portable tape player, and we made love by the fireplace to Mozart and Bach. It was a classical afternoon in every sense. There were carnal acrobatics that defied common decency, gravity, and the laws of several states.

A near-perfect day, with games of chance and prizes for one and all. Tarzan shows Jane what the jungle is all about. Jane wraps a mile or two of legs about my neck, and grips me in a double-scissor twist. Mozart does a tricky allegretto and flips me on my ass. I see I am much too close to the fire. I thrash about and beg Jane to let me go, but Jane is in the throes of sweet content . . .

I woke up sweating, with a bad case of the shakes. The clock said twelve thirty-eight. I had killed six minutes, not a very heavy start. I made it to the living room and poured myself a drink, took the bottle with me, and peeled off my smelly clothes. The apartment had an infinite supply of hot water. I sat on the floor in the shower and let the hard spray beat me back to life.

I was angry and I was scared. Through the magic of special effects, I could see myself clearly from a point across the room, a naked man with knees drawn up against his chest, a thumb across his bottle to keep the water out, hung up somewhere past denial and regret, because I knew I was caught in the goddamn cycle where the only way up is a slug of whatever brought you down.

I tired of hydrotherapy long before the water gave out. Dried off and shriveled, I went through the closets and drawers and borrowed underwear and socks and clean clothes. The shirt fit fine, but the pants were a little too big. Maybe photographers eat a little better than guys at the *Literary Times*.

Going through our host's drawers I found an extra set of keys. Most of them clearly fit home or office doors, but one was for a car. Sherry was still asleep. I took my bottle and closed the door and found my way downstairs. The sun was too bright and the daylight colors hurt my eyes. The car was easy enough to find. The stalls had numbers that matched apartment doors.

Our host had a '91 Cherokee Jeep, four-door, automatic shift, air, roof rack, the works. Plenty of room for photo equipment in the back, perfect for dashing out to floods or uprooted trailer parks. He hadn't used the car much; the little rubber tits were still on the tires.

I got behind the wheel and sat. It was only one-thirty and I still had an hour and a half. What I thought I might do was drive around, cruise by the park and check it out for guys who looked like gangsters or cops.

I thought and I drank. I didn't start the car. I thought about the briefcase and the key that didn't work at O'Hare. It fit somewhere, but it didn't fit there. I thought about Felicia. Every time I thought about her, I took another drink. It dawned on me, finally, that our meeting was a lousy idea. That, consciously or not, I had clearly chickened out on this the moment I hung up the phone.

I felt much better after that. I turned on the radio and took another drink. I thought about Jane and happy autumn days and nights. I thought about keys, and all the places keys fit. The key I had fit a locker. It wouldn't fit anywhere else. Lockers are at airports, and at awful-looking places you go to catch a bus. Lockers are at clubs. Country clubs, yacht clubs, private clubs, tennis clubs. I didn't belong to any clubs. Tony belonged to lots of clubs, but I wasn't a clubby kind of guy.

The answer came to me at once, the way it does in cartoons when a bulb lights up over Daffy Duck's head. I left my bottle on the seat and ran back upstairs. Sherry was sitting up putting polish on her toes. I gathered up what little stuff I had. I dropped my bundle on the floor and sat down across from Sherry Lou.

"I'm driving to Dallas," I said. "It's too risky to take a plane. My key doesn't fit at O'Hare because it fits a locker *there*. At DFW Airport, where else? Why didn't I think of this before?"

"You don't know if it does or not," Sherry said.

"Has to be," I said. "See, the guy at the airport didn't show up. I put the briefcase in a locker and waited for my plane. I got on the plane but I didn't get the briefcase out. I just *thought* I did."

"Maybe so," Sherry said. She yawned, stretched, reached for a smoke, hesitated for a moment and gave me a thoughtful look.

"That old Chevy's not a good idea. It's not going to make it real far. Besides, the cops are likely looking for the plates."

"I'm not taking the Chevy. I ditched it at the supermarket lot. I guess I forgot to tell you that."

"I guess you did. So you're going to drive what?"

"The guy living here, he's got a Jeep. I was thinking of taking that."

"You're going to steal the guy's car."

"I didn't say steal, Sherry Lou."

"It's not okay to steal his booze. It's okay to steal his car."

I looked at Sherry Lou. She looked tired and slightly frayed. One side of her cheek held the cross-hatch pattern from the couch. She didn't look eager for a cross-country trip.

"Listen," I said, "I don't want you to feel that you have to come along. You've done a whole lot to help. I sure wouldn't have gotten this far by myself. You stick with me, you're in for more aggravation and I don't want to put you through that."

Sherry bit her lip and looked away. "You won't . . . you won't think I'm, like, bugging out or anything?"

Her answer took me by surprise. "Not for a minute," I said.

"Good. 'Cause I got to tell you, Russ, I am frazzled right down to the bone. There's too much commotion in my life. I need a chance to get serene. Fun's fun, you know? But homicidal shit is just not my cup of tea."

"Well, then, Sherry . . ."

"I feel awful, Russ. I feel like I'm deserting the ship."

"Now that's silly. You're not doing any such thing."

I went to the couch and held her and kissed her on the mouth.

"Damn it, I think I'm going to miss you," Sherry said. She sniffed and a tear coursed down her cheek. "You be careful, Russ. No offense, but you're not real good at this adventure stuff yourself."

I said good-bye again from the door, and hurried down the stairs. I threw my stuff in the car and checked the panel the way they do on big jets. All the little dials looked fine.

I already missed Sherry Lou. It's easy to make a noble gesture, if you're sure no one will take you up.

I put the car in gear and backed out. I told myself we were

both better off. Sherry didn't need the aggravation, and I didn't need another drunk. Okay, there it is, I thought. It's no fun to face, but it's the truth. You might be able to kick it if Sherry's not around. A fat guy, he's not going to make it in a Hershey-bar plant. He's going to dip a finger in the vat. Hell, I didn't know if I could fight it by myself.

I drove the Jeep out of the lot, turned on the radio and headed for the street and there she was, standing by the curb, hot-pink blouse and purple jeans, hair like an exploding tangerine, pack on her back, and a Nikon bag that was clearly full of booze, a look on her face that said, "Yeah, here I am, so fucking what?"

I stopped, and Sherry tossed her stuff in the back and slid into the passenger seat.

"Don't say a thing," she said, "okay? I don't care to talk about it, Russ."

"Did I say something? What'd I say?"

"Well, don't." She kicked off her shoes and put her feet up on the dash.

"Your toes look nice," I said. "That's a real pretty red."

"It's not red. That's Burgundy Night is what it is, it's not red. I came because I haven't got real good sense, you want to know. I don't know when to quit. Besides, this is my week to help the handicapped. Shit, Russ, I peeked in your wallet last night. You've got two bucks. Just look at that dash. You've got half a tank of gas."

"Jesus, Sherry Lou, poor folks have got feelings too, you know."

"No they don't. They think they maybe do, but they don't. Just shut the fuck up and let me sleep, okay?"

We took Highway 55 out of Chicago, stopped to eat at Springfield, and crossed the Mississippi at St. Louis a little after six. Sherry wanted to see the famous arch, so we screwed around awhile and did that, got lost for an hour and found 44 going west around eight. Missouri's a very pretty state, but there's not a lot to see in the dark.

Sherry took a slug of vodka now and then, keeping on a fairly even keel, not entirely sober, but able to complete every sentence without leaving many words out. Sherry knew her stuff. If you drink for seven hours and you had a good start before that, just staying conscious qualifies you for the drunk's Olympic team.

I had taken a vow not to drink while we were still in Illinois, and my hands were getting sweaty on the wheel. Sherry said this was a dumb idea. That if I got stopped for anything, a cop would take one look at my license and shoot me on the spot. He wouldn't care if I was sober or drunk. She said the autopsy tests would show that. As soon as we hit Missouri, I started looking for motels.

"Who came first?" Sherry said. "Was it Jane or Bambi Dear?"

This out of nowhere, and I nearly ran off the road.

"Okay," I said, "what's with Bambi Dear? You been in my wallet again or what?"

"No I haven't been in your wallet. You said the cops would maybe talk to some bookie you know. Then you said they'd talk to Bambi Dear."

"I don't remember saying that."

"Well you did."

"Maybe I did. A person can't remember everything he said."

"Jesus, Russ." Sherry laughed aloud. "Bambi *Dear? I* think I want to hear about that."

"That's not her real name. That's a professional name is what it is. You're in the entertainment field, that's what you do. You might not use your real name."

"Entertainment field, huh?"

"Sherry Lou, I don't see how my former social life is any concern of yours."

"What I bet, I bet Bambi Dear came right after Jane. Jane's

a classy lady and you figured, okay, maybe quality's not my style, I'll find me a chippie doesn't care if I use the right fork. I'll get me a base-born wench, a girl who's ill-bred and unrefined, a doxy or a tart, a floozy or a tramp—''

"All right," I said, "that's it." I turned off the highway and onto the access road, squealing the tires and slamming Sherry Lou against the door.

"Well for God's sake, Russ." Sherry pulled herself together and gave me a nasty look. "I don't much care for a person can't even take a joke."

"Is that right?"

"You've sure got a—where do I suppose we're going now?"

"I have been driving seven hours," I said, "and I can take a joke just fine. You tell a joke you let me know, all right?"

I passed the gas station and the 7-Eleven store and pulled into the motel parking lot.

Sherry wrinkled up her nose. "Russ, you can just drive on. I am not sleeping anywhere called the Catfish Springs Motel."

"Yes you are," I said. I leaned across and opened her door. "Go in and register. Don't use your real name and pay cash."

"Shit, I guess I know that," Sherry said. She got out and slammed the door.

I watched her prance into the office. I turned on the radio and rolled down the window and smelled the fresh Missouri night air. The motel sign blinked and sizzled and turned the hood red. I lit a smoke and found Sherry's camera bag and poked around for Scotch. The radio was set for Chicago, and the station I had was strong enough to blanket the entire Midwest.

I waited for Sherry and drank, and listened to a teenage singer I'd never heard of before and didn't want to hear again. I thought about the airport and the locker, and the briefcase waiting inside. Once I had it, then what? I hadn't thought a lot about that. What I'll do, I thought, I'll put it in a locker at O'Hare, and call Frank Cannatella and tell him that it's there. He'll say, "Thanks a lot, Murray, you're off the hook. No hard feelings, okay?"

Only that's not the way it would go. I wasn't dumb enough to think that. The mob doesn't like loose ends, they like to tie things up. Like they say on the cop shows, "Sorry, Russ, you know too much."

So what the hell difference did it make if I brought the damn briefcase back or not? Maybe none at all, but I knew I had to try. Maybe Uncle Frank had a heart. Maybe Batman would arrive and straighten everything out.

The radio played a Frank Sinatra, then a Janis Joplin and a Willie after that. I was fairly sure the disc jockey drank. The news came on and I learned all about the Middle East. How the South Chicago potholes were doing, and what the mayor said. How the cops were still looking for Russell Murray in the triple murder case, and how the total had now gone up to four. Felicia Anne Palmer, they said, widow of the late Tony Palmer, had been blown up in her car at ten minutes after three near Lake Shore Park and East Chicago Avenue. The victim was originally from somewhere or other, but I didn't hear that. I was out of the car, stumbling over asphalt and throwing up dinner from Springfield, Illinois, and everything I'd eaten for a week.

I stayed there on my hands and knees and shook, and felt the sweat begin to pop out on my face. I wondered how long it would take me to catch up with Manson and Speck. They'd likely get me for Kennedy and Martin Luther King. They'd never pin the Lincoln hit on me, I had a good alibi for that.

Chapter 21

We slept until noon, and woke to a chilly autumn rain. A very nice start on the day. We were both hung over, mad at each other, and sunk in somber moods. The mad went away after breakfast, dying for lack of support. The gloom lingered on as we headed southwest through Missouri, the whole state obscured by low scudding clouds and drizzly rain.

By silent agreement, we confined ourselves to six-packs of beer, penance for yesterday's abuse. I had not kept up with Sherry Lou, holding to my vow to stay sober in Illinois. News of Felicia Palmer's death took care of that. Sherry slept, and I drank to some excess, threw up twice and fell into bed at first light. The road to St. Louis is paved with good intent.

We passed gray and rain-shrouded towns, roadside blurs with odd and unfamiliar names: Bourbon, Cuba, Sleeper and Hazelgreen. Sherry and I kept to ourselves through the dreary afternoon. We were patients in the convalescent ward, too sick for whimsy and wit. I was grateful for the silence. Felicia Palmer crowded every other thought from my head. I tried, but I couldn't think of anything else.

I knew why they'd killed her—they didn't want her talking

to me. Someone had heard our conversation, or Felicia had told someone about my call. That was the part I understood. It got a little hazy after that. I looked at it backward and forward, and it still didn't make a lot of sense. What did she know that was so damned important it convinced Cannatella to kill his own niece? He'd maybe get her out of town, send her to Las Vegas or the Coast. But, Jesus—someone in the Family, a woman, on top of that, you maybe send her to Sicily for a while. You don't blow her up in her car.

And something else didn't smell right at all. *Why didn't they wait for me?* You want Russell Murray's head, Murray's going to show up at three. I'm ten minutes late, they can't wait, they blow up Felicia's car. I couldn't buy it, it simply didn't fit. But if the Cannatella Family didn't do it, who did? The old lady with the Uzi? And who the hell was *she* working for?

I felt the same sense of helplessness I'd felt last night in the car, when I'd learned Felicia Palmer was dead. Every day I knew a little less than I had the day before. And it didn't much matter what I did or didn't do. I could go for the briefcase or not. I was still dead meat in the end.

This is how a football feels. You're part of the game, but you don't get to call any plays. All you do is get your ass kicked around until the final whistle blows.

There must have been a law, because the rain stopped at once when we crossed the Oklahoma state line. Highway 69 South was the shortest route to Texas, but Sherry said we simply had to go through Tulsa, because her grandmother lived in Depew,which was right on the way, between Tulsa and Oklahoma City. There was, indeed, a Depew, but no one there had ever heard of Sherry's grandmother, and Sherry said it might have been Devola, Ohio, instead, and why the fuck did they have to make towns and states that sounded just alike?

Which is how we ended up late at night in Norman, south of Oklahoma City, at a place called Dwight's C'mon Inn. Sherry said Dwight's was much nicer than the Catfish Springs Motel. This, because Dwight's had towels and TV. Rich people notice things the rest of us might never see.

"Russ, you awake?" Sherry said.

"I guess I am," I said.

"If you're not . . . I mean, you don't have to talk, it's okay."

"I'm awake," I said.

The bed table was between us and I couldn't see her face. Someone in the room next door was watching the "David Letterman" show. Cars whined by in the street. A thin band of light slipped past the curtains, slanted on the floor, and sliced through a weeping clown bolted to the wall.

"Russ, when we were in the guy's apartment," Sherry said, "I was kinda listening in the hall. I heard what you and Jane said."

"I'm real surprised to hear that."

"I wasn't eavesdropping or anything, I was listening, is all. Are you mad about that?"

"No, I'm not mad. You listened, that's fine. What's the point?"

"What it is, what I'm saying to you, Russ, is—you find the briefcase, if it's where you think it is, then you're going to do what?"

"I'm going to give it back."

"I mean then what, after that."

"I don't know what after that."

Sherry sat up. I saw her lighter flare as she lit a cigarette.

"You really don't do you? You don't know what."

"No. I don't know what," I said. "My short-term goal is eating breakfast somewhere everything doesn't come out in a square. My long-term plan is trying not to get shot."

"See, now that's what I'm saying," Sherry said, "that's exactly what I mean."

"Sherry, I don't even know what we're talking about."

"Listen, you want to go to Brazil?"

"Do I what?"

"Brazil. It's a country in South America, Russ."

"I know what it is. We had it in geography class."

"All I'm telling you, friend, is I figure Jane was absolutely right. You're into something big and it's flat going to swallow you up. You're chasing 'round after that *fucking* briefcase, like it's the *fucking* Holy Grail. What you ought to be doing is thinking about your health. You think those mothers, you think they're going to leave you alone, they get their briefcase, you'll start sending each other Christmas cards? Come *on*, Russ, get real!"

How could I argue, when I'd come to the very same conclusion myself? I sat up, thought about a drink, and decided not to start.

"Okay. I think you're right," I said.

"I know I am, Russ."

"And I appreciate, I appreciate your thoughts."

"All right."

"I just thought, you know, if I gave the thing *back*—"

"Russell."

"What?"

"You think you could maybe stop talking, and come ever here and get in bed?"

Beat, one, *two* . . . "Over there."

"Uh-huh."

"You mean me come over there."

"Right over here."

"Yeah, I could do that."

"I thought you maybe could."

Our first and only carnal encounter had barely deserved an "R." This time we plunged wholeheartedly into unrated realms of sweet corruption, back-seat romance and flat-out debauchery and bliss. I saw at once this was a Sherry I scarcely knew, and

perhaps because of that, an aspect of Russell Murray appeared
that had not shown itself for some time. The moment Sherry
held up her arms and let me strip her from the T-shirt she liked
to wear to bed, I stripped away something in myself, the doubts
and misgivings I'd collected from a dozen stale affairs since
Jane and I had burned each other out. With her eyes, with the
lazy set of her mouth, Sherry sent me a silent message that
swept old hurts aside, and let me know this would not be a
repeat of some dreary episode I'd seen before.

A man gains a rare and special sense of wonder when a
woman lets him know, with a smile, with a certain knowing
look, that she is giving herself to him as a gift, that she wants
him to discover every secret of herself. It was clear from the
start that this was not the pale obligatory grope we'd had before.
It was shameless behavior, laughter and mutual assault. It was
passion and horseplay and unabashed delight.

Effort and intent are the ruin of desire. In all the really special
games in bed, everyone recalls the good plays, and no one
remembers the score. Need and want are worlds apart, and yet
the same.

In the morning, after breakfast, we headed south for Texas,
passing towns like Noble and Paoli and Wynnewood and Joy.
Sherry called out names from the map, places off the road we
wouldn't see. Dibble, Civit, Katie and Hennepin. And, just
west of Nebo and Baum, Gene Autry, a town that nearly tempted
us to detour and see if it was there.

And, past the Red River, Muenster and Era and Sunset to
our right: "Russ, last night. That was awful fine."

"I'm inclined to go along with that," I said.

"I feel we made some inroads into prurience and sin."

"Prurience is good," I said. "I kind of like lust and base
desire."

"Lewd and salacious is good enough for me."

We ran through the list, making some effort, it seems, to

deny by definition what we'd had. Still, when we were done, Sherry looked somewhere else and reached out and squeezed my hand, and I squeezed back. Nothing more was said. But we'd told each other that we knew what had happened was more than a romp and a laugh, that it was something more than that.

After our less than sober encounter in Chicago, we had gotten up and gone about our business, pretending that nothing had occurred. The reason, I suppose, is that nothing really had. Now we avoided the issue because something fine had taken place, and neither of us cared to handle that.

Early in the afternoon, we reached the Dallas–Fort Worth Regional Airport, and I found my way through the convoluted roadways to the terminal for American, where I left Sherry Lou and went in with my locker key. There was, to my relief, a locker with a number that matched. I felt a moment of elation, a flurry of anticipation in my stomach, and I believed, for the first time since all this had begun, that there *was* a way out of this mess, that I might get on with my life. And then I opened up the locker and found a rare autographed edition of *Moby Dick,* a sales slip from a Dallas store that deals in rare books, and an empty bottle of Scotch.

All the way from Chicago for this, plus a lesson brought home that it's not the best practice to buy rare books when you're drunk. The son of a bitch who'd signed this lovely volume had misspelled the author's name.

Chapter 22

When I got back to the car, Sherry took one look at me and scooted into the driver's seat. She knew what had happened, but I told her anyway.

"It's all over," I said, "that's it. I don't have anywhere else to look. I can't go on like this, I'm going to turn myself in."

"Shut up," Sherry said, "you sound like bad TV."

"I mean it. That's what I'm going to do."

"No you're not."

"You got a better idea?"

"Get yourself one of those beers."

"Those beers are all hot."

"Then *drink* the fucker hot, okay? And don't talk while I'm driving. I can't drive right and talk too."

I opened up a beer. The foam came out in slow motion and dribbled down the side of the can, too weary to make a show. The sink's clogged up you brush your teeth, the foam looked kind of like that. I put the beer down and lit a smoke. Sherry turned out of the airport onto 183 going east. The road was lined with franchise burger huts, shopping centers and used car lots. A few minutes later we passed Texas Stadium, where the Cowboys yearn for better days.

"It looks like you're going to Dallas," I said. "I'd like to know why we're going there, there's nothing there I much want to see."

"Where did you stay when you were here?" Sherry asked. "You remember that or not?"

"Of course I know where, I ought to know where I stayed. I stayed at the Fairmont, okay?"

"So maybe you left the briefcase there."

"I didn't leave it there. I took it to the airport, Sherry Lou, I know that."

"You had that *Moby Dick,* is what you had," Sherry said. "That and a snootful of booze. Besides, we got to have some-place to stay, and I am flat not sleeping at any more roadside dumps. Those wrappers they put on the toilet, that won't protect you from a thing. I feel like I might've got a rash."

There wasn't any briefcase at the hotel's lost and found, but Sherry liked the Fairmont fine. It has a lobby the size of Central Park, carpets and lots of glitz, and the rates are sky-high. The guy at the desk pretended not to see Sherry's backpack and collection of paper sacks. She was cute and she had a gold card, and the rich can wear anything they like.

The bellboy took us to a suite with a parlor, a small refrigerator, and two big color TVs. Sherry looked around, pointed to the bathroom, and told me to soak for a while. Then she plopped cross-legged on the bed and started ordering shit on the phone.

I could hear her from the tub. She acted like a woman's been stranded in the Congo somewhere, they picked her up and let her out in front of Saks. As near as I could tell, she called everyone in town whose name ended in "store."

I fell asleep in the tub, and woke when Sherry came in. She left a steak sandwich and a Scotch with ice and soda on the floor, leaned in and kissed me on the cheek.

"I'm going out," she said. "I'll be back."

"You're going out where?"

"Just out," she said. "Don't let anything vital shrivel up."

The first Scotch lifted me out of the cellar of depression. The second brought me up to ground level and I started on a third. The steak sandwich tasted great. I walked around naked for a while, then dried myself off. While I'd dozed in the tub, the room-service elves had stocked the bar. All the best brands, plus Norwegian smoked salmon, thin English wafers and Brie de Meaux cheese. Champagne and beer in the fridge. The champagne was Bollinger. The beer was Dortmunder Kronen, and that marvelous Czech treasure, Pilsner Urquell. The rich don't care for domestic beer and nuts.

My clothes looked awful, so I pulled back the covers and got into bed. Sherry had left half a sandwich on the table and I finished off that, leaned back and enjoyed my drink. She had clearly outdone herself stocking the bar. I had a choice of two single-malt Scotches, Glenmorangie or Laphroaig. I felt like a kid on Christmas morning. Which do you play with first, the Daisy air rifle or the swell electric train? I tried the Glenmorangie twice, then switched to the smoky Laphroaig. No soda or ice.

Then I picked up the phone and called Jane. The Scotch had given me courage and purity of heart, in lieu of common sense.

"Jane Kowalski," she said, and I could hear the sounds of business and enterprise.

"Don't say my name," I told her. "They probably got your phone bugged."

"Oh Christ, the mad bomber!" Jane's voice exploded into the phone. "Where the *hell* are you, Russ?"

"Now see, I said don't say my name, you went ahead and did my name."

"The phone's not bugged. We're heavy into freedom of the

press, and we won't put up with that. So where are you? I don't believe you said.''

"I'm in Dallas. And don't do that mad-bomber stuff. That's not real amusing to me.''

"In Dallas.''

"I'm in a hotel. I thought maybe the you-know-what was in a locker at the airport but it's not.''

"Uh-huh. And how'd you get to Dallas? I'd kind of like to hear about that.''

"Oh sure, I figured you'd bring that up. I'm up to my ass in trouble, you're worried about a car.''

"You stole my friend's car. I give you a place to stay, you steal the guy's car, you drink everything except his after-shave, I don't know how you missed that. I know I'm being unreasonable, Russ, that's just the way I am.''

"I'm taking good care of that car," I said, "the car's fine.''

"Christ, Russell. Nothing has anything to do with you is fine, you know that?'' Jane took a deep breath. "You get a chance on your cross-country trip, pick up a copy of today's *Trib.* They've got you flat for this one, friend. Felicia Palmer recorded all her phone calls. I got a peek at the transcript, it's all there on the tape. You were going to meet her at three, she's dead at three ten. That doesn't look real good on your résumé.''

I felt the good Scotch rise up in my throat. I wanted to tell her it was her idea I get in touch with Felicia, but I didn't see how that would help.

"There's more," Jane said, "but none of it makes a lot of sense. A guy, some low-life worked for the Cannatellas, they found the guy dead. They didn't pin this one on you, and I don't know what it's all about, but it might have something to do with this briefcase mess. Also, I dug up some stuff about Felicia Palmer's family. At one time, her uncle Frank was close to Charlie "Pig" Galiano, who is now head of one of the New York families. Cannatella and Galiano had their fingers in the porno, prostitution and extortion rackets. Joseph Cannatella, Felicia's father and Frank's brother, was tied in with all this, and he and Frank were close. At least they were until a guy named Jimmy Riso, who was Joseph's driver and bodyguard, got killed in a shoot-out about 1971. Something happened, I don't know what. But Riso's death had something to do with it. Joseph and Frank had a big falling out, and Joseph got out of the business. He and his brother never spoke to each other after that. Joseph died of natural causes in 1982. Right after that, Felicia married Tony Palmer, the former Antonio DePalma, and the two moved to Chicago. Evidently, whatever bad blood was between Frank and Joseph didn't rub off on Felicia. She and her uncle were fairly close."

The phone cord was long enough to let me fix a drink. I poured half a glass of the Laphroaig.

"That's great stuff," I said, "I'm really into the personal life of hoods. Boy, I'm glad I called. I hadn't called, I wouldn't know any of this."

"All right, Russell."

"No, I mean, what is this shit? What's it got to do with me?"

"Do I know? How do I know?" Jane's voice reached a slightly higher pitch. It told me she had just passed the irritated zone into really pissed off.

"Maybe it's got nothing to do with you, okay? I don't know, I've got no idea. Except a cop on the Organized Crime Task Force, a guy who craves my lovely parts, he's telling me, he's saying there's a couple of heavy hitters in Chicago—from guess where? From the Galiano Family in New York, we were recently speaking about."

"Yeah, so?"

"So fucking wake up, Russell. They've got no business *being* here unless there's some kind of problem between Chicago and New York. Maybe this briefcase is the problem, maybe it's not, I don't know. It's just peculiar, you know, these guys showing up now, right in time for the Russell Murray Shoot-out Show."

"Don't keep saying that. I don't want you saying that."

''Okay, I won't. So what now?''

''What do you mean, what now?''

''Like what's your next cool move? You and the floozy, you going to settle down there and raise little Murrays? You got the china picked out?''

''That is real tacky, Jane. You don't even know Sherry Lou. She's a very nice person.''

''I know floozy when I see it,'' Jane said. ''This is a floozy, Russ.''

''Well, that's it, that's it right there. Now you're impinging on my personal private life.''

''Shit, Russ.'' Jane made an annoying sound in her throat. ''You haven't *got* a personal life. You got floozies and tarts. That's a hormone attack, that's not a life. And I wouldn't use *impinge,* I'd maybe use something else.''

''You'd do what?''

''See, impinge is a thrust or a hit. It means you strike at or collide. 'Encroach' is the second definition. When you can, you want to go with the first. You mean encroach, then say it. Say, 'Jane, you are encroaching on my—' ''

''Listen,'' I said, ''I don't need some *journalism* person tells me how to use a word.''

''Good-bye, Russ.''

''I'm not finished with you.''

''Want to bet?''

Jane hung up. I got some smoked salmon and cheese. I didn't see how Sherry could eat those crackers, they don't have any taste at all.

That floozy stuff, I should've figured that. You're with someone, you're together then you're not, whoever you go with next you found her selling on the street. You're so desperate, you're picking up girls on the street. When Marian and I broke up and I started going out again, someone'd say, 'What's Russ up to, you know?' And Marian would say, she'd say, Russ has got a whore. Russ is going out with some whore. Doesn't matter who it is, it's a whore. Mother Theresa comes to town, Marian tells everyone Russ is going out with some slut in a robe. Gracie and Karen, they saw 'em together in a bar. You're going out with whores, the guy *they*'re seeing after you, he isn't some jerk from the office or the guy who parks her car, he's Paul Newman's brother, he's maybe ambassador to France. You sink to the bottom they go right to the top. I don't know why it works that way, but it does.

Oprah Winfrey had a bunch of people on who had a deathly fear of sheep and I watched some of that. I slept for a while; someone starts banging on the door, it's a guy bringing boxes for Sherry Lou. The boxes have names from big stores. In half an hour four guys come by, and now there's boxes piled up, they fill a corner of the room.

It was clear Sherry Lou was doing Dallas in style, and I wondered what all this stuff was for. Your average felons on the run, you don't see 'em dressing real smart. Of course most of them aren't Sherry Lou, who thinks hiding out means pulling down the shades at Palm Springs. Still, I couldn't knock my own good fortune and Sherry's good taste. If you've got to be on the lam, running with a K-Mart shopper's not near as much fun as a girl who calls Tiffany's "the Tiff."

Sherry showed up about six. Her eyes were bright as Krugerrands; she was flushed with the joy of spending, still on a Gucci high. She looked simply great in a well-cut green suede suit that hugged the Sherry curves just right. There were shoes and bag to match, and someone had done her hair. It looked wild and electric, the color of strawberry jam. No floozy here, I thought, as she came into my arms and offered up a lazy, clearly suggestive kiss. Her lipstick had a peppery taste, and I could tell she'd stopped for nips now and then to sustain her shopping spree.

"Oh Lord, I had fun," Sherry said, kicking off her shoes

and fluffing up her hair. She walked to the bar and mixed a drink, licked her lips and looked at me.

"You have a nice day? I see you made it out of the tub."

"I got a keen insight into daytime TV. You got no idea how many folks are scared of sheep. You walk up and say 'Wool!' there's people go into screaming fits." I didn't mention my call to Jane. There was no use bringing up that. "Boy, you sure got a lot of stuff. You must've bought out the stores."

"I made a real good start," Sherry said. She sipped her drink and nodded at the boxes that filled one corner of the room. " 'Course it isn't all for me, for heaven's sake. Some of that's for you."

"You got stuff for me?"

Sherry grinned "Of course I did, silly. I'm not going to be a fashion statement by myself. We're not shooting *Lady and the Tramp.*"

Sherry padded to the corner and began lugging boxes to the bed. "These are yours," she said, "near as I can tell. You find some high-heel pumps, I figure those belong to me . . ."

Sherry looked up, and saw I was standing there watching, halfway across the room. "Russ, you going to open this stuff or not? I'm likely to get my feelings hurt."

"It's like my fifth birthday," I said. "I was too shook up to start. I think I peed on the floor."

"Well try and hold it back. I'm not up to that."

I went through the boxes and spread out my goodies on the bed. There were shirts in pale Egyptian cotton, two lightweight Oxxford suits, one tan and one white. Half a dozen Armani ties, three pairs of Italian Artioli shoes, so pliable and soft, I figured they were made out of unborn Popes. Assorted socks and underwear, and a natty new belt. Sherry had picked out my lumberman's outfit in Wisconsin, and I was sure all the sizes were right.

"Sherry," I told her, "these are the best-looking duds I ever had. And—listen, I'm not complaining, you understand, everything is real great, but this is all summer wear, looks to me, and it's getting October outside.''

"Well, sure, it is *here*,'' Sherry said, "but here isn't where we're going to be.''

"It's not? Then where do you—'' I turned just then, looked up from the bed, and faced Sherry Lou. I felt a little lurch inside, a quickening of the heart. She had slipped out of her brand-new jacket and hung it on a chair, and let her skirt fall down to the floor. She was standing by the window in the afternoon sun in her pale green panties and a frilly green bra.

"I ought to tell you,'' I said, "I got this thing about lace. I kind of lose control of myself. My, you surely do look fine. I bet that outfit's imported from Paris, France. Those folks have got a way with underthings . . .''

"Just hush,'' Sherry grinned. "Jesus, Russ, you look like a kid at his first peep show. And no, I didn't buy a lot of winter wear 'cause you're going to the tropics and I don't see you'll need a fur coat.''

"Which tropics is that?'' I said, then I recalled our conversation the night before. "Brazil, you still thinking about Brazil? If you are, I have to tell you I don't have a passport, and I doubt they'll want to give me one now.''

"We're not going to Brazil,'' Sherry said. She walked to the bed, pawed through her purse and pulled an envelope out. "Where we're going's St. Thomas, and that belongs to us. It's like the U.S.A., you don't need a passport, you just go.''

Sherry came to me and held up the tickets with a sly little crinkle in her eyes. "We've had about enough of this fugitive shit, don't you think? I figure it's time for some fun.''

I looked at the tickets, and saw we were flying out at noon the next day. I also saw our names.

"Edgar and Eileen Poe. Hey, that's got a certain ring.''

"I thought you'd like that, seeing as how you've got this literary bent.'' Sherry's grin faded, and she gave me her very best deep and thoughtful look. "Russell, I went ahead and did it 'cause I didn't want to argue with you. You've got a real stubborn streak and you tend to get perverse if anyone has an idea you didn't think about yourself. You can't say it's not the right thing to do because it is. You keep pokin' around in this mess, you're going to get us both shot. That's what's going to happen, and I won't put up with that.''

"You're doing a lot of nice things for me," I said. "You have to know I appreciate that."

"Shoot. It's for me too, you know. I'm dead in a ditch somewhere, I won't be buying three-hundred-dollar shoes."

Sherry paused, looked somewhere south of Dallas, then turned back to me. "Russ, I am not saying going away will solve this thing. I don't know, I don't know you're ever going to do that. But we can buy a little time. I know how to do that, I've been at it all my life."

"I sure do admire that bra," I said. "There's not much to it, as far as I can see."

Sherry bit her lip. "I don't think you're listening to me."

"I'm listening. But I'm kind of looking too."

"I see that you are. It's Italian, by the way, it's not French. The Italians got real dirty minds when it comes to doing bras."

"I like those Italians a lot."

I slipped my arms around her waist, and slid my hands up to the small of her back. Sherry stepped in closer and laid her hands on my shoulders.

"This bra you got," I said, "is it one of those that opens in the front?"

"You think it is or not?"

"I'd guess it is."

"There might . . . there might be a way to find out . . ."

I brought my hands around and worked the little catch. Sherry looked right at me, a touch of awe and wonder in her eyes, a green glint of mischief that told me she had thought about this and worked it out, played out the fantasy in her head and was waiting in sly anticipation to see it come about.

When I flipped the catch she sighed and closed her eyes, her lips loose and open, a small vein pulsing in her neck. I cupped both her breasts in my hands and she let her weight sag in against me and I picked her up and carried her to the bed, reached down and swept tropic wear aside, and gently laid her down. I peeled off my sheepherder pants, and she grinned and opened her arms to take me in. Her hair brushed my cheek as I kissed her, and she made a little noise in her throat. I lifted up slightly as she brought her hands down along my back and hooked her fingers in her panties, squirming a little and breathing on my neck. And this is the moment when the sound broke into our pleasant interlude, a sound like someone had tossed a grand piano through the wall. I knew at once what it was because I'd heard the sound before. It happened in another hotel room and in another town, but it was still the same splinter of wood and shriek of metal as the door came off one hinge and swung crazily into the room, the awful sound I'd hoped to God I'd never hear again . . .

Chapter 23

You don't know what you're going to do, something traumatic intrudes upon your life. There's no time to reason, so instinct takes command. The Murray primal self leaped off Sherry Lou, picked up the phone and threw it at the gorilla advancing on our bed. A nice defiant gesture, but not a lot of help. Phones are attached to the wall. It missed Irv Wacker by a good three feet. Wacker laughed, picked me up and tossed me on the floor.

I hit hard and slid against the wall. Sherry Lou was screaming, backed against the head of the bed, clutching a sheet up to her neck. A scarecrow in a black silk suit grabbed the sheet and jerked it free, clutched a handful of Sherry's hair, and slapped her once across the mouth. Sherry cried out, and the scarecrow hit her again.

I came to my knees and shook my head. I said something mean like, "Leave her the hell alone, you bastard," and started for the bed. Wacker stepped into my path, slammed a hand against my chest and sent me sprawling to the floor once again. Nice going, Russ. Naked Man Attacks Wall Safe and Lives.

"Cut the shit," said the scarecrow, "get him up and fix the fucking door."

Wacker grabbed me under the arms, lifted me up like a puppy and dumped me in a chair. Then he straightened out the door and set it back where it belonged. It seemed like an odd thing to do. The door's hanging on a hinge, splinters everywhere, just set it back in place. No one'll notice a thing. I wondered where everybody was. Any other time, a flock of Shriners and half a dozen maids would be running through the hall.

Irv Wacker started toward me. Behind him, Sherry inched off the bed, holding a pillow to her breasts.

"You," said the scarecrow, "where you think you're going?"

"I'm getting *dressed*," Sherry said. "That all right with you?"

"Forget the clothes," he said, "you look fine, you look fine to me."

"Well, I am not going to run around naked," Sherry said. "I don't know who you think you are, but I'm not puttin' on a peep show."

"Sit," said the scarecrow. "You don't want to sit, Irv'll help you sit."

Sherry glared and thrust out her chin, but she sat. She held the pillow close, and I could see she was trying not to cry. The guy's hand had left an angry red welt on her cheek.

The scarecrow found a chair, straddled it backward and folded his arms across the top. Wacker stood behind me, just out of sight. I knew who the scarecrow was, even without the silly hat. The skeletal frame and the rings around his eyes said Ritchie "Bones" Pinelli, Cannatella's number-one hood. I had seen him at a distance in Chicago, and he didn't look better up close. His face was belly-white, skin stretched tight across bone. His eyes never blinked, and his mouth scarcely moved when he talked. It was creepy as hell to hear him talk. He spoke in a dreary monotone, each word the same as the last. Pinelli made a corpse seem cheery and full of life.

He sat there and looked at me and didn't say a thing. He

did this for two or three minutes, and I wondered if his eyes had any lids. This silent shit was supposed to shake me up and it did. I sat there with everything exposed, and all I could think about was what they'd done to Tony, and when they'd do the same thing to me. Pinelli had to know this was going through my head.

"You," he said finally, "you're Murray. What you are, you're a pain in the ass."

"People have told me this before," I said. "I'm trying real hard to quit."

"You got an item, this item don't belong to you. What you want to do, Murray, is tell me where it is."

"See, that's the thing," I said, "I don't *know* where it is. I wish I did. If I did, then I'd—*Jesus!*"

Wacker's fist came down on top of my head. The blow drove my skull down into my collarbone, sending spasms of sharp electric pain along my spine. I heard myself scream somewhere, and Wacker's hand went tight across my mouth. My ears rang and strobe lights flashed before my eyes. The pain didn't stop. It got better but it wouldn't go away. When I could see straight again, I glanced at Sherry Lou. Her eyes were wide with fright, and both hands were pressed against her mouth.

Pinelli's expression never changed. He wasn't interested at all. Nothing happened in the world that had a thing to do with him.

"See, here's the thing," Pinelli said. "What you got to understand, where we're going with this, like Irv does that maybe a couple more times, it don't hurt anymore, you understand? Something kinda snaps in your neck, you're in a fucking wheelchair, someone's serving lunch in a tube. You're thinking maybe T-bone steak, you got stuff comin' out of a tube. You're thinking maybe hey, I want to jump this pretty lady, like you were doing when we come busting in. You can't move nothing, so you can't do that. What you got, you got time for a lot of TV. You want to be a pain in the ass, you got lunch in a tube, you got a lot of TV."

I took a deep breath. "I want to say something, all right? I talk, it's okay I do that?"

"You got something I want to hear it's okay."

"I tell you something, it's something you need to know, it's an answer but it's not—I'm not *saying* it's not, it's a part of an answer, is what it is. I say something like that, then what? He hits me again or what?"

The white disappeared from Pinelli's eyes. "What you're doing, I seen guys do this before. You want to talk, you don't want to get hit. You figure you say something wrong you get hit, you don't want to do that. So you try and think of everything I might want to hear, even if it's not."

"That's not exactly—"

"Yeah, it is. You don't want to jerk me off, Murray. You don't want to be a pain in the ass."

"What I want to do," I said, "I want to talk about the key."

Pinelli hesitated. "You want to talk about a key."

"Look, I had this key. I went to O'Hare and I tried to find a locker, they didn't have a locker that fit. I went to a bar I used to go, it's not there. I think, okay, the briefcase is at DFW Airport, the key fits there. It does, but there's nothing in the locker but a book. I can show you the book. So I come here next. I think I maybe left it here. That's three, no, that's four—that's four places I looked. If I knew where the briefcase was, would I look? I knew where it was, why would I want to do that? You think I'd lie about this, what's the point? You think I want to get hit? I don't want to get hit."

Wacker hit me again. He was real good at this, and he found the same spot he'd hit before. I tried to yell but the sound got stuck in my throat. I knew I was sliding down the cushion of the chair and I sent out messages to stop. Everthing numb, and no one was answering the phone. I collapsed in a heap on the floor. Wacker came around and picked me up.

"Jesus, Murray you're a dope, you know that?" Pinelli shook his head. "A guy sits there, he's getting his brains scrambled up, he's telling me he don't know a thing. He's sittin' there, his pecker's hanging out, he says he don't know a thing. I'm thinking, Ritch, this guy *likes* it in the head, you maybe ought to try somethin' else.''

''You son of a bitch,'' Sherry screamed, ''he's telling you the truth. He doesn't *know* where the briefcase is!''

Pinelli turned to Sherry, moving his head real slow, two inches to the right, like a snake that's heard something and figures it's a mouse, maybe it's a mouse, he ought to look.

''And you ain't no rocket scientist either, lady, you know that?'' Pinelli nearly moved a muscle in his face. ''You're on the run, you do what? You're leaving your autograph every twenty miles. You're buying booze and gas, you're shackin' up in motels. Everyone's climbing up your ass, and you're drawing 'em a map.''

Sherry blinked in surprise and then laughed. ''Now that is a lie and you know it,'' she said. ''In the first place, credit cards are a private and sacred trust. There isn't anyone allowed to do that.''

''Yeah, right,'' said Pinelli.

''In the *second* place—''

''Sherry,'' I said, ''shut up.''

Pinelli looked at Sherry, then at me, and back to Sherry again.

''The lady wants to talk? Okay, so let her talk. Irv, get the lady a chair. Me and the lady are going to talk.''

''Now listen—'' I began.

Wacker was setting a chair next to mine. He stopped and gave me a look, and started for Sherry Lou.

Sherry looked terrified. ''Don't you come *near* me, you fucking ape.'' She backed off and clutched her pillow tight. ''You lay a hand on me, I'll—I'll sue you for every cent you got!''

Wacker grabbed the pillow and tossed it aside. Sherry flailed out with her fists, cursing at Wacker and kicking at his legs. Wacker caught both her wrists in one hand, lifted her off the edge of the bed, and dropped her in the chair.

"You want to talk," Pinelli said, "let's talk."

"I don't *know* where your briefcase is," Sherry said.

"That's it?"

"He doesn't either."

"This is some kinda talk. I'm not hearing anything I want to hear. What I'm doing, I'm gettin' jerked around."

Pinelli looked at Wacker. "The lady don't want to talk to me. Maybe, what? Maybe I got bad breath. So maybe she'd like to talk to you." He looked at Sherry Lou. "That okay with you? You and Irv talk. This is fine, I don't take no offense."

Sherry drew in a breath. All the color drained from her face.

"Don't do this," I said, "she doesn't know anything. She doesn't know a thing."

Pinelli didn't answer. Sherry's bottle of vodka was sitting on a table by his chair. He reached out and took a slug and set it on the floor. I looked at Sherry Lou. All her famous bravado had disappeared. I could see it in her face. All the fight went out of her at once. She huddled in the chair, crossed her arms and brought her knees up high, covering as much as she could. She looked like a small, frightened little girl about twelve, and I knew this whole business was for me, that Pinelli had found a better answer than hitting me on the head, and he wanted me to know what he could do.

"You do this to her," I said, "it won't do you any good. It's not going to tell you where the briefcase is and you know it."

Pinelli looked at me with no expression at all. I was there, but I might as well have been a table or a lamp. He didn't have to talk to Wacker, or tell him what to do. Wacker knew. He always knew what to do. Who to rough up and how much, what kind of doughnuts to get, and who used sugar and cream.

I looked at Sherry Lou again. Her face was tucked into her shoulder, hidden behind a strand of red hair. When Wacker leaned down and picked her up she didn't fight. She flinched at his touch and made a tiny little sound and tried to curl up in a ball. I knew she was thinking if she made herself small enough she might disappear and the man would go away.

Wacker dumped her on the bed and I could see a glint of light in his black bullet eyes, a little smile at the corner of his mouth. He did what he was told all the time and didn't mind. But this was something special, a job he could enjoy. A guy mean and ugly as a bear doesn't meet a lot of girls like Sherry Lou. He drinks a six-pack and sees a girl on TV, he maybe gets a quickie on the street. Now he had a chance for dark romance and he was happy as a clam.

Wacker watched her for a minute, taking in the sights. Then he reached down and hooked his big fingers in her panties and jerked them past her hips. Sherry whimpered, and made a feeble effort to crawl across the bed. Wacker laughed and slapped her hard across her face. Sherry cried out and Wacker hit her once again.

I gripped the edge of my chair. I was scared out of my wits, and the fear fought with anger, helplessness and shame. Wacker would break my neck if I tried to interfere, but I had to do something, I couldn't just sit there and watch. I couldn't let him rape Sherry while I sat buck naked in my chair.

"Go ahead, try it, it's okay you want to try," Pinelli said, "you figure that's what you gotta do."

"For Christ's sake, call him off," I said, the words catching in my throat. "I don't have your fucking briefcase. You think I'd let him do that, I know where it is? *Damn it, call him off!*"

"Maybe something, maybe something'll come to you," he said. "Sometimes, a guy remembers somethin' he thinks he forgot. Something happens, a guy thinks, hey, I better remember that."

"I don't *know* anything!"

Pinelli didn't say a thing. He didn't look at the bed. There was nothing on the bed he cared to see. I made myself look. Wacker had Sherry Lou pinned to the bed like a bug, holding her there with a hand the size of a ham. Her panties were caught around her knees. She kicked out at Wacker but Wacker didn't care. He grinned and loosed the buckle at his waist. His pants fell down to his ankles, revealing the biggest rear end I'd ever seen outside a zoo. Sherry couldn't see him but she knew what he was doing. She thrashed around and screamed and Wacker slapped her on the butt. Sherry gasped and went limp.

Pinelli reached down to get the bottle and I knew I had to try and do it now. I couldn't take Wacker, but I could go for this skinny little bastard and try and get his gun. He had to have a gun somewhere, and if I could get my hands on that—

Pinelli saw me coming. The son of a bitch was quick. His hand snaked under his coat and the gun I was looking for pointed at my head.

I knew he was going to do it. I could read it in his eyes. His eyes said fuck the briefcase, I'd rather put a hole in Murray's head. His finger tightened on the trigger and I crouched there naked on the floor maybe eighteen inches from changing my life-style for good. I heard the sound then and Pinelli heard it too, as the door burst open, swaying on its single loose hinge. Pinelli's eyes shifted quickly to his right. He pushed himself away from the chair and the gun moved in a blur. I grabbed the neck of the bottle, brought it back past my shoulder, and broke it on the side of his head. Pinelli groaned once and went down. The old lady in the pillbox hat came through the door, glanced at Pinelli, and aimed her long pistol at Wacker across the room. The pistol went *phttt!* and a bullet struck Wacker in the ass.

Wacker howled, leaped straight up, and tripped on his pants. He hit the floor like a rhino with a slug between its eyes. The old lady looked at Sherry, then at me, and shook her head in disgust.

"Goddammit, get some clothes on," she said. "You ought to be ashamed of yourselves!"

Chapter 24

I stumbled over Pinelli and took Sherry Lou in my arms. She buried her head in my shoulder and hot tears scalded my chest.

"It's all over," I said, "you're all right, Sherry Lou."

"Oh, Russ, oh, shit." She dug her nails in my arms. "Shit-shit-*shit!*"

"Nobody's going to hurt you now, you're just fine, you're all—"

"Will you stop *saying* that?" The tears stopped. She pulled away from me and glared. "I am *not* all right, you son of a bitch. I've been nearly violated by a giant. I have never been so fucking scared in my life and I am *not* all right!"

"It's okay to get mad. Mad's good."

"Just shut up, Russ. Don't you talk to me, don't you say a thing."

Sherry jerked up her panties, grabbed an armful of clothes, stomped into the bathroom and slammed the door. I heard the lock snap shut. I found a pair of pants beneath a chair, and stepped past the bed to look at Wacker on the floor. He was moaning and rolling about, trying to find his ass with both hands. Pinelli was still out cold. The old lady was sprawled in an easy chair. One hand gripped the pistol in her lap, the other covered her eyes.

"Ma'am," I said, "I don't know who you are, but I'm grateful for your help. That goes for the last time too. Say, was that an Uzi or a Sten? I'm not into automatic weapons, but it looked like an Uzi to me."

"Young man, are you decent?" she said.

"Am I what?"

"You tell me when you got everything covered up. I don't want to see your parts."

"I'm sorry about that. I got my pants on now. We weren't expecting anyone."

The old lady looked at me and blinked. "You wallow 'round in sin all the time, you got to take the devil's due."

"Yes, ma'am."

"I could use a cold drink. Jack Daniels if you got some. Straight up."

"I can handle that."

I found the right bottle and poured half a glass and dropped in a couple of cubes. Then I poured a stiff one for myself. I took the drink to her, watching out for broken glass. The top half of the bottle I'd used on Pinelli was intact. The rest of it was shattered in a thousand sharp pieces on the floor.

She downed her drink like a pro, and handed me the glass.

"Can I fill that up?" I said.

"Don't mind if you do. I don't drink for pleasure, so don't go thinking on that. I got a real bad hip."

"Yes, ma'am," I said, and padded back to the bar. When I returned, she was pawing through an oversized purse. She dumped stuff in her lap, muttered to herself, then handed me some needle-nose pliers and a big coil of wire.

"You want to bind those fellas good and tight," she said, "hands and feet both. Don't go leavin' any slack. That's picture-hanging wire, is what it is. You can get it at the hardware store.

Your ordinary rope's going to give, they don't make it right aymore. I wouldn't use it on a bet.''

I looked at Irv Wacker. ''You think he's bleeding bad or what?''

''Shoot, with a little ol' twenty-two slug in his rear?'' The old lady made a face. ''It wasn't even hollow-point. You don't know much about guns, I'll say that. Didn't your daddy ever take you out to hunt?''

''He mostly liked to fish.''

''Fishing bores me to death. I'd rather sit on a tack.''

''Yes, ma'am.''

I tied Pinelli first. He had a bump the size of a Ping-Pong ball but there wasn't a lot of blood. His eyes fluttered open as I finished. He looked at me but didn't say a thing.

Wacker didn't want to hold still. The old lady told him she'd shoot him again if he didn't, and he quieted down a lot after that. She was right about the wound. There was a tiny purple hole and some blood. Apparently, she'd shot a few guys in the ass before. A butt that size could absorb a lot of lead.

Wacker howled when I pulled up his pants, and I told him Tony Palmer probably had hurt more than that. He tried to spit in my face and I twisted the wire around his arms extra tight. The old lady sat and watched. Now and then she offered household hints. I learned about blood circulation, and how long it took for gangrene to set in.

From the floor, I could see her black hose rolled up around her knees. She had skinny little legs and fat feet. The feet were stuffed into blue Nikes with the toes cut out on either side. The skinny legs didn't go with the body on top. From the knees on up, she looked like a walrus in a flower-print dress. She had a Mary Worth face; putty cheeks and thick wire glasses, and three or four chins. Her gray hair was gathered in a bun behind her head. She wore that silly pillbox hat with a feather on the top.

New opportunities are opening up for women everywhere. The gender gap is closing fast. I had never given a great deal

of thought to hit ladies—or maybe they prefer hit person, I
didn't ask. But why not? A woman can pull a trigger as easily
as a man. I thought about the women I had known. Several
seemed to fit the bill. Maid Marian came to mind at once. She
didn't like guns, but I've seen that woman chase a mouse
around the room with a bat. She does real good with a bat.

Still, when I looked at the lady in the chair, I could picture
her charging through Macy's, shoving other shoppers aside,
but the killer image simply didn't fit. Even when she lectured
me on firearms, and the tensile strength of wire.

Everything was wrong with the image except the eyes. It
took me a while to notice that. I realized then that she and
Pinelli had the same empty eyes. Ball bearings frozen in ice.
The windows were open, but nobody lived there anymore.

I was following instructions, hauling Pinelli and Wacker into
a closet, when Sherry Lou appeared. She was wearing her
orchid T-shirt and purple jeans. She had put on makeup and
combed her hair, but she still looked slightly unhinged, a little
pale around the mouth. When she saw me pulling hoods across
the floor, she stopped and put her hands on her hips, frowned
at me and thrust out her chin in disgust.

"What you go and tie them up for?" she wanted to know.
"Be a lot better if you shot 'em in the head."

"My heavens, child." The old lady shook her head. "Your
folks take you to Sunday school or not?"

"Shit," said Sherry Lou, and stomped across the room to
the bar.

"I don't care for foul talk, young lady."

"I'll fucking drink to that," Sherry said.

She poured herself a Scotch, drank it down fast, and filled
her glass again. I knew she was fairly unraveled. She said she
thought Scotch tasted worse than kerosene.

"So what now?" I said, more or less talking to myself.

"You got two guys in the closet, we can't leave 'em there and we can't call the cops. I don't see this working out."

"We're going to check out, that's what," Sherry said. She gave me a look that said the whole mess was likely my fault. "First place we get's not a dump, I should've known something would screw it up."

"Huh-uh, you don't check out," the old lady broke in. "You go out the back way." She nodded at me. "You go get the car. We meet you out back."

"Oh, great," Sherry moaned, "this'll go on my record for sure. Visa'll have a fit."

"Sherry," I said, "this isn't the time to get upset about stuff like that."

"That's about what I'd expect from you, Russ. You haven't *got* a credit rating, what do you care?"

"Well, if I did, I sure wouldn't worry about it now. And that card of yours is how they tracked us down, by the way. You heard what he said, he said you might as well have drawn a map."

Sherry gave me a nasty laugh. "I didn't see you turning down any meals on that card. I sure didn't see that."

"Shut up, both of you." The old lady glared at Sherry, then at me. She squeezed herself out of the chair, an act that took a great deal of skill, much like getting a potato out of an olive jar. "And you get on a shirt, young man. I don't care to see your chest. I don't suppose you've got a tie. You don't look like a man knows how to dress."

"That's the fucking truth," Sherry said.

"And *you* can watch that tongue of yours, girl." The old lady wagged a finger at Sherry Lou. "Lay off the booze and get packed."

"Don't you tell me what to do," Sherry said. "I don't even know who you are. I'd like to see some ID."

"Sherry," I said, "she doesn't need an ID, she's got a gun."

"That's nice, Russ. Take sides."

"I am not taking sides."

"Well, I guess I know taking sides when I see it."

"I guess you think you do. I guess that's what you think, that doesn't mean it's true."

Sherry ignored me and poured another drink. One of our guests, Wacker or Pinelli, began kicking the closet door. I started rooting around for shoes, and a shirt right for getaway wear. The old lady opened the closet door, said something I couldn't hear, and the pair shut up at once. I didn't want to think about the closet. It was where Sherry Lou and I would very likely be at the moment, if the old lady hadn't shown up. A sobering thought, so to speak.

I felt a little sorry for Pinelli. It couldn't be pleasant, crammed in there with Irv Wacker. Okay, so I lied. I didn't feel sorry for Pinelli. What I did was pray Irv Wacker had a chronic case of gas. I prayed they'd be in there together for a week.

It took three trips to carry all of Sherry's shit down the elevator and out the back. She wouldn't leave anything behind. No one seemed to notice that we didn't check out. The Fairmont was hosting a convention of science-fiction fans, so abnormal behavior was the order of the day.

I brought around the car and loaded up and moved out, following the old lady's directions. She sat in the back, Sherry and I in the front. We quickly left the downtown area behind and headed up the Dallas North Tollway, a trip that cost Sherry fifty cents. A light rain began to fall, and halos circled the tollway's peach-colored lights. I asked where we were going, and our guide said we were driving, we weren't going anywhere at all.

"We've got to talk," she said. "There's stuff I need to know."

"Fine," I said, "like what?"

"Like where you left the briefcase, Murray. I need to know that."

"Lady, we just went through that," I said, "you came in

late. You want to hear it again? I don't *have* the briefcase, I don't know where it is.''

"Wait a minute, Russ," Sherry said. "We don't know who this person is. You don't have to tell her a thing."

"Sherry's got a point there," I said. "I mean, you saved our bacon twice and we appreciate that. But we're kind of in the dark here, you know? We haven't got the briefcase and we don't know where it is. I'm getting tired of telling people that. You *saw* me looking for it at O'Hare. I know you were there. You were outside Tony's office when Pinelli and the Wackers showed up. We were looking for it *then*, okay? What the hell you think we're doing running all across the country, hunting for Easter eggs?''

"Damn right," Sherry said.

The old lady was silent for a while. A sign said our next exit was Lovers Lane. I pictured hundreds of kids from the fifties, smooching in parked Chevrolets.

"Okay," she said finally, "you don't have the briefcase, you don't know where it is. I didn't think you did. So what do you want to know?''

"For starters, I'd like to know who I'm talking to."

"That's none of your business, boy."

"Okay. I can live with that. Where do you fit in with all this? Who are you working for?''

"Next question."

"What's in the briefcase, everyone's so hot to get it back?''

"I don't have any idea."

"You don't?''

"No I don't.''

"Then what do you want it for?''

"The people I work for need it back."

"And who's that?''

"None of your business.''

"Why do I get the idea we're not going anywhere with all this?''

"Because you're asking a bunch of dumb questions, young

man. Stuff that don't mean squat. Shouldn't anything matter to you except finding that thing. Trying to figure how to get it back. You want to turn up there. Get on 635 going west.''

"What for?"

"See, there you go again."

"You don't have to do everything she tells you," Sherry said. "I'd like to stop and eat."

"We'll stop and eat later," I said. "We don't want to stop now."

"Why not?"

"We just don't, Sherry Lou."

"Well, shit."

Sherry slumped down in her seat, folded her arms and stared ahead. She was getting real edgy and her mouth was working funny again. What she needed was a drink. Not later sometime, right now. She didn't care if the chubby old lady in back was in the same line of work as Irv Wacker. That she was talking to us now because her people hadn't told her to shoot Russ Murray and Sherry Lou. Hell, maybe they *had*. Maybe they'd told her to waste us on some lonely road. Sherry didn't think about this but I did.

I turned under 635 and found the ramp heading west. Highway 635 was called LBJ, and it was lined with glass office buildings and glitzy hotels. Everything was brand new. It looked as if someone had gotten tired of Dallas, and started all over north of town.

"Tony Palmer," the old lady said, "he just sent you flying off down here, he didn't say anything else?"

"Like what? He said a lot of things."

"Like who the briefcase was for, anything like that?"

"He said it was a manuscript. That the writer would be at the airport to pick it up. There wasn't any writer, the writer business was just a bunch of crap."

"He didn't mention this Senator Jack Byron, anyone like that?"

"I know who he is. I know he's got some connection with Frank Cannatella, but I didn't hear it from Tony Palmer."

"So who did you hear it from?"

"None of your business."

She didn't like that but she let it pass.

"What did you say to Felicia Palmer on the phone? What did she say to you?"

"I told her I didn't kill her husband. She said we had to talk."

"That was *her* idea? It wasn't yours, she was the one who wanted to talk?" There was a quickening in her voice, as if she found this to be of some interest.

"You think that's important," I said, "that it was her idea? Why do you figure that?"

"None of your business," she said. "Turn in, over there."

There was a cluster of buildings off the highway to the right. The one on the end had a sign that said The Summit Hotel. I turned in and stopped the Jeep in front. The rain had drifted off to the south, leaving the streets slick with neon light.

The old lady wheezed a while and pulled herself up, gripping the back of my seat.

"The way I get the picture is this," she said, breathing down my neck. "You kids don't have the foggiest notion what you plan to do next. You don't know where you're going, you don't know what to do. You'll fall in the sack somewhere and commit a carnal sin. Then you'll try and figure something out. Correct me if I'm wrong."

"Wrong," I said, "we're headed for Brazil."

The old lady shook her head. "Don't. That's a bad idea. You think runnin' off will do the trick but it won't."

"Brazil is the key to this thing. We know the briefcase is tied in somehow with hidden Nazi gold."

"You don't want to get cute with me, boy. You are into real serious stuff."

"Well see, that's the point. I don't know what the hell I'm into, and no one's trying real hard to straighten me out."

"Here, take this." She handed me a card. "You find that briefcase, you give this number a call. It's a toll-free number, won't cost a thing. Someone there'll know where I am. You find that sucker, don't do something dumb like trying to give it back to Cannatella. Those folks'll dump you in a lake. I'd get rid of this car or change the plates. I wouldn't stick around town too long. What you ought to do is find another state. Oklahoma's not far. No one's going to look for you there."

She huffed out of the car, holding down her pillbox hat. When I pulled away and looked in the mirror, she was right where we'd left her, standing in the hotel drive. She might be staying somewhere, but she wasn't staying there. She wasn't in a business where you give everybody your address.

Chapter 25

I didn't know where the hell I was or what I ought to do next. The old lady was right about that. I turned back south on a street called Harry Hines. Right away I could see this was not the very best part of town. There were girls in short skirts on every other corner, and they were clearly not waiting for a bus. We passed cheap cafés, and X-rated video stores. There were places you could buy a pair of camou fatigues or a surplus bayonet. There seemed to be a lot of muffler shops. You see a lot of muffler shops, that is not a good sign.

I stopped at a shabby liquor store and went in, and found I only had twenty bucks. I thought about all the good booze we had left at the Fairmont Hotel. I got a cheap vodka for Sherry, and a bad brand of Scotch for myself. The guy in kilts on the label looked slightly Japanese, and I remembered I'd tried this brand before at Sid and Ann's. Fond memories of Les and Nurse Nina, Clyde Bob, and chilly Wisconsin days and nights. How quickly we forget.

Sherry had said very little since we left the old lady at the Summit Hotel. I knew the signs and let her be. When the nerve ends start to unravel, it is best to leave Sherry Lou alone.

She took the cheap vodka I gave her and didn't complain about the brand. She sat back and fiddled with the radio and drank. I drove around and took in the sights. I turned on Mockingbird to Lemmon Avenue, streets that seemed to circle Love Field. Northwest Highway offered franchise food and topless bars. I found I was back on Harry Hines again.

I could feel the tension easing in the car. A diver goes down too far, he's got to come up kind of slow. Sherry Lou sat up, angled the mirror to the passenger side, and fixed her face and combed her hair. She looked at herself and settled back and lit a smoke.

"I didn't care for that woman at all," she said, curling her toes around the dash. "She's got a real shitty attitude."

"You get in the assassination trade," I said, "you're not going to make a lot of friends. That's what I'd say, you don't get invited to your everyday social events."

"I had a teacher in fifth grade looked just like her. She gave me a D. Mrs. Juanita Cribbs. She wore this lavender stuff all the time. You're walking out of class, you see this big cloud of lavender driftin' down the hall, someone'd say, 'Here comes Mrs. Cribbs.' "

"She had something on her like lilac," I said. "Lilac and lavender, they smell about the same."

"They certainly do not," Sherry said. "Those are entirely different smells. Men don't know a thing about smells." She drew her legs up in the seat. "Listen, how the hell did she know where we were, you figure that? It gives me the creeps, someone knows where you are all the time. And don't you say my credit cards."

"I wasn't going to say that. I was going to say Pinelli and Wacker. They track us, the old lady tracks them."

"You think so?"

"Those boys have got connections all over the place. I bet you could be up in Russia somewhere, they'd get on your trail like that."

"I don't want to hear that, Russ."

"You were asking, I was just saying, I think that's what they'd do."

"And I said I don't want to hear it, okay?"

We passed a big hospital complex on the right The sign said "Parkland Memorial," and I remembered that's where they took the motorcade when John F. Kennedy got shot.

"What she should've done is waste those bastards right then," Sherry said. "I don't see why she didn't do that."

"Professional courtesy," I said.

"Professional what?"

"They're in the same trade. You got your doctors and your lawyers, a doctor or a lawyer, he'll look the other way. A guy does something it's maybe not what he ought to do, this other guy'll look the other way."

"Shit. I hope they suffocate. I hope they lock 'em up about two hundred years."

"Sounds great," I said, "two hundred sounds good."

I didn't have the heart to tell her it wouldn't work out that way. She was flying real steady at the moment, and I didn't want to do anything to throw her off. On a cop show the hoods would get tossed in the can, but it wouldn't work out that way here. A maid would find them in the morning, and Pinelli and Wacker would sell some story to the cops how they were the ones who'd been assaulted and locked in a closet, and the guy who had done all this was Russell Murray, who was wanted for killing four people in Illinois. The cops would check them out, and they'd know in a minute that Wacker and Pinelli had connections to the mob, but they couldn't hold them long on that. One phone call to a big-time attorney and they'd be on the street, and back on the trail again.

And maybe, I thought, they know about the car. The old lady said get rid of the car, and I figured she had a point. Sometimes when you gas up, they write the plates on the ticket when you use a credit card. If Pinelli had tracked us from Chicago with Sherry's credit cards, he very likely knew our plates. We might be okay tonight. If we drove the car tomorrow, we'd probably be pushing our luck.

"We've got to get rid of the car," I told Sherry. "I don't want to do it, but I don't see we've got a lot of choice. I think Pinelli knows about the car."

"So he knows," Sherry said, "so what?"

I looked at Sherry Lou. "You remember Pinelli? Little skinny guy, runs around with Wacker? Big guy, thinks you're kind of cute?"

"You okay, Russ?"

"Sure I'm okay. What's that supposed to mean?"

"I don't like to drive with a guy's in a coma, that's all. You're worried about the car, we don't need no stinkin' car. We drop the car at DFW. We leave it in the lot."

"In DFW at the lot."

"It's an airport, Russ. Where the big iron birds fly out. Take off at noon, you and me? Does fun in the sun ring a bell?"

It came back to me at once. St. Thomas. Natty tropic wear. Edgar and Eileen Poe off on a spree.

"Jesus," I said, "I forgot. How about that?"

"You forgot."

"I've been under a lot of stress."

"Tell me about it sometime. I'd like to hear about your stress."

"We leave at noon."

"Noon, somewhere around noon." Sherry dug in her purse. "We leave about noon, we get there and have a nice dinner somewhere, we go down to the beach."

"We take off all our clothes and splash around."

"If you're lucky. If you're lucky we take off all our clothes, we maybe—Oh, *God,* Russ!"

"What's the matter?" I turned to Sherry Lou and saw a look I didn't like. She looked like a kid who wants a bike on Christmas Day and gets a brown sweater instead.

"Russ. I lost the tickets. I *lost* the fucking tickets.'

"You lost the tickets."

"Goddamn it, what did I say?" She pounded her fists on her knees. "Didn't I just *say* I lost the tickets!"

"They're back in the room somewhere," I said. "Pinelli'll find them. Pinelli or the cops. Okay. It's all right. We can't go there, we'll go somewhere else. Where else you want to go?"

"We're not going *any*where, Russ," Sherry said. "We can't use the cards anymore, I got about eighty bucks cash. In the morning, I got to find a bank. Shit, you see what happens you don't have time to pack? I bet I left some other stuff, too."

I was still back on the part about the bank. "You can do that? You just walk in somewhere, you don't have an account, you say, 'I'm Sherry Lou I need some cash'?"

"Well of course I can do that, Russ." She gave me a kind and very understanding smile, the one you save for the dumbest kid in class. "If you can't get money when you want it, what's the point? That's what being rich is all about."

Sherry Lou spotted some nice hotels, but I found a cheap one on Maple Avenue. The less said about our fine accommodations the better. Our room did little to improve Sherry's outlook on life. She drank to some excess, and we did not engage in carnal vice. The old lady would be pleased to hear that.

When Sherry fell asleep, I did a little nipping myself. I lay on a mattress that was filled with old Budweiser cans, and I watched the lights blink through the shades and listened to the whine of passing trucks. I thought about our day in Dallas and how there almost hadn't been a night. I wondered if I'd learned anything that made sense. I remembered my talk with Jane. I hadn't paid a lot of attention to her colorful history of the mob. It didn't seem to have a whole lot to do with me. That wasn't true, of course, it did. Just because you don't know the rules, it doesn't mean you're not in the game.

I tried to bring it all together, see if I could make the pieces fit. Felicia's Uncle Frank used to be real close to this Charlie Galiano, who was now a big cheese in New York. Felicia's father Joseph fell out with brother Frank. Maybe, Jane said, because Joseph's driver bodyguard turned up dead. Had Frank Cannatella and Charlie Galiano stayed friends throughout the years? Maybe so, Jane hadn't said. But it seemed pretty clear there was now bad blood between Chicago and New York. Heavy hitters were showing up in Chicago from the East, Jane said. Why were they there? I wondered. Because they wanted the briefcase too? They hadn't killed Tony—Cannatella's hoods had done that. But they probably blew up Felicia's car. I couldn't say why, but it didn't make sense to lay that one on Uncle Frank.

Our old lady, then—she almot had to work for Galiano too. Who else was left? There was Texas Senator Byron, who was somehow mixed up in this mess, though I couldn't guess how. Did senators keep a handy hit person on the staff? It didn't seem likely, but Washington is a wonder these days. There are page boys and call girls, and other folks who handle a hardworking legislator's needs.

I fell asleep wondering what assassins did when tax time rolled around. Can you take off travel related to the job? Is an Uzi office equipment, or does that come under professional tools? Who knows? For these and other questions, see the nice folks at H & R Block.

Breakfast was dismal at best. Sherry Lou had the shakes. Her nerve ends were as frazzled as the cord on a flea-market lamp. Back to Harry Hines, which looked a lot worse in the full light of day.

I didn't much care to get close to the Fairmont again, but Sherry said she had to use a bank downtown and that was that. I let her off at a tall aluminum building on the corner of Ervay and Bryan. It seemed to have an abstract shit-kicker boot stuck on the top.

The streets all went the wrong way, and you couldn't just circle the block. I got lost three or four times, then found the bank again. Sherry opened the door and got in, and dropped a fat brown envelope on the seat.

"I take it we're rich again," I said.

Sherry lit up and leaned back. "That's the good part about being a bad seed, Russ. They'll do 'bout anything to keep you from coming back home."

"Sherry, I'm sorry you and your family are out of sorts."

"Don't let it worry your head. It's no big loss to them or me."

I passed Pacific Avenue and headed south on St. Paul. "I guess we ought to talk," I said. "We've got to do something about the car, but first we ought to think about where we want to go after that. The old lady said try Oklahoma. It doesn't seem to me like a real fun place to hide out."

"Turn around and go back the way you came," Sherry said. "You circled Love Field last night, I figure you can find it again."

"We're going to get on a plane. You got any idea where?"

"Florida," Sherry said.

I nearly hit a Yellow Cab. "My God, Sherry, I *hate* Florida. Florida's a swamp. They got dope and shuffleboard, and I don't do either one."

"Russell, *look* at me."

"I can't look, Sherry, I'm driving a moving car."

"I don't know if you noticed or not, but I am coming undone at the seams. I can't take any more abuse. I feel like I'm losing vital parts. I need a little semi-dryin' out. FAR City'll do the trick."

"What the hell's FAR City?"

"Florida Addiction Recovery facility. FAR City. I've been there once before."

Jesus, I thought, a whole new lounge full of drunks named John. Another Les. Another giant coffee machine. Oklahoma looked better all the time.

"Listen," I said, "I don't suppose they've got any rehab

centers in Cancún or Cozumel. I'd sure like to see those pyra-mids.''

Sherry shook her head. ''You can't drink the water down there. You got to drink booze instead. You do that, you kinda lose the effect. You don't have to do this, Russ. I have to do it, you don't have to do it too.''

''I guess I could. I hate to do stuff I've done before.''

Sherry put her feet on the dash and leaned back and closed her eyes. ''Grow up, Russell. That's what life is all about. You do the same thing about two million times and then you're dead.''

''Well that's a real cheery thought,'' I said.

''Fuck you and cheery thoughts. I'm about flat out of cheery thoughts. You want cheery thoughts, you should've hooked up with Bambi Dear.''

It seemed as if I ought to have a razor-sharp comeback for that, but nothing real clever came to mind.

Chapter 26

Southwest Airlines took us to Houston, where we changed planes for Miami. We used two different sets of names and paid cash. Sherry said the Gulf was a lovely shade of green. Maybe it was, I didn't look. I'm flying over water, I make it a point not to look. I know water's just as hard as land if you hit. There's no logical reason for such a fear, but that's what fear is all about.

We didn't talk much on the flight. What we did was have a great deal to drink. Sherry had her own reasons, and it's likely that she shared some of mine. You make it through some really bad shit and it hits you later on that you came very close to being dead. Reaction sets in and you drink as many cute little airline bottles as you can.

I told myself what I was doing was letting down, that I was celebrating life, saying hello to the new Russell Murray, and toasting the one I'd left behind. Even before we left Dallas, I made up my mind to put the briefcase business completely out of my life. I couldn't go back to Chicago, but I could make a start somewhere else. If the cops or the mob tracked me down someday, then they would. There was no use dwelling on that. They didn't have me now.

Maybe I'd go to Wyoming or maybe not. For the moment, I had decided to stick with Sherry Lou, and give FAR City a chance. I had mixed emotions about trying out a detox farm again. I had laughed at such places in Artie's bar, but I learned some things at Wilson Rehab I didn't know. I learned enough that when I left I was full of good intentions, what Sherry liked to call my rookie zeal. Okay, I strayed from the straight and narrow without looking back. Sometimes that's the way it goes.

What hit me in the gut at thirty-two thousand feet was I was flat out scared to put myself through that again. Not because I thought it couldn't work. What I'd learned in Wisconsin was that it *could.* My hands started sweating at the thought. Jesus, what if I dried up for good? I couldn't picture myself without a drink. I didn't *know* anyone who'd ever quit except Les. Did I want to end up like that?

The pilot said we'd be landing in fifteen minutes and the weather in Miami looked fine. Sherry told the flight lady to bring her a double vodka quick. I said I'd have a double Scotch. When the drinks came we slugged them down fast. Maybe, I thought, we could stop for a couple more on the way to the detox farm. You're headed for the desert, you need to tank up. You've got to think about things like that.

The airport was crowded and it took twenty minutes to get a cab. Our driver grinned at Sherry and said she looked fine and did we want to score some coke? He said his homeland was oppressed but it would soon be free, that tyranny could not long prevail. He turned on the radio and assaulted us with sound, a duel between tortured macaws and metal drums.

I studied the pictures of saints and naked girls that were pasted on the dash, and tried to imagine I was anywhere else but where I was. I had been to Florida once and left as quickly as I could. Florida was a tropical paradise until 1513, when Ponce de León dropped by. The place had a few good years, and then the real estate people came along. Now the whole state is crammed with hotels and old folks and alligator farms. Brand-new sun-blinding structures rise out of the paved-over swamp every day. Condos and marinas, shopping malls and monuments to The Mouse. Yet, the new becomes old before the paint has time to dry. The overall impression is perpetual decay, a corpse dolled up in a shiny sequin dress.

When the Last Days are upon us, they'll begin right here. A salesman from Topeka will complain the umbrella in his drink was used before. A waitress, who has just learned her man has a twelve-year-old honey in the Keys, will pull out her Scripto pen and stab the tourist in the eye. Mayhem will spread into the streets, onto the beaches and into the air-conditioned malls, and this will be the beginning of the end.

"Boy, you're sure a lot of laughs," Sherry said. "I haven't had this much fun since New Year's Eve at the Quayles'."

"You didn't spend New Year's Eve at the Quayles'. You just made that up."

"You don't know if I did or not. I had a social life before I met up with you. You still pissed off about Florida, or what?"

"I am not pissed off about anything at all."

"Oh, right."

"Well I'm not."

"You didn't have to come, Russ. Nobody made you do that. You could be in Oklahoma right now."

"I could stay with your grandmother there. The one that doesn't live in Depew. We could talk about my aunt who doesn't live in Santa Fe."

Sherry didn't care to comment on our Oklahoma trip. She crossed her legs and twitched her foot. She had acquired several items of native dress from an airport shop, including very large sunglasses and a chic straw hat.

"You look like a tourist from Cleveland," I said. "You teach third grade and you're here on a two-week package tour. You'd like to meet a man who owns a yacht."

"I already know six or eight guys who've got a yacht,"
Sherry said. "I know a guy who has two. Lord, Russ, life in
the bleachers must really be a bitch. I don't know how you
people hold up."

"Oh, yeah?" I said.

Let's see her top that.

FAR City looked a lot like Wilson Rehab with orange trees
and palmetto palms. Ordinarily, Sherry said, you had to pull a
really good drunk to get admitted on a Title 20, compliments
of the state. Sherry, however, was on a first-name basis with
the rehab staff in ten states, and FAR City welcomed her back.

I was used to the routine at Wilson, but FAR City had a few
surprises in store. Life was fairly easy in the wilds of Wisconsin,
coffee and small talk and plenty of Vitamin B. You were urged
to get with the program, but everybody gave you lots of slack.
Not so at FAR City. These mothers ran a tight ship.

We are scarcely through the door before friendly Nazi nurses
sign me up and lead me off through antiseptic halls. I say good-
bye to Sherry Lou. I get the blood-pressure bit, I get my terry-
cloth robe and funny shoes. Dr. Mengele sticks a rubber-gloved
finger up my ass, searching for tiny vials of Scotch and my
secret stash of coke. Precious bodily fluid is sucked from several
veins. A lady shrink who looks like Barbara Bush wants to
know how much I drink. Do I have hallucinations, do I black
out a lot? Do I want to kill myself? Do I want to sign up for
the volleyball team?

Wilson Rehab liked to think of itself as a second-rate hotel.
Discount lamps and tables, and pictures in the halls. FAR
City favored the clinical and austere. Furniture by NASA, the
decorator colors white and battleship gray.

My room followed the general decor, clean and gray and
spare. Levolor hid ironwork with a Spanish motif. You could
say they were artsy burglar bars, but they were there to keep

the residents in. Drunks who might decide they were 747s, or sparrows on the wing.

"You don't have a roommate yet," said my nurse, "but that doesn't mean you won't. After the weekend we get a lot of newcomers in."

"Whoever she is," I said, "I'm sure we'll get along just fine."

"Now that's real original. How'd you ever think of that?"

"I do it all the time."

"I'll bet."

She was sniffing through the bathroom and the closet making sure the last tenant hadn't left a quart of gin. Her name was Elaine, and she'd told me on the way down the hall she was into body contact sports, including martial arts.

"The evening meal's at six," Elaine said, "try not to be late. You got a Bible in the dresser, and *Twenty-four Hours a Day*. I'd read 'em both if I were you. I got your pills right here. It's Librium and Dilantin and Vitamin C."

"You don't mind, I'll hold off awhile," I said, "I don't need them right now."

"I'll be the judge of that," she said.

"You got a sister works up in Wisconsin, am I right?"

"I had a brother in Ohio but he died. Killed in an auto mishap."

"I'm real sorry about that."

"No you're not. You don't even know who he was."

I took the pills and she left. I thought about checking out the lounge before dinner, but I'd get enough of that. From the window I could see other buildings to the left and to the right. They both looked just alike. In the courtyard below there were shabby palm trees and plastic lawn chairs. The afternoon was pleasant, but no one was about. Drinkers don't care much for daylight, they like it when it's dark. Daylight shows the world like it is. Show me a bar with lots of light, and I'll show you a lot of empty chairs.

While I watched the scene below, a rat as big as a dog loped out across the freshly mowed grass and scampered up the trunk of a palm. Squeals came from the dark and tangled cluster at the top. Daddy Rat home from a hard day in the sewer, happy to see the wife and kids. I wondered where we played volleyball. If it wasn't in the open, away from all trees, I would not go out for the team.

I lay back on my bed and lit a smoke, and wished I had something to read. Reading has always been a part of my life, in my work and in my private time as well. Both of these habits had abruptly disappeared when Tony sent me off to Big D. I no longer had a job, and fleeing from the mob is not a normal way of life. Neither is a hotel for drunks, but at the moment it seemed like the right place to be.

It surprised me to find this sort of thinking in the Russell Murray head. I didn't like FAR City but I did. I had not understood this way of life before, but now I saw what Sherry and the others might feel. Rehab is sanctuary, a haven from the hassles of everyday life. You are safe from the world, and safe, for a while, from yourself. Maybe you get your shit together and you don't come back again. Some do and some don't. Sherry sees FAR City as a pit stop—a place to dry out and get the body back in shape so she can do it all again.

And what was Russell Murray doing here, besides hiding out from the mob? I didn't have an answer to that. Maybe I'd marry Nurse Elaine and go into martial arts. Maybe I'd even do myself some good. Maybe I'd go berserk, and live with Daddy Rat up in a tree.

I thought about a guy at Wilson Rehab who'd boozed his way through two or three fortunes and several wives. He'd been in and out of institutions for seventeen years, and he had come up with an outlook on life. "Russell," he told me, "this would be a great place to be if you could get a fucking drink."

Sometimes you get a handle on life. And a lot of times you don't.

Chapter 27

Sherry Lou didn't show up for the evening meal. No big surprise, I decided. Your average institution serves a lot more tuna casserole than lobster bisque. If I knew Sherry, she was already on the phone, stocking up on smoked eel and pickled octopus—or is it octopi? Maybe that's why the rich have such a shitty attitude. They don't get decent stuff to eat.

It wasn't tuna-casserole night. No big deal, because the meat loaf tasted like fish. The dining room was packed, and I wondered if the people in here had grown up out in the street. Maybe they liked this swill. Maybe the food was *really* bad at home.

I found an empty spot at a table near the door. There were three guys already there. Two were in their thirties, and one was maybe ninety years old. He had the shakes bad, and it was awful to watch him try to eat. Every time he picked up a bite it fell off. He didn't seem to notice this or care. He put the empty fork in his mouth, sucked it through his lips and chewed air. Then he started back through the whole painful process again.

"That's Old Ed," said the guy to my right "He's got a liver

'bout the size of a basketball. You got any mouthwash, keep it locked up. Old Ed's a bugger on Scope.''

"I don't know about Scope," I said. "Nineteen-ninety was a real good year for Listerine.''

"What's that?'' The guy looked blank. "Oh, right you did a joke. Don't waste your jokes on me. A keen sense of humor got me into this mess. I saw life simply as a lark. I'm Dawson Hyde. You going to eat that peach cobbler or what?''

"Russell Murray," I said. "I don't know if I am or not. Listen, how's the tuna here? Does it taste like chicken or beef?''

"Haven't got any idea," Hyde said. "I was born without a proper set of genes. Everything tastes the same to me.''

"Lucky you," I said.

Hyde savored a bite of mashed potatoes, rolling it around in his mouth. All he had on his plate were potatoes. He had two bowls of peach cobbler and a big glass of milk. He didn't have anything else.

I tried to figure who Hyde looked like, and couldn't bring anyone to mind. He was one of those people who has no outstanding features—neutral eyes, neutral nose and neutral hair. If I closed my eyes a moment, I knew I wouldn't remember him at all.

You couldn't say that about the guy sitting next to Old Ed. He was a tall, stringy man with a long and narrow Appalachian face, hound-dog eyes and thinning hair. The bones in his cheeks stuck out like handles on a jar. His pointy ears had little tufts of hair on the tips, and his hatchet nose was veined with a road map to a thousand shabby bars. He hadn't said a word since I'd sat down to eat. He just looked at me and grinned with the biggest set of teeth I'd ever seen.

"What I'm into is color and texture," Hyde was saying. "I like things smooth and I prefer food that's white. I don't care for colored things to eat. Can't stand the sight of toast. By God, I hate that shade of brown. Toast is abrasive to the membrane tissues of the mouth. I'd just as soon eat a plate of broken glass. Say, I got to go. You thought any more 'bout that dessert?''

"You don't mind," I said, "I'll keep it for myself."

"Figures. I had you pegged right off."

Hyde picked up his tray and left. Old Ed continued to miss his mouth. I gave up on the meat loaf and tried the peach cobbler. It was full of cornstarch and tasted like glue. Definitely not abrasive to the mouth.

The hillbilly was giving me the creeps. He kept staring at me, showing off his teeth.

"I'm Russell Murray," I said finally, "I don't believe we've met."

"Corey Lee Banks," the man said. "I wouldn't get mixed up with Hyde if I was you."

"Why not?"

"He's a base violator, that's why."

"I saw what he did to those potatoes. The man's a menace, all right."

The big smile faded. "Sin ain't a joke to me, mister. Let's get that straight right off. The man's a gross defiler of womankind." Banks laid his long spider hands on the table. "Tries to put his thing in 'em, is what he does. I seen him do it."

"You didn't."

"God's truth I did. I know what I'm talking about, friend. Used to do it all the time myself. That's when I was prey to strong drink. I'd have me some whiskey, then I'd go out and violate awhile. I'd violate me two or three before lunch. Then I'd have a sandwich and a Nehi orange and go out and do it all again. I was supposed to be fixin' Buick cars."

"Two or three before lunch."

"Woman is God's sacred vessel. They're not to be touched. Drink's what made me do it." His dark eyes settled on me. "Listen, you ain't a defiler too, by any chance?"

"Hey, I wouldn't touch a vessel on a bet. Nice to meet you, Banks."

I stood and got my tray and left the dining room as quickly as I could.

It's the coast, I decided. Florida's on a coast, and California is too. You got a coast, everyone who's walking the streets is a Looney Tune. So why shouldn't the folks in the detox farm be loonies too? I missed Wilson Rehab and its good-hearted Midwestern drunks. These weren't my kind of people at all.

The lounge looked a lot like the one in Wisconsin, except for the gray and cheerless walls. The coffee urn was enormous, and the room was filled with smoke. Posters on the wall said "Easy Does It," and "One Day at a Time."

I met a lot of people, and immediately forgot all their names. I couldn't find Sherry Lou. I spotted Dawson Hyde across the room, talking to a tall nervous woman with short black hair. I watched for any signs of violation, but all they did was talk.

An incident occurred involving Corey Lee Banks. The TV was turned to "L.A. Law." On the screen, two semi-clad attorneys were locked in hot embrace. Banks spotted this corruption, and switched the set off. Apparently, this was not an unusual event. Two big male nurses appeared at his side almost at once. They talked to Banks earnestly awhile, smiling and cajoling, as if they were all best friends. Banks didn't say a thing. He just stood there and grinned. Finally, he turned and left the room.

It was an interesting scene to watch. Neither of the two male nurses tried to touch Banks or restrain him in any way. They didn't crowd the man at all, they just talked. Both of these guys outweighed him by a good hundred pounds, but all they did was talk. They knew something I didn't know, and they didn't want any trouble with Corey Lee Banks.

I went to bed early, because there was nothing else to do. I was sure I wouldn't sleep, but one of Nurse Elaine's pills took care of that. I dreamed I lived in a tree, next door to Daddy Rat. He was married to Marian now, and they both seemed quite content.

At breakfast, I managed to avoid both Dawson Hyde and Banks. I couldn't find Old Ed. I wondered how Hyde liked his eggs. He probably left the yellows and ate the whites. I like scrambled eggs, but I always have to fix them myself. No one knows how to do them right. You have to squish them up good and add lots of cheddar cheese. Four eggs, and half a pound of cheddar cheese. Swiss is good too. Add a few squirts of Tabasco sauce. That's how to do good eggs.

Nurse Elaine stopped me in the hall. Sherry Lou didn't show up for breakfast, and I was hoping to find her in the lounge.

"You missed the lecture this morning," said Nurse Elaine. "That's part of the program, Murray. Everyone's supposed to go."

"Boy, nobody tells me anything," I said.

"All activities are posted on the bulletin board. It's your responsibility to read it. Don't miss the one this afternoon. Dr. Fry's doing 'Winners Never Quit.' "

"Fry. Tall German guy with a dueling scar? Wears a rubber glove all the time."

Nurse Elaine gave me a frigid smile. "I've got your number, Murray. I can read you like a book. You drink because you've got a lot of pressure on the job. You haven't got a problem and you don't need any help. You can quit anytime. You think everybody here is a drunk except you. You checked in because you scared yourself bad a couple of times. You blacked out and woke up somewhere, and you didn't know your name. So you figure you'll stick around here a couple of days—dry out and drink a lot of coffee, everything'll be fine. Denial's a way of life for you. I'd say you've been married maybe six or eight times. You don't like dogs or cats."

"I've been married once. I like dogs just fine."

"Uh-huh. And what about cats?"

"I don't have any opinion on cats."

"That's what you tell yourself, Murray. You've buried this problem pretty deep. I'd get into therapy quick if I were you. I could talk to Dr. Fry."

"You think that's why I drink? It's got something to do with cats?"

Nurse Elaine smiled. "That's the first step, friend. Start questioning yourself. Stop accepting the way you are. Put Mr. Denial aside. Start looking for Mr. Truth. Murray, I feel good about this. How do you feel?"

"About what?"

"About bringing things out in the open. Getting down to the real basic *you.*"

"I feel fine."

"You'll backslide some, but don't worry about that. Two steps forward and one step back is just fine. Don't miss Dr. Fry. Three this afternoon. I understand there'll be chocolate macaroons."

Nurse Elaine took off on an errand of mercy somewhere, and I walked on into the lounge. The same people were there that I'd seen the night before. I looked for Sherry Lou. I tried not to think about cats.

Dawson Hyde was talking to the same tall woman with the short dark hair. I didn't see Corey Lee Banks. I did see a man I didn't think I'd seen before. I wouldn't have noticed him at all, except he seemed to be looking at me. I got a cup of coffee and watched the game show on TV, and there he was again. He had sandy-colored hair, horn-rimmed glasses, and a nondescript face. He wore a blue blazer and an off-white shirt with no tie. Gray pants and black loafers. The pants had a knife-edge crease, and the loafers were freshly shined. He caught me looking at him and smiled, then backed off casually into the coffee crowd. I deliberately moved to the other side of the lounge, to see if he'd follow me again. He didn't show up, so I bought a pack a cigarettes and walked out of the lounge to the phone booths down the hall.

I dropped about two hundred quarters in the slot, and listened to them ping. The *Trib* operator answered, and put me through to Jane. As ever, I could hear the busy hum of reporters churning out the daily news.

"Hi," I said, "it's me."

"Christ," Jane said, "just when you think your day's working out fine."

"Listen," I said, "you don't have to talk, I don't mind. Say good-bye and hang up, I won't take your time."

Jane breathed into the phone. "Is this some clever new approach, or what? If it is, I can tell you right now it won't work. Where the hell are you, Russ? You still in Big D? You still into stolen cars?"

"I'm not in Dallas," I said. "I'm not going to tell you where I am, so don't ask."

"Why not?"

"Because you don't need to know. Because I'm not involved in that briefcase shit anymore. All that's behind me. I'm starting over, Jane. I'm embarking on a whole new life."

Jane paused for a moment. "What happened, Russ? You want to tell me what happened or not?"

"Who said anything happened? Did I say anything happened? I said I'm starting on a whole new life."

"You don't sound like you. You sound like somebody else. Don't screw around with me, Russ. Just tell me what happened, okay?"

I told her what happened in Dallas. I told her what Pinelli and Wacker had done to Sherry Lou and me, and how the old lady saved our hides. I told her I did not intend to go through anything like that again.

"My God," Jane said, "I don't blame you for feeling a little shaky, pal. You and What's-her-name all right?"

"What's-her-name and I are fine. Her name is Sherry Lou, by the way."

"I know what her name is, Russ. I'm being a little bitchy, is all. That's the way I am. Listen, I've got a make on that old lady of yours. She wasn't hard to find, seeing as how there aren't a lot of seventy-year-old hit ladies in the mob. Her name's Maria Pianezzi. She works for guess who?''

"She works for Charlie Galiano in New York," I said.

Jane was surprised. "How the hell did you know that? Who told you that?''

"Nobody told me. I figured it out for myself. Sometimes I do that, Jane. I figure things out for myself.''

"Okay, Russ . . .''

"You know what? You want to know what else? I don't *care* who she is. I don't care if she works for Daffy Duck. I don't care about old ladies with guns, or guys named Vinnie and Sal. I do not give a shit, Jane.''

"That's fine, Russ. The only thing is, they still care about *you.*''

"That's not my problem," I said.

"You don't think so, huh?''

"Please deposit another three dollars and seventy-five cents," the operator said.

"I'm out of quarters, Jane.''

"Russ, get some more change and call me back. I think we need to talk.''

"I don't think so," I said. "Listen, Jane, you have a good life.''

"*Ru*ssell—!''

The phone went dead. I stood there and listened to the awful empty sound. I didn't want to say good-bye. I didn't really want another life. What I wanted was to somehow fix the one I had, cut out a few chapters, and work it out right. It's like your favorite pair of pants. They're not perfect in every way, but they don't ride up in the crotch. You start a new life, it's sure as hell going to ride up in the crotch.

Chapter 28

Sherry Lou showed up for lunch. I saw her across the room and started for her, then stopped. I wasn't real sure. For a moment, I thought it was someone who *looked* like Sherry Lou—Sherry Lou if she'd been run over by a truck, if she'd somehow survived the black plague. Her skin was the color of ash, and dark hollows framed her eyes. Her hair had all the luster and sparkle of a mop.

I felt like a fool. I wanted to run over there and hold her, but I wasn't sure what I ought to say. Sherry, you're really looking fine? You going out for volleyball? While I stood there and wondered what to do, Sherry turned and spotted me and gave me a weary smile. My expression must have given me away, because she rolled her eyes and shrugged her bony shoulders, a gesture that clearly said, hey, I can't help it, Russ. I'm sorry but I guess it's really me.

Tears welled up in my eyes. Hell, I couldn't help it. She looked so goddamn pitiful and lost in her shabby blue robe, and I went to her quickly and took her in my arms. She nuzzled her head against my shoulder. I could count every rib beneath my fingers, and I wondered if she weighed a hundred pounds.

"Sherry Lou," I said, "God, I missed you a lot. I looked all over the place. When you didn't show up for any meals—"

"I kinda went downhill is what I did," Sherry said. "Don't guess I have to tell you that." She pulled away then, and laid a hand on my chest. "You don't mind, Russ, I think I need to sit down. I'm not too steady on my feet. Besides, they don't encourage huggin' in here. They say it leads to kissing and holding hands."

"They're just guessing," I said, "they don't have any proof."

We sat. We looked at each other and grinned for a while, then Sherry said for me to go ahead and eat. I said I wasn't hungry. She said she'd like a large orange juice and plain toast. I went through the line and decided on a piece of chocolate pie for myself.

Sherry cast a wary eye on my pie, and took a mouse-size nibble of her toast.

"*Vogue* called and canceled my cover shot," she said. "I'm just sick about that. I said listen, you get in a jam next month, don't come whinin' to me. I won't put up with that."

"I wish you wouldn't try and be funny," I said. "You don't have to do that. No one expects you to be entertaining when you're feeling like you do."

"When I'm *looking* like I do is what you mean. Russell, I won't be funny if you won't be kind. I am fully aware that I look like shit. Don't you say I don't."

"You look pretty awful," I said. "You look like shit, Sherry Lou. What the hell happened? I mean, I know you were feeling pretty poor when we got off the plane. You bought a real silly hat."

Sherry ran a hand through her hair. She didn't look at me. "Hard drinking's bad enough during ordinary times. You toss in mobsters and a load of mental stress ... I crawled kinda close to the edge is what I did. I got convulsions and the sweats. Malnutrition and some dehydration on top of that. They said they used 'bout half a carload of IVs. I don't remember that."

She studied her broken fingernails. "As an added attraction, I had a little alcohol poisoning on the side."

"Jesus Christ, Sherry . . ."

"You want to try and figure that? *Al*cohol poisoning, old Sherry Lou? What'll they think of next?"

"You're going to have to take care of yourself," I said. "I mean, that's what you're going to have to do." It sounded sort of foolish, but I said it anyway.

"I know I am, Russ." She glanced at me quickly and looked away. "I'm thinking real hard on it, too. I really am."

I knew this was something she didn't want to talk about at all. Experience had taught me not to push the standard lecture too far. Sherry had made the trip before, and she knew all the answers by heart. If she wanted to stop, then she would. If she wanted to go for the liver-of-the-year, then she'd do that, too.

To break the spell between us, I told her amusing stories about Corey Lee Banks and Dawson Hyde. She'd spotted Corey Lee, but didn't know his name. She grinned at Hyde's bizarre food habits, but she didn't crack a smile at Old Ed. Old Ed had been there when she'd stayed at FAR City before. He had been there long before that. He was more or less a permanent fixture, a reminder that things didn't always work out the way they should.

So I switched very quickly to Nurse Elaine. I told her that science was now quite certain that drinking was caused by cats. I did what I started out to do, which was to make Sherry laugh. Nurse Elaine reminded her of Nina in Wisconsin, and Nina reminded her of Les. Les opened up a whole new vista, and we coasted for a while on that.

Then I screwed up good. I told Sherry Lou about my phone call to Jane. Sherry's smile disappeared. I could feel her withdrawing from me, pulling away.

"I don't want to hear this," she said, anger pitching her voice a little high. "I don't want to *know* anything, I don't want to *hear* anything about Jane."

"Sherry," I said, "it's no big deal. I just called, that's all."

Sherry's eyes drilled right through me. "You say you're through with it, Russ, but you're not. You keep hanging on. You won't stop, you won't let it go."

"That is exactly *why* I called Jane. That's what I told her. I told her I was through with the briefcase business. I told her I was starting on a whole new life. That . . . I told her I wouldn't be calling her again."

Sherry made a noise in her throat. "Jesus, Russ. You called her to tell her that you wouldn't be calling anymore. So tomorrow you can call her up *again*, and say, 'Listen, Jane, I just wanted to call to make sure you understand that I called up to tell you that I won't be calling anymore.' Listen to yourself, you stupid shit. Do you hear what you're saying?"

"Now that's not fair and you know it. It sounds different when you say it like that. That's—taking stuff out of context, Sherry. You do that, something's not going to sound the way it should."

"Okay, Russ."

"Okay what? What kind of okay are we talking about here?"

"Okay. Just plain old simple okay. Okay you—you want to call up and chat with old Jane. Okay you want to fuck around with gangsters and drive around in cars. What is . . . *not* okay is you keep—on—bringing—that shit to me. I'm—out of it, Russ, I cannot *take* it anymore!"

"Sherry—"

"No. You shut up and *listen* to me!" Tears filled her eyes. Her hands started shaking and she doubled up her fists and tried to stop.

"Maybe—maybe I'm d-drinking myself to death, all right? I don't—goddamn need you to tell me that. Maybe I don't give a shit if I do, did you ever think of that? That it's—it's—none of your b-business if I—if I—"

Sherry screwed up her face and squeezed her eyes shut. Her mouth kept working, but nothing came out. The trembling wouldn't stop. It moved through her hands and her arms and her shoulders, until her whole body was shaking violently out of control. Her arms and her legs slammed hard against the table, and I thought she might shake herself out of her chair.

It scared the hell out of me to see her like that. I didn't know what to do. There were people all around, but no one seemed to notice or care. They were busy eating lunch. Maybe this sort of thing happened all the time, but it didn't happen all the time to anyone *I* knew.

I looked up then and saw Nurse Elaine running quickly across the room, one of the male attendants on her heels. She gave me a dirty look that said I'll get to *you* later, then the two of them took charge of Sherry Lou, and got her out of the dining room.

I looked down at my chocolate pie. It looked like something I'd eaten the day before. I shoved it aside and got out of there as fast as I could.

I felt bad about Sherry. I asked myself if I'd been responsible for that. Part of it, maybe, but not the whole thing. Sherry Lou was a bomb just waiting to explode. I had seen her, more than once, nearly reach the point she'd reached today. Sherry herself had said: "I guess I was crawling kind of close to the edge." You do that enough, you're sure as hell going to fall off.

I wasn't hungry anymore. I didn't want to go to the lounge and I didn't want to sit in my room. I headed outside to the courtyard and the perfectly mowed lawn and the shabby palm trees. It was September, but Florida hangs on to summer as long as it can. After close to a day of frigid air, the heat nearly brought me to my knees. I eased into one of the cheap lawn chairs and thought how it might be cool in Chicago right now, and how great it would feel to be walking down Michigan Avenue in a coat. I could stop in at Artie's and watch a game on TV. Maybe some of the guys would be there. I'd have one of Artie's hot pastramis on rye. Maybe I'd have a drink or maybe not.

Maybe not? Now where the hell had that come from? I pulled up the tail of my shirt and wiped the sweat off my face. It was a pretty scary thought, but there it was. I'm not sure the idea that I might have a choice had occurred to me before. Maybe I really didn't. Maybe I just thought that I did. You go in a bar you're going to what? You're going to have a drink like everybody else. You're going to have two or three. There's nothing to do in a bar except drink. You watch TV, you have some pretzels and peanuts, you have another drink. Everyone you know is there, and everyone is having a drink—

I jumped up, startled, suddenly aware that someone was standing behind my chair. The guy looked surprised and backed off.

"Jesus," I said, "what the hell you think you're doing? Don't ever do that!"

"Sorry," he said, "didn't mean to sneak up on you, friend."

I saw it was the guy in the blazer and the well-polished shoes, the one I'd spotted looking at me in the lounge.

"Your friend looks pretty sick," he said. "Withdrawal can be a painful experience. Hard drinkers take it hard. That's what they say."

"I don't know you," I said, "what the fuck do you want?"

"I want to talk to you."

"Fine. Go ahead."

"Not here."

"Why not?"

"Let's go back to your room."

"No offense, pal, but I'm not into that. Find yourself another friend."

The guy actually blushed. He took off his horn-rimmed glasses, frowned at them a minute, then dropped them in the pocket of his shirt.

"I'm Max Walker," he said. "FBI."

"I'm Russell Murray. Scotland Yard." Christ, another Looney Toon. "It's been swell talking to you, Max. Have a nice day." I turned and walked away.

"I'm not a patient here, Murray," he said. "I got into this

place to talk to you. I know about the briefcase. I know the whole bit.''

I stopped. Something turned over in my stomach and started up my throat. It tasted like chocolate pie.

"Come back and sit down," Walker said. "I think we're going to get along fine. I think we're going to have a nice talk."

Chapter 29

Max Walker was a very thoughtful guy. He said if I had to throw up he could wait. I said I'd be fine and could I see some ID. He had a plastic card and a badge in a little black wallet, just like they do on TV. He said, "Wait here," and then he left and went inside.

I thought about running. I could maybe steal a car and hide out in the Everglades. Wait until things cooled off, then hitch a freight and head out west. Did they still have freights? There weren't a lot of trains anymore. Did the modern-day hobo catch eighteen-wheelers or what?

While I thought about that, Walker returned with two Pepsis in big paper cups full of ice. I took a big swallow, and wondered if anything had ever tasted that cold before.

"Let's get something straight right off," Walker said. "The Bureau doesn't think you killed anyone. We're not after you. If we thought you were a murderer, we'd lock your ass up like that. We don't want to lock you up, we want to talk."

I downed some more of the Pepsi, and rubbed the cold cup against my head. "This is going to be a short conversation," I said. "I've been through all this shit before. You ask me where the briefcase is. I say I don't know. You say you don't believe me and I'd better find it quick. Am I close so far?''

Something rustled in the palms overhead, and Walker paused to take a look. He lost a few points on that. It seemed to me a real agent of the FBI would know all about Daddy Rat. Ephram Zimbalist, Jr., would know all about Daddy Rat.

''We already know that,'' Walker said. ''It's obvious you don't know where it is.''

''You might pass that along to the mob. I don't think they got the word.''

Walker showed me a patient smile. ''Murray, your criminal types are a very suspicious lot. They don't trust each other. They certainly don't trust an outsider like you.'' He tapped his cup to get the last of his ice. ''Now. Let's take it from the top. I've been on you since you found Tony Palmer. I witnessed the shoot-out in the alley. I saw the old lady, which by the way is Maria Pianezzi, alias Mary Penn, alias Martha Payne. She works for the New York mob. New York is going to the mattress with Chicago. They both want the briefcase. You probably figured that out yourself.''

Walker hesitated to make sure I did. He had dealt with civilians before, and knew you had to go kind of slow.

''I followed you from the alley and lost you,'' Walker said. ''So I got on Pinelli's tail and tracked him to Dallas. I intended to talk to you there, but it didn't work out. It was easy enough to follow you here. That's what they train us to do. We get a bunch of courses on that. You can use as many names as you like. Doesn't matter to us. We can find you anywhere.''

Walker pulled his chair up close, and rested his elbows on his knees. ''Murray, to put it in layman's terms, you are up shit creek. I know all about the airline tickets. My guess is you'll try and skip out again soon. With or without your girlfriend. What I'm telling you is *don't.* Just put that out of your head. Try a stunt like that and we'll forget you're an innocent party. We will throw the fucking book at you, friend.''

I wiped my face again. My brains were beginning to bake,

but I figured Max Walker would shoot me in the foot if I said something foolish like let's get out of the heat. They get courses in shooting people, too.

"This is all really great stuff," I said. "I'm impressed, okay? I'm convinced you can lock me up forever somewhere if that's what you want to do. What I'd like to know, Walker, is why waste your time scaring *me?* You know I don't have the damn thing, you said so yourself. We can sit and drink Pepsis forever, you still won't get the briefcase back."

Walker grinned. "Yeah, but *they* don't know that, do they?"

"They don't know what?"

"That you don't have the briefcase. If we can convince them that you do, all the rats will come out of their holes and we can wrap this sucker up."

"Oh, shit." I stared at Walker. My stomach started acting up again. "Listen, I don't like this. I don't think I want to hear it. Whatever it is, I don't want to hear it."

"Hey, Murray, relax, okay?" Walker spread his hands. "It doesn't matter if you *like* it or not. That's the way it's gotta be. You help us, we help you. You don't, we will eat you for lunch. Period. That's it. No offense intended. We're your government in action, pal. All we want to do is get this mess cleaned up. We're grateful for your cooperation. Don't think we aren't. We've got you in our files. Pull any funny stuff and we'll dump you in a hole somewhere."

"Boy," I said, "I sure feel a lot better now. For a while I had this dumb idea my fucking government in action wanted my ass in a sack. I'm glad you cleared that up."

Walker looked at me a minute. His expression suddenly changed. I could see him shifting gears, going into his "friendly agent" mode. He must have skipped class that day, because the whole bit was as subtle as a bear in heat.

"You're absolutely right," Walker said. "I came on pretty strong. Totally out of line. You could take me to court. I hope you won't consider that. What I do, is I get wound up sometimes. Murray, this business is bigger than you think. There are fundamental principles at risk. Some very important people are involved. I'm talking top level here.''

"Like Senator Jack Byron," I said.

Walker sat up straight. His eyes swept the whole courtyard. He didn't spot any gangsters or spies, so he turned back to me.

"Hey, I can't reveal that. Okay, you said it, I didn't. Byron is presidential material. That concerns the Bureau a lot. There are people who'd like to see Byron get mud on his face before the primaries roll around again. We know what they're up to, don't think we don't. They'd like to make it look like he's involved with the mob. We've got files that won't quit. I can tell you right now that he's not.''

"What about Byron and Cannatella?" I said. "They knew each other a few years back.''

Walker aimed a finger at my chest. "Watch yourself, Murray. They knew each other. That's all. There's nothing else to it.''

I thought about Jane. She had a lot of files, too. "You're sure about that? I've heard a lot of talk.''

"Of course I'm sure." Walker thrust out his chin. "We've got evidence to prove it.''

"What kind of evidence?''

"That's strictly need-to-know, pal. I can't go into that.''

"Oh, well, that's just great." I stood and glared at Walker. "That irritates the hell out of me, *pal*. If anyone needs to know it's me. You give me this crap about rounding up the mob, using Murray's ass for bait. But I don't need to know. Well fuck that, mister. I am *out* of this mess.''

"No way." Walker shook his head. "You're in, you're not out. You help us, we help you.''

"Don't tell me that again. I don't want to hear that again. Walker, if I was dumb enough to go along with this shit, whatever it is—which I'm not, by the way—but if I was, what makes you think you could convince these hoods I've got the briefcase when I don't? We're not talking your comic-book mobsters. These jokers are for real. They make people dead. They do that a lot. They're not going to fall in your lap you give them some phony-baloney story how I've suddenly got the briefcase back.''

"They'll believe it," Walker said, "count on it, pal."

"You want to tell me how you figure that?"

"Need-to-know, Murray." Walker stood and inspected the crease in his pants. He looked straight at me. "Don't do anything stupid. The Bureau never sleeps. We've got eyes everywhere." He aimed his finger at me and popped off a shot. "You get my drift, pal?"

Walker strolled off, a man looking easy and confident, as if he owned the place. Hell, I thought, maybe he did. Maybe the government had a whole chain of detox farms. They could keep everyone on drugs. Anyone they wanted to disappear, they could dump him in here and tear up the files. Maybe Old Ed was a Martian defector from 1952. Maybe he knew how to use a fork before they put him in here.

It was a ridiculous scenario, but it fit right in with my paranoid feelings of the moment. I didn't have any delusions that my taxpayer dollars were working for me. Walker had me by the balls and he knew it. I was nothing but a case with a number, and he'd use me in any way he could. I was certain that whatever crazy scheme he had in mind wouldn't fool an old fox like Frank Cannatella for a minute and a half. The whole thing would fall apart, and I'd be hanging in the middle somewhere. Walker wouldn't be there, of course. Walker would be somewhere else, out of the line of fire. Later, he'd write a nice report. It would fully explain how the plan got really fucked up, through no fault of his own. Russell Murray would be shipped home in a box, and Walker would find another jerk to take his place.

It was a very dreary story, and I didn't like the way it came out. If I stayed at FAR City, it would very likely happen that way. I had no doubts about that.

Okay, I told myself, all you've got to do is get away. The Bureau never sleeps, but it has to doze off sometime. I vaguely recalled that I used to be an editor for the *Literary Times*. Now what I did was get away. What does your son do, Mrs. Murray? Oh, Russell gets away. It's a real fine job, but he doesn't get home a whole lot. Most of the time he gets away.

I made a big decision. I went to my room and took a nap. It seemed like the right thing to do at the time.

I decided the best thing to do was do nothing at all. Or at least make it look that way. Normalcy was the key. I would think and I would plan. But I wouldn't do anything to arouse Max Walker's suspicions in any way. All this, of course, is another way of saying that I didn't know what the hell to do. I couldn't think of any clever plan that would get me away from FAR City without the Bureau's finest on my tail.

I took my pills like a good boy. I showed up and mingled in the lounge. I even went to hear Dr. Fry tell us "Quitters Never Win." Either that, or "Winners Never Quit," I can't recall. I can safely say I never heard so many clichés strung together in my life. Dr. Fry would drive old Ben Franklin up a tree.

Oddly enough, what he said made sense. It was just the way he said it. It doesn't take long to understand that a rolling stone gathers no moss. It doesn't take an hour and a half. Still, I made points with Nurse Elaine. Several times I caught her approving grin across the room.

After the lecture, I looked for Nurse Elaine in the hall. I wanted to ask her about Sherry Lou. I couldn't find her at first, then I spotted her by the cigarette machine. She was in what I guess you'd call rapt conversation with Dawson Hyde. You can tell when two people are rapt. They moon at each other, and appear to be oblivious to the world.

I could have waited but I didn't. Perversity is the key. I walked right up and said, "Boy, wasn't that a terrific speech? Never heard anything like it in my life."

Hyde and Nurse Elaine looked startled, like deer caught in the headlights of your car.

"Yes, it was—uh, very nice," said Nurse Elaine. One hand raced to the vee of her highly starched blouse, as if this gesture might somehow contain the color rushing from her throat up to her face.

"Hey, gotta be going," said Hyde. He grinned too much, got his feet in gear and took off.

"Just wanted to ask you," I said, "how's Sherry Lou, do you know?"

"She's—better," said Nurse Elaine. "Doing much better this afternoon." She looked at the floor and the walls. She looked everywhere except at me.

"That's great. I'm sure glad to hear it. She's had a rough time."

"The thing is, she's had a really rough time."

"Is that right?"

"She's much better now. She's a whole lot better this afternoon."

"That's good."

"Well, then . . ."

"Nice talking to you, ma'am."

"Nice talking to you, Mr.—"

"Murray. Russell Murray."

"Nice talking to you, Russell Murray."

I left her there, recovering from her daze. Halfway down the hall I looked back and saw Max Walker lurking by the entry to the lounge. Clearly, he had witnessed this shameless encounter too. You can't fool the FBI. They see this sort of thing all the time.

The entree at dinner was "Broiled Tenderloin and Cheddar de París." I swear to God, that's what the sign said. Maybe this fooled the less sophisticated diners, but I can spot a cheeseburger a mile away. Still, everybody seemed impressed. The dining room took on a very continental air.

Corey Lee Banks sat down at my table. He didn't waste time
with hellos.

"I seen you at lunch," Banks said. "You was holdin' that
redheaded gal real close. Looked to me like you had something
nasty in your head. Thinking is just the same as doing, don't
think it's not. God'll make your thing rot right off."

I put down my cheeseburger "de París" and looked Banks
squarely in the eye. "Banks, I take great offense at that. It just
so happens that's my sister you're talking about. You take that
back, or I'll tell Jesus to put a bunch of snakes in your bed."

All the color drained from Corey Lee's face. He picked up
his tray and fled.

First Nurse Elaine and Dawson Hyde. Now Corey Lee Banks.
I seemed to have the power to cloud men's minds. I decided
not to let this go to my head. I would not buy a cape and a
mask until I turned Walker into a rat.

Chapter 30

I lay in bed and looked at the ceiling. My mouth tasted foul from cigarettes. A 40-watt bulb burned in the courtyard below; it cast a dim shadow of palm leaves on the wall.

I hated to admit it, but Jane Kowalski was right. I couldn't simply toss the past aside. I could hide out in Florida, or head up north and hunt seals with Eskimos. The problem wouldn't go away. Every hood and cop in the country would still be on my tail. On the plane coming down, I earnestly believed I could put all the briefcase business behind me and start a new life. I really felt I had a way out. Max Walker's appearance had put an end to that.

It scared the hell out of me to imagine what goofy trick Walker had in mind. Whatever it was, it would put me somewhere I didn't want to be. Back with freaks like Wacker and Pinelli, people I did not want to ever see again in this life or the next.

How had I gotten myself into this mess? I wondered. Why was everything going wrong? I tried to recall all the private-eye stories I'd read in the past. What happens is the guy gets involved in a case, and right away he meets a pretty girl. Some hoods show up, and he gets beat up a lot—but in return, things begin to come together. Clues start to fall in his lap. "Look, Sheila, it's obvious the necklace they stole from Mrs. Dexter is a fake. Harrington knew this, and that's why he had to kill Fred."

I had been shot at and chased several times, and clubbed severely on the head. My parts had been exposed to gangster eyes. By now I should have come up with several good clues, and I didn't know shit. Maybe I wasn't doing this right. Maybe the problem was deeper than that: I was still Russell Murray, an unemployed editor who drank too much. I was not Sam Spade. I didn't even have a roscoe or a hat.

Sherry Lou showed up for breakfast, looking much better than she had the day before. Correction: She didn't look *better,* she looked terrific—a little thinner here and there, a little hollow in the cheeks, but I confess to a weakness for knobby hipbones. In fact, her outfit of the day revealed several top selections in the Russell Murray fetish catalog. She wore a pair of wheat-colored jeans that hung low on her hips, leaving her belly button exposed. I like belly buttons a lot. They fill up with suntan oil. They look very fine in the flickering light of a fire. As an added attraction, she had cut off the bottom of a pink T-shirt, the cut-off line coming daringly close to her breasts. If she had some occasion to stretch, this act would sober every man in sight, or drive him back to drink.

"You're looking great," I told her. "Hey, if those bozos from *Vogue* could see you now."

Sherry smiled, and gave me a peck on the cheek. "I bounce back pretty good. Us rich folks go in for nifty genes. Plus I follow the basic rules of health. You treat your body right, why, it won't let you down."

"Sherry, God'll get you for that," I said.

Sherry laughed. "Russell, I'm chock-full of orange juice and

Vitamin B. I feel okay, but I look a lot better than I feel. I've got a lot of good makeup skills. That fools 'em every time."

"I like that outfit," I said.

"I see that you do. As I recall, you've got an abnormal interest in navels, and indentations of every sort."

"I've got to admit that I do."

Her green eyes sparkled with mischief. "You got some real kinky habits, Russell Murray. I sure do admire that in a man."

As we went through the line, I tried to think of ways to avoid telling Sherry what I knew I had to say. I couldn't just leave her without a word. But if I told her, I'd have to tell her why, and that meant bringing up Walker and the whole can of worms, a lot of stuff she didn't want to hear. She was coming out of it, feeling good. What if I sent her screaming out of the dining room again? Hell, I couldn't do that.

Maybe, I thought, I could work up to it somehow. Kind of lead into it, so it wouldn't upset her too much. Say something like, "Sherry, I know you don't want to go through that brief-case business again, and I don't either. I don't even want to mention it, okay?" Start off kind of subtle, and see how it went from there.

Sherry got hot tea and toast, and a large V-8. I got sausage and a cinnamon roll, and potatoes fried in lard. I ate a bite of sausage and tried the roll. It was one of those rolls that comes out of a paper can and tastes like a chemistry set.

"Sherry," I said, "I know you don't want to go into that briefcase business again, and I don't either. I don't want to even mention it, okay?"

Sherry had her teacup halfway to her mouth. She set it down slowly, and looked at me across the table.

"Russ, you aren't any good at this. You ought to know it by now, but I see that you don't. Don't stumble around, just say it. You drive me nuts you do somethin' like this."

"I was trying to do it right."

"Well, don't. I flat can't stand it, you try to do something right."

I looked across the room. I didn't look at Sherry Lou.

"There's a guy here from the FBI. His name's Max Walker. He wears a blue blazer all the time, the kind they sell at Sears. Either that or maybe Ward's. He knows all about the briefcase. He's going to do something, I don't know what. Something real bad. I got to get out of here. I didn't want to go without saying good-bye."

"Jesus Christ, Russ." Sherry didn't go into a spasm or a fit. She bit her lip and went a little white around the mouth.

"I don't want to hear this," she said. "Why did you have to tell me that?"

"See, that's what I said. I said I didn't want to tell you any stuff like that. Sherry, you'll be okay. He's after me. He knows about you but he's only after me."

"How did I get *in*to this mess? That's what I want to know. Why *me?*" Sherry's voice started squeaking up the scale. Her mouth starting working real funny and I didn't like that.

"Just take it easy," I said, "Don't get hysterical, Sherry Lou."

"Don't you tell me what to do. I won't put up with that." Sherry's eyes closed to mean little slits. "A lot of drunks lead semi-normal lives, but shit, not me."

Sherry picked up her toast, frowned at it, and threw it down again. "Goddamn it, Russ, I was going to say I was sorry. About what I said yesterday, I mean. I was going to say, Russell, I know you didn't ask for all this. I know it mostly isn't your fault. Every time I start feeling sorry, you come up with something else."

"I didn't ask this guy to show up," I said. "That sure wasn't my idea."

"Shut up, okay?" Sherry ran her hands through her hair. She pressed her fingers to her temples and closed her eyes, like she was working on a trance.

"Where you going to go? You got any idea?"

"I don't know. I don't even know if I can get out of here. He might have agents everywhere. That's how they do it. They look like they're fixing up something in the street. They might be in a laundry truck. They use laundry trucks a lot on TV."

"Never mind the fucking TV. You got any money, anything at all?"

I shook my head. "I have a few bucks. They took all my stuff, like they do when you first come in."

Sherry looked disgusted at that. "Don't you ever learn anything, Russ? Don't *ever* give 'em all your stuff. You got to keep a stash. I've still got a lot of dough from the bank. You can have that."

"I couldn't take your money, Sherry Lou."

"Why not? It never stopped you before."

"Yeah, but I didn't like to do it. I've got a little pride. Maybe not a whole lot, but I've still got some."

"Fine. You ever try to eat on it, friend? It's only money, Russ. I can get some more."

"I keep forgetting that."

"Most of you folks in the working class do. You get the dumb idea that it's going to run out. I'll get you the money. When you think you're going to go?"

I thought about that. "I guess after dark tonight. Maybe midnight or one or two. No, wait—That's what he'll expect me to do. Unless, unless Walker thinks *I'll* know that *he* knows what he expects me to do. If he does—"

"Stop it, Russ." Sherry gave me a wary look. "I'm better, but I'm not in shape to listen to that."

"I'm sorry," I said. I picked up my tray and stood. "This thing's got me on edge. I know a threat when I hear it, Sherry Lou. Walker flat out dared me to try and run. There's no telling what he's going to pull. I'm just sitting here, waiting for the other shoe to drop."

"I know that, Russ."

I stood there looking at her. I didn't want to go. I wanted to stand there, be with her as long as I could.

"I'm sorry I got you into this," I said. "I really am. I wouldn't have put you through all this for anything. I hope you know that."

"I know that. I know you just—" Sherry looked away. I knew she didn't want me to see her cry. I turned and walked off and put my tray in the rack, and went out into the hall.

It made me feel awful to see her that way. I had put her through a lot, brought her trouble she didn't need, on top of all the other problems she had. Still, if someone's crying, it means she feels something for you, right? Someone cared about me. Someone was flat out miserable, and didn't want to see me go.

Murray, I thought, you're an immature, self-centered jerk. You can't feel good because someone else is feeling bad. I couldn't help it, though. I needed something I could hold on to, and Sherry's tears were all I had.

Chapter 31

The way from the dining room led down the long polished hallway, past the lounge to the glass front doors. I knew the doors were there, but for the moment they were lost in the harsh blazing glare of the Florida morning sun.

The Florida state motto is "Nothing Exceeds Like Excess." You can see this motto in action if you squint up at the sky. The sun is a constant intrusion. You can't keep it out. It doesn't just hang up in the blue like it does in other states. It explodes like a nova, searing the eyes and bleaching all the colors but white. Florida is a great place for lizards, mobsters from New Jersey, and other forms of reptilian life. I'm not really sure what else it's for. Florida's major export is oranges. Its major import is coke. People come here to bake in the sun, play shuffleboard, and die.

So where do *Florida's* old folks go to retire? An alarming thought, indeed. I decided I didn't care to dwell on that.

I walked down the bright hall and went into the lounge. I didn't *think* about going to the lounge. I didn't want coffee, and I didn't want to see anyone. It's just something you do in a place like this, an automatic reaction, because there's no place else to go.

To hell with it, I thought. I don't have to do this, I can do something else. I turned and started back, the soft-drink machine by the stairs a sudden image in my head, a cold Pepsi to cut the taste of breakfast that lingered in my mouth.

My left foot made it just fine. The right veered off somewhere, pitched me off-balance and nearly dumped me on the floor. I reached out and grabbed at the wall. Nausea started in the pit of my stomach, lay there like a lump, then rolled in dizzying waves up to my head.

I nearly went down. The shakes hit me hard and my mouth went dry. I could feel the stinging fever in my face and the sweat in my palms. I tried to blame it on the greasy potatoes and sausage, but I knew it wasn't that. I had been through this before and I knew what it was and it made me mad as hell because I hadn't missed the booze that much and I was feeling pretty smug and the pills were working fine.

Now the goddamn thing was kicking in again. My body didn't want a fucking pill. I had thrown all the chemistry out of whack, and body was telling brain it better send down a drink real quick or it would make things very uncomfortable for us all, and what did I think about that?

I stood there and breathed in and out. The nausea didn't go away, but after a moment it seemed to taper off. Enough, I decided, to let me climb the stairs and get up to my room and fall into bed.

I started down the hall, staying close to the wall in case the thing hit me again. A Pepsi still seemed like a good idea. I stopped at the machine and dropped in fifty-five cents. The cold can felt good in my hand. I turned and there was Walker, leaning against the wall, hands folded across his chest.

Seeing him again brought all the fears back that I'd tried to tuck away, and I tried not to let him see that.

"I'll bet they've got a course in sneaking around," I said.

"I bet they teach you that. I bet they give you special sneaky shoes."

Walker wasn't amused. "You were talking to the girl. Don't try and deny it, we see everything you do."

"You've got a little video cam. It's hidden in a button on your coat."

"That's need-to-know. What did you talk about? You tell her anything about me? That's classified, Murray. I could get you on six or eight counts. Don't think I can't."

"I can talk to anyone I want to," I said. "I've got certain rights."

Walker grinned at that. He'd tell the guys at the office. "You'll never believe this, Bob. You know what the jerk said?"

"We've got to talk," he said. "Let's go outside for a while."

"Let's don't. I'm not feeling real good at the moment. I think it's something I ate."

"I'm not taken in by that."

"You didn't have the fried potatoes."

Walker smiled. "Let's cut the shit, okay? You're a dead giveaway, Murray. We know all the tricks. A trained observer can see right through your feeble efforts at deceit. You've got guilt around the eyes. You're sweating like a pig. You got a little tic about the mouth. It all adds up."

"I can't wait to hear this."

"Jest if you like," Walker said. "Levity won't hide the truth. You're thinking unauthorized departure. It's written all over your face."

"Unauthorized departure?" The sickness rolled over me again. I didn't know whether to laugh or throw up. "Do you guys really talk like this all the time? How about 'skedaddle'? I kind of like 'intent to flee.' "

Walker took a step forward and poked a big finger in my chest. "Get it all out of your head, pal. You're not going anywhere. You and me. Fifteen hundred hours this afternoon. That's when it's going down."

"When—what's going down?" I didn't want to ask.

Walker looked irritated. ''Don't you ever listen? What did we talk about yesterday? We're clearing up this briefcase mess.''

''Oh, Jesus,'' I said, ''here we go again. I'd like to hear how you plan to do that.''

''Need-to-know. I can't reveal that.''

I looked at Walker, making yet another effort to see behind the nondescript, government-issue eyes. He looked sane enough but that isn't how you tell. Sometimes the real batty ones don't show any signs at all. I wondered if it made any sense to try and talk to this clown. I wondered if I'd fall on my ass and pass out.

''Why do you keep on *doing* this?'' I said. ''I don't know where the thing is. You want to dazzle the mob with your plan, go ahead. You don't need me for this.''

''I know you don't know where it is,'' Walker said.

''Now we're getting somewhere. We agree on that.''

''So we're going to find out.''

''We are. You and me.''

''You and me, Murray.''

''Shit. We're back where we started. Now I say, how are we going to do that? And you say—''

''You know what's the matter with you? You've got a bad attitude. I bet you don't vote. Your federal government's trying to work with you, Murray. We are putting our tails on the line. We do it every day, to keep this country safe for jerk-offs like you. That's fine. It's what they pay us for. I don't expect your gratitude. I do expect you to do your part.''

''Fuck that,'' I said. ''You're trying to get me shot. I don't intend to help you do that. Go polish your badge or something, Walker. Have a Coke. I'm going to take a nap.''

I turned and left him there and started down the hall. The sun bored a hole through my eyes, right through the back of my head.

''Say, you do that sick act pretty good,'' Walker called out. ''You almost had me going for a while. Training pays off. You gave yourself away. You want to know how?''

No, I didn't want to know how. Sweat was oozing out of every pore. I felt dizzy as a duck.

"Fifteen hundred hours," Walker said. "Don't try anything dumb. I'm armed and I'll drop you in your tracks."

I don't remember making it up the stairs. I remember the tile floor turning to mush, the pretty pink and purple stars. I remember Nurse Elaine coming up on my starboard side, looking anxious and concerned.

"You all right, Murray? You're not looking too good."

"I'm okay," I said, "I just need to lie down."

Nurse Elaine looked at her chart. "You're not due for medication. I can get you an extra Librium if you want."

"No," I said, "no pills, absolutely not!"

"Well you don't have to shout."

"Right. Sorry 'bout that."

Nurse Elaine was looking quite bizarre. Her hair was full of neon lights, and her eyes kept running down her face.

"You want to help," I said, "get me on my feet. Get me in the goddamn bed."

"You're already on your feet, Murray."

"Good. Then we've got a head start."

My head was screwed up real bad, but one thing was perfectly clear. I knew I didn't want any pills. Pills would put me under and I had to stay awake. Lie down a minute, then get the hell out somehow before—what? It was getting hard to think. Fifteen hundred hours. Was that two o'clock or five? Take away four, carry your nine.

I hit the bed like a rock. Nurse Elaine tapped the side of her nose, something nurses like to do.

"I think I ought to get Dr. Fry."

"No you don't."

"I'm in charge here. Don't you tell me what to do."

"Fine," I said, "go get Dr. Fry. We'll have a nice talk. We'll talk about Dawson Hyde."

Nurse Elaine screwed up her mouth and gave me a killing look. "You're a real asshole, Murray. I should've expected that."

"Get out of here, okay? I got to throw up."

"Go ahead. I hope to hell you choke."

Nurse Elaine closed the door and left. I leaned over the side of the bed and threw up. I started shaking and couldn't stop. I gagged and heaved, then I gagged and heaved again. Breakfast came up early, but my throw-up machine was on a roll and it didn't want to quit.

As they say, everything went dark. It was a classic withdrawal blackout, complete with happy dreams full of bogeymen and snakes, and red-eyed demons of every sort.

Karla Stark was there, sitting beside me on the plane. Tony Palmer and Felicia were just across the aisle. All three of them were dead. But that was okay, because everyone else aboard the plane was dead too, except me. Nurse Elaine came down the aisle, rolling her metal hospital cart, and I said I'd like a drink. Sorry, she said, I'm not allowed to serve you, sir, until you're properly deceased. What kind of rule is that? I said, I never heard of such nonsense before.

Nurse Elaine disappeared. Irv and Mort Wacker came rumbling down the aisle like a pair of tanks. They wore flight-attendant suits, with cute little hats and short skirts. It seemed to me that they ought to shave their legs.

Suddenly, as it happens in dreams, Uzis appeared in their hands. Irv and Mort began to spray the plane, and everyone screamed and died again. I tried to get away, but a hundred cold hands grabbed my legs and pulled me down. I yelled and lashed out, smashing at the dead and empty faces, but they wouldn't let me go . . .

I sat up and stared, trying desperately to remember where I was, the end of my scream still trailing me out of the dream.

I was covered in clammy sweat, and my heart pounded rapidly against my chest.

I remembered the dream. I remembered Karla Stark and I remembered something else. It had happened once before, when I blacked out in Wisconsin at the cigarette machine. Things I'd forgotten had fallen into place. I'd recalled the trip to Dallas, and the plane trip back with the girl. Now I knew the rest. Buried in the dream was a thread of something real, something apart from dead faces and the Wackers on a nightmare killing spree. The thread came with me out of the dream, and I saw it in the harsh light of day.

I knew where the briefcase was. I knew exactly where it had to be.

Chapter 32

I looked at my watch. It said two twenty-four, and I suddenly remembered very clearly that fifteen hundred hours meant three.
Christ! My gut clenched up in a knot. I had slept through lunch right into the afternoon—right through the precious hours when I should have been flying the coop. Going over the wall. Making my unauthorized departure from the clutches of the FBI.

Standing seemed to work okay. I was shaky but I could walk. I smelled like a junior-high gym, but a shower would have to wait. Desperadoes have other things to do. They don't have time to wash up.

I grabbed a smoke and hurried to the john, thinking how I shouldn't take the time to pee and brush my teeth both, when the rest of Russell Murray woke up. What the hell was I thinking about? I didn't *have* to run. My dream was a tangle of alcoholic fears, but the part about the briefcase was real. There was only one place the thing could be. I didn't have any doubts about that.

I felt as if a weight had been lifted from my back. Walker could forget his goofy plan to con the mob. We could work things out. I didn't have to herd sheep. Sherry and I could maybe take a long trip.

I felt joy and relief. I felt my troubles melt away. I felt great for a minute and a half. Then someone who talked like Daffy Duck said, "Hold it there, Murray, your mind's not working right yet, you better stop and think this mother out."

Reason seemed to take command. Before it deserted me again, I played out the scenario in my head. I tell Walker where the briefcase is. Walker says, "Bullshit, Murray—you didn't know before, how come you know now?" Good point. Still, he has to check it out. But in the meantime, he's not about to let me go. If I'm wrong, then I'm up the creek again. He puts me out for bait. If I'm right, he doesn't need me anymore. But he's got me on a string, and he figures some clever way to screw me anyway. I go a few rounds with Pinelli and Wacker, and Walker writes me up in his report.

Daffy Duck was right on the money again. The briefcase was the only ace I had. I had to get it back myself. Get it back, and see what was *inside*. After that, I might call Walker in to help. Then again, I might not. Who did I trust the most, Iran or Iraq? My government in action, or Frank Cannatella and the mob?

My plan seemed sound enough, but like all plans, it had a flaw. It wouldn't work too well unless I got away.

The courtyard was out. Even if the windows weren't covered with decorator bars, I'd never make it safely to the ground. I never trusted that bed-sheet trick on TV.

The hall outside my door was empty. I pictured the layout of the place in my head. Other rooms and a dead end to the left. More rooms straight ahead, and the main stairway at the far end of the hall. I wanted to avoid the main stairway if I could. I found a laundry closet and two doors that were locked. Then, at the end of the corridor, where the building jogged right in an "L," I found a narrow stairwell behind an unmarked door. If I was right, it would come out below somewhere near the dining hall. And if it didn't, so what? They were the only stairs I had.

Peeking out the door, I could see the lounge off to my left down the hall, and the front entryway beyond that. My watch said two forty-eight. As I'd guessed, the dining hall was just to my left. It was the dead time of the day at FAR City, right between lunch and dinner, and there were very few people about.

I slipped into the hall, and into the dining room. I wished I hadn't passed out. There wasn't time to find Sherry Lou. I had no wallet, and no ID. I couldn't walk into a bank like Sherry Lou, and have Daddy wire me a wad of cash.

In the *The Great Escape,* James Garner and Steve McQueen escaped from a Nazi prison camp. They had money, and forged IDs, and clothes that made them look French. I had a sweaty pair of pants and a dirty T-shirt, and very little money. I didn't feel I had properly prepared myself for this.

I could smell food cooking, and people talking in the kitchen. A good time to flee. Unless I missed my guess, tonight was chicken à la king.

I passed the kitchen and a big supply room stacked with institution-sized bottles of catsup and cans of green beans. Beyond the supply room was a dark and narrow corridor that dog-legged to the left. Feeling along the walls, I found the warped wooden panel of a door and pushed it out.

After the semi-darkness, the sudden light of a Florida afternoon was especially harsh. I squinted against the glare. A cyclone fence, a concrete alleyway. Rows of garbage cans. The side of the building, then. I could walk up the alley, past the parking lot and onto the street that fronted FAR City. Once I got across the street—

Something moved behind me to my right. I turned around fast, and nearly had a stroke. There were two male attendants in whites. One leaned against the concrete-block wall and smoked. The other squatted down, munching a Milky Way.

"Hi," I said, grinning as well as I could, "how you fellas doing, okay?"

The man with the candy bar looked up. "What you doing out here, friend?"

"Same as you," I said. "Getting a little air."

"You're not supposed to be here," Smoker said. "Clients are supposed to use the other door."

I tried another grin. "Well, now, I didn't know that."

"You know it now."

"Right. I sure do know it now."

"Better be getting on back."

"That's what I'm going to do. I'm going to do that right now."

Candy Bar stood. "We'll walk back with you."

I shook my head. "Hey, you guys are on your break. You don't have to do that."

"No trouble at all, Mr. Murray," said Candy Bar.

"Glad to do it," Smoker said.

Something gave way in my knees. "Do I—do I know you fellas? I don't guess we've met."

"We're new," Smoker said.

He took a step toward me, casual but quick. Before I could move, his hand closed around my left arm like a vise. Candy Bar took up the same position on my right.

My throat went tight. I forgot how to breathe. "Wait a minute," I said, "we can work this out." A waste of time, but it seemed like the right thing to say.

"Let's go, Mr. Murray," Smoker said.

They opened the door and led me past the storage room. My feet scarcely touched the floor. I thought we were going to the hall, but they turned off into kitchen, past the cutting tables and the big chrome ovens. The two cooks glanced up, then looked away. They decided this was something they didn't want to see.

There was a door beyond the freezer, and we went through that. I didn't know where the hell I was. There were stacks of wallboard, and scrap lumber lying about. Plaster had fallen from the ceiling and the walls. It looked as if they'd started to repair this end of the building, then run out of money·and quit.

Sometimes I'm kind of slow. This time my mind raced straight to the answer with the dizzying speed of light. These clowns didn't work for FAR City. They worked for somebody else. And if there were two of them waiting in the back, there was another at the courtyard exit, and a couple of more out front. Maybe some guys out pretending to fix the street, or in their phony laundry truck. What did all this shit cost the taxpayers? I wondered. Twenty, thirty grand? Likely more than that.

Max Walker stepped out of an empty room. He looked at his watch and frowned.

"You're late, Murray. It's fifteen hundred ten."

"I had a tap lesson," I said, "we ran a little late. What the fuck is this, Walker? I want to see a lawyer. I'm entitled to a call."

Walker grinned at the guys in white. The guys in white grinned back.

"Get him in there," Walker said. "I got to catch a plane at five."

The two jokers in white hauled me into the room. The place was empty, except for a wooden office chair. The windows were boarded up. There was another door at the far end of the room, and a dried-up can of Sears paint on the cement floor.

Smoker and Candy Bar tossed me in the chair. They whipped out canvas straps from their pockets and quickly bound me to the chair's arms and legs. They did the job with no wasted motion, as if they'd handled this several times before. I'd been more than a little anxious when they brought me into the room. I was flat out scared shitless now. This would not be a friendly discussion of any kind. You tied people up to make them talk. They could hook up a wire to your private parts. This happened in South America all the time. Laurence Olivier drilled a hole in Dustin Hoffman's teeth. He forgot to give Hoffman a shot. I tried not to think about Tony, and the way I'd found him.

Walker came into the room carrying an attaché case. He looked at me and seemed satisfied.

"Wait outside," he said. Smoker and Candy Bar left and closed the door.

"You better stop this," I said. "I'm not represented in any way. I haven't been charged with anything. You can't get away with this."

Walker squatted down and opened up his attaché case. "That's really a dumb line, Murray. Everybody says, Walker, you can't get away with this. I mean, it's obvious I can, but they feel they have to say it anyway. Just once I'd like to hear somebody say, looks like you got me tied down good. Hey, I bet you can get away with this. Just once, I'd like to hear one of you jokers say that."

Walker straightened up, and I saw the hypodermic in his hand.

"Oh, Jesus," I said, "oh, shit!"

"Perfectly safe," Walker said. "Used it a dozen times. Hardly ever get a side effect."

"Walker, I got to throw up."

"No you don't. Listen, this isn't some Mickey Mouse stuff like those Agency bozos use. This is approved by the FDA."

Walker shot a spurt out of the needle, and turned to my chair.

"Wait a minute, hold it," I said. I tried to dance my chair across the floor. "You don't have to do that. I know where the briefcase is."

So much for Russell Murray, trained superspy. One look at the needle and I completely caved in. *Fuck* my ace in the hole. I'd tell him whatever he wanted to hear. Hell, I'd give him Bambi Dear's unlisted number, and I'd never done that before.

"You guys, I'll swear." Walker grinned. "That's another thing they always say. Textbook answer we get in a course.

'Subject won't cooperate. Show subject the needle.' Clears up those pesky memory losses fast.''

"I'm not lying," I said. "I know where it is."

"How come you know now?"

"I held out on you, what do you think? Isn't that what everybody does?" I couldn't tell him I'd seen the briefcase in a dream. I didn't think he'd buy that. Your average federal agent isn't into the mystic side of life.

"Okay," Walker said, "so where is it, pal?"

"You won't use that stuff if I talk?"

"Sure I will. That's SOP. You tell me what you know. I confirm it with this."

"I don't think that's fair."

"Yeah, it is. What I do, I make a note on your record. There's a square that says, 'Did subject cooperate or not?' Hey, your FBI record stays with you all your life. Let's do it, okay?"

Walker leaned down and ripped a long tear in my sleeve.

"Listen," I said, "that's my good shirt!"

"Jesus, Murray, don't you ever take a bath?" He rubbed my skin with cotton. I could smell the alcohol.

"Goddamn it, Walker, don't do this. I hate to get shots."

"Hold still. I'm not very good at this. I might break it off."

"Don't tell me that. Why did you tell me that?"

Walker pinched my skin between his fingers.

"Don't do it," I said, "let's talk about this."

"Shut up," Walker said.

He checked the needle again. He frowned in concentration, hesitated, then stopped, as if something had crossed his mind. He glanced up past me and blinked. His eyes looked glazed, slightly out of sync, as if he'd suddenly noticed something and couldn't imagine what it could be.

"What the fuck," he said, "what are you doing in here?"

I hadn't heard the door open. I twisted my head to see and there was Corey Lee Banks. Banks looked at Walker and then at me. He looked curious and confused.

"What you doin' in here, Mr. Murray?" he said. "How come you're all tied up?"

"Get out of here," Walker said. He stood up straight. "This is government stuff. It's none of your concern."

"Corey Lee—"

Walker shot me a look. "Murray, keep out of this."

"You in some kinda trouble, Mr. Murray?" Corey Lee stood there, a tall and skinny hillbilly specter, a scarecrow who'd wandered from the field. "You shouldn't oughta tie a feller up," he told Walker. "That ain't a good thing to do."

"How did you get in here?" Walker said. He jerked his head toward the door. "Jackson, Hobert, get your sorry asses in here right now!"

Nobody came in. Walker looked appalled. Corey Lee still looked confused.

"Corey Lee," I said, "here's the way it is. This clown here wants to put his thing in my sister. I said he couldn't do that. He said he'd do it anyway, so here we are. That's about what's happened so far."

"What? What?" Walker looked stunned.

Corey Lee turned his dark eyes on Walker. Two things happened at once: Walker shoved his hand inside his jacket, going for his gun. Corey Lee made a real awful sound in his throat, and began to come unraveled at the seams.

Chapter 33

Corey Lee grabbed Walker under the chin and lifted him straight off the floor. Walker kicked and flapped his arms and tried desperately to get away. Corey Lee ignored him. He held Walker up in his big, gnarly hands with no apparent effort at all, as if he did this sort of thing every day. He held Walker up there, his hound-dog eyes focused somewhere else, and that's when it occurred to me that Corey didn't have a big finish for his act, like maybe putting Walker down. Walker's skin was turning purple and his eyes were beginning to bulge, but Corey didn't seem to notice that. He had forgotten that Walker was there.

"Corey Lee," I said, "it's okay now, it's all right to put him down."

"He's a craven violator," Corey said. "You tol' me so yourself."

"I know he is, Corey, but see, he didn't really *do* anything to my sister's, uh—sacred-vessel parts. You stopped him before he did that."

"Thinkin's the same as doing," said Corey Lee.

"Right. I remember that. That's what you said."

"The Lord smites a sinner. He strikes 'em with his great and mighty—"

"Damn it, Corey, put him *down!*"

Corey Lee blinked. He came back from wherever he'd been. He opened his fist and let Walker fall from his grasp. Walker hit the floor like a rock. He choked and gagged and gasped for air.

"He's got a gun beneath his coat," I said. "Get that."

Corey Lee did as he was told.

"Now come over and get me out of this thing."

Corey didn't bother with the buckles on my straps. He simply ripped them off and tossed them away. He ruined two straps before I could make him stop. Nice going, I thought, now I didn't have a damn thing to bind Walker up.

Corey Lee helped me get Walker to the chair. Walker glared and tried to talk, but nothing but a sandpaper whisper came out. I used the two straps I had left to tie Walker's arms to the chair. I wished I had some of the old lady's picture wire. Picture wire seems to work best.

"Those guys outside," I said, suddenly recalling Smoker and Candy Bar. "What did you do with them?"

"They tried to touch me," Corey said. "I don't like folks touchin' me none."

"I know you don't, Corey Lee."

"Them other fellers, they know I don't like that. They don't do it anymore."

"Corey Lee," I said as patiently as I could, "what did you *do* with them? You remember that?"

"I come in here all the time. I like it lots better'n the other place. Ain't anyone around. They said I couldn't come in. They wasn't actin' nice."

"And you did what?"

Corey Lee's narrow face split into a grin, and I got another look at his awesome set of teeth.

"I kinda hit 'em some. I hit 'em real good."

Oh, Jesus, I thought, real good to Corey was possibly very bad.

I opened the door and looked out. Smoker and Candy Bar were sprawled out on the floor. I bent down to check. They were both out cold, but fortunately, alive.

"Corey Lee," I said, "I need to go find my sister. What I'd like you to do is watch these three for a while. Don't *hurt* them or anything. Just watch them, okay? Until I can get my sister safe. Will you do that for me?"

Corey blinked his big dark eyes. "Sure, Mr. Murray. Whatever you say."

Corey Lee still had Walker's gun stuck in his belt. I hoped I could handle this right. I wasn't going to leave him with that.

"I'd like to have that," I said, nodding at the gun. "Is that okay with you?"

Corey Lee looked slightly distressed. "I never had a gun before. It sure is nice."

"I know it is, Corey. That's why I need to take it with me. What if I don't have it, and someone tries to do you-know-what to my sister?"

Corey Lee's face clouded. "I guess you better then," he said.

I took the gun with some relief, and walked back to Walker's chair.

"I wouldn't screw with him a lot," I said. "It wouldn't be a sound idea."

"I don't need your advice," Walker said with a rasp. "I've handled fruitcakes all my life."

"I'd find a better word if I were you." I reached into his jacket pocket and took his wallet, and his badge and ID.

"That's a federal offense," Walker said. "You'll never get away with this!"

"Everybody tells me that," I said. "Just once I wish you guys would think of something else."

I left him there muttering to himself. Corey Lee took my arm and led me to the back of the room.

"You can use this door," he said. "It comes out right near the courtyard. You won't have to see no people that way."

"Thanks a lot," I said, and stepped through the door.

There was a blanket on the floor, and some cookies Corey had filched from the dining hall. I scarcely noticed the blanket or the food. All I could see were the pictures on the wall. Corey Lee had clipped dozens of pictures from girlie magazines. He had every conceivable pose on display, every unlikely contortion of the female form. There was nothing unusual about the shots, they were ordinary soft-core porn. The only thing was, Corey Lee had carefully inked out every breast, every crotch and every shapely rear. There was no hint of anger in his work, no intent to mutilate the images he'd pasted on his wall. He had taken great care to draw the little black squares. Every one was neatly done.

I was conscious of Corey Lee hovering behind me, and the hairs rose up on my neck. Maybe he'd forgotten I'd see this. Maybe he didn't want me to know this gallery was here.

"I'm tryin' to do God's work," Corey said. "I do the best I can."

"I—I'm sure you do," I said. "It looks real fine, Corey Lee."

"They was dirty stuff before, but they ain't anymore. You see a woman's holy parts an' maybe think somethin' bad. You can't do it now."

"I'll tell Jesus what you're doing, Corey Lee. He'll appreciate that."

Corey Lee grinned. "I won't let them fellers get away. Don't you worry 'bout that."

I made my way down the hall. I didn't look back, but I felt that Corey Lee was still there. I wondered how good old Dr. Fry had let Corey Lee Banks slip through the net. He didn't belong in here. He had a few problems more pressing than alcohol.

Corey Lee's hallway led me exactly where he said it would. When I cautiously opened the door, I could see the courtyard entry to my right. I decided my luck was holding. People were now mingling in the hall. The pre-dinner coffee crowd were up from their naps, wandering in and out of the lounge.

Moving into the open, I kept one eye on the main entryway, watching for guys in white. I was grateful for the crowd. All I had to do was slip into the dining hall, get past the kitchen and out the alley door, a post that was no longer occupied.

The best-laid plans do—you know what. Timing is the key. Someone shouted down the hall. Everyone stopped in their tracks to turn and look. Two men in whites raced toward me, scattering the crowd. I took cover at once, ducking behind a woman the size of a minivan. The legend on the back of her lime-green sweats read "Dora Loves to Dance."

The two men looked alarmed. One spoke into a walkie-talkie on the run. They disappeared through the courtyard door. What the hell had happened? I wondered. Something had clearly stirred them up, and I couldn't think it was Corey Lee. Corey Lee was diligent to a fault, and it didn't seem likely he'd let his captives get away. The walkie-talkies were a clue. If the agents had a check-in time, they'd know that Walker, Smoker and Candy Bar were somehow out of touch. Great news, I thought. That meant they'd check the alley door. I couldn't go there, I'd have to—

"Russell, you want to tell me where the hell you've been?"

"*Good God!*" I leaped a good foot. Sherry was standing there, twitching her mouth and looking out of sorts.

"Don't sneak up like that," I said. "I don't like it when you do that, Sherry Lou."

"I waited at lunch and you didn't show up," Sherry said.

"You shouldn't tell people you'll be somewhere, it's not polite. Especially if someone's bringing you a whole bunch of cash."

"Listen," I said, "I've got about a two-second lead and I don't have time to talk. I got to get out of here quick. This is good-bye, Sherry Lou."

I left her and started down the hall for the front entryway. It seemed like the quickest way out. Sherry caught up and matched my stride.

"Those fellas were after you, huh? Figures. Somethin' hits the fan, you're going to find old Russ nearby. Who is it, that joker from the FBI?"

"He and his friends. He tried to give me a shot. I think it's that truth drug the Nazis used to use. I don't know if it is or not."

I stopped and looked at her. "I've got to *go* now, Sherry. If I can get off the grounds I've got a chance. When we came in, I thought I saw a mall close by. I can lose myself in there for some time."

Sherry Lou shook her head. "You'll never make it on foot. You'd better take a car."

"Sherry, I don't *have* a car."

"I know you don't have a car. Don't you think I know that? You don't have a car, you use someone else's car. Seems to me you ought to remember that."

"That's easier to do if you got some keys. I don't have any keys."

Sherry Lou shrugged. "I'll hot-wire you one. I haven't got anything else to do."

"No, you won't," I said. "You're out of this now. You don't need any more shit. The Bureau's already got your name. You get a lot of stuff in your file and you'll never get it off."

"Shoot." Sherry made a face. "I'll bet my daddy knows the guy who *runs* the FBI. I bet they play golf."

"I wish you'd told me this before," I said.

"Let's go find you a fucking car," Sherry said.

* * *

The parking lot was six rows deep. The concrete baked in the afternoon sun, and waves of heat rose from the cars. We kept low, checking for unlocked doors. I popped back up now and then to check out the front door. Once I saw a guy in white running toward the left wing, but no one came toward the lot. Sherry was right. With so much cluttering up my head, I'd forgotten we had a way with cars. If Walker had checked our MO, he'd know Sherry Lou and I were strangely attracted to other people's automobiles.

Sherry met me at the end of row three and shook her head. I took the left of row four, and she took the right. I wasn't too shocked to find everyone had remembered to lock up. Florida is a hotbed for crimes of every sort. It wouldn't surprise me to find these bozos stole a lot of cars.

I was trying the door of a Buick when I heard the peculiar sound. It seemed to be close by. Edging past the rear of the Buick, I heard the sound again. It was coming from the next car over, a white Chrysler four-door, one of those low-slung numbers with racing stripes. Marian had tried to get me to buy her one once. I told her *Consumer Reports* said the differential was shot. It didn't say that at all, but I knew a guy at Artie's who could get me a Toyota at just above wholesale price.

The sound came again. It was sort of a moan, as if someone might be badly hurt. All the windows in the Chrysler were down. I put my hands flat against the side of the car, worked my way up and peeked inside.

A frightening sight met my eyes. A very large, naked male butt was only inches from my face. It moved rapidly up and down. The man attached to it went "Huh! Huh! Huh!" This wasn't what I'd heard. Whoever was underneath him was making the painful sounds.

I had to make a hard decision fast. Accept the hand of fate, or search for another car. I weighed the odds for a second and a half. Then I drew Walker's weapon from under my shirt, opened the door and stuck my arm inside.

The man jerked around and stared. He said "Wha-wha-wha," his mouth working like a fish. His face was so uniquely forgettable, I recognized him at once as Dawson Hyde. He sat up straight, pawing at his pants, a motion that revealed Nurse Elaine.

Hyde was terrified. He looked as if he might pass out. Nurse Elaine looked surprised, but managed to keep her cool.

"Murray, just what do you think you're doing?" she said. "Get out of here at once."

"I'm sorry about this," I said. "I'm going to have to take your car."

"The hell you are."

I pulled out Walker's badge and ID, whipped it by them fast and snapped it shut. "FBI," I said. "You know me as Russell Murray. That's a cover name. Dr. Fry's mixed up with some drug lords, I'm afraid."

"Bullshit," said Nurse Elaine.

"I hope you're off duty," I said. "This doesn't look good. Maybe you'd like to tell us why you're driving such a big expensive car."

"Maybe you'd like to go fuck yourself," said Nurse Elaine.

Sherry Lou appeared beside me. '*Uh*-oh," she said, "what have we got here?" She suddenly noticed the gun. "Jesus, where'd you get that?"

"What do you mean, where'd you get that? I always carry a gun."

Nurse Elaine gave me a nasty laugh. "If you're from the FBI, I'm Saddam Hussein."

"We'll look into that." I turned to Sherry Lou. "Thanks for everything. I can take it from here."

"I guess I better tag along. Looks like you might need some help."

"No way," I said. "You're out of it. I mean that."

"I'm the one with the money, Russ."

"I don't care about that."

"Yes, you do, Russ."

"Oh, shit, Sherry Lou." I turned back to Nurse Elaine. "You get up front and drive. Hyde, pull up your pants and sit still."

Hyde blinked. "Wh-where are we going to go?"

"That's need-to-know. Nurse Elaine, I suggest you get dressed. We're running out of time." I felt I was speaking with authority and force. Being an agent wasn't bad.

It was hard to look away while Nurse Elaine got dressed. She was really quite fetching without her clothes. The starched white uniform somehow blurred her charms.

Sherry got in back with Dawson Hyde and took the gun. I told them both to keep low. I got in front with Nurse Elaine. We drove out of the parking lot without incident. I thought I spotted Walker standing by the front door, but the sun was too bright to be sure.

I didn't see any agents disguised as repairmen in the street. I did see a laundry truck. It might have been full of laundry, you can't ever tell.

Chapter 34

The less said about our journey out of Florida, the better. It was not a pleasant trip. Nurse Elaine was the picture of contempt. She said we'd pay dearly for our crimes. She said we'd rue the day we stole her car. You don't hear people use ''rue'' a whole lot anymore, and I respected her for that.

Dawson Hyde moaned and carried on, complaining of this and that. He was certain we planned to shoot him and dump him in a swamp. As the miles rolled by, this idea gained some appeal.

We left them on a back road off 441, west of Coral Springs. I told Nurse Elaine that if she wanted to keep her job, she ought to say we'd taken her as a hostage, along with Dawson Hyde. I said I didn't feel Dr. Fry would approve of their backseat romance. Nurse Elaine said I knew what I could do with my advice. I felt she was a very nice person overall, but she had a quick temper and seemed inclined to hold a grudge.

If I thought I'd shed my cares, I was wrong. You never appreciate the troubles you had until the new ones come along. Things had been moving so fast, I hadn't had a chance to bring Sherry up-to-date. I certainly couldn't tell her with Hyde and

Nurse Elaine in the car. As soon as they were gone, I explained what had happened with Walker, Candy Bar and Smoker, and how I had left them in the care of Corey Lee. I left out the bit about God's sacred vessels and their missing private parts. I didn't feel she had to hear that.

I saved the big news for last. I told her how the briefcase had come to me in a dream, and that I now knew exactly where it was. I didn't just hit her with it *wham!* like that. I am not entirely dense. I had certainly not forgotten how they'd carried her off, shaking like a bad carburetor, when I told her that Walker was on my tail. So I knew how she'd react to the briefcase news, and I had a disclaimer all prepared. You don't want anyone to have a fit inside a moving car.

"What I'm saying," I told her quickly, "is I know where it *is*. That doesn't mean I *care* where it is because I don't. I mean, I can't help it if I know, I just don't *care* if I know."

Sherry gave me a very cool and cautious look. "Where is it?" she said. "Where is the briefcase, Russ?"

"It's in Chicago," I said.

"Where in Chicago?"

"I don't—what difference does it make exactly where? I am not going near it, Sherry Lou. I thought I made that clear."

"Jesus Christ, Russ." She closed her eyes and leaned back in her seat.

"What? What did I say now?"

"I thought for a minute, I said to myself, I said I do believe Russell's finally showing good sense. I believe this boy's coming around. I wonder why the hell I thought that?"

"Sherry, you aren't paying attention. I told you that was finished. I have flat put it out of my head."

Sherry opened her eyes and turned to face me. She looked very weary, as if she'd missed a lot of sleep. "You are flat out lying," she said. "You're lying to me and to yourself. You say it's done, but it's not. Russell, you son of a bitch, I can see it in your squirrelly little eyes. You've got me running somewhere in another stolen car, and you're just dyin' to dive back into this whole pile of shit. Don't tell me that you're not."

Sherry wasn't mad. I know Sherry mad. She looked totally calm, and that worried me a lot. I decided it wouldn't be wise to remind her it was her idea to steal a car and come along. I didn't see how that would help.

"You think you know everything, but you don't," I told her. "You got this idea you can peek inside everyone's head."

"I can sure as hell peek in yours."

"You maybe think you can, but you can't."

Sherry lit a smoke, and looked out the window at Florida's bright and garish east coast. It stretches north from the Keys without end, the largest tourist trap in the world, obscuring all the natural wonder of the place, and polluting as it goes.

"I know you, Russ," Sherry said without turning my way. "You mean to do right, you just don't have a lot of smarts. You won't be happy till you get your fucking head torn off."

"Well there you go again," I said. "You're going into your gypsy-lady act."

"You've got some good points too, I'll give you that. You've got a lot of gentle in your heart. You try to show me kindness, and not a lot of men'll do that."

She turned to me and gave me a weary smile. "I know you don't want to get me riled up, and I appreciate that. But you don't have to treat me like I'm made out of import glass. I'm tougher than you think. And if I was any smarter than you, I'd scream and jump out of this car and start runnin' the other way. Jesus, I ought to see a shrink. I would, but most of 'em are crazier than I am, and I won't put up with that."

"I don't think you're crazy," I said, "I think you've got a real fine head."

"How would you know?" Sherry looked appalled. "God, you could've said anything but that. What the *fuck* am I doing here with you? Just tell me, I'd like to know that."

I didn't have an answer. I didn't know why I put up with myself. I wanted to run and hide, stop somewhere and get a steak. Get a cool room, and take Sherry's T-shirt off. I didn't want to go to Chicago any more than she did.

Maybe we both had a strange genetic flaw. A chromosome slightly out of whack, pickled in alcohol. The whole world's out of sync, and there are mysteries to life we can scarcely comprehend.

We didn't talk much for the rest of the drive. There wasn't much to say. We did decide what to do next. Sherry Lou shared my views of Nurse Elaine. The woman had a thirst for revenge. It was likely that she'd rather face a scandal than miss the chance to turn us in.

We ditched the car at a small airport near West Palm Beach, and Sherry Lou chartered a private plane. The plane winged us over Florida's fading afternoon and set us down at Valdosta, Georgia, where we caught a feeder flight to Atlanta, and Delta to O'Hare. Thus do the rich fly away from their sins, while the poor folk stay on the ground and get caught. "Life-styles of the Rich and Simple-Minded" strikes again.

Our motel was a mile from O'Hare. It fell somewhere between Sherry's idea of minimum standards and mine—which means it was cleaner and nicer than anywhere I'd ever lived.

I could say I was seized by a strange sense of *déjà vu*, as if all this had happened before. The reason I was seized is that it had. We were holed up again, hiding out and using other names. We were all out of clothes. The expensive tropic wear Sherry Lou had bought in Dallas was back in FAR City in our rooms. Or maybe it wasn't by now. Maybe Dawson Hyde was even now trying on my very soft Italian shoes. Old Ed was looking natty, spilling soup on a silk Armani tie.

I tried to picture Corey Lee Banks in something nice. The image kept fading every time, and all I could see was that gaunt hillbilly frame clothed in an outfit a scarecrow would use to mow the lawn. I felt real bad about Corey Lee. I had left him in a touchy situation back there. I hadn't meant to complicate his life but I had. Maybe, I thought, it would work out for the best. They can't prosecute you if you aren't of sound mind. Maybe someone would notice that he needed more care than he was getting at the detox farm.

According to our custom, I soaked in the tub while Sherry shopped. Scrubbed clean and rid of the sour sweats, I couldn't stand to get near my old clothes. Wrapping myself in a towel, I stuffed the clothes in the wastepaper basket and set the basket far across the room. No wonder I hadn't made a lot of friends on the plane.

Sherry returned with new duds for us both, nothing as fancy as before, just your basic everyday wear. She complained that there weren't any decent places to shop nearby so late at night, and I said she'd done fine.

I watched her as she talked, as she moved about the room. I don't remember what she said. I remember the flush of color in her cheeks, the way she moved in jerky little motions like a bird that can't decide where to light.

Sherry Lou believed she could see things in me I couldn't see myself, that I was the proverbial open book, as predictable as the dawn. She made a big thing about that. Maybe she was right, but I could read her fairly well myself, and I knew, the instant she entered the room, flitting all about, telling me a little of this, then jumping around to that, a liquid sparkle in her eyes as she talked—I knew, for dead certain, that she had started drinking again.

I wasn't too surprised. Even in the frantic throes of fleeing FAR City, it had crossed my mind that Sherry wasn't leaving solely because she couldn't stand to be away from me. That she missed the feel of danger in her veins, the keen anticipation of mayhem and rape at the hands of our prankish gangster friends.

Maybe, as she had said about me, she couldn't see this cycle of abuse in herself. She had just pulled herself out of the pit, but that was all forgotten, and now she was ready to fly again. I hadn't told her about my own adventure with the demons and the sweats. I don't know why, but I wanted to keep that to myself.

So I talked to Sherry Lou and tried on my new pants, my new shirt and new shoes, and a nifty bomber jacket that didn't quite fit but looked fine. She also bought me a colorful cap with a snap on the bill. She said I could use it if we stole any fancy foreign cars.

I told her I really loved the jacket and the cap, and I pretended not to notice that she made frequent trips to the john with her oversized purse, that she had, for reasons of her own, decided not to drink in front of me. Maybe she thought I'd nag, and she wanted to keep the peace. Or maybe she didn't entirely approve of herself. At any rate, Sherry, in turn, pretended that she didn't know I knew, and we let it go at that.

It was after twelve at night, but we found a fairly decent café still open and near the motel. Both of us nearly went to sleep at the table, and when we got back to our room, we fell into bed almost at once and went to sleep. A little semi-conscious cuddling occurred, but no carnal efforts of any sort.

The same café served us breakfast at noon. Sherry's appetite had returned, and she did not order tea and dry toast. I wolfed down an omelet the size of my dinner plate, several link sausages, biscuits and juice. After FAR City, everything tasted simply great.

"I guess you're going to do it," Sherry said. This without warning at all. "I guess I could tell you all the reasons why not. I don't figure that'd help."

"I know all the reasons already," I said. "I don't want to

do this, Sherry. It's the last thing in the world I want to do. But I can't keep doing reruns of 'The Fugitive' all my life.''

Sherry started to speak, but I politely waved her off. ''I know what you're going to say and you're right. Finding the briefcase doesn't mean I get away free. Nobody's going to give me a medal, I'm quite aware of that.''

Sherry gave me a narrow look over the rim of her coffee cup. ''What they're going to do is put a bunch of bullets in your head. I'd count on two or three.''

''I intend to avoid that if I can.''

''That's brilliant. It really is.'' Sherry made a face. '' 'I intend to avoid that if I can.' Jesus, Russ.''

''Okay, Sherry.''

''Say you get the thing, then what?''

''I don't have the slightest idea.''

''How come I knew that?''

''How come you asked me if you did?''

''Okay, *time*.'' Sherry made a referee's ''T'' with her fingers and sat up straight in her chair. ''I don't want to do this, Russ. I don't want to fight.''

''I don't either,'' I said. ''Let's not.''

''Good. Then we won't.''

Sherry hesitated, and studied me through her purple granny specs.

''You're not going to tell me where it is, are you? You're going to make me guess.''

''You've been very patient about that.''

''Hell I have. I been frothin' at the mouth. But I said to myself, if he won't tell you, I'm damned if I'm going to ask.''

''I had a good reason,'' I said.

''And what's that?''

''If I'm wrong, I don't want to look like a nut.''

Sherry laughed. ''If you're wrong, you're going to look like a nut anyway, whether you tell me or not.''

''I'm next to certain that I'm right. I just don't want to say anything until it's done.''

"Is it bigger than a breadbox?" Sherry said.

"What are we talking about?"

"Where the briefcase is."

"Yes, it's considerably bigger than that."

"Will you tell me if I guess?"

"No, I won't tell you if you guess. Are you finished here or what? Sherry, I got to go and do this before I back out. I feel as if I might start to crack all over and fall apart. Like what's-his-name, that cartoon cat."

"Jerry," Sherry said.

"Jerry's the mouse. The cat's Tom."

Sherry looked at me. "Is there something I could do to make you stop? I could lure you with my physical charms."

"You could, but I don't think I'd be any good."

"You going to finish that biscuit or not?"

"Be my guest," I said.

Sherry reached over and took my hand. "Be careful. Try and think smart. I am fairly pissed at you, Russ. I guess you know that."

"I guess I do," I said.

I bought a pair of sunglasses to go with my jacket and my cap. I took a cab to O'Hare, walked through the terminal to American, and asked the girl where they kept their Lost and Found.

"Right here, sir," she said.

"Good. You've got a briefcase. It was on your flight from Dallas September seventh. Someone left it on the plane."

"I'll look," the girl said.

She disappeared for a while. For some strange reason, I was totally calm. All my fears of returning to O'Hare had vanished as soon as I walked through the doors. I was invulnerable. The cops wouldn't spot me, no one would know who I was. I wondered if Sherry had put some kind of drug in my eggs. Whatever the cause, I hoped this goofy feeling would last.

The girl came back. She had the briefcase in her hands. My heart started pumping three or four times faster than it should.

"There's no tag," she said. "This was carry-on, right?" She gave me an airline smile. "Can you describe the contents, sir? I'll need to see some ID."

I flipped out my badge and ID case, and fanned it by her fast.

"Max Walker," I said, "FBI."

The girl blinked. "Oh, my."

"We knew it had to be here. Von Stroesser came through here before he sold the plans. We nailed him in Berlin. Forget I said that. Strictly need-to-know."

I picked up the briefcase and looked at the name on her breast.

"Betsy McNabb. You've done your country a service today, Miss McNabb. Pretend I wasn't here. The Bureau won't forget."

I left Miss McNabb looking awed and impressed, walked out of the terminal and took a cab back to the motel.

After all the fucking running about, finding dead bodies and racing around in cars, it was as simple as that. I had the briefcase in my hands. It was right where my alcoholic nightmare said that it would be. When Karla and I got back from Dallas, we were both half-looped and I left the briefcase on the plane. Everybody wanted it, and now it was there in my lap.

I told the driver to stop two blocks from our motel. I got out, paid him, and threw up breakfast on the ground.

Chapter 35

Sherry met me at the door in white jeans and a Minnie Mouse T-shirt cut off at the sleeves.

"Jesus, Russ . . ." She stared at the briefcase as if it might be full of snakes. "You got it, that's it?"

"I got it," I said, "this is it."

Her expression was an odd emotional mix—one part anxiety, two parts relief. This, along with slightly droopy eyes and a lopsided mouth, told me I'd better add six parts of vodka on the rocks. I noticed the bottle was on the table, along with a plastic tub of motel ice. Apparently, we weren't playing drink-in-the-john anymore, and I was glad to see that.

I sat down on the sofa, pulled up a straight chair and laid the briefcase on that. Sherry sat down close beside me, leaning in to see. Another big moment in my life. Something like Christmas when I got my first bike. Russell Murray is a guy who knows how to have fun.

I flipped up the snaps and opened the lid and there it was—a set of galley proofs, the same ones I'd seen when I took a quick peek on the way to Big D. At the time, I hadn't even given them a second look. Tony had sent me to DFW with galleys. That's what was *supposed* to be inside. If I'd bothered to read a line or two, I would have noticed the galleys were from a book we'd reviewed the year before.

This revelation pissed me off a lot. Tony Palmer hadn't bothered to try and make the farce look real. He had tossed in the first stack of papers he could find. Hey, it's only old dumb-ass Russ. What difference does it make?

Sherry picked up the galleys. She didn't have her glasses, so she squinted and held them close.

"That's it? We been chasing our tails for a bunch of shit 'bout Daniel Defoe?"

"No, that's not it," I said. "You got a knife of any kind?"

Sherry gave me a look. "Of course I don't have a knife. Why would I have a knife?"

"Because I need one, that's why."

I got up and left the room and walked over to the lobby. They had one of those machines that sells combs, toothpaste, stuff you forgot to bring from home. I bought a pack of single-edge blades and went back to our room.

Sherry had made another drink. She was sitting on the sofa, getting in pretty deep with Defoe. That's what I want, I thought, a drink. God knows I need one, give the old nerve ends a break. Habit and chemistry led me across the room. It's like lighting up, you don't even have to think.

I stopped just before I reached the table. Reason crowded need aside for a second and a half, then need got its bearings and knocked that sucker flat. I told myself one wouldn't matter and I knew damn well it would. One isn't ever enough. I'd have one or two, then I'd go and get a bottle of my own. By evening, I wouldn't even care what was in the briefcase. I'd be watching guys bowl on TV, and crying about my first dog.

Sherry looked up from her reading. "You don't look too good, you okay?"

"No I'm not," I said.

"You know Queen Anne had this guy locked up because he didn't want to toe the Tory line? Boy, what a bummer."

"Sometimes it's hard to be a Whig."

"I'll say."

They like to call them attaché cases these days, like you're really not on the road selling term life, you're a big diplomat. You're not in Dayton, you're taking something vital to France. The one I had was like several billion others you can buy in any store—not first-rate, but good enough. Black, a little over three inches deep, with the "feel of genuine leather," as they say.

First I cut out the inside lining in the part where you keep all your stuff. Then I did the same to the inside of the lid. Nothing there. The outside was harder. Whatever the material was, it didn't want to come off. There was nothing on the bottom of the case. But there was something behind the top.

The brown 9 x 12 envelope was glued solidly to the case. I left it there, opened the clasp, and slid out the items inside.

"Holy Shit!" said Sherry Lou. Her words came out in one rapid breath. She was sitting very close, and I could feel her go stiff.

Holy Shit was good enough for me. I couldn't do better than that.

There were six 8 x 10 glossy black-and-whites. Two men and two girls appeared in every shot. The men were in their twenties. The girls were maybe seven or eight. The lighting wasn't all that good, but I could see a lot more than I really cared to see. There is no need to say what the two men were doing to the girls. What they were doing was everything they possibly could.

One of the men had a dark Mediterranean face, a full head of black hair, and heavy black brows that bridged a classic Roman nose. The nose had been broken more than once. The other man had no face at all. Someone had neatly scissored it out.

Sherry stood up and walked away. She didn't say a thing, she just left. I could hear her behind me, scooping up ice. My

mouth was dry as dust, and I tried to shut out the sound of
vodka hitting the glass.

I concentrated on the photos, trying, for the moment, to
ignore the missing head, and the brutal assault on little girls.
I saw there were no dark shadows like you get when you use
a flash. Another thing was the way the men looked. You can
always tell when someone poses for stuff like this. They get
in some position and hold it, like the couples in porn magazines.
They look stiff and awkward, and you know they're keeping
perfectly still. Usually, everyone looks at the camera and grins,
so you'll know they're having fun.

There was none of that here, and I was ready to lay heavy
odds these bastards had no idea their antics were being captured
on film.

It pained me to look at the girls. They were children, with
gangly arms and legs, their bodies straight and shapeless, too
immature by several years to do more than hint at the female
form. Like children that age, their bellies were still slightly
swollen, and their heads were a little too large. One of the girls
had tight black curls that clung to her head like a cap. The
other girl's hair was much lighter, pale brown or blond.

It was the faces of the girls that left a cold lump of anger
in my gut. Their faces were empty, there was simply nothing
there. They suffered every kind of degradation, every terrible
offense, but their eyes remained empty as holes in white stone,
their small mouths open and slack. They had to be heavily
drugged to ignore what the men made them do. They scarcely
seemed to know they were there, or at least I hoped that this
was so. Or maybe they did know, I thought. Maybe they knew,
and they were screaming inside.

I couldn't tell when the pictures were taken, but it had to be
some time ago. The background, a hotel room or a bedroom
in a home, clearly showed a Philco table radio and an old-
fashioned stand-up lamp. The men in the shots were naked,

except for socks as thin as women's hose. The socks were held up by garters that strapped around the calf.

How long ago had men stopped doing that? It was still a stylish thing in the forties—I remembered them from a friend's collection of magazine ads. But I couldn't recall when the custom had started, or when it had begun to die out.

I sat back and lit a smoke. The room seemed unusually dark, and when I turned I saw a hard rain lashing against the window by the bed. Sherry Lou was gone. The damn pictures had completely absorbed me. I hadn't heard her leave, and I was totally unaware of the rain.

Okay, I told myself, settle down and think this thing through, try and work it out:

Two men in a picture, one without a face. Why? Someone wanted to expose one man, and keep the other out of sight. That seemed to make sense. And Jane Kowalski had talked about possible blackmail from the start. In spite of Max Walker's assurance that Senator Jack Byron was pure as baby's breath, street talk said he had somehow been connected to Frank Cannatella in the past. A presidential candidate wouldn't want a thing like that to get out. Especially if there was more to reveal than a couple of shady deals. Like Byron had a yen for baby girls.

My theory came together in a flash, and just as quickly fell apart. If Cannatella was blackmailing Byron, the picture bit simply wouldn't fly. A man's not going to panic over a picture if he isn't even in it anywhere.

I crushed out my cigarette and got up and looked out the window at the rain. It was coming down in oscillating waves, whipping like misty ghosts before the wind. I hoped Sherry Lou hadn't left the motel. If she had, I hoped she didn't get the itch and start slogging through the rain. It was the kind of thing she'd do. If she didn't like where she was, she would by God be somewhere else.

I decided it was nearly impossible to work this puzzle out. The Italian- or Sicilian-looking guy in the picture could be a

young Frank Cannatella. Or Charlie Galiano of New York. Or
Joseph, Frank's brother and Felicia Palmer's father. They were
all—except Joseph, who was dead—about the right age now,
if the picture was taken in—what? Say, 1945, around that. The
guy cut *out* of the picture could be any of those people, too.

Okay, I could eliminate Frank Cannatella as the man in the
picture. He wouldn't be sending his picture to Byron to blackmail himself. Hell, I thought, maybe it wasn't *any* of the characters I knew about. Maybe the guy in the picture wasn't anyone
I'd heard of before. A lot of hoods have gone down the pike
in the past fifty years.

Still, if it *wasn't* any of the men I knew about, why was
Frank Cannatella sending the picture to Dallas? The face I
was looking at had to mean something to Senator Jack Byron,
someone from the past he'd just as soon forget.

I got a piece of hotel stationery and sat down on the couch.
I intended to write down everything I knew, which wasn't
really a lot, mostly stuff I'd picked up from phone calls to
Jane:

1. Frank Cannatella (Chicago), who used to be close to
2. Charlie Galiano (New York), are major players in the game.
3. Tony Palmer sent me to Dallas to deliver the picture. Logi-
    cally, one of Cannatella's hoods would pick it up at DFW,
    and make sure it got to Senator Jack Byron.
4. Something went wrong. No one picked the picture up.
5. Now there's bad blood between Chicago and New York.
    The trouble between Cannatella and his one-time pal Gali-
    ano *has* to have something to do with the picture.
6. Question: *Why* is Charlie Galiano just as determined to get
    his hands on the picture as Frank Cannatella?

I looked at my list, wadded it up and tossed it at the wastebas-
ket in the corner. As usual, I missed. Shit. I didn't really know
any more than I had when I got mixed up in this mess. I knew
a lot of names, but names without facts didn't do me any good.

I simply didn't know enough to get off the ground. If I knew who the guy in the picture was . . . That would be a start. It might not solve anything, but it might tell me something I didn't know now, which was why these pictures had gotten a lot of people dead.

The rain seemed to be letting up. Either that, or taking an evening break. My stomach was growling, and I tried to remember when I'd eaten last.

I knew what it was I had to do and I didn't want to do it. Don't think about it, I told myself, just do it. Determination is the key.

I went to the phone and called Jane. Who else? I silently prayed that she was still at the *Trib,* and hadn't gone home. I added a codicil to that, a prayer tacked on to the end that Sherry wouldn't catch me on the phone.

The *Trib* operator put me through. Jane picked up on the very first ring.

"Hi," I said, "it's me."

"Go stick it in a wall," Jane said.

The amenities behind us, I told her what it was I had to have. Jane said forget it, absolutely not. I told her I'd found the briefcase, that I knew why everyone was so hot to get it, and did the words "Pulitzer Prize" ring a bell? Jane said fine, she'd be awfully glad to help. She'd send the stuff out in a cab. It was four-forty now, and I should have a package by six. I told her I admired her journalistic zeal, and her unwavering search for truth. Jane said to stick it in a tree, and hung up.

An hour and twenty minutes. I figured it out in my head. I'd probably go stark raving goofy by then. I wished I had a drink. Whisky soothes the nerves and makes the hours fly by. I tried to get the image of a twenty-gallon bottle of Glenmorangie out of my head.

The rain started up again. Doubt and apprehension were setting in. The more I thought about the whole mess, the more depressed I got. What difference did it make if I learned who the man in the picture was? What was I supposed to do then? Sherry Lou had said it more than once and she was right. Even if I stumbled on something that would clear this mess up, what the hell could I do with what I had?

Chapter 36

Sherry Lou showed up a little after five. Her clothes were soaking wet. Her Orphan Annie hairdo was plastered to her face like wet strands of kelp. To keep the marine-life analogy intact, her skin had the white sickly pallor of the belly of a fish.

"I had to get out of here," she said. "I went out for a while."

"I see you did," I said.

"It's none of your business where I've been. Don't you nag me any, Russ."

"Okay I won't."

"You got to know, I went out and had a drink. I guess I had more'n that."

"Did I ask? I didn't ask."

"Well don't. I won't put up with that."

Sherry glanced at the sofa, saw the pictures there and quickly looked away.

"I couldn't handle that. It flat made me want to throw up."

"I don't blame you," I said. "It's pretty rough."

"Jesus, you know stuff like that happens, but you don't sit around and think about it. You know who the guy is?"

"I don't have any idea."

Something in the way I said it tipped her off. She liked to do that. Pick up little intonations, little hints here and there, then make something out of it, whether there was anything to it or not.

"You're still playin' Dick Tracy, though, right?" She ran a hand through her stringy hair. "You're still hanging on."

"I've got the pictures," I said. "They got me into this mess, and I'd like to find out what they mean."

"Uh-huh." She gave me another look. "And what you got so far?"

"I told you. I don't have anything."

"You got this little line around your mouth. When something's going through your head, it kinda kinks up tight. Every time you start thinking too much, there you go. That little line kinks up real tight."

Tight is the key word in this conversation, I thought, but kept this comment to myself.

"You hungry?" I said. "You want something to eat?"

She shook her head. "I'm taking a bath and going to bed. You go on if you want."

"I think I'll stick around here."

"What for?"

" 'Cause I want to, that's why."

"There goes that little kink again."

Sherry Lou struggled with her T-shirt, finally peeling it over her head. Then she slicked out of her jeans and her blue bikini panties, hopping about on one foot, and nearly falling twice. Vodka can hinder your balance quite a lot.

I watched her as she wavered toward the bathroom, naked, enticing, and also awfully cute. My throat, and several other parts, experienced some distension at the sight. I wondered if it might be possible to work a little fun into the evening's events. More than likely not. The cab would bring my stuff from Jane, and I couldn't predict what would happen after that. So romance was out. Timing, as ever, is the key.

* * *

Waiting was as hard as I'd expected it to be. Every minute slogged by in heavy boots. Sherry Lou slept. The rain continued to fall. Doubt continued to cloud my head. What if the stuff from Jane didn't help? Worse still, what if it did? What was I supposed to do then?

I sat in the room in the dark. The rain cast teary shadows on the floor, where I'd dropped the photographs. Teary shadows seemed more than apt. I thought about Corey Lee. He thought he knew what violation was all about, but there were things he'd never dreamed about here.

I was outside waiting at ten to six, standing below the dry entryway of the motel. The cab didn't come at six. It came three or four hours later, at six-eighteen.

I had asked Jane to go through the morgue at the *Trib,* and get me every mobster shot they had—plus pictures of Senator Jack Byron. I wanted current shots, but mostly I wanted pictures from the past, as far back as she could go. Jane came through and then some. There were two hundred and nine pictures in all. Gangsters and politicians are in the news a lot.

I spread them by individual on the floor, oldest pictures first and newest last. I went through them one by one. It didn't take long. I knew right away that the face in one of Jane's pictures and the guy in the porno shots were the same. He was much older now, but this was the guy. The dark hair and heavy brows were white, the flesh hung loose on his cheeks and there were bags beneath his eyes, but there wasn't any doubt. If there had been any question at all, there was the nose. That nose with the break right on the bridge belonged to only one person, and nobody else.

The only trouble was, now the whole thing didn't make a bit of sense. It turned everything upside down and left me back at square one. I kept staring at the picture, waiting for the features to change, shift around somehow and show me some-

one else. Everything remained the same. It couldn't be the right
guy but it was.

Lightning hit somewhere and shook the room. Sherry moaned
and put a pillow on her head. I thought how most things that
happen, just happen and then they're gone. But sometimes they
hang on and follow you down the years. The pictures were
taken before I was born, but the poison they'd created was
stronger than ever now. People had died in the last few days
because two men raped a couple of kids nearly half a century
before.

I wondered about the little girls, and what had happened to
them after that terrible event. It was hard to believe they'd be
in their middle fifties if they were alive. Grown women, possibly
with grandchildren now. Maybe they didn't remember anything.
Maybe they'd mercifully blanked it out. Or maybe the nightmare had followed them down the years.

I looked at my watch. It was twenty past ten. I'd been sitting
in the dark for three hours. The answer was still right there
before me and it wouldn't go away. I had simply kept plugging
in new scenarios, trying to think of every reason why it might
work out some other way, because I couldn't afford to get it
wrong. I was caught in an unforgiving game, where the players
never got a second chance.

Sherry Lou was thoroughly pissed. You wake up a three-year-
old and tell her she's going on a trip, you've got a Sherry Lou
on your hands. Only this little kid wasn't merely asleep, she
was close to cataleptic, deep in the leaden embrace of alcohol.
Getting her up and dressed was as easy as getting a tree sloth
ready for the fifty-yard dash.

"You've got to do it," I said, "you can't stay here, Sherry
Lou." "Whasa-whasa why?" Sherry said.

I was holding her up with one hand, attempting to run a cold rag across her face. She didn't care for that at all.

"I just told you why. You forgot. I have to do something here. And I don't want you here when I do."

"Do wha'?"

"Get things, uh—straightened out if I can."

I let her go a moment, and she sagged back onto the bed. I took this opportunity to stick her legs into her jeans. When I lifted her up again, her eyes told me she was close to being semi-aware.

"You're gonna do somethin'—dumb again, right?"

"I don't know if I am or not."

"Fuckin' Jane . . ."

"What's that?"

"You been—talkin' to fuckin' Jane. Shit, I knew it."

Now how did she know that? "You don't know that," I said. "You don't know who I've been talking to."

"Fuckin' Jane," said Sherry Lou.

I sat her upright in a chair and called a cab, found her purse, and stuffed her new purchases into a sack. By the time we made it out to the front of the motel, she was dangerously close to being fully alert, fast approaching nasty and mean.

"Goin' to do something dumb," she said again.

"I guess I am, Sherry Lou."

"I think I better throw up."

"You don't want to do that."

"Don't tell me what to do. Know when I gotta throw up."

The cab arrived out of a misty rain. I got Sherry Lou in the back. She gave me a crooked grin.

"Hey, Russell," she said.

"Yes, Sherry Lou."

"Hope you get your ass shot off."

"Thanks very much," I said.

"I don't mean it, okay?"

"I know you don't," I said.

I told the driver to take her to the Chicago Hilton. I said she was my sister and she wasn't feeling well, and I wanted him to help her check in. I gave him one of Sherry Lou's fifty-dollar bills. He said, "Sure, pal," and let me know with a wise cabbie look that he fully understood this kind of thing. Fun's fun, but you don't want to wake up in the morning with a drunk.

I watched the cab pull away, and I imagined that she turned and looked back, and that I saw understanding in her face, and possibly affection and regret. The light wasn't good, and more than likely she was telling the cabbie what an asshole Russell Murray was.

Jane wasn't asleep, but she wasn't at all happy with my call. I told her what it was I had to have. She said I was out of my mind, and I ought to go to bed. I tried the Pulitzer Prize bit again, but it wouldn't work twice. She said she'd try. I might as well forget it but she'd try.

It took her an hour and a half. I wished I'd gotten something to eat. My stomach had the queasy, hollow kind of feeling that tells you you've somehow missed a meal. And, a few moments after that, I felt the first hint of something else, the beginning of the sweats, the cotton-dry mouth, the nerve endings crawling out to the end of every hair.

God, I thought, not now, I certainly don't need this! I told myself it wasn't the start of a major quake, that it was only an aftershock from my FAR City bout. But I wouldn't know for sure until it happened or went away.

Jane was surprised she was able to get the numbers I had to have.

"I started, you know, to call back and say I couldn't do it," she said. "I thought about that a long time. I told myself, this is Russell Murray you're talking about. If he doesn't do this, he'll maybe do something worse. Call it off, Russ. You *don't* want to do this. Whatever it is you're going to do.''

"You've got a deep-seated longing for me, Jane. It's there but you don't want to let it out, because the memories hurt too much. It's like Bergman and Bogart, she knows she's got to get on that plane, that two people can't hang on to happiness in this crazy mixed-up world. They'll always have Paris, but she doesn't know how she can let him go.''

"Shut up, Russ. We've never been to Paris. We went up to Michigan once.''

"That doesn't mean you can't care.''

"Okay. So I care. Don't do anything stupid. I know you probably will, but don't.''

"Good-bye, Jane," I said.

I looked at the numbers Jane had given me. I didn't look long. I knew if I waited I'd probably never do it, so I made the first call. We talked for some time. I hung up, and made the second call. That one didn't last long at all. The third call was the worst. I knew I had to be tough, determined and resolute.

"Six o'clock," I said, "and I'm talking six o'clock sharp. My contact's watching the motel. You show up before that, he takes the pictures to someone else. Don't try and cross me. I mean business, pal.''

I didn't sound a lot like Bogart. Somewhere to the right of Woody Allen, a touch of Don Knotts. I put down the phone and threw up.

Jesus, what had I done? There were any number of ways I could kill myself. Some of them wouldn't even hurt. Nearly anything was better than asking Ritchie Pinelli to drop by in the morning for a chat.

Chapter 37

I lit a smoke, and by the flare of the lighter I saw it was ten after two. Nearly four hours to wait. Plenty of time for whimpering in the dark, for doubts and second thoughts. A lot of people get in deep shit through fate and happenstance. Not many get the chance to arrange some disaster for themselves. The worst thing about these acts is the perpetrator truly believes they are practical and sound. As George Custer said, it seemed like a good idea at the time.

The rain had let up, leaving furry halos around the street lamps. Traffic signals winked away the long dead hours of the night. A lone car sizzled over wet and oily streets, leaving pools of neon behind.

It didn't have to go wrong. It could turn out right. The thing is, that's two choices and I could have stuck with one. I could have listened to Jane and Sherry Lou and tried to make a new life. Screw the whole thing and start over somewhere else. Clearly the reasonable thing to do. So what the hell was I doing, sitting there waiting for killers in the dark?

You know the answer to that one, pal, but you don't have the guts to spell it out. You're tired, sick, and scared enough

to fill your pants, but you're too pissed off to care. You don't
want to do this shit anymore . . .

Sherry's bottle of vodka was on the floor by the couch. The
light from outside said maybe half a fifth, a little less. I worked
it all out, measuring the shots in my head. If I paced myself
right, I could make it last the night. I could chase the blues
away, smooth all the wrinkles out. I told myself this would be
strictly preventive, a therapeutic move and nothing more.

Maybe if I hold it. I thought, *that couldn't do any harm.*
Doesn't mean I'll drink it, simply means it's there.

I reached down and picked it up. I studied the label with
care. A good domestic brand. All vodka tastes alike to me, it's
a great drink for drunks.

Okay, now we know what you are. Let's get on with it, pal.
I didn't say that.
Didn't say what, Murray? That you don't want a drink?
I didn't say I was a drunk.
If it looks like a drunk, and it drinks like a drunk—
That's what I used to do.
Bullshit, Murray.
Okay, I get the point. I did, but I don't want to do it anymore.
You want to get the sweats, you want to be crawling on the
floor when Pinelli and his buddy get here?
I'm not that bad right now. I can make it just fine.
Sure you can. You and Sherry Lou.
I'm not like Sherry Lou.
Yeah, right.
Well, I'm not. Sherry Lou can't stop. Sherry's a—she's an
alcoholic, she's a drunk.
And you're Captain Marvel. Shazam, you dumb fuck.
Goddamn it, it's not like that! She has to do it, I don't! I
can quit anytime I like!

* * *

I sat up with a start, coming out of it like you think you've maybe dropped a thousand feet. I looked at my watch. It said twenty after five. I stared at it again. Christ, I couldn't believe I'd drifted off!

The bottle was still in my hand. I put it down and got up and went to the john and washed my face. My stomach felt queasy, but I told myself that was hunger and nerves and nothing else. There was a row of machines down the hall. I could get a candy bar and a Coke, something to keep me off empty for a while. I still had time for that.

There was a small pile of change on the dresser. I scooped it up into my hand, crossed the room and opened the door. Ritchie Pinelli was standing there, his fist curled up for a knock.

"Morning, asshole," he said. "You going to stand there, ask me in or what?"

I didn't move. I stared at the bony ridges of his face, at the raccoon eyes. Irv Wacker loomed behind him, like a redwood guarding a hockey stick. Everything inside me fell apart. All the things I'd said I wouldn't do when this moment arrived, I went ahead and did—the knot in my gut, the rope around my throat so tight I couldn't breathe.

"You're—early," I said, because I couldn't think of anything else. "I said—I said don't come before six."

"No shit," Pinelli said. "Asshole here says I'm early. On the phone he says, be here at six. He says, he's telling me on the phone, he says, 'I mean business, pal.' "

Pinelli raised his chin a bare quarter of an inch. Wacker couldn't possibly have seen him but he did. He squeezed past the scarecrow, shot his big hand out flat, and knocked me to the floor. I hit hard, saw him coming and tried to scoot away. He grabbed a handful of shirt and jerked me up. He slapped me hard twice, snapping my head from side to side, the pain bringing tears to my eyes. He held me there an inch off the floor, a serious, beetle-browed look on his face, like he didn't know whether to stop or start all over again. Finally, he threw me at the couch. I bounced once, and sprawled on the floor.

Pinelli looked down at me, shaking his head. "You tell me on the phone, you're saying, hey, don't cross me up. You're saying, 'I mean business, pal.' I'm thinking, I've seen assholes before, this guy is something else."

Pinelli's hand blurred at his side, whipped into his jacket and came out fast as a snake about to strike. He squatted down and shoved the muzzle of his pistol up my nose.

"You mean business, fine," Pinelli said. "Let's you and me do some business, asshole. So where you got the pictures? I don't want a lot of shit, I want to know where they are."

This wasn't going the way I'd planned. In my scenario, I held all the high cards. He knew it, and he wanted the pictures bad, and I didn't get knocked around.

"Okay," I said, "let's talk. The pictures aren't here. They're somewhere else. You don't think I'm dumb enough to keep 'em here, do you? What do you think I—"

Pinelli took the gun out of my nose and slammed the butt against my head. I heard myself yell and the pain nearly swallowed me up. Pinelli hit me again, using the Wacker technique, working from left to right.

"That's enough," someone said, "let him talk."

Pinelli stopped. A face swam into focus. Max Walker stood just above Pinelli. He had traded in his blazer for a three-piece, official-looking suit.

"I hope you gave this a lot of thought," I said. "These guys have got a lousy dental plan."

Walker ignored me. "No one's got to get hurt," he told Pinelli, "we talked about that. I don't want this going any further than it has."

Pinelli stood. He slipped his gun back under his coat, took a quick step and got up in Walker's face.

"I don't want to hear we had a talk," Pinelli said. "We had a talk, I don't give a fuck about a talk. You'd done what you shoulda, I wouldn't be getting out of bed in the middle of the night, talkin' to this asshole on the phone. Don't come telling me we had a talk.''

Pinelli nodded at Wacker, and Wacker hauled me roughly to my feet.

''I'm asking you again,'' Pinelli said. ''You got the package, you tell me where it is.''

''It's not here,'' I said, ''I told you that.''

''I know you told me that. I didn't ask you where it's not, asshole, I asked you where it is.'' He paused, glanced at the door, and back to me. ''The girl. You give the stuff to the girl?''

''The girl's gone. She's out of it, she's got nothing to do with this. Forget about the girl.''

Pinelli just stood there, looking at me with no expression at all, no feeling, no emotion of any kind, as if I weren't even there. He had looked at me that way in Dallas, just before Wacker started pounding on my head.

Max Walker was something else. He looked around the room, studying the furniture, the carpet and the walls, as if he had some decorating ideas. He wouldn't look at me. He didn't want to be here but he was. Whatever reasons he'd thought he had for selling out to Pinelli, they weren't holding up well now, but he was in too deep to get out. It had been a long night, and a lot of things had fallen into place before I made my phone calls. Not everything, but a lot, and now that Walker was here, I wasn't all that surprised he'd shown up.

''I told you on the phone,'' I said, ''I told you how it works. I give you the pictures, you forget about me, you forget about the girl. All I want is out.''

My mouth was dry as dust. I tried to make the words come out right. ''The pictures are in the lobby. They've got a safe, you're staying here, they'll keep stuff you want in the safe.''

Pinelli nearly broke his rule and grinned. ''You put the stuff in a safe.'' He looked at Irv Wacker. ''Asshole here, he put the stuff in a safe.''

"What's the matter with that?"

"It's not very original," Walker said. "Somebody's hiding something, they put it behind a picture, they put it in a safe. That's the first two places you're going to look."

"I'm sorry," I said, "I'm real new at this."

"Okay, so let's get out of here," Pinelli said. He looked at me. "You and me, we walk up to the desk. You tell the guy, you say you want your stuff. You don't do nothing else, you do that. That's all you say, you want your—No, fuck that." Pinelli stopped and looked at Walker. "*You* go up to the desk. You flash your badge, you tell the guy it's some kinda government shit. You get the package, you walk real easy out the door."

The color rose to Walker's face. "Uh, I don't exactly have a badge. I mean I don't right now."

"What you mean, you don't got a badge? You're a fuckin' fed, you got a badge."

"He's got it."

"Who has?"

"Him. Murray. He's got the badge."

"Jesus." Pinelli stared at Walker, then at me. "The asshole's got the guy's badge. How you figure that? Don't tell me. I don't want to know. Irv, look in the guy's pockets, see if he's got a badge."

Wacker jammed his fat hands in my pockets, ripping out the seams. He came up with Walker's ID case, and held it out to his boss. Pinelli raised a palm, as if he didn't care to handle anything like that. Irv gave the ID case to Walker, and Walker looked pained. He had thrown in with Pinelli, but the Bureau was still in his heart, and this wouldn't look good in his personnel file.

"Let's get the fuck out here," Pinelli said again, and we did.

* * *

Max Walker led the way down the hall, with me, Irv Wacker and Pinelli behind. It was a little after six and the hallways were empty, as cheery as a Russian mausoleum. I waited for something dramatic to happen, the way it does on TV. Batman should be here anytime. Hopefully before we reached the desk, and everyone discovered that the pictures weren't there.

The candy and soft-drink machines were straight ahead. The hallway was a "T," with more rooms to the left, the way to the lobby to the right. Walker turned right. He took half a step, made a funny little sound in his throat and jumped back.

Three guys stepped quickly around the corner, guns held straight out in their hands. They looked like the front line of the Bears, crammed hastily into cheap suits.

Walker looked shaken and pale. Irv Wacker stood perfectly still. Pinelli showed no reaction at all. He had been what he was a long time, and he didn't need a lot of time to think.

"Listen, you're doin' what you think you gotta do," Pinelli said, "I know that. Maybe this is not the right move, maybe you could do something else."

The first guy shook his head. "You got a problem, Ritchie. It's something, I don't know, maybe you get it worked out."

"This problem," Pinelli said, "it don't get worked out."

The guy shook his head, as if he didn't know how to answer that. He didn't take his eyes off Pinelli when he talked.

"One of you two, which one is Murray Russell?"

"Russell Murray." I said. "Everybody gets it wrong."

The guy moved his gun an inch. "You stand over there. Out of the way by the wall."

"What I'd like to do," Pinelli said, "is you and me talk. What's it going to hurt, we maybe talk."

The guy shook his head. "This problem, it's like I said, it's maybe something you get it worked out."

"Like I'm saying, it ain't a problem like that."

"Maybe, maybe not. It's maybe somethin' you can—"

The guy suddenly stopped. He looked past me and blinked, like the picture wasn't coming through right and he couldn't

figure what he ought to see. I was standing by the wall, I didn't
have to turn and look. Sherry Lou was twenty feet behind us,
trying to find the door to our room. She wore a bright-green
gown she'd picked up on her latest shopping tour. She had it
on backward and wrong side out. She had lost one shoe somewhere, and I figured that couldn't help a lot when you're blotto
as a loon. Makeup hadn't worked out any better than the dress.
She had missed her mouth a mile, and a bright pair of lips ran
down one side of her nose. Eyebrow pencil was applied with
equal skill. She looked like Tammy Faye after three rounds
with Holyfield.

I took all this in in a second and a half. Pinelli was quicker
than that. He didn't turn around and look. He didn't know why
the guy with the gun had glanced away for an instant and didn't
care. His hand moved into his jacket and came out incredibly
fast. I never saw *any*thing move that fast in my life.

Chapter 38

A tiny blue hole appeared between the guy's eyes. He opened his mouth and looked surpassed. The man beside him did a fast pirouette, grabbed his gut and hit the floor. Irv Wacker swept past me with a sawed-off shotgun in his hand, spraying the weapon like a hose. Someone yelled *"Son of a bitch!"* Max Walker dropped and howled like a dog. As Zane Grey used to say, guns were blazing everywhere.

I didn't stick around for the rest. I was racing for Sherry Lou, praying nothing lethal found my back. As I reached her, Sherry looked up. It was clear she didn't know who I was.

"Hi there," she said, "Whasa-whasa-whoo?"

I grabbed her by the waist, picked her up and turned a corner fast, out of the line of fire. A door marked EXIT in red was straight ahead. I pushed it open with my shoulder and stumbled outside.

"Lost m' fuggin' shoe," said Sherry Lou. She giggled and waved her arms, clearly enjoying the ride. We wouldn't get far like this. I tossed her over my shoulder, hoping that she wouldn't throw up.

The dawn was streaked with red. I looked around to see

where the hell I was. There was nothing to the right but closed shops. A tall parking garage was to the left. I jogged for the entryway as quickly as I could, while Sherry made very peculiar sounds.

What a screw-up, I thought. It isn't supposed to work like this. Then again, things hardly ever did.

Sherry didn't weigh too much, but I wasn't used to lugging ninety or a hundred pounds around. Up to now, three or four books across the office was my personal best.

I got her nearly up the first ramp and let her down. She leaned against a fender for a second, then flowed to the ground like a cartoon cat. I lifted her up and set her straight.

"Sherry," I said, "it's important that you listen to this. I can't do that anymore. You're going to have to stand up. You think you can do that, you think you can maybe stand up?"

She looked at me and blinked. *One . . . two . . . three . . . four . . .*

"Hey, ol' Russ. Whasa doin' here?"

"Sherry, you listen to me." I glanced over my shoulder, where the ramp circled down into darkness and the street. Nothing so far, but it wouldn't be long. Sherry Lou grinned and looked blank.

"God*damn* it, Sherry Lou!" I shook her hard, and she seemed to like that. She narrowed her eyes into focus and gave me a fuzzy grin.

"Y'know wha'? Got a cab to the . . . wrong hotel. Had a hell of a time . . . gettin' back. Made it, though . . ."

"Right. What a lucky break for us both. Come on, we can't stay here."

I grabbed her hand and pulled her along. The lights in the garage were too bright. Not a great place to hide, but it was too late to think about that. If I could make it to Level 2, we could head back down. Maybe get out while our pursuers were going up. I didn't have the slightest doubt that they would come. If Pinelli came out of the shoot-out alive, he'd be on my ass like glue. And if he made it, I'd know for dead certain I wasn't getting any help.

"Gettin' . . . sick," Sherry said. She stopped and sat down.

"No, you're not." I jerked her back up. "Don't throw up and don't sit. That's two things not to do."

I led her behind the line of cars, doing my best to keep her low. The clock in her head was running slow. It took about four or five seconds for a message to make it through. It was very irritating, like talking to a drunk on Mars.

"*Don't* stand up," I said. "Keep your head down low."

One-two-three-four . . .

"Hey, ol' Russ, wanna dance?"

"I don't think I want to dance. Keep down."

"Why not? Why you don' wanna dance?"

"Maybe later, not right now. Right now you've got to keep your head dow—"

The shot made a god-awful noise, rolling like thunder and bouncing off the cement walls. A windshield by my head suddenly shattered and blew apart. So much for safety glass. I yelled at Sherry Lou and dragged her down as another blast peppered the hood. I crawled two feet and risked a look. Irv Wacker was laboring up the ramp. He broke open the shotgun, tossed out his empties, and rammed in two more shells.

Sherry looked wide-eyed and awake. A shotgun has a sobering effect. If you don't have coffee or a cold shower handy, a shotgun will usually do the trick.

I led Sherry down behind the cars, heading for the turn and Level 2 after that. We had a good start, and I figured we could lose Irv Wacker and hit the exit ramp before he reached the top. Pinelli worried me a lot. If Wacker was coming up behind us, the scarecrow was somewhere else . . . It struck me then that this somewhere almost had to be the exit ramp from Level 2. Exactly where I wanted to go, where I didn't want Pinelli to be.

But if we went back *down* the way we'd come . . . The idea

of heading back toward Wacker coming up didn't have much
appeal, but I couldn't see any other way.

I tapped Sherry on the shoulder and stabbed a finger down
the ramp. Her lag time was improving. She stared at me and
shook her head *no!* No time to argue the point. I grabbed her
and pulled her along. She tried to jerk away and I could hear
her say ''Shit-shit-shit!'' beneath her breath.

I took it slow, going down on my hands and knees. I had to
let Sherry go, and hope she didn't do something dumb. The
cement was cold, and the air smelled like oil and old exhaust.
I knew Wacker had to be close. Going flat, I peered beneath
a Buick. The guy had a bad muffler and probably didn't know
it. My heart nearly stopped. Wacker was standing right in front
of the car. All he had to do was step around to the side, take
two easy shots and blow us into stew right there.

I held my breath. Sherry's hand tightened around my ankle,
nails biting into my skin. Wacker seemed to be listening. Or
maybe he was trying to think. He stood there some time. Thinking wasn't Wacker's major skill.

Finally, he moved off up the ramp. I counted to ten, then
came up in a crouch and led Sherry down the way we'd come
in. Five or six cars and we'd be back on the street. I didn't
know where the hell we'd go and didn't care, as long as Wacker
and Pinelli weren't around.

We passed a Chrysler and a Ford, and a van I couldn't name.
Vans all look alike to me. Then I heard something scrape
cement. I turned to tell Sherry to hold it down, and remembered
she'd lost her shoes. If you don't have shoes you don't scrape.
Something hard touched the top of my head and I looked up
into the raccoon eyes and the granite face. Pinelli looked at me
a second, then slammed the muzzle hard against my head.

A chain saw ripped through my head. I fell back and hit a
Dodge Charger, bounced off the fender and sat down hard.
Sherry Lou screamed somewhere. I could hear Wacker puffing
his way back down the ramp. I tried to stand, but my legs
wouldn't work. I could see, but everything was in pairs. Two

Pinellis and two Sherry Lous. I shook my head and the images came together and something ice-cold crawled up my back.

"Jesus," I yelled, "don't! Don't do it, Pinelli!"

Pinelli gripped one of Sherry's wrists, tossed her roughly over the ledge above the street and held her hanging in the air. He held her with his right hand, and pointed the gun in his left straight at me. Sherry started screaming and couldn't stop, a high, frightening shriek that threatened to go off the scale.

"Okay, asshole, where you got the stuff?" Pinelli said. "I got to ask you twice?"

"Behind the picture," I said at once. "I put it behind the picture in the room. Jesus, that's the truth, pull her up from there!"

Pinelli shook his head. "Nobody puts nothin' behind a picture. You, you'd put somethin' behind a picture."

"Goddamn it, it's *there,* pull her up!"

"Or you'll what?" Pinelli's dark eyes bored a hole through my head. "You get me up in the middle of the night, I come down, I see some guys I don't want to see. I'm askin' myself, what the fuck are they doing here, who invited them, right? I'm thinking, I bet the asshole did that. I'm thinking, I am havin' a real bad night, I am getting pissed off."

"You want the pictures, you got 'em," I said, "that's what you want, so go ahead and—"

A sound like the Indy 500 ripped through the garage. Rubber screamed on cement and headlights swept across the walls. An oversized pickup roared up the rampway and shrieked to a stop. Ritchie Pinelli stared. An old lady in a hat poked her Uzi out the window spraying everything in sight. Glass shattered, and lead thunked into cars. Irv Wacker howled and dived for cover, his shotgun discharging in the air. I came off the floor and threw myself at Pinelli. He said something under his breath and squeezed the trigger twice.

Hot powder blistered my skin. I felt something sing through my hair. I didn't care about Pinelli, I went for Sherry Lou, fighting to reach her, straining to get her hands.

Pinelli let go. Sherry screamed and dropped out of sight.

For a quarter of a second I thought about her falling and hitting the street below and how she'd look after that and then something tore loose of me inside. Russell Murray was gone and there was nothing left but rage and the tears that burned my eyes, nothing left for Sherry or Karla Stark or Tony Palmer or anyone else, nothing but the sound coming out of my throat and the feel of my hands as they pounded at Ritchie Pinelli's face. Somewhere in some other place I thought how fine it was to hear cartilage snap and feel flesh tear away and I wanted to keep on doing that I didn't want to stop. It was a noble and totally spiritual high to know I didn't have to run from Pinelli anymore or do anything he said, that now all I had to do was stand there and pound him into shit . . .

I stopped, and sucked in a breath. Pinelli groaned and crawled along the floor. Blood came out of his cheek and one eye was closed shut and his nose angled off to the right. I stepped over and kicked him in the face. He yelled and I kicked him again. *Oh God, Sherry, I'm sorry as hell, Sherry Lou . . .*

I didn't want to look but I did. The street was two stories down and she'd be there twisted and broken, the ground underneath her stained red. My throat closed up completely tight and I made myself lean over the ledge and look down. Sherry Lou looked up and said, "Get me *out* of here, you stupid shit! Don't just stand there starin' like a loon!"

She was hanging on a shaky piece of pipe, a foot below the ledge. I leaned down and stretched out my hands and grabbed her wrists and pulled her up. She collapsed against me and cried and I took her in my arms. She jerked away at once. Her green eyes suddenly went Sherry Lou mean.

"Don't you give me that cuddle-up crap," she said. "I'm not speakin' to you again."

"Fine," I said, "let's get the hell out of here."

I looked at Pinelli. He was moaning and dragging himself away, trying to squeeze under a blue Chevy Corsica sedan. I knew he'd never make it. Those cars don't have the clearance for that.

The nasty rattle of an automatic weapon split the air. Good, maybe the old lady had Wacker on the run. Her pickup was idling on the ramp, twenty feet away. I took Sherry Lou by the arm, opened the passenger door, and pushed her inside.

The Uzi rattled again, and I saw her, loosing a burst of fire at a Ford. If Wacker was there, he was wishing he were somewhere else. The old lady was dressed in a black leather jacket, black pants and black boots, and her pillbox hat with the feather on the top. From a distance, she looked like two ripe melons in a sack.

I ran around the back of the truck and got in the driver's side. I could apologize later for borrowing the truck. She had an Uzi, and all I had was Sherry Lou.

I stepped on the gas, braked into an empty space, then slammed the gears into reverse.

"Where do you suppose we're going now?" Sherry said.

"Out of here," I said, "what do you care?"

"Don't you yell at me. I am not havin' a real good night."

I tore off down the ramp. The truck had a hell of a lot of lights—lights on the bumper on the sides and on the top. We could light a night game for the Bears. I shifted into second and looked at Sherry Lou and something hit the truck hard. I slammed on the brakes. Sherry Lou screamed and came at me, elbows and knees punching holes in vital parts. I looked past her and saw Irv Wacker trying to squeeze his way into the cab. He had his head and one arm inside. His little pig eyes were blood-red and he was grabbing for Sherry's legs. I yelled at Sherry and tried to fight her off, but Sherry didn't hear. She had one mission in life—to get across my lap, away from Wacker, and out the other side.

"Sherry, stop it, goddamn it!" I yelled. Sherry's butt hit me in the face and her foot came down on my knee, slamming my foot against the gas.

The truck had several mad horses beneath the hood. We

burned rubber, racing down the ramp. I hit the brakes and
turned half around, heading the other way. Wacker howled and
hung on. Sherry was out the window, clawing for the top of
the cab. My lights caught the old lady in the middle of the
ramp. Her eyes went wide and she clambered up a Toyota
hood.

I made a sharp turn, taking off fenders and ripping hoods,
trying to shake Wacker off. Wacker spotted Sherry on the top,
growled and went after her. He reached out a ham-sized fist
and grabbed the windshield wiper. He grasped the window with
his other hand and pulled himself onto the hood. He went to
his knees, hanging on with one hand, clawing for his pistol
with the other. Sherry screamed. Wacker waved his gun around,
trying to get a shot. I stuck my head out the window and yelled
at Sherry Lou.

"Jump in the goddamn back," I said, *"now!"*

I heard her feet hit the bed, rammed my foot through the
floor and made a sharp turn to the right. I headed straight
for an empty stall and the low cement wall after that. The
speedometer read sixty-five as I jammed my foot against the
power brakes. Wacker looked alarmed. He yelled and loosed
a round through the windshield, turning the glass into frost.
Centrifugal force did the thing it liked to do, and he sailed out
into the morning light. He hung there for an instant, arms and
legs extended like the sky divers do on TV, then he dropped
out of sight.

I jumped out of the cab and went back to Sherry Lou.

"Jesus, you all right?" I said.

"Oh sure, Russ, I'm just fine," she said.

"I know you're not *fine*, I didn't mean fine—"

"I know what you meant, Russ, just shut the fuck up."

I looked back and saw the old lady coming up the ramp.
She was limping a little, like a duck with a flat. I wondered
why she was waving, flailing her arms about. She'd never been
that excited to see me before.

"Hey, asshole, over here," Pinelli said.

I jerked around fast, saw him leaning against a car. His face looked like a rare Porterhouse but the big gun was steady in his hand. I saw his finger tighten, saw him grin for the very first time and decided I liked him the other way.

"Just hold it. Don't do it, Ritchie—"

I saw him out of the corner of my eye. Max Walker had lost his coat somewhere. He was holding one arm to his side and blood was soaking through his shirt. Pinelli looked at him and moved his gun quickly to the right and Walker shot him in the knee.

Pinelli said, "Shit!" dropped his gun and sat down.

Walker turned to me. His face was white and he looked very tired.

"Things don't always seem to work out right," he said.

"I noticed that," I said.

Chapter 39

I went back to Sherry. She seemed okay. She was sitting in the cab of the truck, looking like she might pass out or throw up. Max Walker stood where he was and didn't move. He was probably wondering what kind of jobs were open in Chile or Peru. I didn't look at Pinelli. I didn't want to see him anymore.

The old lady was sitting on the cement floor. Her hat was on crooked and the Uzi was resting in her lap. I squatted down and asked her if she needed any help.

"Twisted that pesky hip again," she said. "Likely popped right out of the socket. Did it once before. Don't guess you got a little nip on you, boy."

"No, ma'am," I said, "I don't."

"Figures," she said. "See if you can get me upright. Damn floor's colder'n a Minnesota night."

"Is Minnesota where you're from?"

"None of your business, young man."

"Right."

I helped her up. I recalled the day lightning struck my grandfather's farm, and we had to lift six dead horses into a truck.

"I'm glad you came," I said. "I appreciate that."

She held me with her coal-black eyes. "You get this mess settled up, I'd get into something else if I were you. You're not real suited for this line of work."

"I guess you're right." I said.

Bright headlights swept up the ramp. A black limo braked to a stop, and a dark blue Chrysler after that. Wonderful, I thought, not more than ten minutes late.

Eight or ten doors opened at once. A lot of men in dark suits got out. They were mostly broad and short, like the guys Pinelli had shot in the hall. They spread out over the garage, and two of them walked up to me.

"You Murray?" the first guy said.

"I guess I am."

He nodded at the limo. "Get in."

"The girl in the pickup," I said, "she's with me."

"Wrong," the guy said, "get in."

I looked back at Sherry Lou. The old lady nodded, as if everything would be just fine. Yeah, sure it will, I thought.

They led me to the limo and I climbed in back. All the doors *wooshed!* the way they do in big cars. The engine purred like a well-fed lion and we were gone.

The man sitting three or four feet across the seat had neatly trimmed silver-gray hair, a broken nose and bullet eyes. He wore a pearl-gray suit, soft imported shoes, a white shirt buttoned at the top and no tie. I didn't have to ask his name. I had a Frank Cannatella photo album in my room. I knew how he'd looked for the last fifty years.

"You're Murray," he said. "You got something belongs to me."

His voice made the hair stand up on my neck. He sounded like he might be chewing rocks.

"I hid it in the motel room," I told him. "It's behind a picture on the wall. I think the picture's got ducks."

"Jesus," he said. He didn't look at me. He leaned forward and spoke to his driver. The driver nodded and picked up a phone.

"You got a phone number," Cannatella said. "Don't anyone got this number. I don't give it out."

"You're going to ask me where I got it," I said. "I'd like to ask you not to do that. I hope you won't."

Cannatella muttered to himself. "You call me, you call Ritchie. You call this old lady works for Charlie Galiano in New York. You like to call people on the phone. You're calling who else? Who else you wakin' up in the middle of the night?"

"That's all. I didn't call anyone else."

I knew I had to do this right. You're riding with a guy like this, you're not sure where he'll let you off.

"I called you first," I said. "I thought I had some answers, but I had to make sure. And I had to be certain nobody knew about the call except you. As soon as you told me you didn't know a thing about the pictures, I knew I was right. I told you I wanted to call Pinelli and have him there at six. You gave me the okay on that, and said it was all right to call Mrs. Pianezzi too."

"You know a guy a long time, you think you know this guy, you don't know the guy at all."

"No, sir," I said, "I guess not."

The car windows had thick tinted glass. You can't see in and you can hardly see out. I guessed we were on the Tri-State heading south.

"I'm guessing a lot of this," I said. "It doesn't matter much if I get it all right. I wondered who had taken those pictures. It wouldn't be an easy thing to do. I figured maybe Jimmy Riso because he was your driver at the time. Maybe he had some bone to pick with you, I don't know. Maybe he thought he could make a buck sometime. Like I say, I'm just guessing, I'm talking about people I didn't know.

"There was another man in the picture, and I thought it might be Charlie Galiano, because I'd heard that you two were close about then. So I wondered—if I was right about Riso, who got the pictures after Riso died? They had to come down through the years somehow, so maybe Riso arranged to have them go to your brother, Felicia's father, after Riso died.''

Cannatella didn't speak. He listened, but he didn't say whether I was on the track or not. He wasn't a man who gave anything away. Which is maybe how he got to the top in the business he was in. You listen, while the other guy talks.

"About the time Riso died, you and your brother stopped speaking to one another and Joseph retired. I don't know why, that's none of my business. Anyway, the pictures were still around, so maybe Joseph left them to his daughter, Felicia, since he didn't have any sons. When you told me that you didn't know the pictures existed, I knew it had to be Pinelli running the show. It didn't make any sense that you'd send pictures like that to Senator Byron. So that kind of turned things around. The word on the street was that you were blackmailing Byron somehow, because there was some kind of connection between the two of you in the past. When Max Walker found me in Florida, he made a big thing about Byron being pure as snow. I didn't think anything about it at the time. Then, when I learned you weren't involved, I thought maybe Walker was working for Byron. Maybe the Bureau knew it, but I don't figure they did.

"So now it was the other way around. Byron, or someone in his camp, was trying to blackmail you. They wanted to make sure you wouldn't try to hurt Byron's presidential bid. It had to be Ritchie Pinelli who went to them with the deal.''

"Jack ain't nothing," Cannatella said, a sharp touch of venom in his voice. "He's a fuckin' politician. Those guys, those guys got no honor. They do business like pigs. I did him plenty of favors. He don't understand that. A guy like that, he forgets. He don't want to remember something, he forgets.''

Cannatella paused. "This guy Tony, my niece, she marries this guy, I think he's maybe okay. He's got a good name, but he's got no connections to the business. I don't see him sticking his nose into somethin' like this.''

"I don't think he did," I said. "Pinelli used Tony. Tony

didn't have any idea what the hell was going on. This friend of mine, this person tells me someone who . . . worked for you was found dead. It didn't seem important at the time. I think he was the man Pinelli sent to Tony. He had this guy tell Tony that you had something important for him to do. I knew Tony, and I'm guessing he was flattered. He was that kind of guy. He couldn't guess the request came from Pinelli. He was excited to be doing something for 'Uncle Frank.' ''

"Ritchie sends a guy to Tony Palmer," Cannatella said, "then Ritchie has to knock the guy off."

"I'm guessing again," I said, "but I'd say Pinelli used this deal to take you down. That's the only thing that makes sense, taking a risk like that. He makes a deal with Byron's people: He gives them your pictures, and promises his support. If Byron wins, Pinelli's got a very powerful friend in high places."

"Ritchie covered his ass," Cannatella said. "He tells me, he says, 'This Tony, I don't know what he's up to, he knows somethin' about the business. Maybe he hears somethin' he shouldn't ought to know.' Ritchie tells me, this Tony, he's working something out with Charlie Galiano in New York, they got something going, he doesn't know what. I'm thinking, what the fuck? What does this joker know that he shouldn't oughta know?"

"Maybe Pinelli sent Mr. Galiano one of the pictures anonymously. With *your* face cut out. Maybe he said you were working a deal with your old school buddy Byron. Byron gets the picture and throws Galiano to the wolves. That'd be a nice bit of publicity for a man who wants to be President.

"You think about it," I said, "that's maybe how New York got involved. Mr. Galiano sent Mrs. Pianezzi and maybe some other people here to track down the picture."

"I got no problem with Charlie," Cannatella said. "He ought to know that."

"Yes, sir," I said, "but he doesn't know you're not involved in anything. All he knows is there's some kind of trouble in Chicago.

"I don't know if Pinelli went to Mr. Galiano or not. I do know he made a big mistake using Tony. He didn't know Tony very well. Tony *did* have a hot session lined up with one of his ladies, so he sent me instead. I lost the briefcase and everything got screwed up. I don't know why the briefcase wasn't picked up in Dallas, something went wrong there. Tony's man missed the connection, I don't know. There's something else here too: I was supposed to bring the briefcase *back*. So maybe Pinelli was supposed to get some money from Byron's people. Anyway, Pinelli's got to get the pictures back, so he calls in Byron's trained FBI agent, Max Walker."

Cannatella took a cigarette from a silver case. "I keep seein' something here I don't like. I keep seeing my niece in here somewhere, I don't like what I'm seeing. If Joe left her the pictures, she did somethin' she shouldn't have done."

"Yes, sir," I said. "I can't see any other way the pictures could have gotten into Pinelli's hands. Maybe they had something going, I don't know. She had to know Tony had a lot of women on the string. When I called her up, I think she saw a way to help this thing along. Mrs. Pianezzi said something to me in Dallas. She kept asking me if it was my idea or Felicia's that we meet and talk. She thought that was important. Now I think it is. Felicia tells Pinelli we're going to meet. He gets a chance to nab me then, only he doesn't."

Cannatella nodded. "He figures, he's thinking he can get to you soon enough anyway. Pinelli don't think anyone can keep him from gettin' what he wants. I know the guy. He'd take a chance like that if he had somethin' else in mind."

"Fine," I said, "but why did he blow up Felicia in her car? So he could blame it on Galiano's people, maybe, strengthen the idea in *your* mind that New York was involved, that Galiano was sending you a message by killing your niece?"

"Huh-uh," Cannatella said. "He maybe blew her up. I think he did something else. He don't know whether Felicia's squirreled away another set of pictures with someone. Somethin' goes wrong—like getting blown up in a car—the stuff comes to me. Ritchie's smart. He wouldn't take a chance like that. I'm thinking he gets his hands on some broad on the street, she takes Felicia's place in the car.''

"So what happened to her?"

"She's sunnin' her ass somewhere. She's thinking it's warm in Bermuda, some fucking island somewhere. She's waiting for Ritchie to work things out, she's drinking stuff with umbrellas on the top.''

Cannatella was silent a long moment. He snuffed out his cigarette and loosened the button at his neck.

"So now I got you," he said. "You're thinking, you're saying to yourself, Felicia had the right idea. I'll keep a set of prints for myself, I'll tell Cannatella if anything happens to me, the pictures get out.''

"I didn't do that," I said. "You don't have any reason to believe me, I understand that. It scared the shit out of me to call you, Mr. Cannatella. I don't mind telling you I'm still scared now, but I had to get this behind me. I was willing to take the chance.''

Cannatella was looking straight ahead. I looked at him until he had to turn and face me.

"I did something for you," I said, "and the chance I was taking was that you'd see that too. A minute ago you said people ought to remember favors. What I'm doing—I'm betting you'll think about that.''

Cannatella didn't answer. He leaned back in the seat and lit a smoke. I wanted one too, but I didn't want to ask.

"That stuff Charlie and I did," he said. "That was somethin' we shouldn't have done. It was a wrong thing to do. It didn't happen but a couple of times. A guy's young, he makes mistakes, he don't make that mistake again.''

I didn't comment on that. Maybe it was something he'd thought about a lot. I didn't know if he had or not. All the things a man like Frank Cannatella does down through the years, maybe there's one thing he'd like to forget.

* * *

When we stopped, we were somewhere near the lake. I hadn't been in this part of town for some time, but I guessed we were somewhere near East Chicago, right across the Indiana line.

The blue Chrysler, along with another just like it, was already there, along with a Lincoln sitting off by itself.

Three men got out of the first Chrysler and brought Maria Pianezzi and Max Walker to the car. Walker still looked awful, but someone had bandaged up his arm.

The window on Cannatella's side whirred down. I tried to look past them to see if I could see Sherry Lou.

"Tell Charlie I appreciate the help," Cannatella said. "You tell him there's no problems between us. Tell him it's straightened out, that me and him'll talk. You tell him that. You give him my regards."

The old lady nodded. "I'll tell him," she said. "I will give him your words, Don Cannatella." One of the men led her off. Cannatella turned to Max Walker.

"You," he said, "you get back to Jack Byron. You tell him I don't give a fuck he's dog-catcher, President, what. You tell him nothin' happens, that's another favor from Frank. You tell him I'm running out of favors fast."

Max Walker didn't answer. He nodded, and looked relieved that he was going to get a ride back, as if he hadn't expected that.

A man took Walker away. Cannatella looked out the window a long time. I could tell he was looking at the second blue Chrysler. He didn't have to tell me, his eyes told me who was in the car.

"The girl," he said finally, "she got a look at the pictures too?"

"No, sir," I lied, "no one but me."

Cannatella turned in the seat and looked me straight in the eye. No one had ever looked at me that way before. I hope no one ever does it again.

"I'd sleep a lot better if you and Jesus was playing tennis tomorrow afternoon. You understand what I'm saying to you?"

"Yes, sir," I said, "I certainly do."

"I don't know you, you don't know me. You never seen me before. Leave town. Take a vacation somewhere."

"Yes, sir," I said, "I've been thinking about that. That's a very good idea."

"Get the fuck out of here," he said.

Chapter 40

Two days later, the papers ran a front-page story how one Carl Rickey of Detroit had been charged with the murders of Tony Palmer and his wife Felicia. Rickey, who had a mile-long record of armed robbery, extortion, and assault, and a background of mental instability on top of that, confessed that he had broken into Tony Palmer's office, when Tony was working late at night. He had stolen Tony's valuables and cash, then shot him in the head.

Rickey also gave the Chicago police a detailed account of how he'd gotten Tony's home address from his wallet, how in this wallet had been a picture of Tony's wife. Being of unsound mind, he later assaulted and raped Felicia in her home, and, to cover his tracks, blew her up in her car, thinking the police would see no connection between the two killings.

The murder of Karla Stark was still unsolved. However, the police were now certain this was the work of two misfits looking for money to buy some coke.

Most important of all, in my mind, the police now admitted that Murray Russell—they got it wrong again—had been a false lead, and that Murray Russell was not involved in any of these crimes.

In an unrelated story, police were investigating a shooting in a motel near O'Hare. Three men, identified as "local business executives," were gunned down in a pre-dawn robbery attempt. Two of these men were dead, and the other was in critical condition.

There was no mention anywhere of a large man who had apparently fallen from a parking garage. There was no account at all of one Ritchie Pinelli. If he was missing, and I assumed that he was, no one seemed to care.

I never learned what happened to Felicia Palmer. At times, I imagined her reluctantly taking her vows in a convent in Palermo somewhere, let off the hook by Uncle Frank, because the people in his line of work had a thing about women, that you shouldn't knock them off.

I have no idea what happened to Walker. Did he come out on top or take a fall? Who gives a shit, okay?

We were sitting in Jane's apartment, looking at a cold and drizzly rain outside, the kind of day when you don't have to go outside, all you've got to do is look to get the flu.

Jane had made chili, which she makes real well, because she gets it at a deli from a guy who used to live in Fort Worth. It was a very nice occasion all in all. Dinner, and two people who managed to keep from sniping at each other more than four or five times during the night.

It was not, in any way, a romantic interlude. There wasn't much chance of that happening again, though I wouldn't be unhappy if it did.

I tried to keep the talk away from mobsters and recent events, but Jane worked her way back to it every time. She had been involved in the mess, and she felt that gave her certain rights.

"I'm grateful," I told her, "I think I told you that."

"I don't know if you did or not," Jane said.

"I did. I said thank you very much. I don't know what else to say than that."

"You couldn't have done this without my help."

"I'm aware of that."

"And don't think I helped because I bought that Pulitzer Prize bullshit. I didn't just fall off the truck, Russell Murray. I'm a veteran newspaper person. Maybe you don't know it, but I'm pretty damn smart."

"I know you're smart, don't you think I know that? A guy asks sometime, who do you think is smart. I'll say Jane Kowalski's smart. That Jane Kowalski's smart."

Jane gave me a look that all but closed her eyes. "You don't want to rile me, pal. I'll put you right out in the cold."

"I'm not a wanted felon anymore," I told her. "I don't have to hide out, I can go anywhere I want to go."

"Good. What you ought to do is run over to Bambi Dear's. That girl's got a fine mind. You can have a little wine and talk about God and Henry James."

"You mean William," I said.

"No, I don't."

"Yes, you do. William did the philosopher stuff. He's the guy to see about God. Henry wrote books. *Daisy Miller. The Golden Bowl.* The—"

"Fuck you," Jane said, "what do I care?"

It was that kind of evening. We'd bitch at each other for a while, then we'd recall some times we'd had and we'd treat each other nice for a while. Still, I could tell by the way she looked at me that Frank Cannatella, Jack Byron, and the contents of the briefcase were always on her mind. She knew that I couldn't tell her any of that, and it made her mad as hell she couldn't ask.

So we said we'd get together real soon, but I didn't think we would. The hurts of the past were still with us, and now I'd disappointed her again. I had the story of the year and it would never come out. She could maybe forgive the past, but she couldn't forgive that.

Sherry Lou spent six weeks back at Wilson Rehab in Wisconsin. I wanted to go and see her but she said she wasn't ready for that. I didn't hear from her again until a few days before Thanksgiving. I'd been looking for a job, and thought I had something lined up. The guy sounded good on the phone. He said my literary background would fit the job fine.

After I'd braved the snow and the cutting wind that swept in off the lake, I found this joker had an office the size of a shower stall. What he wanted me to do was go out on the road and pitch his books. I said, "What kind of books?" and he handed me a stack. These books had titles like *Horny Housewife* and *Sorority Slut.* Plus, I could make a little extra if I'd carry his line of marital aids. He said the stuff was the top of the line, and after I'd proved myself I could have an exclusive on Inflatable Irma, and he didn't do that for everyone. I told the guy thanks, that I was looking for something more basic, something with a little less class.

When I got back to my apartment, Sherry's message was on the machine. I called the number, which turned out to be her hotel. She said she was leaving that night, and could I meet her at O'Hare.

I gave myself two hours, and wondered if that would be enough. The weather was dismal and the cabbies didn't need to look for fares. I got there with maybe ten minutes to spare. She was waiting where she said she'd be, in front of the British Airways desk.

She came into my arms and I held her for a while, thinking how good it was to feel the familiar warmth of her again.

Finally, Sherry pulled away from me and grinned. "You look real fine," she said, "just as good as you can be. Lord, you're the only man I ever cared for didn't know shit about clothes. I bet you got that suit at a Beirut close-out sale."

"Sherry," I said, "you're looking great too. Cute as a bug."

She was, too. Her hair was alive with shiny apricot curls. She wore a smartly tailored suit in deep blue that was cut to fit the Sherry Lou frame. She had a Russian sable coat that could keep me in rib eyes the rest of my life.

She looked good, but there were definite signs of wear. There were shadows beneath her eyes, and a few extra lines around her mouth. Her stay at the detox farm must have been hairy, I thought. It had to be, if Sherry hadn't gotten the itch and left.

"I'm cute, like you say," Sherry said, "there's no denying that. And I'm feeling some better than I did." She showed me a weary grin. "We went through some rough ones, pal."

"Yeah, we did," I said. "A couple of them right here, too. I don't know if I'll ever grow fond of O'Hare."

"Russ, you ought to come with me," she said. "I'm stopping in London and going on to France. We could have a lot of fun."

I started to answer, but she quickly pressed a finger to my lips. "Hey, you don't have to say a thing, Russ. I can see that *no* real good."

"I don't guess I'd better right now. I kind of need to—"

"Shut up, Russ. I said it was fine."

"I'll miss you a lot, Sherry Lou. You know that."

"Course I know that. But it wouldn't work out, and we both know that. I'm kinda stuck wherever it is I am. And I don't know how to be anyone else. I guess I can't help that." She gave me a sad little flutter with her eyes. "What I got, I got this funny little strain keeps running through my head."

"Strain's good," I said. "I kind of like chant and air."

"Don't forget lay," Sherry grinned. "That's kind of good too."

We talked for a minute or two, and then she gave me a teary kiss and ran for her plane. I watched her until she was out of sight. I remembered how she looked and how she smelled and how warm she felt in bed. Her words kept pushing the good parts I remembered aside because I knew Sherry Lou and I knew she was right. *I'm kinda stuck wherever it is I am,* is what she said, and I didn't want to think about that.

The cab let me off ten blocks from my apartment. The snow was melting some and the streets winked back the evening lights. I opened the door and went in and climbed the stairs and took a seat near the back. I thought about Sherry. I tried to remember Karla Stark. I could picture her dark-night hair and her long legs tangled in the sheets, but I couldn't see her face.

A little later I stood and went up to the front. I saw a lot of familiar faces, and a lot I didn't know.

When my turn came around, I said, "Hi, my name's John and I'm an alcoholic. I haven't had a drink for two months and nine days."

"Hi, John," everyone said.

I figured I was getting real close. Next time I'd probably say Russ.